The door opened
The dark-skinned w
at her, then raised h
an incredulous, deli
man in the hall simpl gazed at her.

'I'm Mrs Wendover. I would like to see Alex, if that's possible.'

The maid, her eyes still round, took Elizabeth's overnight bag and led her towards a great pair of doors. She opened one and ushered Elizabeth in.

'Señora—' she began.

A blonde girl stood up and turned around. Behind her was her own portrait, the one in which she seemed about to recognize someone and speak. She hesitated for a moment, her blue eyes widening as the maid's brown ones had done, then 'It's you,' she said. 'It's you, isn't it?'

Also by Victoria Petrie Hay:

FORSAKING ALL OTHERS

Every Purpose Under Heaven

Victoria Petrie Hay

WARNER BOOKS

A *Warner* Book

First published in Great Britain
by Michael Joseph Ltd in 1991
This edition published by Warner Books in 1993

A CIP catalogue record for this book
is available from the British Library.

ISBN 0 7515 0070 4

Typeset by Vivitext Creative Services

Printed and bound in Great Britain by
Richard Clay Ltd, Bungay, Suffolk

Warner Books
A Division of
Little, Brown and Company (UK) Limited
165 Great Dover Street
London SE1 4YA

Every
Purpose Under
Heaven

Prologue

THEY TRIED TO BREAK IT to her gently, but there was no gentle path to this. She put her hands over her ears to block out what her mother was saying and when that did not work she began to scream.

No! She would *not* leave home and Daddy and live somewhere else with Mummy and Uncle David. What they were doing was wicked. Nanny said so. And *Uncle* David was no such thing. She knew that because Nanny had snorted and said, 'Uncle, my foot!'

Her mother put her arms around her and said, 'Alex, darling—' but Alex kicked her – kicked her own mother! – and pulled free and shouted and shouted for Daddy and Nanny, and the door had opened and there they were, the two of them, everything she most wanted in the whole wide world. She ran to Daddy and clung to him and said she would never leave him and Nanny, never *ever*. She hated Mummy and never wanted to see her again, and Nanny said, 'There, there, my ducks,' and Mummy said, 'Alex, darling,' again and sounded as if she was crying, which was impossible, of course, because grown-ups didn't cry. And Alex yelled again that she hated her and at last Mummy and Wicked Uncle David went away and Alex was left alone with Daddy and Nanny.

She had to go and see an important man who Nanny told her was a judge. He asked her lots of questions and she told him over and over that she wanted to live with Daddy and Nanny, that she hated her mother because she was wicked. The man said she could live with Daddy and Nanny, though she'd have to see Mummy sometimes, but she soon sorted that one out. When Mummy came to Montly and said she and Alex were going to have a lovely weekend in a hotel by the sea and wouldn't that be fun? Alex clung to Nanny and screamed and screamed and, again, Mummy had gone away.

Alex never looked at the pictures on the postcards that came for her, though Nanny said some of the stamps were interesting and cut them off with a pair of scissors. She opened the parcels that arrived at Christmas and on her birthday, tearing the wrappings away quickly to get the whole business over with as soon as possible. She never played with the toys the parcels contained. She hated her mother, and wanted nothing more to do with her.

She hated her even more when she learned the facts of life. Belinda and Amy had found a book hidden in their brother's chest of drawers and brought it to the secret place they had made among the hay bales in the barn at Montly. This is what grown-ups do, they insisted, and while they giggled and squealed over the pictures Alex sat quietly, the sweet hay tickling her legs, and thought.

So it was because of that – *that!* – her mother had gone away with Wicked Uncle David. She had preferred doing that to being with Daddy and Alex.

Well, Alex didn't need a mother any more than her mother needed or wanted a daughter. She had Daddy and he was all she would ever want. She didn't mind one little bit – because he explained it all so lovingly and carefully – when he decided, after having asked Alex's approval, to marry again. Jess was a super person, and she came from New York in America. She took Alex shopping in London and treated her like a grown-up friend. Nanny disapproved of the clothes she and Jess had bought, but Alex didn't. She wore one of the new dresses to the party after Jess and Daddy's wedding – which couldn't be in a church because, Nanny explained, of what Mummy had done – and everyone said how pretty she looked. Aunt Celia took her to one side and said she mustn't mind about Daddy wanting a new wife, she mustn't be jealous, and Alex gave her the wide smile she had been practising so it looked like Jess's and said, 'But I don't mind a bit. I love Jess.'

Alex took photographs of Daddy and Jess to school.

'My new mother,' she told everyone. She didn't

think life could hold any more when Daddy and Jess came to Open Day, and all the girls said how beautiful Jess was, how super her clothes. And yet life *could* hold more, because a year later Jess presented Alex with the most beautiful baby brother.

Chapter One

JESS WATCHED ALEX, WEARING SCRUFFY jeans and a checked shirt, playing croquet with five-year-old William and three-year-old Annabelle.

'She's so sweet with them,' she said. 'Richard, do look.'

Her husband did. His elder daughter was helping his younger one – whose mallet was almost as tall as she was – to send her own ball into a distant flower bed. Annabelle's little dungareed body leapt about with triumphant joy and then she took careful and inaccurate aim at her brother's yellow ball.

Richard went back to the file he was studying. 'It would be a pretty poor thing,' he remarked, 'if she tried to win.'

'That's not the point. It's how she loves them and gives up time for them.'

Richard raised his head once more and gazed appraisingly at Alex as she showed William how to hit his ball so it would go through the hoop. 'I thought that finishing school would turn her out elegant and sophisticated. She seems to have regressed since she left Roedean.'

'She's seventeen, Richard! She's got plenty of time to be an adult.'

'What is she going to do with herself?'

'She doesn't have to worry about that just yet. She's learning to drive, she's instructing at the Pony Club rally next week, and she's going to the disco with Henry Glover.'

'A Pony Club rally and Henry Glover – the height of rural gallivanting! Jess, you're becoming more English than the English!'

She did not like the sarcastic and critical tone in his voice, had never heard it before. 'I daresay I am,' she said stiffly. 'I haven't been home in more than five years and I have two British children, one of whom will inherit this great place—' She indicated with a sweep of her hand the old house and the downs it nestled among. The limit of Montly Manor's grounds was, literally, the sky, and truly Sir Richard Mountfield was master of all he surveyed. 'When I married you, you said I would have to forget I was an American.'

He was immediately contrite. 'Jess, my darling, I'm sorry,' he said, laying aside the file and taking her hand. 'I've got things on my mind, that's all. Are you and I going to the Pony Club disco?'

'No, you fool, we are not,' she said, forgiving him and affecting an accent that was more English than the English. 'Unless you want to cook sausages or mix the punch. Adults at these affairs are strictly functional.'

'I'll cook the sausages.'

'Richard, you've got to be kidding!'

'Why? . . . An American at the Pony Club,' he mused, sitting back in his deck chair. 'It sounds like a musical.'

'Richard Mountfield cooking sausages sounds like a miracle,' she countered.

The croquet game finished amidst excited yells. William leapt upon his father with the news that he had won, while Annabelle, equally loudly, said it was only just. Alex ordered the two black Labradors on the rug at Jess's feet to remove themselves and flopped down in their place.

'I came third,' she said.

Jess smiled at her. 'I want a witness to what your father just told me. He's promised to help with the barbeque at the disco next week.'

'Wow! What prompted that?'

'I don't know,' Jess said, again vaguely troubled.

Richard rid himself of his son and heir. 'I hear you're instructing at the rally,' he said to Alex. 'That sounds very superior.'

'Hardly instructing. Just helping out with the tinies.'

William bounced on her and she squealed in mock hurt. 'I'm a tiny, Alex, aren't I? Me and Pickles.'

'You are,' she said, hugging him. 'One of the tiniest tinies.'

'I'm the tinierest of all, though,' Annabelle said,

clambering on to her mother's lap. 'When'll I be going to the Pony Club?'

'When you're old enough.' Jess stroked Annabelle's curly chestnut head. 'It's teatime. What would you like?'

Annabelle whispered in her ear.

Jess laughed. 'Okay, but don't tell Daddy.'

'Secrets?' Richard said awfully. 'What's this?'

Annabelle squirmed in an ecstasy of confusion.

'I bet I know,' William said, getting to his feet. 'Come on and tell me then, man to man.'

'No!' yelled Annabelle.

'It's all right,' Jess told her. 'You say.'

Annabelle was now one big giggle. 'It's – it's peanut butter and jelly sandwiches. Only' – and this was even more exquisitely amusing than anything else – 'only it's not jelly, but jam!'

'Yippee!' William pulled his sister from their mother's lap and, telling her to stop laughing because it really wasn't all that funny, ran with her towards the house chased by Alex and the dogs.

Jess stood, picked up the rug and said, 'Well, perhaps they aren't entirely British after all . . . Oh, you've had a letter from Frank. How is he?'

Richard, in the act of folding Jess's deck chair, dropped it, bent and swiftly tucked the letter away in the file. 'He's fine. Very well. This is just business.'

'I didn't mean to pry. The letter was handwritten and I thought it might be gossip.'

'Just business. He's having problems with the old man.'

'When didn't he?' said Jess, remembering the furious phone calls between Franklin Benjamin Stanford Junior in his office on Third Avenue and Franklin Benjamin Stanford Senior in his mansion on Long Island, to which he had supposedly retired the previous year. Over six years later he was, apparently, still refusing to exit gracefully.

'I was thinking,' Richard said, as he tucked the file and the two deck chairs under one arm and put the other around his wife and they walked across the lawn to the house, 'especially after what you said earlier – about not having seen home for so long – that perhaps we should go to America.'

She stopped and stared at him. 'All of us?' He had suggested often enough before that she go with him on his business trips to New York but she had refused, not wanting to take the children with her or to leave them while they were so young. It was another way, she reflected, in which she was not English, for she had never employed a nanny to take care of William and Annabelle, even though Alex's old one – and she had been Richard's and his father's as well – was a pensioner of theirs and more than willing to come out of retirement and take charge. Now Jess thought about it, it was because of Nanny Mountfield that she had not wanted a nanny and nothing to do with being an American at all: it would have been most awkward to give someone else the job when the prejudiced and smothering old lady had been there ready to do it. Alex adored her, and Jess tried to like her for everything she had been to the poor motherless child, but she did not want her having any influence over her own children. Nanny baby-sat, which pleased both parties, Jess because in spite of everything Nanny was reliable, and anyway William and Annabelle slept away her visits, and Nanny because she could still boast of her connection with the big house among her cronies in the village.

Jess stood there under an English sky, the folded rug over her arm, and waited for Richard's reply. If he would not agree to the children coming – for Annabelle was old enough now to be aware of her surroundings – she would have to wait longer before seeing her homeland again.

'Well?' she asked as Richard, too, seemed deep in thought.

'All of us,' he said.

'Alex as well?'

'Oh, yes. Alex as well.'

'When? Richard, when?'

He shifted the deck chairs under his arm and flicked his head to remove the lock of hair that persistently fell on to his forehead. 'After I've cooked the sausages,' he said.

She sighed. 'The whole thing's a joke then. I knew it.'

'It is not. We'll go in two weeks.'

'Two weeks! I'll have to buy clothes. That could mean a trip to London. I suppose there's time,' she fretted, and he roared with laughter.

'Jess, Jess, you've become a xenophobe. We're going to America, my darling. *New York* – to begin with, at least. Buy what you need there, for God's sake.'

'New York,' she said wonderingly. 'And where else?'

'Long Island, of course, if your parents can cope with us. Can they?'

'You bet they can. They'd sleep in the yard if it came to it. But Richard, why so sudden?'

'I have to see Frank. He thinks both of us may be able to talk the old man round.'

'Are things that bad?'

'No! I told you, it's just the usual problems. Christ, Jess, I thought you'd like to go.'

'I would, I would!'

'Let's tell the children, then.'

Henry Glover pulled Alex closer to him as the disco music thudded around the barn. Strobe lights flashed and the other dancers appeared to move in spasm, like puppets.

'They're all kids here,' she shouted into his ear.

'What did you expect?' he shouted back.

She pushed him away and he looked down at her, his face leaping in and out of the light.

'Want to go?' he mouthed.

She nodded, and he took her hand and led her towards the door of the barn.

'I've been too old for this for years,' he yelled over his shoulder. 'I'm glad you've decided you are.'

They went outside. It was wondrously still and a moon glowed on the humps of the downs. Behind it was an infinity of stars. The music from the barn punched the night and seemed an insult to it. Henry put an arm around her shoulders.

'What shall we do, Alex?'

'Let's go for a walk,' she said.

'Okay. Where?'

'To the top of the Long Man.'

He laughed and kissed her cheek. 'That's easy enough,' he said. 'I was worried that your fancy finishing school had taught you to say' – and here he raised his voice into a falsetto – '"Oh to the Ritz! Where else?" What did they teach you there, Alex?'

'Lots and lots. I learned how to cook, after a fashion, how to go to the theatre, how to visit the turgid sights of Switzerland, and how to write.'

'*Write?*'

'Cheques. It was a joke,' she explained. 'The idea was that that's the most important thing we'll ever have to do after we capture our rich husbands.'

He was silent, and she realized what a very bad joke it was away from the spoiled darlings in their school above Lake Geneva and in front of Henry Glover. Henry's father was the local vicar and the family was far from rich. Neither the vicar nor his

wife minded, or their son and daughter, but as
Nanny had told her often it was not done to refer to
one's wealth when in the company of those less well
off. She touched Henry's arm.

'Are we going up the Long Man, then?'

He unlocked the passenger door to Jess's car,
opened it and bowed. 'We go wherever *la demoiselle*
wishes. In you get.'

'Henry, how cosmopolitan!'

'Wot's that mean?' he said.

'Where has she gone?' Richard Mountfield asked
Jess.

'Off with Henry Glover.'

'But where to? What's she doing?'

'Walking, talking, kissing, perhaps. Richard, she's
seventeen. You said yourself it's time she grew up.'

'Not all the way up, though.'

'She's safe with Henry. You know that.'

He relaxed. 'Yes, she is. Safe as houses with
Henry.'

'How were the sausages?'

'I got detailed to do the hamburgers. They only
needed cooking on two sides.' He took off the white
chef's hat and apron he had insisted on wearing. 'It
was quite fun once I'd got into the rhythm of it, and
I got smiled at by lots of pretty girls.'

'Oh, did you?'

'Alex was the prettiest, though. I hardly
recognized her wearing a dress . . . Hey, let me do

that,' he added as a woman came out of the dark carrying a bucket of water in each hand.

'Bless you, Richard,' she said. 'Tip them on the coals, will you? I don't like the idea of leaving them burning. We'll take everything else away tonight.'

Richard went around dousing the barbeques. Steam hissed into the air and music thudded from the barn behind them.

'You must be exhausted,' Jess said to Jane Patterson.

'Only terminally,' she replied, affecting a faint. 'Every year I swear never again and every year I find myself doing it. Why? None of my children has deigned to attend. Why should I do it for other people's?'

Jess laughed. 'You do it because you like it,' she said.

Jess had been led to suppose that the British were reserved and unfriendly, was told it would be decades before she would be accepted in this little Sussex village in a fold of the South Downs near the sea. During their mad, three-week courtship in New York, Richard had spoken of Montly and how she would love it; he had told her his wife had left him and they were divorced, but after that had not said a single word about her, and Jess had half-feared a Rebecca-like atmosphere, with everyone silently measuring her up to the previous mistress of Montly Manor. She could not then and still could not now understand how a woman could fall out of love with

Richard – Richard Mountfield who, having explained about his daughter and saying Jess would have to meet her, then asked her to marry him while they were in a cab stuck in a traffic jam on Fifth Avenue. When she had said yes, he had paid off the driver and dragged her along to Tiffany's, only two blocks away, and bought her a ring.

If that was British reserve she loved it, though she often wondered what would have happened if Alex had rejected her as a stepmother. And she could not imagine how people could have been more friendly. The new Lady Mountfield ('Jess, for heaven's sake. Jess!' she had kept saying) had been welcomed with dinner parties and drinks parties, had been co-opted on to committees, asked to lend her name to charitable enterprises and invited to open the new Scouts' hall.

'Say no,' Richard had urged when Jess complained of tiredness.

'I try to, but it comes out as yes.'

The tiredness turned out to be William in the making and saying no had become easier after that.

But Jane Patterson, beside her now, had become a very close friend. She had met Jess in Eastbourne during the first school holidays that Alex had spent with her new stepmother, while Jess was still wrestling with the currency and the different brand names and the difficulties arising from two nations divided by a single language.

'My dear,' she had said. 'I was going to phone

21

you to say what a different child Alex is. She's confident and smiling and is obviously very happy. We all noticed it and put it down to you.'

'Oh – oh, thank you,' Jess whispered, and Jane had seen the tears coming and had borne Jess off for a cup of coffee. Which is how Jess had become involved in the Pony Club and why she was here outside one of Richard's barns as a Range Rover pulling a trailer, driven by Jane's husband Ralph, bumped into the clearing. Richard put the empty buckets in the trailer as Ralph got out.

'Roped you in at last, have they?' he said.

'I roped myself. Do you want any help?'

'I've got the boys. On parade, you two.' His twin sons climbed from the Range Rover and nodded greetings.

'So you don't need me?'

'Only if you haven't anything better to do.'

'I rather think I have,' Richard said. 'I want to dance with my wife.'

'Ah, how sweet!' Jane sighed, and Jess protested that they would embarrass the kids, or be embarrassed by them.

'They won't be able to see us,' Richard said. 'It's practically pitch dark in there.'

It was true. The lights had been turned very low and only music was coming from the barn. Richard took Jess inside where youthful couples were revolving vaguely in time to the music. Richard tilted Jess's chin upwards.

'To blend in,' he whispered and kissed her. 'Though why are we here,' he added a little later, 'among this adolescent frustration when we could be doing more interesting things at home?'

She laughed softly. 'Because I'm supposed to be making sure these kids don't do anything interesting here.'

Panting, Alex and Henry drew parallel with the right foot of the Long Man of Wilmington. The rest of him, etched into the hillside, stretched away above them and, above all, the moon floated.

'Isn't he splendid,' Alex said, 'standing here with his two great staffs?'

'He is. Are we really going to the top?'

'Of course! We must reach the moonlight and the barrows up there.'

She scrambled up the glassy-grassed hill and he followed, trying not to fall more in love with her than he had been since he was fourteen and she was twelve. Up beside the Long Man's right staff they went, past his outstretched arm and his strangely empty head, on hands and knees on the near-vertical slope at the top, then through a gate. They flung themselves on the springy moonlit turf and lay there catching their breath.

Alex turned on to her stomach and, her chin in her hands, gazed from this rabbit's eye view across the downs to the distant glitter of the sea. She was glad they had come up here, away from the music and the manic lights.

She wriggled over to Henry. 'Hello,' she said.

'Hello,' he replied gravely. 'Fancy meeting you.'

'This is the first weekend you've been down from London since I've been back, isn't it?'

'I believe it is.'

'Why? Do you have a girlfriend? I didn't think to ask when I invited you to the dance.'

'Would you mind if I did?'

Would she? She had set up Henry Glover as her boyfriend for the benefit of the girls at school, and certainly she was very fond of him. He had never made unreasonable demands at the dark ends of teenage parties, unlike other boys who seemed to think their slobbery kisses and groping hands were interesting to girls. When Henry was at home, and not in London being an articled clerk in his uncle's solicitors firm, he had always taken her to parties and brought her back because Daddy and Jess trusted him and lent him a car and knew he would not get drunk or take drugs. And when the lights went out she would end up with Henry, whose kisses weren't at all slobbery and whose hands did no more than hold her as close as was strictly necessary. She always assumed that she turned to him to avoid the slobber and because of one of Nanny's sayings, which was that a girl should never ignore her escort as she might not find a taxi home (and where, for heaven's sake, had Nanny learned that?), but now she wondered if it wasn't simply that she liked Henry's kisses and the feel of his arms around her.

'Yes,' she said at last. 'I think I would mind a bit.'

'A bit!'

'Have you, then?'

'Thousands of 'em.'

She moved further over and placed a hand on either side of his head. The grass felt very solid beneath her palms. He put his hands into her hair and drew her down to him.

This kiss was fierce and demanding and most un-Henry like. She pulled back and he nibbled her ear and murmured, 'Oh Alex,' over and over again.

Something was wrong and she did not know what it was, but then Henry kissed her again in a firm, friendly way – which was nice – rolled away from her and stood up. He held out a hand, and she took it and he heaved her to her feet.

'Let's walk,' he said. And: 'I hope your nice dress hasn't been ruined.'

He took off his jacket and put it and an arm around her and they strolled across the turf. Sheep ran from them like woolly ghosts.

'I wonder what I'll do,' Alex said.

'Do? With what?'

'With my life. I just realized, you see, that from now on I'm in charge. Even though I've been to that silly finishing school I hadn't thought of it as ending anything. It was the Pony Club dance that brought it on . . . being too old for it and suddenly knowing that you can't stop growing up, however hard you try.'

'Don't you want to grow up?'

'I suppose I do, eventually,' she said, and he laughed.

'In your own time, is it? God, stay your hand for me?'

'You're not being very helpful, Henry.'

'Sorry. So let's find you a career. You always said you wanted to be a journalist. What happened to that plan?'

'I don't know how to go about it.'

'Alex!' he exclaimed. 'This isn't like you! What did they do to you in Switzerland?'

'Not a lot, I told you. In a way I wish I hadn't insisted on leaving school. Perhaps I should have done A levels.'

Henry sighed. 'It's not too late. You're only seventeen and nothing is closed to you.'

'How would I know if I'd be a good journalist?' she asked.

She felt him shrug. 'I don't think people do know. I think they try it and find out. Tell you what,' he said. 'When you're in America, why not make a serious effort to write articles about it? Pretend it's an assignment and you won't eat unless you deliver the goods.'

She considered this and the idea took hold of her and filled her with purpose. She ducked away from Henry's arm and danced in front of him. She was sure she could do it and could hardly wait to begin. The future, so uncertain when she came up here to the top of the downs, leaving her childhood in a booming barn in a valley below, now lay clear before her: Fleet Street beckoned her with a curving finger.

'Henry, I'll do it,' she said. 'And will you read what I write and tell me truthfully if it's any good?'

'Okay, but I'm no expert.'

'No, but you're wise and you're honest and you'll say what you think.'

He doubted the last bit, so he said: 'No schoolgirl essays, Alex. No "How I went up the Empire State Building" rubbish. You must find an angle and work each article around it.'

'Yes,' she said. 'Do unusual things . . . talk to interesting people.'

Henry groaned and said, 'New York isn't Eastbourne, Alex. I meant beware of self-indulgence. This stuff you write won't be sold. It's just an exercise between you and me.' He put his hands on her shoulders and shook her gently. 'So no wandering the streets at night in search of "interesting people" – all right?'

'All right,' she said, wondering why he thought she would do such a thing.

He stroked her hair, bleached white by the moon, and in spite of his best intentions their lips met again. She wasn't for him – she couldn't be – and the reason he hadn't come to Sussex for weekends since she had been home was that he hadn't wanted, or he wanted too much, to see her.

They turned and began to walk back the way they had come.

'You've always known exactly where you're going, Henry, haven't you?' Alex said after a while. 'So sure of everything.'

'Sure of where, but not when.'

'But you're going to be a solicitor,' she said, puzzled.

'For a while.'

'Then what?'

He pointed at the star-flecked sky.

'It depends on the man upstairs. One of these years he'll call me.'

She stared up, thinking for an absurd moment that she would be able to see who was going to call Henry, and then she understood. 'A priest like your father? Henry – no!'

'Why not? My father is the most fulfilled and contented person I've ever met.'

Yes, she wanted to say, but his best suit is one discarded by my father and his daughter has always worn my old clothes and, Henry, you have been poor all your life and you deserve something better. 'It's sad,' she whispered.

'Sad? Rubbish! Some people want to be journalists and some want to be priests. Some want to be dentists, and isn't that lucky for the rest of us? – because, personally, I can't imagine a worse job than looking into other people's mouths. Would you say it was sad if I told you I was going to be a dentist, Alex?'

'No.'

'Well then.'

'You're right. I'm sorry. It's just that I care what happens to you,' she said, loving him.

'I forgive you,' he said, more than ever in love with her, though he must not be – for how would Alexandra Mountfield be a vicar's wife?

And they slithered back down the hillside alongside the Long Man, not realizing there is a gulf the size of the Milky Way between loving someone and being in love, not knowing, indeed, that the gulf existed – not even Henry, wise though he was considering his nineteen years. He allowed himself to hope that, given time, it might turn out right for him.

But then Alex met Ben.

Chapter Two

FRANKLIN BENJAMIN STANFORD III WAS blond-haired and blue-eyed. He was muscular and tanned and when Alex first saw him he was swimming in the pool on his grandfather's Long Island estate. He heaved himself out in one graceful movement, picked up a towel and, having wiped his impressively furry chest with it, he padded over to where his father stood with Jess, Richard, Alex and the children. He shook Richard's hand, smiled deprecatingly as Jess exclaimed how he had grown since she had last seen him and turned to Alex. He had the whitest teeth she had ever seen, which he showed off now as he said, 'Well, hi there.'

'Hi,' she said, feeling rather shy before this magnificence and trying to think of something witty and sophisticated to say; but then Annabelle created a diversion by yelling, 'I'm hot!', and before anyone could move she angrily tore off her dress and jumped into the pool.

Jess screamed and Alex gasped. Franklin Benjamin Stanford III calmly slid into the pool and held up Annabelle as she surfaced and spluttered indignantly (and untruthfully), 'I can swim.'

'Sure you can,' he said, tactfully placing a hand beneath her stomach, 'but the water here is pretty deep. Let's go to the shallow end.'

He bore her along as he sidestroked powerfully, and she put her arms backwards in the air and pretended she was a speedboat. No amount of remonstration when she was retrieved by her mother could alter her view that the whole experience had been wonderful.

'I was hot and bored,' she said, and she looked up at Franklin Benjamin Stanford III and said, 'Can we do it again – please?'

He squatted in front of her. 'We can if you'll promise me one thing. Will you do that?'

She nodded.

'Never, *never* again,' Franklin Benjamin said, 'must you jump in the pool like that. The water is deep and a little thing like you could get lost in it. You promise?'

'Promise,' she said.

William stamped his feet and Franklin Benjamin turned to him and said, 'You look like a man who could use a swim.'

'I could,' William said fervently. 'Mum, do I have to wait for my trunks?'

Jess helped him off with his T-shirt and shorts and he leapt into the pool wearing only his underpants. She had been feeling so guilty about the children. How could she have forgotten that New York in

July was no place for two country-bred kids who were used to English summers? They hadn't minded shopping because they could be in the air conditioning and they'd liked the boat ride around Manhattan Island, but the trips to the Statue of Liberty, up the Empire State Building and to the zoo in Central Park had been a disaster. She hoped their experiences had not given them a life-long aversion to her home town. She had wanted to get them to her parents' house immediately, but Richard had persuaded her they should accept the flattering invitation to spend a few days at Franklin Benjamin Stanford I's mansion, and now she was beginning to think it had been the right move. Her parents couldn't wait to get their hands on their grand-children, and the last thing William and Annabelle needed after the frustrations of New York was to be smothered by the attentions of the two people they had not remembered from their visit to England the previous year when they'd seen them at the airport.

William was now getting the speedboat treatment, and the magnificent Franklin Benjamin seemed to be deriving almost as much enjoyment from giving it as William was from receiving it. Then he released William and, laughingly fighting off Annabelle's pleas, he shaded his eyes and looked at Alex.

'You coming in too? It's great in here, isn't it, kids?'

'Love to,' she said, 'but – well – I need to change properly.'

32

Jess touched her elbow. 'You do that in the poolhouse. I'll get your bikini and the children's things while you keep watch here. You don't mind me going through your suitcase, do you?'

'No,' Alex said. William and Annabelle didn't need watching while Franklin Benjamin Stanford III was in the pool with them, but it gave her a chance to watch him. He was the most handsome man she had ever seen, and had been so splendid when he rescued Annabelle. She was longing to get to know him properly.

Yet fifteen minutes later, when she was in her bikini, she was reluctant to go outside again. She looked at herself in the mirror. Her figure was all right and the bikini was okay, but her body was so white! She'd look like a slug compared to Franklin Benjamin's tanned hulk. And should she wear a swimming cap? Her hair had been washed that morning in the hotel salon. The chlorine meant she would have to wash it again, and it wouldn't look nearly as good. She imagined herself with her white body and her white schoolgirl's cap and decided the sacrifice would be worth it. She put on her towel robe – a present from Jess – and stepped into the sunlight.

William was standing on the broad brown shoulders until, with a triumphant yell, he bellyflopped into the water. Jess handed Alex two pairs of armbands.

'Put them on, will you? I'm going to change. I

can't wait to get in there.'

'Where's Daddy?'

'Talking business, I expect. He'll be out soon.'

As Jess wandered away Alex slipped off her robe and into the water while Franklin Benjamin's back was turned. He saw her as William lunged towards her and he gave her another of those brilliant grins. To overcome her shyness, she grabbed William and, over his protests, began putting on his armbands. A large pair of hands removed Annabelle's.

'You're not going to make a fuss like your brother now, are you?'

'No,' said Annabelle, standing on the steps and trustingly stretching out her arms. When the bands were in place and blown up Jess called the children so she could put on their bathers and Alex was alone with Franklin Benjamin Stanford III.

'I don't even know your name,' he said. 'Thanks to your sister we didn't get properly introduced.'

'Alexandra. Alex for short.'

'I'm Ben,' he said.

'Oh! But I thought you were called—'

'After the statesman and scientist, but backwards? I am, but when I was eight years old I figured if Granddad was Franklin senior and Dad Frank junior there wasn't a lot left for me, so I decided to call myself Ben.'

'Ben's a nice name,' she managed, thinking how strong-minded and sure you must be to change your name at that age. William had decided he wanted to be called Gary, after the farm manager's son, but that had lasted less than a day.

'Alexandra's kind of nice too. How long are you staying?'

'Just a couple of days, I think.'

A frown marked his smooth forehead. 'That all? It's too bad.'

'On Long Island for another three weeks, though,' she hastened to assure him.

The grin lit his face. 'Not so bad, then! Say, do you sail? Would you like to come out on the Sound tomorrow?'

She smiled back at him. 'I haven't done much sailing, but I'd love to learn.'

'Great . . . oh, no! Here come the tornados,' he yelled as William and Annabelle, now in more proper attire, jumped into the pool.

Jess knocked at Alex's door as Alex was dressing for dinner that evening.

'The kids pronounce themselves satisfied with America, thank God,' she said, 'and, having demanded to be said good night to by young Hercules, both fell asleep like angels. Have you finished with the hair drier?'

Alex handed it to her.

'Did he say good night?'

'Who?'

'Ben.'

'Yes.'

'He's asked me to go sailing tomorrow.'

'That will be fun.'

'Yes . . . Jess, is this dress okay? I'm worried about the neckline. It sort of flops all over the place and my bra shows.'

Jess surveyed her stepdaughter. This was the first time she had ever paid much attention to what she was wearing – and she had paid a lot, Jess thought, seeing the discarded outfits on the bed. The first thing that came to hand was good enough for Henry Glover. Still, perhaps it was time some handsome prince awoke Alex's sleeping emotions and no harm could come of a brief flirtation with Franklin Benjamin Stanford III, who seemed hardly older than William as he played in the pool.

'Well?' said Alex, and Jess looked properly.

Alex's blonde hair fell in natural shining waves to past her shoulders and the dress she had chosen to wear was a bright, fresh green. Green and golden she was, like a summer's day.

'You look lovely,' she said warmly.

'But the neck . . .'

Jess tweaked the top of the dress and it settled into place. 'There you are.' She turned to leave the room and Alex gripped her arm.

'I don't want to go down alone. Will you and Daddy come and fetch me?'

'All right,' Jess said, trying to keep a straight face. 'Lord, is that the time? I'll have to forget washing my hair. Franklin does not like to be kept waiting.'

36

She fled. Alex picked up the clothes from the bed and hung them up, as Nanny had told her she always must, then went to the open window and looked out. The grounds, she now saw, ran down to the water's edge. Was that the Sound they would be sailing on tomorrow? And, as she picked out a mast alongside a launch moored to a jetty, was that the boat?

She gave herself a mental shake, took out her notebook and pen, turned the pages until she found an empty one and headed it determinedly, 'Long Island. First Impressions'. She closed her eyes and thought about it. Annabelle fractious in the car, William impatient . . . who would want to read about that? That or a lyrical description of a powerful, tanned body rolling through the blue waters of a swimming pool.

Henry Glover, the Long Man of Wilmington and the undertaking she had made in the moonlight on the top of the downs in far-off Sussex were a million miles from her mind.

Ben was not there when they entered the huge drawing-room, but his father was. Franklin II said he had been sorry not to see more of Alex in New York and how had she liked the Big Apple? Alex replied that she had liked it very much, but would have preferred it to have been a bit cooler. Franklin II said his wife would agree with her; she always spent the summer in Maine. A maid brought drinks and Alex took her white wine and sipped it and listened as Jess and Frank recalled the old times when they had worked together until Richard Mountfield – who had seen her dozens of times before – had suddenly noticed her on one of his New York trips and that, they concluded, had been that.

Alex looked at Jess. Presumably to disguise the fact that her hair had been in a swimming pool and not been washed, she had put it into a chignon kept in place by a tortoiseshell clip. She was wearing a silk dress of deep crimson and she looked most beautiful and elegant.

'How could you have not noticed her?' Alex asked her father.

'I must have been blind,' he said. 'I think I still am, for I've only just noticed how very lovely my daughter is.'

She did not have to reply to this, for the doors opened at the far end of the room and Franklin Benjamin Stanford Senior came in on his grandson's arm. Both of them – like the other two men present – were wearing dinner jackets and they were followed by an elderly grey-haired woman in a plain brown dress.

Franklin II went to meet the little procession and took the old man's other arm. 'How are you, Dad?' he asked.

Franklin I shook off his son's hand. 'Ill. Dying probably.' The woman behind him tut-tutted and he issued a curt 'Shut up' over his shoulder, then looked around the room. Brown his eyes were, and very sharp – quite at odds with his apparently infirm physical condition – until they softened as they came to rest on Jess.

'You!' he exclaimed. 'Learned to type yet?

Mr Stanford, sir,' she said, 'you know I was the best goddamned secretary you ever had.'

'Maybe so, maybe so. I trained you well, mind. That was why you could be such a help to my fool of a son – at least until that limey carried you off.' He walked forward, reached out a leathery hand and touched her cheek. 'You been happy?' he asked.

'Very. As you know – or would do if you read my letters, for you sure as hell don't answer them – I have two wonderful children, who I hope you'll consent to meet tomorrow, an even more wonderful husband and, as an extra special bonus, a stepdaughter.' She beckoned to Alex. 'This is Alexandra, Franklin.'

The brown eyes raked her from head to foot and Alex wondered if she should curtsey, so regal did this old man seem. Then, unbelievably, he winked at her. Jess turned to the woman who had followed him and Ben into the room.

'Maisie, how are you?'

'She's well,' Franklin said angrily. 'Five years older than me and not one damned thing wrong with her, except for her brain and that's never been right.'

'Alex, this is Miss Stanford, Mr Stanford's sister.

Without her this great place would fall apart.'

Franklin gave out a growl and his sister Maisie said, 'I hope your room is comfortable?'

'Yes – yes, thank you,' Alex said, for the woman seemed to be speaking to her. 'Most comfortable.'

'Let me know if you lack anything.'

'I will, but I'm sure I won't need to.'

'How very polite she is,' Miss Maisie Stanford said, as though to someone standing beside her. 'And what a pretty dress. I wonder how much it cost . . . now, dear, where shall we have our drinks? By the windows, I think.' She took two glasses from the tray the maid was offering her, marched across the room and sat down. The maid, used to her peculiarities, solemnly pulled up another chair and placed a table between them.

'It's an improvement,' Franklin said, regarding this performance. 'She used to have three of 'em. The shrink says he's got to leave her with one or she might go plain crackers with me as the only other company.'

He went off with Jess, and Ben came to join Alex. The white of his collar and cuffs was startling against his tan, and the fact that he was fully clothed enhanced the muscular power of his body rather than masked it. Now his hair was dry, she could see that it had little crinkles in it and, like the rest of him, it glowed with vitality.

He took a beer from the maid. There was a faint scowl on his face. 'Aunt Maisie's kind of

40

embarrassing,' he muttered.

His unease dispelled her shyness. 'All families have them. One of Daddy's cousins had her dog stuffed and still treats it as though it was alive.'

He stared at her. 'You're kidding.'

'No,' she assured him. 'It is – was – a Pekinese, and last time she came to stay she complained because it was off its food. When Daddy asked her how long this had been going on, she said, "I can tell what you're getting at, but me and Tinky know better" – and then she kissed it.'

'Kissed a stuffed dog?' Ben was laughing so hard he spilled some of his beer. 'Boy, that makes Aunt Maisie sane,' he gasped. 'You know, she used to insist that places were laid at table for her "friends"? Anyway,' he added, suddenly serious, 'she was right about one thing.'

'What's that?'

'Your dress. It is pretty.'

'Thank you,' she said, feeling the colour rise to her cheeks.

'How about going out later? There's a place a crowd of us meet up.'

'Well, yes,' she stammered, 'but really you don't need to take me along, Ben. I'm not your guest.'

He showed his devastating white teeth. He had a dimple. Just one, on the right cheek.

'I'd like to take you,' he said.

At the end of dinner, Ben asked his grandfather and

great aunt if he may be excused and then sought Richard and Jess's permission to remove Alex. This having been given, they escaped into the hall. Ben tugged at his black bow tie.

'I've got to get out of this,' he said. 'You want to change too?'

She nodded uncertainly. 'Meet you back here in five minutes, then.'

He zipped up the stairs and Alex hesitated, wondering what she should change into. She had no idea where they were going and what would be appropriate; obviously what she was wearing now was not. As she began walking up the wide staircase, Jess came out of the dining-room and Alex turned to her in relief.

'Jeans,' Jess said, when Alex had explained the problem. 'Jeans, of course. This is where they were invented, remember?' She slapped Alex on the bottom. 'Hurry along! You mustn't keep the man waiting.'

Alex zipped as Ben had done and Jess smiled affectionately after her. Being smitten by a beautiful young man was enough of an ordeal, but being smitten in a foreign country when you didn't know the dress code was overwhelming. Reflecting that she was glad she wasn't young any more, Jess pushed open the door to her children's room. They were profoundly asleep, away from the traffic noise and the air conditioning of New York. Jess pulled up William's sheet and gently unravelled the cocoon

Annabelle had made of hers, kissed them both and waited until they were settled once more before she left. Alex, having effected a lightning change, was waiting for her at the top of the stairs and they went down together. Jess could feel her stepdaughter relax as she took in Ben's jeans and his open-necked shirt.

'I'll take real good care of her, Mrs Mountfield,' Ben said.

'Sure you will. Have a good time, both of you,' Jess replied, registering, to her own astonishment, her shock at not being called by her (or Richard's) title – and she a born and bred Republican.

Ben led Alex through the back of the house and into a garage where five gleaming cars stood, including the one Richard Mountfield had rented, and opened the door of a white convertible. Alex got in.

'Do you mind the top down? It won't muss up your hair or anything?'

Of course it would, but she had a brush in her handbag. 'I like an open top,' she said.

He drove very fast through the dark, the motion and the noise of the car making conversation impossible, until he drew up in a car park. Blackness opposite indicated water, but on this side of the road there were lights and activity. Ben opened her door as she was tugging the brush through her hair and she stepped out feeling like a princess and wondering if Ben was exceptional or if all Americans had manners like his. They went into a big, barn-like bar above which 'Roscoe's Place' flashed in blue neon.

'Hi, everyone,' Ben said, cutting short the chorus of shouts that greeted him. 'This is Alex – from England.' He began to tell her their names and then said, 'Aw hell, they can introduce themselves. I'll get you a drink, Alex.'

He disappeared and Alex was surrounded by friendly, open smiles. Before she could think she had been invited to a barbeque the following night, a picnic the day after that and a dance the next week.

'Well, thank you,' she said. 'I'm not sure about the dance, though, because I won't be staying at Mr Stanford's then.'

'I love the accent,' a dark, curly-headed girl called Nancy murmured. 'Say some more. Where will you be staying?'

'I don't know, but it's not very far away,' Alex said a little self-consciously, and explained about Annabelle and William and how she would be at their grandparents' house.

'Sounds a drag,' Nancy said. 'You'll have much more fun with us.'

Of that there could be no doubt, and Alex tried to work out which of the half-dozen girls there was Ben's girlfriend – for surely such a man would have one. She would not dare go to the dance, even if she was able to, without him. How, for a start, would she get there?

'He takes Marilyn,' Nancy said, apparently reading her thoughts, 'but that's only because Alan's working nights this summer waiting tables. He doesn't have a regular date. But what about you? Do you have a boyfriend back home?'

Alex thought of Henry and shook her head. 'A boy who's a friend,' she said.

Nancy laughed. ' "A boy who's a friend," ' she repeated. 'That's good. I like it.'

Ben came over and handed Alex a glass. 'A dry white wine. Isn't that what you like? It's from California. Is it okay?'

She sipped it. 'It's delicious,' she told him, and was rewarded by a flash of the teeth and a glimpse of the dimple.

'Okay, gang,' a tall man called Mike yelled. 'What are we going to do tonight?'

'Movie?' someone suggested, and they all groaned.

'Skinny dip in the Sound?' another voice said.

'Play strip poker.'

'Stay here and get canned.'

'Go someplace else and get canned.'

In the end they piled into their cars, drove through the dark and piled out again into another bar which seemed very like the one they had just left, except this one had a piano player and a few couples were dancing. Mike – with whom Nancy was 'sort of' going steady – and some other boys pulled tables together and they sat down.

Alex could not believe how friendly they were as

they asked her about England and herself, except they would keep commenting on and imitating her accent. Ben noticed her irritation, though she had tried not to let it show.

'Come on, give it a break,' he said. 'How would you like it if someone did that to you every time you opened your mouth?'

The girl so admonished, whose name was Christine, was genuinely distressed. 'I'm sorry, Alex,' she said quickly. 'I just didn't think, but, honest, it's just because you sound so cute.'

'It's all right,' Alex said, touched by how upset Christine was and even more by how Ben had recognized her dilemma. A boy, Rob, sitting on her other side, who had been punctuating every remark with 'Anyone for tennis?' and 'Oh, I say!' thrust out his chin.

'Hit me. Go on – sock me one.'

Alex balled her fist and touched him lightly on the jaw. He fell back, clutching his face.

'The revenge for the Boston Tea Party,' he howled, 'and I get it! . . . Alex, I forgive you. Will you forgive me?'

'Ah guess Ah wi-ill,' she said.

'Jesus, that's terrible. Where did you get it from?'

'Hollywood, Ah guess. Where you got your British acc-ent.'

'Okay, okay. We're quits.'

No one ever teased her about her accent again.

She loved them, loved their energy, their freedom,

their quick acceptance of her. They were living life for all it was worth this summer, for they had finished high school and were going to their separate colleges in the fall. Sure, they said, they would be back next summer, but things were bound to have changed.

'We don't admit it, not out loud, but it's got to be the last summer of the old gang,' Nancy said, taking a T-shirt off the rack and holding it critically against Alex. 'I mean, Mike's going to Harvard, Ben and I are off to Miami. Donna's going to UCLA, California dreamin'. Alex, try this on with the shorts. I think it'll look great.'

Alex took the T-shirt along with another one Christine handed her and went towards the changing rooms. She did not have the right clothes for picnics and tennis, so the three of them were having a 'girls' morning' shopping, spending the thick roll of dollars Richard Mountfield, having been told of Alex's difficulties, had laughingly handed over.

'But didn't you want to be near Mike?' Alex asked through the cubicle door, stripping off her boring British T-shirt and putting on the exciting American one.

'Maybe I did,' Nancy said, 'but since we were kids Ben and I had this crazy idea we'd be Olympic swimmers and Miami was the place to do it from. Anyway, I didn't get the grades for Radcliffe.'

Ben hadn't got the grades for Harvard and Alex

had gathered at dinner last night that this had annoyed Frank, but his father who seemed to delight in anything which annoyed his son – had said he'd never been to college, it hadn't done him any harm and why shouldn't Ben graduate in swimming or whatever he liked at Miami? Even in two days Alex had discovered that grades were all-important, though she hadn't worked out exactly what they were. Different from the GCSEs she had acquired, certainly, but beyond that was mystery. Another boy in the group was also going to Florida, but to somewhere which was not even next door to Miami. How huge this country was! Was it really true that if you stood in Shannon, in the west of Ireland, you would be closer to New York than New York was to Los Angeles? And then there was the distance between the Canadian and Mexican borders – snow in winter in the north and the stuff only known in legend and Christmas cards in the south.

She shook her head to rid it of things too big for it to contain and put on the shorts.

'How about it?' she asked the others.

'Knock out,' Christine said. 'Try the other top on, and these, too.' She gave Alex another pair of shorts.

'I want shoes like yours,' Alex said. 'Where can we get them? Can I afford it?' she added, handing Nancy the roll of notes.

Nancy flipped through it. 'No prob,' she said. 'Your daddy's been very generous.'

'Will there be enough to take you out to lunch? I'd really like to.'

Christine grinned at Nancy. 'Oh hell, Nance,' she said, 'I suppose we might take the price of a hamburger off her.'

Alex loved them, she loved them.

They moved into Jess's parents' house the next day and Betty and Austin Mitchell gave Alex a spare set of keys and demanded – begged – that she treat the place as her own. They had no interest in her and were longing to get down to the serious business of spoiling their grandchildren rotten for the few precious weeks they had a chance to do so.

To Jess the visit to Franklin's now seemed providential. First of all, William and Annabelle had forgotten the horrors of New York and were relaxed and ready to submit to the adoration of their grandparents, and secondly Alex had met Ben and his crowd and was obviously going to be fully occupied. And the crowd was a wholesome, energetic bunch of kids, who did not take drugs or do anything silly and who had apparently welcomed Alex to their all-American heart.

'It couldn't have worked out better, could it?' Jess said to Richard.

'No,' he said. 'It couldn't.'

Alex, if consulted, would have agreed. Ben came and collected her each morning, greeted his reception committee with smiles and hugs, would tell William – with real hurt in his voice, so William felt bad about doubting him – that of course he had not forgotten he was taking him out in the boat that afternoon, pretend he had indeed forgotten Annabelle was coming too (intuitively knowing that Annabelle could take the teasing and William could not) and then allow himself to be dragged off to inspect the children's growing collection of horseshoe crab shells, having somehow managed politely to wish Jess, Richard, Betty and Austin a good morning and give Alex a friendly wave of the hand as well.

Who could blame her for falling in love with him?

They played tennis, they swam, they sailed, they danced, they had picnics at lunch and barbeques in the evenings. They went to movies and Ben, as the other boys did with their girls, put his arm around Alex and held her hand. The first time he kissed her was at the dance she had been invited to on the evening she had arrived on Long Island. As the lights were turned down and couples moved closer together, Ben pulled her to him.

'Alex, oh Alex,' he whispered.

Their lips met and she did not know how her legs supported her.

'Alex,' he said again, and stroked her hair. 'You are one special girl.'

'Franklin Benjamin Stanford the Third,' she responded, trying to sound normal, 'you are one special guy.'

'Hey, you're learning American!'

'We say "guy" in England.'

'Don't lose your accent, Alex. It's so—'

'Cute?' she supplied.

They both laughed and kissed again and were comfortable with each other.

But there was so little time. Two weeks were left, twelve days, ten . . . And what after that? Not only would she and Ben be three thousand miles apart, but what was she returning to England for? Everyone here was amazed she wasn't going to college, that she had finished her education. 'But what are you going to do?' they asked, and she said, 'I don't *know*,' and envied them their four years' grace before they had to decide. And remembered with an impatient stab of guilt Henry and a distant hilltop, and the page in her notebook headed 'Long Island. First Impressions', and nothing more written there.

One more week. Richard Mountfield encountered Alex coming down the stairs. '*Another* new outfit?' he asked, smiling at her.

'No. I've had it for ages.'

'More than two weeks, you mean?' She raised her eyes heavenward and was about to speak when he said, 'Your young man has arrived to sweep you off for the evening.'

'Why didn't you say?' She brushed past him and ran to the door.

Richard gazed after her for a moment, then went to change. He'd had a torrid day – in more ways than the weather – with Frank in New York; William had told him he looked like a man who could use a swim, and William was right. He put on his trunks and went back downstairs. Jess was on the verandah. He stole her glass, took a sip of her drink and watched his two younger children attempting to beguile their hero into staying a few minutes longer by promising him a view of the *biggest ever* horseshoe crab shell if he would bowl them some balls so they could practise with their plastic baseball bat.

'Not bowl,' Ben said, 'pitch.'

'Pitch! Pitch!' they pleaded.

Ben glanced at Alex, who shrugged, kicked off her shoes and prepared to act as fielder.

'Coming for a swim?' Richard asked Jess.

'I've been in the water so often that my skin is turning into a prune.'

'No, it isn't.' He kissed her cheek and handed back her glass. 'Where's Alex going tonight?'

'Dinner at Franklin's and then off somewhere. Franklin has asked us tomorrow night, by the way, all of us. Mom, Dad and the kids.'

'Alex two nights running?'

'Oh sure. If he doesn't have Alex he doesn't have Ben. Anyway, he likes her.'

Jess had gone to visit the old man that afternoon.

'I haven't seen enough of you,' he had snapped, as though it was Jess's fault he hadn't asked them over more often.

'You've seen plenty of Alex, though.'

His face had softened. 'Your girl and my boy,' he said. 'They sure make a pretty pair.'

'She's not my girl and he's not your boy,' she pointed out.

'He's my boy,' Franklin had said. 'Since he was thirteen he's all but lived with me. He's more my son than his father ever was.'

Okay, so Ben preferred to spend his vacations at his grandfather's Long Island mansion than in the apartment belonging to his parents in New York's Upper East Side, but what healthy boy who liked the outdoor life would not?

'Have you heard what they call them?' the old man had asked her.

'The golden couple, you mean?'

'It suits, 'em, doesn't it?'

The two blonds, one muscular and deeply tanned, the other glowing with sun and first love.

'The golden couple,' Franklin said. 'Their beauty and youth are a great joy to me. They brighten the last summer of my life.'

'Nonsense, Franklin,' Jess said, exasperated and concerned, and had added, without thinking, 'Are you really dying?'

He took her hand. 'Ah Jess, my dear, we are all dying. The only relevant question is when.'

Richard nudged her and gestured to Alex, who was leaning against Ben and putting her shoes back on. 'She's so happy,' he said.

Jess sighed. 'I know. She's really flipped over Ben.'

'That's all right, isn't it? I flipped over you, in about the same amount of time, too.'

She stared at him. 'Richard, in God's name what can you mean? They are children. Look at them!'

Ben, egged on by William and Annabelle, was threatening to put the biggest ever horseshoe crab shell down the back of Alex's dress. She was fighting him off, half laughing and half in real fear.

'Go *on*!' Annabelle yelled.

'No.' Ben handed her the shell. 'Alex really doesn't like them. Do you?'

'They are,' said Alex, '*gross*.'

Ben looked at his watch. 'Jesus, we should be gone. Come on, I'll race you to the car.'

They ran, Ben easily outpacing Alex, but he had to scoot round the back of the big gas guzzler to get to the driver's side and Alex scrambled into the passenger seat and, panting, declared it a dead heat.

'See?' Jess said. 'Children.'

That night, when William and Annabelle were in bed, Betty Mitchell, as achingly aware as Alex was of the short time left, hesitantly asked if they had to go back so soon.

'William's school doesn't begin for a while,' she said. 'Maybe you could stay a bit longer.' She put a bowl of salad on the table and turned away. 'Never mind. I expect you have important things to do.'

Austin Mitchell leaned across the table towards Richard.

'If it means paying to transfer the airline tickets . . . well, I'd cover that, of course.'

Jess's eyes filled with tears. Her father wasn't rich. Their retirement from New York City to Long Island had been precisely calculated and they lived comfortably but modestly. Jess had had a running battle with her mother over the grocery bills during their stay here and, naturally, William and Annabelle had been bought several presents. She was already worried about how much this visit had cost her parents, and to hear her father offering money he could not really afford so he could have a little more time with his grandchildren was almost more than she could bear. She knew Richard would refuse the offer, but it made no difference to the spirit in which it had been made. Absurdly, she felt guilty for marrying an Englishman and causing such hurt and heartbreak.

'I won't hear of you paying,' Richard said, true to form. 'I must get back, but it's up to Jess if she, Alex and the children stay.'

Betty stood in suspended motion, and Austin said nervously, 'What do you say, Jess?'

'Sure we'll stay,' Jess said. 'If you'll have us.'

'Oh you!' her father said, and her mother relieved her emotions by serving both Richard and Jess impossibly large portions of clam chowder.

'Will you survive without me?' Richard asked, nuzzling up to Jess as he got into bed.

'For two whole weeks? It'll be tough, but I'll manage.'

'You sound more American since you've been here.'

'I keep being accused of being British.'

'Poor Jess. An American in Britain and British in America. You'll end up a dual personality.'

'Thanks.'

'Jess, shall we let Alex invite Ben to England for Christmas?' he said.

Jess pushed away her husband's distracting hand. 'See the old country, broaden the mind and all that crap, you mean?'

'It's not crap.'

'Richard, what are you up to?'

'Nothing! I just thought the prospect of seeing Ben again at Christmas would make Alex more cheerful about going home.'

'I suppose it would do that,' Jess said. A long plane journey with two small children and a heart-broken teenager was not something to be anticipated with relish.

'Well then.'

Jess couldn't be bothered to think it through. If Richard wanted his daughter and his business associate's son to make a match of it, so what? Ben had four years of college to go through, and if his and Alex's friendship (or whatever it was) survived for that long – which was, surely, unlikely – then it would be very suitable. Right now, Jess was thrilled to have an extra two weeks to watch her children, browned by the sun and like little seals in the water, learn to love their grandparents. Jess remembered how Austin had introduced William and Annabelle to Oreo cookies. They had downed a whole pack at one go and been unable to eat the 'proper American' – as opposed to improper British, Jess assumed – hamburgers they had demanded and Betty had cooked for their supper, and Jess had thought the low-voiced argument between her parents on the subject of her children's diet was the loveliest thing she had ever heard.

'Well then nothing,' she said.

'Really?' Richard murmured. 'I was hoping you might like a little something.'

'Oh were you?' she whispered, her children and stepdaughter vanishing from her mind as her husband hijacked her attention.

Yet Alex was not as overwhelmed and enthusiastic about the news that she was to have an extra two weeks in Ben's company as she might have been, for something even better had come up at dinner at Franklin's. It was daft Maisie who suggested it.

The old man and his sister were sitting in the drawing-room when Alex and Ben arrived.

'What took you so long?' he said sharply, for his insistence on punctuality at mealtimes was legendary and never challenged.

Alex ran forward and kissed him on the cheek.

'My brother and sister's fault. They wanted Ben to play baseball with them.;

'Turning them into proper Americans, are you?' Franklin said to Ben, mollified by that and by Alex's disarming kiss.

'Doing my best,' Ben replied. 'And Alex shows great potential as an outfielder.'

'A girl playing baseball!' Maisie exclaimed. 'I call that very odd, don't you, dear?'

Franklin scowled at her and offered an arm each to the golden couple to help him out of his chair. 'Okay, so now you are here *at last*,' he said, trying to inject sarcasm into his voice, 'perhaps we can eat . . . though,' he went on as he was settled into his place at the head of the table and Maisie sat at the foot, 'it's a wonder you want to have dinner with me, considering the other places you could be.'

'True,' Alex said, smiling at Ben as he held her chair out for her on Franklin's right side, 'but it's cheaper here and the food is much better.'

'She's in for it now,' Maisie said, nodding significantly to her invisible companion and the maid, hearing this as she entered the dining-room, paused and waited for an exhibition of her employer's famous temper.

But Franklin was delighted. 'Cheaper and better!' he cried. 'Damned right it is! Conchita, be sure you tell Juan, though you will anyway.' The Puerto Rican woman's face broke into a relieved smile and Franklin took Alex's hand. 'We're going to miss you like hell when you go back to cold, grey England. Isn't that so, Ben?'

'Yeah,' Ben said softly, his eyes on Alex and his handsome face suddenly sad. 'Like hell.'

'Please don't,' Alex begged, 'don't say that. I have another week here.'

Conchita served the first course, a delicious fish pâté made by her husband Juan. Franklin poked at his minute portion.

'Have you decided what you're going to do back home?' he asked.

'No,' she wailed. 'Don't talk about it – please!'

The notebook still with the empty page . . .

'But why aren't you going to college?' he said. 'A bright girl like you?'

'In England it's not the same,' she explained for the hundredth time. 'Colleges and universities aren't the same thing.'

Maisie clattered her knife on her plate. 'I don't understand,' she said, 'why they are making such a fuss. If the girl wants to go to college, why doesn't she attend one here?' She continued to eat until the fact that the three other people seated at the vast table were staring at her penetrated her disjointed brain.

'Is the pâté all right?' she asked. 'Shall I get Conchita to bring something else?'

'She's right,' Franklin said. 'For once the stupid old woman is right . . . No, no, the pâté's fine,' he added as Maisie reached for the bell to summon the maid.

'Could I go to an American college, though?' Alex wondered.

'Sure you could. Find one to take you and pay, like everyone else.'

Alex looked at Ben. There was only one American college she wanted to go to and if he didn't want her there then it was back to square one. But Ben laughed and whooped and congratulated a most bewildered Maisie on her idea, wrote down the address and made Alex promise to apply to the University of Miami the moment she got home.

Alex ambushed her father the next morning and, scarcely assimilating the tidings of the extra two weeks and that she could ask Ben to Montly for Christmas, she asked him to come for a swim so she could speak to him privately. They walked down to the Sound, swam to the raft anchored a little way out and Richard listened as his daughter poured out her reasons for wanting to go to college in America. What would she do back in England? she argued. Be some dumb secretary in some idiot office in London and wait to get married, that's all.

'What happened to being a journalist?' he enquired.

Alex played her trump card. Nancy had handed it to her last night. 'That's just it! I could do a course in journalism. Colleges here have them.'

'Don't they have them in England too?' Alex sighed dismissively. 'Which college would you go to if Miami didn't accept you?' Richard went on.

She was silent for a while. 'Okay,' she said at last, 'so quite a lot is to do with Ben, but if Miami won't take me I'll find a college that will and go there. My other reasons for wanting this are valid with or without Ben.'

It was Richard's turn to be silent, then: 'Very well,' he said, and was about to add a lecture on how she was to follow the whole thing through and not waste a year trying to get to where Ben was and give up if she didn't, but Alex was hugging him, telling him he was a darling and the best father ever, thanking him for letting her ask Ben for Christmas and wanting to get back to the house so she could thank Austin and Betty for putting up with her for another fortnight.

While she was doing this Ben arrived and was told the news by William and Annabelle.

'Alex, is it true?' he asked. 'And about me going to England?'

'If you'd like to,' she said, annoyed that the children had got in first. She had planned to bring the matter up indirectly so Ben could refuse if he wanted to. She'd go any distance to see him, but it didn't mean he felt the same way about her and she didn't want to appear pushy.

'You bet I would!' he said.

The time went by as swiftly as it had done before, but now Alex was filled with purpose and certainty. She would see Ben again at Christmas – four months really wasn't long – and she would use the time to make her application to the University of Miami and also to do some academic work. She would have to do SATs and, once at college, Nancy had said she could take CLEPs and get credit hours and if she worked hard she might be able to graduate at the same time as Ben. It was all double Dutch to Alex, but if it was a good thing she'd do it. Her teachers at Roedean had always said she had a brain but showed a remarkably consistent lack of interest in using it. She would use it now, and she was, in a curious way, looking forward to going home so she could get on with everything. Except that Franklin kept saying how much he'd miss them, his golden couple, for Ben would be leaving shortly after Alex; Alex said falteringly that perhaps Ben should not come to England for Christmas, perhaps he should be with his grandfather, but Franklin told her not to be so goddamned stupid. He'd have the company of Ben's parents, no doubt, and silly Maisie, and that was about as much as an old man like him deserved.

Two nights before Alex left Franklin allowed Ben to give a farewell party for her. Such a crowd came, people who in five weeks had become real friends. They sang 'Auld Lang Syne' for her and she cried a bit, and so did Nancy and Christine. They made Alex promise that she would get herself into a college here and, if not that, she would come back to America by next summer at the latest.

'Or we'll come over and get you,' Christine added.

'You do that,' Alex told them. 'Please do that.'

The next night Ben took her out to dinner at a restaurant. It was, she realized, the first time they had spent a whole evening on their own. He ordered champagne, saying this was the beginning and not the end of anything, and, aching with love for him, she watched him trying to enjoy drinking it, until she told him to forget it and order a beer, which he did, grinning in relief. At the end of dinner he gave her his farewell present to her, a gold chain with a pearl in a cage hanging from it.

'To remember me by,' he said, and she stared at him, amazed he should think she would need anything to help her remember him.

'I didn't get you a present,' she said. 'Now I feel awful, but thank you for this.' She put it around her neck and began the speech she had prepared for this occasion.

'Ben, if you meet anyone else and decide you don't want to come to England—'

'You write and give it to me straight,' he said. 'I was going to say the same to you.'

They both agreed such a thing was impossible.

Impossible, though, not to feel sad as she received her last goodnight kiss from her golden boy for four months, and heard him promise to pick her up the next day in good time to take her to say goodbye to Franklin before driving her to JFK instead of to some assignation with the gang. And no cheer to be had from Austin, Betty and Jess as they sat up late, comforting themselves that they had so well succeeded in putting on a positive front for the children that William had gone to bed declaring he was looking forward to seeing his pony Pickles again, and pleased he had won sole ownership of the baseball bat in return for Annabelle's total possession of the biggest ever horseshoe crab shell.

What a melancholy place an airport was to say goodbye; except, suddenly, tumbling through the crowds towards them came Nancy, Christine, Donna, Mike and Rob, yelling, 'Surprise, surprise!', and they presented Alex with a T-shirt they'd had specially inscribed with 'I WILL RETURN (to Long Island)' and a book in which they had written special messages to her and included their photographs and ones taken over the past weeks, which would, they said, keep her occupied during the plane journey. They pushed her through the departure gate shouting, 'Go, go, go, but not for long,' and, 'Long live the golden couple,' and then she was on the plane and glad to have the distraction of helping Jess with the children.

And back to grey old England.

Chapter Three

ALEX WENT ABOUT THINGS WITH devastating determination. She railroaded herself into various courses at the college in Eastbourne, and she studied hard. She passed her driving test and bought a beaten-up Mini with her savings which Richard, terrified by the look of the thing, spent more than Alex had paid having it made roadworthy. She received application forms from the University of Miami which demanded an essay from her and she concentrated most mightily both to be honest and tell the university what she thought it would like to know. She wrote to Ben often and had a number of letters back, talking about frat houses and rushes, the great bunch of guys he had met and, more satisfactory and understandable, that he missed her and couldn't wait to see her. When Henry Glover came home for a weekend she told him about Ben and her plans. He listened, resisted informing her that the last thing Fleet Street would want was someone who claimed she knew about journalism because she had done a course at an

American university; and he agreed, a little sadly (though Alex didn't notice this), that he would like Ben and even added – since more seemed to be expected of him – that he looked forward to meeting him.

Alex worried about keeping Ben entertained when he arrived. Sailing, swimming and tennis were obviously not possible in England in midwinter and although a crowd of people tended to meet up in the Montly Arms on Saturday nights it was hardly comparable to Roscoe's Place or the other bars frequented by the gang on Long Island.

'Stop fussing about it,' Jess scolded. 'Ben's an easy-going boy and he'll find plenty to do. And,' she added, 'if you can't keep him occupied, William and Annabelle will. They've made all kinds of plans.'

They had, her darling children, though William's biggest treat for Ben – a ride on Pickles – had been vetoed since Pickles was too small; William had compromised and decided Ben was to be invited to watch him ride.

'Ben this and Ben that!' Nanny Mountfield exclaimed. 'Can this family talk of nothing else?'

She did not approve of Alex's scheme and told her so, saying this falling in love and going off to America was nonsensical, but for once Alex paid her no attention. Jess privately agreed with the old woman but was wise enough not to voice an opinion. She hoped it would fade away, though Alex's determination showed no sign of diminishing.

On a cold December morning, Alex drove to Heathrow Airport. She arrived far too early and as she waited for Ben's flight to land she suddenly became nervous. They hadn't known each other for long. What if it had been – as Nanny said – the equivalent of a shipboard romance and only due to sun and summer? But then his flight was announced and soon after there he was, her golden boy, pushing his luggage trolley out of the customs hall and coming at a run towards her, wearing jeans, a shirt with a loosely knotted tie, and a jacket and overcoat, both unbuttoned. He stopped the trolley, ducked under the rail and picked her up in a bearhug.

'It's you,' he said as he put her down. 'It's really you!'

The doubts vanished.

'It's me. How was your flight?'

He shrugged. 'The plane took off, flew and then landed. What more could you expect? Let's get out of here.'

He grabbed her hand and with his free one got the trolley moving again. She had to trot to keep up with him. It was all there, the energy, the power, the confidence that the world would be kind to him. She felt as if a little slice of America was beside her.

'This is a *car?*' he asked, horrified, when they reached her Mini. 'Oh boy. And what's the steering wheel doing here?' He slung his case into the boot, found the passenger seat and crammed himself into it. 'Okay, Alex, get this tin can moving.'

He was very brave about it, really, especially when they reached the winding country roads.

'I guess I'll get used to it,' he said, 'but honest, Alex, I don't feel there's anything between me and eternity. And why in hell do you drive on the wrong side of the road?'

'Because here it's the right side of the road. You'd be even more nervous if I drove on the right.'

'That proves it's insane. The right is wrong, left is right, and that's impossible.'

Between his squeals, he managed to tell her about his new life in Florida, how he'd been taken on by the swimming coach though he didn't have a hope of making the team, how his courses were going, how Nancy sent her love and he had a letter and a present for Alex from her. And everything he said made it obvious that he expected Alex to be there with him in the fall.

'Have you been working?' he asked her severely.

'Yes. The SATs seemed okay, but I don't know what these CLEPs are like, whether I'm doing the right things.'

'You keep working. You'll be fine. Alex, can we stop at a pub? I met a guy who'd been to Britain and he said I had to go to a pub and have a warm beer.'

'You and your beer,' she said, overtaking a tractor while he hid his head in his hands. 'Any excuse to get at it.' She found a pub and they went in. Ben exclaimed over the low beams and the brasses, the inglenook with a great log burning in the grate and, most of all, at the landlord's casual admission that the place was four hundred years old. He liked the beer, too.

'It's not really warm,' he said. 'It's just not cold.'

'Cold beer is an abomination,' the landlord stated. 'An abomination.'

'Yes, sir,' Ben agreed politely, while Alex had a fit of the giggles.

Alex rang Jess (as she was supposed to have done when Ben's plane landed) and they set off again. Twenty minutes later, she turned off the main road and went up a tiny lane that could not have taken two cars abreast, though to Ben's relief none appeared from the opposite direction. She stopped the car and told Ben to get out.

'Why?' he asked, but obediently unfolded himself and emerged into the December bluster.

'Look.' She pointed, and he looked and gasped.

The Long Man of Wilmington, 230 feet high, shook his two staffs at him from his hillside.

'Oh my,' Ben whispered. 'Who put him there?'

'No one knows.'

'How old is he?'

'They don't know that either, but he's believed to be Iron Age.'

Luckily Ben didn't enquire when this was.

'That's some hill he's on,' he said.

'Yes,' Alex said, 'I climbed it one night last summer.'

In a short while they were at the gates of Montly Manor, where Annabelle and William were waiting to greet them. They pulled open the door on Ben's side of the car and tried to clamber on top of him.

'No, no!' he cried. 'There isn't room.' He tipped them off. 'I'll walk with them,' he said to Alex. 'I want to stretch my legs anyway.'

She waited for him to shut the door and drove away. In her mirror she could see Ben breaking into a jog trot, the children scampering at his heels. How he hated to be still. He must have loathed the plane journey.

Jess came out of the front door, and the children ran up to her breathlessly shouting, 'It's Ben! Mummy, it's *Ben!*' as though they had just invented him.

'Hi, Lady Mountfield,' Ben said, taking her outstretched hand. 'What a beautiful house, and don't you look the part?'

The two Labradors were obligingly posing on the step beside her. With those and her old tweed skirt she supposed she did look like an English country gentlewoman – except that Labradors originated in Canada so really all three of them were fake.

'I expect you'll want to change after your journey,' she said. 'I'll show you to your room.'

They went inside and began walking up the stairs, William and Annabelle, against the rules, inviting the dogs up too.

'I went to see your parents yesterday,' Ben told

Jess. 'They are well and send you their love.'

Jess stopped and stared at him. 'Ben, how very kind of you,' she said, touched. 'How *very* kind. Thank you.'

'No trouble, Lady Mountfield.'

Was it possible he was thoughtful and sensitive as well as everything else? What defence could Alex have against that?

'How is your grandfather?' Jess asked.

'He's pretty well. He sent you his love, too.'

They reached the top of the stairs and the children ran down the corridor, lined with paintings of their ancestors, and stopped expectantly outside a closed door. Their hero did not disappoint them.

'Gee! Did you do this? Surely not!'

'We did, we did,' Annabelle crowed.

'Mummy helped us with the letters, though,' William said.

'"Welcome to Montly, Ben,"' Ben read. 'Well, that's real nice. And is this a picture of us swimming?'

'Yes, and I did one of you and Alex playing tennis,' Annabelle said, aware that grown-ups – inexplicably – often needed to have her drawings explained to them.

'So you did.' Ben hefted his suitcase into his left hand and gravely extended his right one to each of them in turn. 'Thank you very much. I couldn't have dreamed of having a nicer welcome. Hey, and you haven't introduced me to these guys. What are their names?' He stroked the glossy head of the dog nearest to him.

'They are called Silas and Marner,' Jess said. 'Come on, you two. Leave Ben alone now.'

She shepherded the children and the dogs away and Alex opened the door to the bedroom. Ben threw his suitcase on the bed and went to the window.

'When was the house built?'

'In the late seventeenth century but the site is much older. The pond there is part of the moat of the original manor.'

She showed him the bathroom across the corridor, and told him she'd see him downstairs. She waited for a bit, hoping he would kiss her, but he had turned away and was unpacking his case.

'All right?' she prompted.

'Yup. I'll change my shirt and get out a sweater.'

'I've never seen you in a sweater before,' she said.

'There's a first time for everything, Alex.'

She left him to it and went downstairs to the kitchen, where she found William and Annabelle planning Ben's afternoon. Jess caught Alex's anguished look, smiled reassuringly and reminded her children that they had a rehearsal for the church's nativity play to attend.

'But what will Ben do?' said Annabelle.

'He may want a sleep after his long journey. Anyway, he's Alex's guest. It's up to her and him.'

To Alex's relief Ben said that he did not want to

attend the rehearsal of the nativity play, adding tactfully he would instead look forward to the final production. The idea of sleep seemed extraordinary to him, and what he really wanted, he said, was some exercise – if that was okay with Alex.

His sweater was an enormous woolly affair and the crinkles in his hair shone. He looked most huggable and anything he wanted to do was okay with Alex.

'Fine, then. We'll go for a walk,' she said.

Richard lent Ben a pair of wellington boots and Alex struggled after him as he strode up the hill behind the house, the boots picking up a weight of mud he appeared not to notice until they were out of the clay and up on the chalk and turf at the top of the downs.

'There's the English Channel,' Alex said, waving at a distant grey glitter. 'If we were out there you could see the chalk cliffs of Beachy Head. *Much* more impressive than the white cliffs of Dover.'

She was gabbling. She couldn't help it. It was either that or a wind-filled silence between them.

He put his arm around her. 'Sounds like a bit of local prejudice,' he said.

'But it's true!' She used local prejudice to turn towards him within the circle of his arm.

'Really?' he said, and then he did kiss her, and their lips were the only warm things in a high, cold world.

'I thought you must have found another girl,' she

said, snuggling up through his coat to his sweater.

'I show 'em your photograph and they can't take the competition.'

'Do you? Honestly – do you?'

'Sure I do.'

He did. Like Alex with Henry, the girls Ben had taken out had been friends before they were girlfriends and the ground rules had always been clear. Being good-looking, sweet-natured and not short of money, he had attracted a lot of attention when he arrived at college and they scared him, those girls with their overt sexuality. They seemed to know so much more about that sort of thing than he did, and he was terrified they would demand more of him than he wanted to give. He had, in any case, been seduced by the idea of the golden couple, and his first few weeks at college had convinced him that he wanted to give whatever it was he had to no one but Alex, whose innocence matched his own and whose existence – and the photographs he had of her – he indeed used to repel female advances. Nancy's absence from Mike had fulfilled the proverb and made her heart grow fonder, and she had bolstered the edifice by telling Ben that when they needed a partner they could use each other, and had also spread the word about Ben's beautiful British girlfriend. Alex had not only made him immune to and safe from other girls, she had also made him glamorous (flying to England for Christmas so he could see his girl!) and invested him with a hint of tragedy. Beguiling stuff, even for a straightforward and uncomplicated boy like Ben.

'Am I still one special guy?' he said into her ear over the howling wind on a cold shoulder of the Sussex downs.

She removed a glove and touched his glowing hair, as she had been longing to do ever since he had erupted out of the customs hall at Heathrow.

'You know you are.'

'It's great to see you, Alex,' he said softly. He took her bare hand and shoved it into a pocket of his coat along with one of his own.

She wanted to tell him that she loved him, had done so almost from the first moment she had seen him when he had – as she thought – rescued Annabelle from drowning before their very eyes, and had then introduced her to a lifestyle and a crowd of people she had fallen for so that everything since then had seemed dull in comparison. And she, who had been escorted to the formative parties of her life by Henry Glover – who, most cruelly, she now consigned to the dull part of her life so far – was also content with just holding hands and kissing, though the difference between doing that with Henry and Ben was like comparing a weed with a rose. But all she did was squeeze Ben's hand, so intimately close to hers in the warm dark of his pocket, and say, rather feebly, 'It's great to see you too.'

*

They went to London to view the sights, many of which, Alex had to confess, she had not seen before; they went to the theatre; at Montly they walked to the pub for a drink most evenings so Ben could continue his study of English beer and where he met Alex's old friends, including Henry Glover, home for Christmas. Then came Christmastide itself. Ben was amazed at the commonplace of a thirteenth-century church where they went for the carol service which had the nativity play intertwined with it. Annabelle was an angel and William a shepherd, and when they and the other children of the parish sang 'Away in a Manger' and their little voices splashed among the wooden vaulting and into the corners of the ancient place, Ben gripped his service sheet and blinked hard. He was not the only one but had the least cause, and Jess, standing on the other side of him to Alex, noted this with a warring mixture of apprehension and approval.

'That was so beautiful,' he said as they went out into the frosty dusk. 'I won't forget it as long as I live.'

He would not be shaken, even when the angels, the shepherds, the three Wise Men and even Mary and Joseph displayed unholy signs of being 'over-excited and above themselves', as Nanny Mountfield put it at the tea in the church hall afterwards.

Christmas day, and the vicar and his family came for drinks at Montly Manor after the morning service and before lunch. Henry shook Ben's hand in a friendly way, kissed Alex and gave her a small packet. She thanked him and went to find her present for him while Ben, innocently ignorant, showed Henry Alex's gift to himself – a leather wallet embossed with his initials in which he had already stowed the contents of various pockets.

'I've never had one before. It'll be real handy,' he said.

'I'm sure it will,' Henry agreed.

The Reverend John Glover took the whisky Richard offered him and turned to Ben. 'How do you like your first English Christmas?' he asked.

'*Very* much, sir,' Ben replied. 'The service this morning was just about like home, I guess, but that one when the kids did their play . . . that was special.'

'It was, wasn't it? And that is entirely due to my wife. She wrote it, you know, and got the children to perform.'

Ben's eyes widened. 'Is that so? I thought it must come from some book.'

'It did,' Emily Glover said. 'The Bible.'

Everyone laughed, but Ben brushed the noise aside. 'It was special,' he insisted, 'and if there were Oscars for church services, Mrs Glover, you'd get my vote.'

'Why, thank you, Ben,' Emily Glover said, overcome by Ben's sincerity and, like the others listening, warming to this big young American.

'He's nice, isn't he?' Alex whispered to Henry.

'He is,' Henry said, regretting the fact that it was nothing but the truth.

Then time started playing its devious tricks again. The two weeks so looked forward to for four long months steadily leaked away, and after Christmas came the realization that in six days Ben would be back in America and there was no certain prospect of seeing him again until Alex joined him at college in the autumn if, that is, she was given a place there. No mention had been made of another summer on Long Island and there was talk instead of Betty and Austin Mitchell travelling to England, of renting a villa in Italy.

'Would you be able to come here again?' Alex asked Ben.

'I could, I guess, but I'd feel kind of bad leaving Granddad for too long, having seen so little of him this vacation.'

'Yes, of course,' she said, her heart lifting. Even a short time would be better than nothing.

'And maybe,' Ben went on, throwing a stone for Silas and Marner to chase (they were out walking, this being the only way they could be sure of not being ambushed by William and Annabelle; the dogs, Richard had remarked, had never been better exercised), 'maybe you could come over and stay with us. Would your dad pay? . . . Oh no,' he added, subsiding, 'that would mean two flights over, wouldn't it?'

'Only if I get into college,' she reminded him.

'Don't talk about not,' he said.

'I have to. What if I don't?'

'You will,' he said. 'You must.'

Jess watched the golden couple wilt. She felt sorry for them but was powerless to help. In retrospect she wished she had not agreed to the extra time in America, that the idea of Alex going to a college there had never been thought of, that Richard had refused to give the scheme his blessing and had never told Alex she might invite Ben for Christmas. Alex would have been lovesick for a while, but five weeks in the sun could not have sustained her heartbreak for long. Now she and Ben had seen just enough of each other to decide that their feelings were more than a fad and to ensure that adversity (and months and thousands of miles apart was quite a lot of adversity) would strengthen them, yet not enough for boredom and familiarity to set in – as Jess was sure it must. It had to! Like Henry Glover, Jess had searched for flaws in Ben and, like Henry, could find none apart from a certain immaturity which, by the nature of the beast, time would most certainly cure. He had even charmed Nanny Mountfield, who had declared him to be a very pretty-mannered boy. Perhaps, Jess thought hopefully as she examined the roast potatoes for Ben's last Sunday lunch in England, perfection itself would lead to boredom. But there again, Alex was not going to see enough of Ben to find that out.

Jess gazed absently at Silas and Marner, who

gazed back. 'He'll meet another girl,' she told them. 'He's bound to, a lovely boy like him. Isn't he?' They clattered their claws on the quarry tiles and wagged their tails in agreement. 'Yes, he's bound to,' she repeated, not knowing the peculiar place Alex occupied in Ben's pantheon at college. 'And then Alex will be committed to four years in America, and you can bet she'll be too stubborn to admit the whole exercise was because of Ben so she'll stay there and be miserable . . . And my God, no!' she exclaimed, at last realizing the reason the dogs were paying her such polite attention was the beef she had taken out of the oven. 'You touch that and you'll be hung, drawn and quartered. Count on it.'

'Count on what?' Richard asked, coming into the kitchen and handing Jess her drink. 'It was getting lonely. What's taking you so long?'

Jess explained, having made sure the door was closed and there was no possibility of being overheard. 'See?' she concluded. 'The whole thing is a mess. An absurd mess. It should never have gotten started.'

'Calm down,' Richard said. 'Jess, my darling, for heaven's sake calm down.' For Jess had indeed become quite agitated, picturing vividly the whole scenario: Alex going mournfully to class being ignored by everyone, while Ben grew his hair and he and his new girl dropped out of college and spent their time travelling around the country attending demonstrations. That college kids no longer thought long hair fashionable or demonstrated against the Vietnam War made no difference: Jess could imagine how Alex would feel because something very similar had happened to her – and she had only gone from home in New York to Chicago.

She blew her nose and took a healthy pull of her gin and tonic. 'I'm sorry, Richard. It's because I know this whole thing is disastrous. Alex isn't my daughter and you'll probably tell me to mind my own business—'

'Jess, you must be ill or overtired or something! Have I ever said that to you? Ever?' She shook her head and he continued, 'You know how grateful I am for what you've been to Alex. Why, everyone – her teachers, everyone! – said how much more settled and happy she became almost from the moment you and I were married.' He paused. 'Perhaps I never actually told you, but I am grateful.'

She managed a smile. 'I don't want your gratitude, Richard. Maybe I would have if I'd done it out of duty or to make myself more important to you. I did it – well, I didn't do anything, it just happened – because I love Alex. Which is why I'm so worried about this. I don't want her to be unhappy.'

He kissed her and held her close. 'Do you think I do?'

'She's going to be whatever happens. Don't you see? It's gone too far.'

'You're exaggerating, Jess. Why are you so convinced Ben will meet someone else? So might

Alex, come to that.'

'Not before she gets to this damn college she won't. You know what she's like once she's decided on something.'

He did, none better, and Jess's tears unnerved him. He did not want Alex alone and friendless thousands of miles from home. A thought came to him, and he almost rejected it: surely it was too soon? But Alex would find out if she was accepted by Miami some time in the next month, and if she wasn't? It was Richard's last chance and would solve every problem, Jess's included, though she might not see it like that.

'I'll think of something,' he said, stroking his wife's hair.

She pushed him away. 'What? What on earth can you do?'

He grinned at her. 'I could,' he said lightly, 'play the heavy-handed father and ask the young man his intentions.'

She thought he was joking.

The next day was New Year's Eve, the day before Ben was flying home. Alex was going into Eastbourne to have her hair done for the party that was traditionally given at Montly to welcome the New Year, and it was easy enough for Richard to persuade Ben that he would rather take a gun out with him and the dogs than hang about in town waiting for Alex.

'Go,' Alex said, though every second with Ben was precious.

'I'll shoot you a pheasant,' he promised.

Alex left, and Richard, Ben and the dogs set off up the track behind the house.

'It sure is a fine day,' Ben said, indicating the downs shining in the sun against the blue sky, their shadowed flanks filled with frost.

'It is,' Richard said. 'Ben, can you slow down? I'm not as young and fit as you are.'

'Oops, sorry, sir,' Ben said, easing his swinging stride.

Richard leaned against a gate to catch his breath. What he had to say to Ben was tricky enough without the added complication and indignity of panting as he tried to keep up with him. Ben stopped too, and laid his breeched gun on top of the gate.

'I'm sorry,' he said again. 'Alex complains I go everywhere too fast. I like to get there quickly, I guess.'

'I want to talk to you about Alex,' Richard said, grabbing his cue.

'Yes, sir?' No wariness in his voice, only innocent enquiry.

'She's set her heart on being at college with you, hasn't she? Do you think she'll get in?'

'I hope so. It'll be great to have her there.'

'Jess and I are worried about it, Ben,' Richard said, man to man.

Ben turned to face him, a concerned frown between his blue eyes.

'Why is that?' he asked.

Richard hesitated and then said, 'You don't have a sister, but can you pretend you have? A younger one.'

Ben nodded, mystified. 'Okay, I'll try.'

'It's probably easier than imagining you have a daughter . . . Anyway, this sister of yours meets a boy from England one summer, and before you know it she's arranging to move three thousand miles, to a foreign country, to be with him. Now, don't get me wrong. You like the boy, but you love your sister. She's young for her age and she doesn't know half as much about the world as she thinks she does. You wonder what would happen if things between her and the boy go wrong and there she is, far away with no big brother to turn to or to look after her – as you have always done. How would you feel about this, Ben?'

Ben put his hands in his pockets and hunched his shoulders. 'I'd be worried,' he said at last, staring at the ground, 'if I couldn't persuade my . . . sister not to go. I'd tell the boy to make darned sure he takes real good care of her and if he didn't I'd promise to punch his teeth in.'

'And would your mind be at rest then?'

Ben kicked at the gatepost. 'No, it wouldn't.' He looked directly at Richard. 'You want me to persuade Alex not to come to college. Is that it?'

The boy was too good to live.

'Is there anything else,' Richard said carefully, 'that would satisfy you? As the older brother, I mean?'

Ben sighed. 'I'll talk to Alex,' he said. 'But I love her, you know, and I'm pretty sure she loves me.' He took the gun from the top bar of the gate. 'Come on,' he muttered. 'I said I'd get her a pheasant.'

Richard whistled to the dogs and followed him, all kinds of conflicting emotions sprouting in all directions inside him. Guilt about the unhappiness of the young man walking up the hill ahead of him, so disturbed that his manners had been forgotten and he no longer cared if he left his host behind. Hope that when this conversation was relayed to Alex she and Ben would come to the obvious conclusion. Or perhaps not. Had Richard ballsed the whole thing up? Worry, because was what he was doing – had done if he'd played Ben correctly – right? If he really thought so he would have told Jess about it; he hadn't, quite simply, because he knew she'd be furious . . . Yet what had he done other than to voice Jess's own concerns? Guilt again, because he knew (hoped?) he had done a lot more than that. Then again and again: wasn't he only ensuring his daughter's happiness? Yes he was. He was.

Ben had stopped and was waiting for him by a fallow field, part of Richard's setaside land.

'This looks a likely place,' he said, his eyes not meeting Richard's.

Richard sent the dogs on. 'Okay,' he said. 'We keep abreast. Anything to the left is yours, to the right is mine. No poaching it's dangerous.'

'I know,' said Ben stiffly and moved forward parallel to Richard, evidently determined to lay dead birds at Alex's feet, poor substitutes for dragons though they be.

When Alex arrived home, she made her way through the clutter of the party preparations and eventually ran Ben to earth in one of the back pantries where, hindered by William, he was cleaning the guns he and Richard had used that morning.

'How did you get on?' she asked.

He nodded towards the old wooden draining board. 'I got you your pheasants. A pair of 'em.'

'Ben, well done! What did Daddy shoot?'

Ben pulled an oily rag through one of the barrels of the gun he was holding. 'He winged a pigeon.'

'So you did better than him. What fun!'

He smiled slightly. 'I was lucky, I guess . . . Hey, you, scoot,' he said to William. 'I have to talk with your sister.'

William stood up reluctantly. 'But you'll watch me ride this afternoon? It's your very last chance.'

'Yeah,' Ben said. 'I'll watch you ride.'

Alex waited until William had closed the door

behind him. 'What's the matter? Ben, whatever is the matter?'

He washed his hands, then pulled the rickety chair William had been sitting on over next to his own and patted the seat. They both sat down, and he took her hand and told her everything Richard had said to him.

'But it's absurd,' she exclaimed when he had finished.

'No, it's not. The way your dad put it to me made me realize.

He and your stepmother are right to be concerned. I know I won't let you down or desert you, but why should they take my word for it? I wouldn't in their place.'

'If you know you won't let me down and I know it too,' she pointed out, 'then they can go on being concerned until they get bored of it. Unless . . . Ben, did he say he wouldn't pay for me to go through college?'

'No, but he could do that, I guess.'

They stared at each other, youth confronted by perfidious adults, the image of Richard between them growing the devil's horns and tail.

'I'll talk to him – now,' Alex said. 'He promised, and he's not going back on his word.'

Ben took her arm. 'Listen to me, Alex. There's a way round everything.'

She sat down again, her head drooping. 'What is it?'

With one forefinger, he swept back the shining blonde curtain of hair nearest to him and tucked it behind her ear.

'I like to see who I'm talking to. It could be anyone behind there.' He turned her face towards him. There were tears in her eyes. 'So that's what you're trying to hide.'

'It's awful, Ben,' she whispered. 'Bad enough you leaving tomorrow, but now this—'

'Listen, and please don't cry. Alex, I told your dad something today that I haven't ever told you. It just came out and when it did I knew it was true.' He dropped his hand and fiddled with the gold bracelet on her wrist, his Christmas present to her. 'I told him that I love you and said I thought you loved me too. Alex, was I right?'

'Oh, Ben,' she breathed.

'Because if I was, I began to figure it out. Like what would make me feel comfortable about my kid sister going off to a foreign country to be with some boy. And the other side of it, too – if you don't get into college, I mean—'

'But you always say I will! Ben, I can't bear this!'

'You do or you don't. It wouldn't make any difference.'

'How wouldn't it?' she said drearily.

'Because we get married.'

Each year everyone said it was a miracle how Jess managed to give a New Year's Eve party of such magnitude and with so little apparent effort. Jess always smiled and said it was no problem and they praised her all the more, but the secret was so simple that Jess dared not reveal it, except to Jane Patterson who knew it anyway.

When she had been pregnant with William and ordered to rest for two hours every afternoon, she had found in the library an account of life at Montly during the nineteenth century written by – Jess tried to work it out – Richard's great, great grandmother. At first the cramped, crabbed writing had daunted her, but the enforced idleness had made her persevere. It was, she soon realized, not so much a diary as a practical guide to running Montly, written, so Jess presumed, for the purpose of helping the wife of her eldest son when it was her turn to be mistress of the house. In every true sense, although it seemed most strange, Jess was its latest inheritor and the wife of the thing inside her – if it was male – would be the next in line. The idea that she was but one small cog in the recurring cycle of birth, marriage, parturition and death that had ensured the continuance of the Mountfield line, from the time Robert Mont le Fleuris had stepped on to English soil with William the Conqueror not so very far from here up until now, half elated Jess and half depressed her.

'I'm hideous and horrible,' she wailed, when Jane came to see her. 'Just a brood mare. Richard only married me because he wanted an heir.'

'Nonsense,' Jane said briskly. 'And I wish women would not compare themselves to brood mares. Ours have a lovely life. Much less frazzled than mine. It's newsletter time, my dear. Could you bear to do the necessary?'

'Sure,' Jess said, taking the sheaf of envelopes and the list of the Pony Club members' addresses. 'Even a brood mare could handle that.'

'You didn't get my point. They don't have to handle anything. They laze about in the field and get looked after by me.'

'But they spend most of their lives pregnant,' Jess said, feeling much sympathy with this however pampered they were otherwise.

'Yes, but they love their foals dearly, as you will yours, and forget about how uncomfortable it was.'

Jess began to laugh. Jane always cheered her up. 'If I give birth to a foal, will you admit I'm a brood mare?'

'Oh,' Jane said crossly, 'you know what I mean.'

Soon any emotional reactions to her Victorian predecessor's book were swamped by fascination. Georgiana Mountfield had given several parties a year, most notably the one on New Year's Eve 'for all the People of the Locality', and after William was born (who Jess did indeed love dearly) and her usual energy was restored, Jess had the idea of reviving the custom and learned that, in fact, it had persisted until a few years ago. Ah. Until Richard's first wife had left him, then. Jess knew the signs. She had a moment's jealousy as she wondered if her immediate predecessor had read Georgiana's book and, on examining it for clues, she saw that her own reading of it was damaging the spine. She bought a book for herself and followed Georgiana's first maxim: 'Write Everything down. You do not know when it might be Useful.'

She did not plan to give a Victorian party; that would be absurd. But she did like the idea of taking Georgiana's advice and was intrigued to see how valid it was well over a hundred years later. Jess did not have, of course, Georgiana's unlimited servants to command, nor did she have to remember 'by Oct ltst' to book Mr Paynton's 'excllnt Orchestra' from Eastbourne, but the use of various rooms for 'Dancing, Card-playing and Sitting Out' (Georgiana bewailed the fact that Montly had no ballroom, but Jess did not) held up pretty well and so did – most extraordinary to Jess – the information about which pieces of furniture should be moved where to make room for the throng, for it was all still there and in the same places, though there had been some additions.

By substituting Richard for the butler, who must order in 'sufficient Beer, Wines and Spirits', herself for the housekeeper to 'instruct Cook to prepare (cold) three Gammon, ten brace Pheasant and (hot) two haunch Venison' (Jess blanched at the roasted Ox on a Spit and other of Georgiana's more labour-intensive recipes), Cynthia and Sue George, mother and daughter from the village, for the cook and other local people for Georgiana's endless supply of serving men and maids, Jess managed. It was very much a community affair. The so-called servants took their turn in the disco and the guests did a stint of clearing plates and washing up. Most people walked to the party, their torches flickering up the drive rather less romantically than the lamplight of the past, bringing their children with them. Those over twelve were allowed to come to the party while the younger ones were tucked into their sleeping bags and left in the old night nursery under the charge of Nanny Mountfield, whose high spot of the year this was.

The routine was now firmly established, the only major change being that people had expressed a wish for more traditional music. The church choir, a trifle merrily perhaps, sang carols in the hall as the New Year approached and the disc jockey shared the rest of the night with a band of musicians who played anything from foxtrots to Scottish reels, so Jess had had to find a substitute for Mr Paynton's excellent orchestra after all.

Georgiana's book was in a locked cabinet in the library and Jess's would eventually join it there, for after last year's party Richard had taken it away and returned it bound in leather. It made her feel a bit intimidated when she wrote in it, especially when Richard had made her inscribe on the flyleaf:

Jessica Claire Mountfield (née Mitchell)
of New York City, New York USA
Married to Richard William Robert Mountfield Bt
of Montly Manor, Montly, East Sussex

So there was her little share of immortality. But had she not been working towards it? She had always used a fountain pen when writing in her book, liking the scratching sound, the drag of the nib across the paper and, most of all, the ink spatters which needed frequent application of blotting paper. Georgiana's ink blots were wondrously eloquent and spluttered from her pen in anger, enthusiasm or frustration, making some pages nearly impossible to read.

Before this latest party Jess laid out the makings of a picnic lunch in the morning-room. The children were already bored of ham and cold turkey, but there was nothing else apart from cheese. They would probably be too excited to eat much, anyway. It was Annabelle's first year outside the baby category in the night nursery and she had been practising with her sleeping bag this morning; William had been trying to frighten her with horror stories about Nanny Mountfield, but Annabelle wasn't fooled. She knew about the goodies that were sent upstairs.

Jess took stock. Cynthia and Sue were in full control of the kitchen, the women who made the puddings had rung to say they would be bringing them over at five o'clock, Henry Glover's sister and Jane Patterson's daughter were rolling cutlery into napkins and laying out plates in the dining-room, the drink and glasses had been delivered and the furniture had been moved the previous day. 'If,' Georgiana had written, 'the Staff are well trained and carry out their Orders, there is no reason why the Lady of the House should not retire to her boudoir for a quiet afternoon before the Night's Festivities begin.' Jess thought that after lunch she may well have retired to her boudoir if she'd had one, and wondered if a snooze in her and Richard's bedroom constituted a substitute.

And then the golden couple, looking radiant, burst into the room with their shattering news.

They did not seem to notice that she did not react. As she sank into a chair, her mouth dropping stupidly open, they demanded the whereabouts of Richard and, too impatient to await her answer, rushed out again.

She had dreamt it. She must have done. It was some strange hallucination arising from exhaustion after the preparations for the party. It could not possibly be true . . . but the door of the morning-room was open and she knew she had to believe the evidence of her ears and eyes: Alex and Ben had been in front of her announcing that they were getting married.

She heard Richard shout, 'No!' and then 'No!' again, and footsteps in the corridor. She stood up shakily as he came striding in.

'Good God, Jess,' he said. 'Have you *heard* what these two plan to do? I won't allow it. I will *not* allow it.'

William appeared in the doorway, his eyes wide with interest, and the house seemed to have fallen silent and be full of listening ears. Jess led William to the dining-room and asked the two Sarahs – Glover and Patterson – if he could help them with their tasks. Politely they nodded, their eyes, like William's, wide with speculation; Annabelle came down the stairs dragging her sleeping bag and was shoved into the dining-room too.

Jess returned to the morning-room. Alex and Ben, hand in hand, were standing in front of Richard, Alex looking defiant and Ben unaccustomedly determined.

'You wanted to be sure she'd be taken care of,' he was saying. 'This way makes it sure.'

What had Richard said to Ben? Jess wondered as, evidently distressed, he ran his hands through his hair and muttered, 'I need a drink.'

'Champagne,' Alex said solidly. 'To celebrate.'

'No!' Richard yelled.

Alex turned to Jess. 'You understand, don't you? Ben and I have decided we will never love anyone else so we may as well get married now.'

'Now?' Jess said carefully.

'Well, soon,' Alex amended.

'It's nonsense,' Richard stated, and Jess stared at him warningly. Did he not realize that a bit of healthy opposition was all that was required to force the golden couple to the altar?

They sat down and talked the whole thing through. It did not take long, for it was soon obvious that no opposition was needed to force Alex and Ben up the aisle. They were going there of their own free will and nothing would stand in their way. Alex drove Richard's objections back at him with equal or greater power than they were delivered, and the objections, anyway, only amounted to the well-worn pair of twins – that Alex and Ben were too young and did not know each other well enough – which adults always produce on such occasions and which inflame both sides of the debate since both know they are right and neither can prove it.

The guilt Richard had felt this morning had coagulated into a horribly unpalatable mess, and just at the moment when he wanted to put an end to the thing he had created it had developed a mind of its own, escaped from its cage and had no intention of being recaptured.

'But I don't want you to go and live in America,' he said, knowing he sounded petulant.

'We'll come over, won't we, Ben? Every year.'

'Sure we will.'

'And we'll announce our engagement at the party tonight.'

'No,' Jess said suddenly, standing up.

Alex glared at her, her cheeks flushed and the light of battle still in her eyes. 'Why not?'

'People are coming here to celebrate the New Year. I am not calling for silence in order to tell them about an engagement that will cause more shock than anything else. "Announce" indeed! Why in hell should your "announcement" – thrust upon us at a few hours' notice – upstage the New Year? Ben's parents don't even know about it yet. Will you call them this afternoon, Ben, or wait until you see them?'

'I'll – I'll call them, I guess,' he said. He was sure what he was doing was right, but he needed Alex's strong presence at his side as he gave his parents the happy news.

'And your grandfather,' Alex said. 'He at least should be pleased.'

Jess sighed. 'If you say so, Alex. If you say so.'

'I don't understand. I would have thought you'd want me to be happy.'

The fight had gone from her, and she appeared vulnerable and terribly young.

The blond giant beside her took her hand once more. 'And I will make her happy. Sir, ma'am, believe me I will.'

He was so handsome, so earnest and so damned *nice*, but dear God they were a pair of children. Jess already regretted her flash of temper and wondered what on earth her attitude should be. She touched Richard's shoulder. 'I'd like that drink,' she said. 'Then we must have lunch.' From somewhere she found a smile and offered it to Alex and Ben. 'You can't expect us to be pleased, not straight away. You must give us time to get used to the idea. Don't say anything to William and Annabelle yet because they won't be able to keep it secret and will tell everyone they see. That is the last way, surely, you want news of your . . . engagement to get out. I suggest we talk again after Ben has spoken to his parents.'

They agreed and smiled happily back at her, the beautiful golden couple, and she went to collect her son and daughter. It was only an engagement, she told herself. Only an engagement and at least there had been no mention of a wedding date. An engagement didn't necessarily become a marriage, did it?

And who was she trying to kid about that?

She did, in the event, retire that afternoon, but to have a council of war with Richard and not to rest. Ben's parents had been spoken to and Alex interpreted their stunned silence as delight. Franklin, as Alex had predicted, was pleased – overjoyed, in fact.

'It's all very well for him,' Richard said. 'He gains Alex. We lose her.'

He was so upset that Jess found herself playing devil's advocate. 'Maybe it's not so bad. Ben's a nice boy' – why did she always use that word, the blandest, most all-embracing adjective in the English language, to describe him? – 'and if they were a little older you couldn't wish for a nic . . . more charming son-in-law.'

Is that what sons-in-law were supposed to be? Georgiana had ended up with six of them, and her criteria were money and breeding. Ben didn't do badly on those scales either: his was a respectable New York family; his father was reasonably well-off and his grandfather had untold millions. She explained this to Richard and he laughed for the first time in hours.

'You and Georgiana,' he said.

The phone rang on their bedroom extension and Jess picked it up, automatically registering the fact that Ben and Alex were out with the children, supervising their riding, and so would not be listening in on a telephone downstairs. It had come to that so quickly, the feeling that she and Richard were besieged.

It was Franklin. 'See?' he said. 'Your girl and my boy.'

'They're too young, Franklin.'

'Like hell they are! If I'd waited to marry Mary I'd have been a widower first. I've never regretted those few years I had with her.'

Mary Charman Stanford had died of pneumonia at the age of twenty-two, and her perfections had made the second Mrs Stanford's life a hell from which she had escaped through bottle after bottle of Bourbon.

'Anyway,' the old man went on. 'You're not about to stop 'em, not from how they sounded to me, so I want you to know that I'll take care of 'em. Rent an apartment down in Miami and make sure they don't starve. I thought you may be concerned,' he added, his voice softening.

It had been the last thing on Jess's mind, but if Ben and Alex were really going to get married and set up a home together she supposed she and Richard should be grateful. 'But don't encourage them to marry too soon,' she told him. 'We're relying on an engagement of at least a year.'

It was unlikely, but worth a try.

'Don't you worry. It'll work out just fine.'

Jess put the phone down. 'We're on our own,' she said to Richard. 'We have to make the best of it we can.'

'How do we do that?'

She shrugged and smiled slightly. 'Wholesale surrender, I guess.'

He put his arms around her. 'I'm sure it's my fault,' he said, hoping to be released from some of his guilt.

'Nonsense. They met and this was the result. No one could have predicted it. Anyway, lots of young marriages work out, don't they? This one will probably be very happy and prove us both wrong. But what,' she said, snapping him to systems alert once more, 'did you say to Ben this morning? Something must have brought this on.'

'Only that we were worried about Alex alone in a foreign country,' he replied, with nearly perfect truth. 'And don't forget that they are parting tomorrow for heaven knows how long.'

'I suppose that must be it. It's why you proposed to me, isn't it?'

'That and because I loved you – still do.'

He kissed her and, as her arms tightened around his neck in response, he felt himself absolved.

Alex grabbed Henry as soon as he arrived that evening and whisked him into the library.

'Can you keep a secret?' she asked.

'I don't think so,' he said. He didn't want to hear it. His sister had reported the goings-on at Montly this morning and obviously he was about to find out that her and Sarah Patterson's speculation had been correct. 'Why is it a secret, though?'

'But you don't know what it is yet.'

'Okay. Tell me.'

She did so and he said, 'Congratulations.'

'Daddy and Jess are furious.'

'I'm not surprised. Going to college in America is one thing, getting married at your age and living there permanently is something else. Why should they like it?'

'Is that all you have to say?'

'What could I say that would make any difference? If you really want to know, I don't like it either.' He turned to go out of the room. 'Thank you for telling me, Alex. It would have been . . . hard hearing it from someone else.'

That was not why she had told him. She had been

hoping for a joyful and positive reaction to her engagement, and thought Henry might provide it. Nanny had gasped then muttered darkly about handsome being as handsome did and snapped, 'I certainly will not!' when asked not to inform anyone else. Alex was beginning to feel that she and Ben were reading from a different script to everyone else – except old Franklin, which made up for a lot – and now she could see Henry was in fact saddened by her news. She remembered their times together.

'I'm sorry, Henry,' she said.

'That we'll go no more a-roving, you and I, by the light of the moon? So am I.' He opened the door for her. 'Come on, it's time to join the party.'

'Will you dance with me later?'

He smiled his sweet Henry smile. 'Yes, I'll dance with you, provided I don't have to fight your enormous fiancé for the privilege.'

The identical reaction from the people she loved most (apart from Ben) could have been daunting if Ben hadn't been leaving tomorrow and their future together, until he proposed, so uncertain. But Alex had never been particularly daunted by what her seniors considered to be her best interests, and when Ben took her into the disco and pulled her to him for the last time in months, she knew that what they had decided was right.

'Sure it is,' he said. 'Don't you see? It's because they love you that they don't want you to leave them. So we'll have to come back often – and invite them over to see us – and then everything will be.'

A golden future for the golden couple. What could tarnish that?

Chapter Four

YET NOT EVERYONE REACTED BADLY. When the announcement appeared in the newspapers Alex received many letters from school friends saying how romantic and exciting it was and when was the happy day? She also had ecstatic letters from Nancy and other Long Island friends. Ben's parents wrote and even Franklin put pen to paper – to both Alex and Jess (he seemed to ignore Richard as comprehensively as he ignored his son) – inviting Alex to stay for part of the summer, and Jess and the children if they cared to come, and reassuring Jess that it would be all right. A girl of Alex's intelligence and strength was exactly what Ben needed.

'Which,' Jess said, taking back the letter after Richard had read it, 'begs the question of whether a boy like Ben is what Alex needs.'

'Will you accept his invitation?'

'No. Mom and Dad are coming over here, remember? We and the Pattersons are going to Italy.'

'Only for three weeks.'

'They'll be this side of the Atlantic for six.'

'Alex has asked me if she can go.' 'She's asked you?' Jess exclaimed. 'She tells you she's getting married and asks if she can go to America for a while. Why would that be, do you suppose?'

'You know. She needs me to pay for the air fare.'

'No kidding.'

'Shall I say yes?'

'It's not for a while yet. Why not make her sweat?'

'I'm worried Franklin will offer to pay. I can't allow that and it will make me appear petty when I end up paying anyway.'

'You are quite right, of course,' Jess said, after a moment's silence. 'Richard, I apologize. This whole damn mess is making me sound off at everyone. Let her go, and how about inviting Ben to Italy? The more they see of each other the better. It's the only thing that's going to stop this marriage.'

'Will there be room for him?'

Jess worked out that they could accommodate Ben and rang Jane Patterson to ask if her family would mind if he joined the party at the house they had taken outside Siena.

'My dear, I'm afraid they would love it,' Jane told her. 'The boys think he is wonderful and Sarah has a crush on him. She wants to bring Sarah Glover too, so they can both gaze on him soulfully.'

'Maybe he'll marry one of them instead,' Jess said.

'Unfortunately,' Jane said cheerfully, 'they are

both under-age and thus can be locked up on a diet of bread and water until they come to their senses.'

Alex was showing no sign of coming to her senses. A day in August was chosen for the wedding. She received from Ben, by courier, a ruby and diamond ring. It was, Ben wrote, his grandfather's first wife's engagement ring and Franklin was anxious she should have it. They could choose a ring together when they next met, but in the meantime she should wear this on the fourth finger of her left hand and pretend Ben had put it there. The University of Miami accepted her (thanks to some sugaring by Franklin, though Alex didn't know that), but she continued her academic work, reading whatever books she thought appropriate to passing the mysterious CLEPs. She'd need thirty credit hours (whatever those were) to catch up with Ben, for if she didn't she would end up being at college longer than he would and that would be a bore and a nuisance. Whatever anyone thought she was determined to graduate and show doubters she wasn't playing games.

Another letter contained details of the fees and this caused something of a dilemma. Who should pay: her future husband (in the person of his grandfather) or her own father? It seemed appalling that she was dependent upon men, but she didn't have any money of her own. If she wasn't working so hard she would have taken a job, and even began searching for an evening one. Jess or Richard – Jess, most likely – found the local paper with bar work and waitressing jobs marked, and Richard told Alex wearily that he had promised to pay for her to go through college and he wasn't in the habit of breaking his word.

She did feel bad about the air fares and the money, about the disruption she had caused and the distance that had come between her and Richard and Jess. She tried to talk to Jess about it, and Jess stroked her hair away from her face and smiled at her.

'Honey, it's you,' she said. 'You're not with us.' She waved a hand vaguely westward. 'You've gone.'

It was true. Alex was marking time in the Old World while everything exciting was happening in the New. Nancy wrote saying a couple graduating this year had an 'adorable apartment' near the campus, and enclosed photographs. Wasn't it great? Ben liked it, the rent was well within what Franklin had stipulated and Nancy reckoned the young Stanfords-to-be should get in there quick. Alex looked at the photographs, finding it odd that this was where she and Ben would live as man and wife. The place was more modern than she was used to, but that was America, she supposed. She told Ben and Nancy to do what they thought best.

The young Stanfords-to-be, though, were to have a main residence apart from the apartment in Florida. This was one wing of Franklin's mansion on Long Island. Maisie was delegated by her brother as secretary and general dogsbody. Alex was pleased to discover her censorious 'friend' did not take part in Maisie's correspondence, but Maisie asked Alex for impossible decisions. What colour carpets would she like for the living-room? What kind of and colour bathroom suite? The space available for the kitchen and dining-room was so many square feet – how much did Alex want allocated to each? It depended, she said, on how much formal entertaining Alex planned to do. This last Alex had no trouble with. The idea of Nancy, Christine, Rob and the gang sitting in a dining-room waiting to be formally entertained was hilarious. A big kitchen, obviously, so they could sit around and eat take-out meals.

'As for the rest,' Alex wrote to Maisie, 'can it not wait until I come in July? I find it hard to visualize the details and am not acquainted with the brand names you mention.'

'Wowee!' Nancy wrote in reply to Alex's letter telling her what she had said. 'That sounds brilliant and – well – so married. Can I help choose? We'll have a shopping spree like never before.'

No wonder the English spring passed with all thoughts and emotions three thousand miles away. Alex received the news that Ben could come to Italy with a casualness bordering on indifference. If he had not been invited, or did not want to come, she would have gone to America instead. But Ben accepted and Franklin agreed to pay for his flight over. Franklin himself was coming to the wedding and was astonished that anyone should be surprised.

'You think I'm not going to see my boy married?' he roared at Jess down the telephone. 'Any fool can sit still on an aeroplane for a few hours. I haven't done it too often before because there hasn't been a single darned place I wanted to go.'

'All this to-ing and fro-ing across the Atlantic because of you,' Nanny Mountfield scolded Alex. 'You've become a spoilt little minx.'

Alex hugged the old woman. 'I have, haven't I?'

'I always let you have your own way, and now see what it's come to.'

'You did not! Nanny, you were as strict as anything!'

Nanny allowed a tear to escape from her eye. She would be in the family pews at the wedding and was getting into training.

'Don't cry, Nanny. *Don't!*'

These burdens tethering her to the ground. She could not wait to fly away with Ben and be free of them – most particularly since the enthusiasm for her and Ben's marriage was so palpable and positive on the other side of the Atlantic, the latest example of which was Franklin's offer to bring over six of Ben's friends for the wedding.

'Not Nance, obviously,' Ben said, and an outraged yowl came at Alex along the phone line. 'She wants to be maid of honour . . . I think.' There was a minor scuffle as Nancy grabbed the phone.

'Can I, Alex? I should wait for you to ask me, but there isn't any time.'

'Of course you can!' Alex shouted over more scuffling as Ben took the phone back.

'Alex, you don't know him but Clint's going to be my best man. I couldn't choose between Mike, Rob and Tim. This way I get to offend them all. Do you mind?'

'He's your best man, Ben. I don't need one – I'm having you.'

He laughed and then lowered his voice. 'Not so long now, Alex.'

'Not so long.' Thirty-seven interminable days before she saw him, and she found the weekly telephone calls difficult. Unless there was some momentous bit of news to exchange, like this evening, she found she had forgotten everything she wanted to say. Letters were much easier. In them you could write what you felt and take time to think about it. Ben wrote her letters but relied more on the telephone calls, which disappeared into so much air and could not be cherished and reread.

Never mind. Not so long now. Ben would soon be finishing his year at college, would spend a few weeks with his grandfather – and she could not complain about that; the old man hadn't seen Ben since the New Year either – and then he would be here. Alex went to the kitchen to inform Jess of the latest developments. She didn't appreciate it, but Jess was admirably calm.

'Nancy's to be maid of honour?' she said.

Alex took a radish from the salad Jess had prepared for supper. 'She wants to be so I said she could. That's okay, isn't it?'

'She needs to wear something, Alex. Can you find out her measurements, please? And what's her colouring? It would be dreadful to order something in pink and discover she's got red hair.'

'Nancy has black hair,' William said, dunking bread into his boiled egg. 'It's Donna who has red hair.'

'Well, thank you, William,' said Jess.

'Does that mean she'll walk down the aisle with us?' Annabelle asked.

They were at their angelic best, the two of them, bathed, pink-cheeked, in their pyjamas and dressing gowns and smelling sweetly of soap. Alex gave them each a kiss. 'She'll walk behind you and keep you in order.'

'I'd like to go down the aisle with Nancy,' William said. 'She's sexy.'

Jess spluttered and Alex's eyes flew to hers. For the first time in ages there was the old friendliness between them, and more than that: it was two adults communicating about the funny things children say. Wanting to cement this new relationship, Alex offered to put William and Annabelle to bed, first taking them to say good night to Richard who, in the mystified but determined company of Silas and Marner, was admiring his garden.

Richard kissed William and Annabelle, and then Alex too. The lack of restraint seemed to have followed her out of the house and she felt relaxed as her father put his arm around her shoulders, though the only thing he said was, 'Bloody greenfly! What do they think they are doing here at this time of year?'

Three days later this accord was threatened when the wedding invitations arrived, along with the printed cards of its announcement which would be sent to those people – mainly Ben's parents' friends – who could not expect to attend the event itself. The lists of who should receive which card had already been compiled, but there was one important name missing from both of them. Jess thought it was wrong, from her own, from Richard's and from Alex's point of view, but Alex stood absolutely firm. She was not intending to inform her mother about her marriage let alone send her an invitation to it. Whatever the woman had done, Jess could not believe she deserved this.

'I don't know where she is, anyway,' Alex said.

But Jess did, for she had always made a note of the return address on the parcels which came for Alex in case there was some undefinable emergency. The previous Lady Mountfield was now Mrs David Wendover. Her husband was a diplomat. They moved around a lot and at present were at the British Embassy in Tokyo. Jess hoped she had other children. She wondered what she would do if Annabelle and William cut her out of their lives and shuddered so violently she had to sit down.

But there were other concerns just as pressing.

'Have you and Ben decided where you're going for your honeymoon?' Jess asked one day, and Alex stared at her in surprise.

Jess had a moment of perfect panic. Did the child know the facts of life?

'I'll talk to him,' Alex said finally. 'There's lots of time.'

'Alex, there is not. As soon as we get back from Italy you and Ben fly to the States. You are returning a week before the wedding and Ben only days before. At least decide which side of the Atlantic you plan to be on afterwards. In any event, you'll have to book a hotel for your wedding night.'

'Okay, okay. I'll talk to him.' There was uncertainty in her voice at last.

'And there's something else I've been meaning to say to you,' Jess went on. 'Have you thought about what kind of birth control you'll use?'

'No,' muttered Alex.

'You do plan to use something, I hope?'

'I suppose so.'

'Will you make an appointment to see Dr Tommy, then?'

The pencil Alex was fiddling with broke. 'Must I?'

'I really think you must.'

The idea of this pair of children producing a baby was horrific if, that is, they worked out how to go about it. Most parents worry about pre-marital sex, but Alex and Ben, apparently, hadn't considered the idea even of fully consecrated and legal acts of love.

'I'll come with you if you like,' Jess offered. 'Thanks,' Alex said. 'But—' She stopped.

'But what?'

'Nothing.'

Had she been about to say she didn't think she'd need anything? If so, it was the most absurd element in this whole absurd business, but at least Jess had sown some seeds of doubt in Alex's mind. But what use was that? Seeds were not going to stop the juggernaut of this marriage.

Her conversation with Jess did worry Alex for a short time. She truly hadn't considered sex as part of the package, and the idea of having to go to a doctor to prepare herself for it was repugnant. She soon realized how silly this was. Of course she and Ben would make love. Ben would know what to do and it was bound to be very pleasant – like kissing and holding hands, only more so. Thank goodness she hadn't revealed her ignorance and stupidity to Jess, and to prove she was adult and sensible she made the appointment with the family doctor, went to see him, acquired six little packets of pills and instructions on how and when to take them and presented these facts to Jess as a fait accompli. It was a shame this had to be done by manoeuvring Jess to a place she could be alone with her instead of letting it come out casually, but Austin and Betty Mitchell had arrived and there was no way Alex was going to bring up the subject in front of them.

Then Ben flew in and took her in his arms at Heathrow and gave her a long and lovely kiss.

'It's okay,' he said, grinning around at the crowds waiting outside the customs hall. 'She's my fiancée.' He picked up her left hand and showed them the ring, and the people smiled back at him unable to resist his happiness.

'It's been one hell of a long six months, Alex,' he said, kissing her again before bustling her away. 'What's been happening?'

She told him about the wedding plans, about how they had to have talks with the Reverend Glover on the meaning of marriage and choose the hymns and music for the service.

'Honestly, it's such a bother. Why can't we simply get married?'

'We must do it the traditional way in your old church. I'm going to wear one of those tail coats so I really look the part. Hey, Alex, do you like that ring or shall we get another one?'

'I like it,' she said. Franklin had told her over the phone what it meant to him and she would have found it difficult to reject even if she had hated it.

They drove back to Montly through the summer

countryside and any tiny doubts which Alex had not admitted even to herself vanished in Ben's company, especially when he asked her where she would like to go for their honeymoon.

'I don't know, Ben,' she said, thankful he had brought it up. It hadn't occurred to her, but Ben wasn't such an idiot. 'Is there somewhere you have in mind?'

'Yeah. Scotland. I haven't seen much of Britain and my mother's family came from Scotland. How about it?'

'Great.'

'There's supposed to be good fishing there. Do you think we could get some in?'

Never wanting to be doing nothing, her Ben. 'I don't see why not,' she said.

'We'll have to sort that out too. There's our pub, Alex. Let's stop. Jesus, it looks beautiful with all the flowers out. What's Italy like? Is it this beautiful?'

'I haven't been before either.'

'It'll be terrific, I know it. Hi,' he said to the landlord, as though he expected to be recognized from his one previous visit, 'I'd like a pint of your best bitter, please.' He placed a huge tanned hand possessively on Alex's blonde head. 'And, for my fiancée, a dry white wine.'

An hour with him and it was as though they hadn't been apart. She and Ben were right, and anyone who denied them wrong.

She tried to convey this when they reached

Montly, but there wasn't a chance as William and
Annabelle flung themselves on the one they had been
rehearsing to call their brother-in-law and Silas and
Marner, after a quick check-up sniff, recognized the
man who had taken them for so many exciting
walks and added greeting barks to the mayhem.
When this had subsided, Alex could find no quarrel
with the way Jess welcomed Ben, kissing his cheek
and telling him that perhaps he would now call her
Jess, or with her father's friendly handshake, after
which Ben turned to Betty and Austin Mitchell.

'I guess we never expected to meet here.'

'Long Island comes to Sussex,' Austin said.

'I don't reckon we can take it. We're pretty much
outnumbered and Lady Mountfield – Jess I mean –
could be a turncoat.'

He was so sure of his welcome that he got it. No
one could deny his charm and they had to laugh
when he begged Richard to insure the car so he
could drive it when they got to Europe.

'I might have to be driven by Alex on the wrong –
that is the right – side of the road,' he said. 'There
are some things a man can't be expected to take.'

'See?' Jess said to her mother later, after Ben had
thanked her and apologized for the hard work their
wedding was involving her in, something Alex had
not thought to do. 'He's so *nice*.'

'What's the fuss? You can't stop it so you'll have
to roll with it.'

'They're too young,' Jess insisted.

*

A few days later Jane Patterson, Jess, Austin, Betty and the children flew to Pisa, where they would pick up a hired car and make their way to the house outside Siena. The rest of the Patterson party and a load of luggage went in the Range Rover, crossed the Channel and drove south in convoy with Alex, Ben and Richard.

It was Alex's eighteenth birthday and they celebrated it with a five-course meal at their first overnight stop, at Reims in Champagne country, where the French kings had been crowned in the wedding-cake cathedral. Which Ben dragged Alex and Richard round in every detail, marvelling that they were in the place where Napoleon had once stood, for he had been driving that afternoon and had gained a good two hours on the Range Rover.

Alex's eighteenth birthday, then, toasted in champagne where Napoleon had crowned himself and Josephine emperor and empress of France. On down the empty roads, another night, then up into the Alps, the air getting cooler with every bend, the trees disappearing and the meadows, dotted with unmelted snow, containing more flowers than grass. Over the Col de Montgenèvre, where they stopped and took photographs, and down the other side and into Italy where suddenly everything was pandemonium with cars, trucks and buses sounding their horns and Vespas buzzing in and out of the traffic like hornets, and everyone seemed to be waving their arms at each other and arguing, though

Ralph Patterson said they were most probably simply saying hello and discussing the weather.

A night in Bologna, where they arrived during the *passeggiata,* that enchanting custom whereby the people stroll about the marble-floored, arcaded pavements of their city to greet each other and discover the latest gossip. The speediest of showers and a change of clothes and the travellers joined them, Ben and Alex's golden presence causing heads to turn and murmurs of admiration. Deterred from ogling Alex by the size of Ben, the Italian boys ogled the two Sarahs instead until Simon Patterson took Sarah Glover's arm, which he had been wanting to do ever since they had left England, and glared the boys away. His brother Edward, younger by half an hour, nobly took on the task of protecting his sister while Ralph and Richard, missing their wives but not daring to admit as much to each other, wandered along behind, for to stroll through a Renaissance city on a warm evening with your loved one at your side is the most romantic thing there is.

Alex certainly thought that and perhaps Ben did too, but he was already stunned by this country, by Piacenza where they had eaten lunch, and now Bologna. Yet he did not, as the others feared he might, act like a typical American tourist and loudly exclaim over each new wonder – as a group of his compatriots could be heard doing – or look at everything through the lens of a camera instead of using his eyes, or speak arrogant English to waiters and shopkeepers without attempting to communicate in their native language. He took charge of the phrase book Alex had brought with her and studied it before every transaction, asking Ralph for help with the pronunciation so that, until he identified the same words spoken by Italians and could imitate them, he was unique in being an American speaking Italian with an impeccable English accent. The waiters at dinner that night were delighted with him and showed wonderful patience at his determination to be understood, laughing and clapping him when he succeeded. One by-product of which, as Ralph told Richard as they drank grappa while the others explored the Piazza del Nettuno, was that his children were becoming less inhibited about speaking Italian in an effort to impress Ben.

'And about time too, considering Jane's efforts to teach them, and we've been here often enough. What a super chap your daughter is marrying.'

'He is, isn't he?' Richard said, the unease that had kept him company for the past months lifting. 'It's only that they are so young, and we'll miss Alex when she goes to America.'

'The world's a small place these days. You'll see her often enough,' Ralph said, and frowned fiercely in the direction of a party of British tourists, who were being noisily merry, taking flash photographs of each other with no consideration for other diners, and arrogantly speaking English to the waiters without attempting to communicate with them in their native language.

Early the next morning, Ben crept out of the bedroom he shared with Richard (who had wanted his future son-in-law under his eye, though Jess had told him it was unnecessary: and, indeed, the thought of creeping into Alex's room did not enter Ben's head) and out into the streets of Bologna. He watched the place come alive, astounded and thrilled at the way the people did not treat their town with any special reverence. They opened the shutters of their shops and cleaned the sidewalks outside, shifting the accumulated cigarette butts and other rubbish across the marble and into the street as casually as their New York counterparts would do, replying to Ben's increasingly confident 'Buon giorno' with a nod and a 'Giorno' and often some other remark, after which Ben had to admit, 'Non parlo Italiano.' But he wanted to, he wanted to! He had to unlock the magical door of language and be allowed admittance. He found a bookshop where, with the help of an English-speaking assistant, he bought a dictionary and an English-language *Green Guide to Italy* and took his spoils to a cafe where he successfully ordered himself a cup of coffee. While he waited for it to be brought to him he gazed at the astonishing triangle of space between the two leaning towers in the Piazza di Porta Ravegnana. One tower had surrendered to gravity and broken off, but the other continued to defy it and tilted crazily away into the sky. All the buildings Ben could see were old when the first foundation stone was laid in what was then called New Amsterdam. The university here had been founded in 425, over a thousand years before Columbus sailed the ocean blue and discovered what he thought were the East Indies.

The feeling of vertigo caused by the towers and time increased abruptly as Ben leafed through the guide book and realized that Bologna only rated two stars as somewhere for tourists to visit whereas Siena, a few miles away from where they would be staying for the next two weeks, had three bestowed upon it. A place more worth visiting than here! What kind of country could this be?

He arrived back at the hotel to find Alex and Richard in the foyer.

Richard, who had woken up, seen the empty bed and feared the worst, said to Alex, 'There you are. I told you nothing could have happened to him.'

He went into the dining-room, and Alex turned to Ben. 'Where have you been?'

'Exploring.' He showed her the *Green Guide,* the touring programmes in the front. 'Alex, let's forget Scotland and come back here. Venice . . . imagine Venice for our honeymoon, and a whole load of other places. We rent a car and just take off. Alex, say yes!'

'Yes,' she said. What other response was there?

Ben drove that morning through the decidedly non-Renaissance outskirts of Bologna, where Richard feared for his car as Ben played the traffic game with the *brio* if not quite the skill of the Italians, and on to the autostrada going south, where Richard quite frankly feared for his life.

'I can't go any slower,' Ben called over the noise. 'There's a great mother of a truck on my tail and if I slow down it'll be in the back seat with Alex.'

Somehow they survived and took the turn off to San Gimignano. The fact that they were to have lunch here (a three-starred site) reconciled Ben to them not stopping at Florence. Ralph had told him a couple of hours there would be a frustration, while he could take in San Gimignano in that amount of time. In the event, thanks to Ben's driving, they had three hours. Richard, shaking after the journey, found a bar, sat himself outside, ordered a brandy and told Ben and Alex he would meet them and the others, as arranged, outside the *duomo* at one o'clock. They left him there and went to tour the little medieval town with its plethora of crooked towers to delight Ben. Swallows darted above the roofs of the houses and across the streets, some trick of the sun causing their shadows to bounce up and down the walls like manic yo-yos.

'Oh my,' Ben said, over and over again. 'Oh my!'

'You sound like Toad,' Alex said.

'I do *what*?'

'Don't you know about Toad in *The Wind in the*

Willows? The first time he ever saw a motor car he sat in the road and gazed after it saying, "Oh my!" And,' Alex added conscientiously, ' "Poop poop." '

Ben shook his head at her and tweaked the brim of her sunhat. 'You've gone mad,' he said fondly. 'The sun's gotten to your brain.'

'It was because he was so amazed, you see,' she explained.

'I'm amazed all right,' Ben said, latching on to the one word he understood. 'Well and truly amazed.'

A less frantic journey after lunch, with Richard at the wheel keeping pace with the Range Rover. Off the main road and on to miraculously empty ones in the country outside Siena, past fields of wheat already yellow, their dramatic gradients punctuated by the dark green exclamation marks of cypress trees, silver groves of olives interspersed with grape vines and hazed with the red of poppies, fields of sunflowers which seemed to smile when you were sunward of them and to hang their heads sulkily away when you were not. Through sleepy villages, light and shade black and white on their one main street, each scarcely changed – in its centre at least – from the time it was built in the Quattrocentro, or before. Off the road, then, following the Range Rover up a rough track where the sunflower fields, the vines and the olive groves ceased to be part of the general landscape and became recognizable as individuals: tatty yellow petals and drooping yellow-green leaves, and the trunks of the olive trees appearing so fat and gnarled and old that they ought, in some way, to be ashamed of the meagre sprouting of branches and leaves they produced.

The cars stopped and their engines died, the sounds of insects taking over until these were superseded by William's and Annabelle's cries as, wet from the pool, they rushed out followed by Jess and Jane, while Austin and Betty Mitchell hovered in the background with the diffidence of those who have no relative to greet. Neither did Sarah Glover, and they spoke kindly to her, and neither did Ben, though this seemed hard to believe as William and Annabelle, having said hello briefly to their father and half-sister, began dragging him towards the pool, insisting he looked like a man who could use a swim.

'I sure could,' he said, laughing and disentangling himself, 'but I've got to find my room and unpack and change first.'

'Hurry *up*,' they said.

To make sure he did, they accompanied him as Jane Patterson showed him his room next to the one her twin boys would be sleeping in and – as a sop to Richard – as far away from Alex's as was possible. The house was normally let out as two separate units and Jane supposed it was sensible to keep the boys and girls apart, particularly after the intelligence Ralph had managed to convey about Simon and Sarah Glover going around Bologna hand in hand. Not that, of course, Jane thought for a moment they would do anything, except children grew up so quickly these days and the handsome blond boy in front of her now was going to be married to Alex in a couple of months' time. Little Alex Mountfield who only a few years ago had zoomed around at the Pony Club rallies, her fair plaits sticking out at odd angles from under her riding cap.

And she could understand Jess's frustration. Ben and Alex were ridiculously young to be embarking on married life, yet Ben was as Jess had often remarked in exasperation – so damned *nice*. Here he was, not minding at all that Annabelle and William were rummaging in his bag in search of his swimming trunks and, looking out of the window, he asked what the place was he could see in the distance.

'Siena,' she replied, unable to keep a rich note of pride from her voice.

'Ah, Siena! Your husband told me. Your grandmother came from there – right?'

'Right. And when I'm there I feel my blood stir.'

Ben turned away from the window and stared at her. 'I understand that. Seeing Bologna and San Gimignano and this countryside, I understand how your blood might stir. Mine does, too. Do you think maybe I've got Italian blood in me?'

Six-foot-two and blond, and his blue eyes gazing at her so intently, sincerely and anxiously.

'Maybe you have, Ben,' she said. 'Maybe you have.'

Annabelle and William had found his trunks and were clamouring for him to put them on. The contents of his bag were scattered over the bed and Jane knew that under the same circumstances (which she could not imagine them allowing in any case) Simon and Edward would leave them there until dire sanctions were threatened, but she would be prepared to bet Ben would clear the mess up.

'Of course he will!' Jess snapped as she cooked her children's supper while Jane began preparing the sauce for the gigantic pasta the rest of them would eat tonight. 'I told you. He's perfect.'

Everyone agreed on that. Alex, of course, and William and Annabelle as he swam with them in the pool and always made sure they were included in the other games – badminton, table tennis, cricket-cum-rounders-cum-baseball – which Simon, Edward and the two Sarahs would have considered too juvenile an occupation had not Ben instigated and endorsed them. Ralph Patterson for those reasons he had expounded in Bologna, and Jane Patterson because of Ben's continued determination to master Italian, and because of the way he fell so comprehensively for her grandmother's home town of Siena.

They went to other places – Perugia, Arezzo and Assissi, and to Florence, where they stayed the night.

They toured the Uffizi Gallery and experienced the shock of seeing paintings so familiar from myriad reproductions here before them, each brushstroke laid on this very canvas by the long-dead hands of Raphael, da Vinci, Botticelli. They admired the Madonnas and Child painted by lesser artists who, in the backgrounds, had depicted with loving tenderness the hills and towns of Tuscany as though Christ had been born in this blessed land. They saw the Ponte Vecchio and the *duomo* and the doors of the baptistry. They saw Michelangelo's David and his unfinished statues of the captives who, it seems, need only to flex their muscles and stand up to shake off their imprisoning marble. They saw just about everything they could see in the two days they were there but Ben had no desire to join Austin and Betty on the return trip they were planning to make, for this would keep him away from Siena.

He took upon himself the task of collecting the quantity of bread that fourteen people ate each day, but instead of going to the nearby village he borrowed Richard's car and drove through the dew-soaked morning to the magical city of Siena. He made friends with (not surprisingly) the baker and his wife, with the woman who had a newspaper kiosk near the *duomo*, with the owner of a cafe where he drank a cup of coffee. He gazed upon the Piazza del Campo, the scallop-shaped space ringed by palaces with the Palazzo Pubblico as its hinge, and he marvelled at the drone who translated

Palazzo Pubblico as 'Town Hall' in the *Green Guide* as though every city in the world could house its mayor in such glory.

One morning he heard drumbeats, followed them to their source and found three boys of about his age, two of them waving flags while the third beat the drum. They were, they told him in a mixture of Italian and English, practising for the Palio. Had Ben heard of the Palio? Ben said he had and was looking forward to seeing it. They said their names were Paolo, Giovanni and Giorgio and they let him try waving their flags, which was much harder than it looked, then they draped a blue and white scarf with the figure of a fish on it around his neck and said he was *onda* like them. Ben strode off wearing the scarf. He had learned enough about the history of Siena to realize the boys were being kind, for no outsider, no one who was not born and bred of Siena, could be a member of *onda* or any other contrada, or quarter, of the city, but he felt proud nonetheless. Until Franco, the owner of the café, let forth a torrent of what, even considering the histrionic ability of the Italians and their language, sounded like vitriol. He was gesturing at the scarf so Ben quickly removed it and stuffed it in his pocket, after which Franco simmered down and served him his coffee.

He brought the scarf out and displayed it at breakfast. Jane looked at it in mock disgust as Ben recounted what had happened.

'It's not a fish, it's a dolphin,' she said. 'What colour were the flags on your café's street?'

'Purple, sort of,' Ben said after a pause for thought. 'With some yellow maybe.'

'My dear Ben,' Jane said, 'the café owner must be *torre*. *Onda,* down to the last *bambino,* hate *torre's* guts and *torre* aren't keen on *onda* either. No wonder your Franco was not happy at you wearing their colours.'

'I thought it had to be something to do with that. I didn't realize they take it so seriously.'

'Oh it's serious, all right. My grandmother was *torre* and so am I, which means you'd better put that thing away or you won't eat in this house again.'

'Do you really feel strongly about it?' Jess asked.

'Well, no,' Jane admitted, 'but the true Sienese do, especially during the run-up to the Palio.'

Ben folded the scarf. 'Franco felt strongly,' he said.

He saw Paolo, Giovanni and Giorgio the next morning and the one after that, and on the fourth day he saw them they were transformed, transported from the twentieth to the fifteenth century. Giorgio led the *onda* parade with his drum followed by Paolo and Giovanni, one hand on their hip, the other waving their flag, their faces grave under caps of a circlet of blue velvet encased in silver netting. Behind them walked a huge man in armour carrying a sword and after him, bewigged and berobed, came other members of the contrada bearing banners and flags on the trident of Neptune, for *onda* means the wave.

'It must all signify something,' Ben said. 'I just wish I knew what.'

He hurried Alex through the city, listening for drumbeats and homing in on them, and each of them heralded, around the corner of a narrow street, another Renaissance procession.

'Oh my,' Ben said. 'Oh my, oh my . . . and I don't care if I sound like a toad.'

Near the Piazzo del Campo they encountered Jess, Richard, Austin, Betty and the children who were entranced by this spectacular fancy-dress parade.

'But it isn't fancy dress, is it?' Jess said, and Ben turned eagerly to her.

'No, it's not, and I've been trying to figure out why. I reckon it's because they wear these costumes as a right. It's their heritage, as their city is. They've never rejected their city, never once in hundreds of years have they thought it not good or modern enough—'

'That's true,' Alex said. 'I mean, how much of London would Queen Elizabeth recognize?'

'Right! Whereas the Piccolomoni guys and the rest who built the palaces here would be able to find their way around now without any trouble.'

'What has this got to do with whether or not it's fancy dress?' Betty said.

'They're part of their own history.' Ben shook his head. 'I need more time to understand it.'

They went into some stables containing four white oxen. They would, Ben learned, be in a procession later. The little man in charge of one of the beasts, perhaps taking a shine to the golden couple, lifted up a rope and beckoned them all through. Alex, keeping a nervous eye on the enormous feet and her own skimpily sandalled ones, patted the animal's shoulder, which was as high as she could reach, while Richard and Ben held up the children so they could stroke the smooth white coat. Jess stayed a safe distance away and made admiring noises. The ox looked amiable enough but it was about as big as a medium-sized elephant.

Alex joined her. She held out her hand, the palm of which had a film of white on it. 'Talcum powder,' she said. 'Smell it.'

Jess did. It was indeed talcum powder and she wondered at the devotion of the little man as he coated his animal with it to make it that much whiter, and at the patience of the ox to stand while this was being done. Jane had told her the Palio had nothing to do with tourism, that it was the Sienese's own affair and they didn't mind sharing it but wouldn't care if no one else came. Jess had found this hard to accept, thinking every effort expected a monetary return, but the man and his ox convinced her. If this had been a tourist show, off-white oxen would have done.

She understood a bit of what Ben had been trying to say about the oneness with the past. The costumes weren't any kind of coy return to the Renaissance; they were worn because the Renaissance was a living entity here. The fact – as Ben had pointed out – that the Sienese had seen no need to change their city was proof of that. Look at New York, constantly changing, London forever redeveloping, each decade dissatisfied with what the previous one had done. Here in Siena they had been satisfied for five or six hundred years – so what, given that, was remarkable about coating an ox with talcum powder?

They thanked the man and went outside. Richard looked at his watch. 'An hour before we meet the others. Where to next?'

'The *duomo,*' Ben said. 'They go there. Anyone want a ride?'

Two small people did. Richard took Annabelle on his shoulders and Ben, groaning about how big and heavy he had become, carried William.

'Am I really too heavy?' William asked with anxious delight.

'I can manage, but don't do any more growing, okay?'

They reached the Piazza del Duomo and watched as each contrada came forward, flags bristling, drums beating, the supporters chanting, to be blessed by the bishop in the palace by the marble-clad cathedral. The drumming was hypnotic, the excitement of the people epidemic, and Jess was startled when Richard touched her elbow and reminded her of the time. It seemed she had been there only a few minutes – or then, perhaps, for a few hundred years.

The Patterson contingent was waiting for them at the rendezvous they had agreed on. Edward and Simon scouted out an uncrowded bar and the women, relieved to be off their feet, sat while the men organized drinks and ice cream. Ben swallowed his beer and watched the television mounted above the bar while everyone discussed what to do next. The original plan had been that only the young people would stay on while the rest of them would take the children back and do sensible things, such as having a swim and a gin and tonic, but after witnessing the build-up to this most extraordinary of horse races they were reluctant not to see the thing through to its conclusion.

'There's plenty of time,' Jane said, noticing Ben's impatience to be off. 'The race won't begin until at least seven o'clock.'

'Seven o'clock!' Alex said faintly. 'That's another two hours!'

'The parade's begun already.' Ben indicated the television which showed a costumed brass band marching in stately fashion around the Piazza del Campo. 'You want to see that, don't you?'

Alex finished her ice cream and tried to look eager and Jess caught Jane's eye, knowing they were both thinking the same thing: how ironic it was that Alex had fallen for the New World while here was Ben enthralled by the Old. He contained himself, however, as people availed themselves of their last opportunity to go to the lavatory, everyone over the age of seven was instructed to keep an eye on anyone under that age, William and Annabelle were told on no account to stray, directions were given about where the cars were parked, bottled water was bought and, as though they were going into battle, they crossed the road covered with impacted earth on which the horses would race and entered the maelstrom of Siena's Piazza del Campo.

The scenes outside the *duomo* were only a dress rehearsal for the spectacle now. The band were taking their seats in the stands in front of the Palazzo Pubblico and they were followed by a parade of – Jane said, digging into her memory in response to an enfilade of questions from Ben – the guilds of Siena and the flags representing the towns and villages of the province. Then into the piazza, the bell in the Torre del Mangia ringing on one monotonous chime, came the contrada of *lupa*, the she-wolf, the symbol of Siena and Rome, its procession enhanced by the horse that would run for it, its jockey in Renaissance costume led on another horse. *Lupa's* drum echoed around the piazza and its flags flew high, were caught, then swirled on and stopped and in came *giraffa*, its drum frenzied. *Lupa's* and *giraffa's* flags in the air, on in a slow, measured fluttering, the band playing a strangely discordant chorus of bugles calling in *pantera*, then *torre* . . . until around the piazza the flags of six *contrade* were in the air and six drums beat against the sky. *Lupa's* procession took their seats, *giraffa's* flags were flung into the air at the foot of the tower and, not far beyond, *onda* entered the piazza. Giorgio's drum sounded against the rest and Paolo and Giovanni's flags shot high, higher, surely, than anyone else's.

Slowly the wave moved around the piazza, its flags the only evidence of its progress, until it reached the fifth of its six halts, and Ben could catch a glimpse of Giovanni and Paolo's faces, their silver-netted caps, their blue-clad arms as they threw up their flags, caught them and moved off after their drum under the solemn tolling of the bell. *Onda's* jockey rolled past on his fat horse, the one he would ride in the race tossed a white-blazed nose as it jogged behind, unable to understand why it should be in this cauldron instead of among the quiet hills of home. *Nicchio* the shell came next, then *civeta* the owl and the dragon *drago,* and then there were eight drums battering the encircling palaces, sixteen flags in the sky as the shorter processions of the *contrade* who had no horse running were in the piazza amid the chants and cheers and bugles. Grim horsemen rode by, their faces hidden behind steel and their helmets topped with fearsome figures: no flags or drums for these, the defunct *contrade;* only fluttering penants and a diminuendo of sound as the processions before them reached the Palazzo Pubblico and their drumbeats ceased.

The cart drawn by the four white oxen passed, and on it was hung the *palio* itself – nothing more than a not very well painted banner surmounted by a silver plate and decorated with the black and white banners of the City of Siena. The crowds greeted it by waving their scarves at it, and Ben had a momentary urge to pull his *onda* one from his pocket and wave it too, but in that same instant he knew he could not. He was part of this, but only as a witness. It did not belong to him and never would, not if he learned to speak the language like a native, and although he was surrounded by – packed in by, now the sun had left this part of the piazza – thousands and thousands of people he felt a sudden and inexplicable thump of loneliness.

In the moments of relative calm as the occupants of the cart took their seats and the *palio* was detached from it Austin Mitchell let out an astonished breath. 'Let me get this straight,' he said to Jane. 'The only prize is the banner and the plate. There's no betting on the race, the contradas can't buy, or even choose, the horses that run for them, the jockeys can be bribed and winning isn't that important. Is that it?'

'Yes, except the *palio is* valued above the plate and winning is important, but it's just as important to make sure your enemy doesn't win.'

'And that's where the bribery comes in?'

'There are rumours of millions upon millions of lire.'

'Okay,' Austin said, his pragmatic American brain getting to grips with this. 'Why don't the contradas teach their kids to ride and have their own jockeys? I wouldn't like to go round here bareback, but you would've thought they could find one boy from each contrada willing to do it. Wouldn't that be better sense? And cheaper, too.'

Jane laughed. 'I suppose you're right, but it would spoil it. The fact that the jockeys can be bribed means a contrada which has drawn a bad horse still has a chance to influence the result. No one knows, though, if the strategy has worked until the race is on since the jockey may have been offered a bigger bribe by someone else. They do deals between themselves at the start and prosecute their employers' feuds. That's why their whips are kept by the carabinieri and only handed out at the last moment.'

'Crazy,' Austin said. 'Crazy but wonderful. This must be the greatest free show on earth.'

'You can pay,' Jane said, gesturing at the stands lining the piazza. 'You can pay money and get a better view.'

She had never wanted to, though, for then she would see horses die – the shadow on the colour of the Palio.

The oxen were led away, dragging the empty cart. The *palio* was carried onward amid its escort of black and white and the drumming began again. Seventeen flags, one from each contrada, moved on to the track and billowed to and fro. One by one they were thrown, caught and retired to the stands until only *onda's* remained. Ben craned his neck. It was Paolo. He flung the flag high and the pole came down into his right hand as though it knew it belonged there. Ben forgot his feeling of isolation and cheered.

'If he'd dropped it,' he said to Alex. 'Je-sus!'

'He'd probably have had to emigrate,' Jane said. 'Ben, your friend was *brave*.'

'Yeah, he was,' Ben said, proud to have such a friend as Paolo.

The horses entered the piazza on a roar. Only the caps and shoulders of the jockeys were visible. Ben picked up William and held him so his head was under his chin, and Austin took care of Annabelle. There was desperate tension, the adrenalin sparking from body to body, as the jockeys manoeuvred for position at the start, and the thousands of people in the piazza and the stands surrounding it fell quiet until a second roar signalled the race was on.

The crowd in the piazza turned, following the horses like the sunflowers in the Tuscan fields follow the sun; twice it turned the full 360 degrees, and then *'Onda!'* shouted Ben. *'Onda!'*, as the blue and white cap fled away and the colours behind were reduced as horses and jockeys fell. 'ONDA!' And down past the Palazzo Pubblico and round the far turn. A gun fired, a race had been won. The crowd surged forward, a band of T-shirted *onda* moved in a wedge singing the chanting song that in one version compares *torre* to the things that come out of the rear ends of animals. The ranks of people who had earlier been in the processions leapt from their stands and ran to where the *palio* was being lowered from its place and claimed by jubilant masses of blue and white. The flags of the other contrade of Siena, to honour it, escorted it out of the Piazza del Campo, and those and the jigging banner of the *palio* were all that could be seen above the tide of humankind that swirled and flooded away into the city, there to brood in defeat or celebrate in triumph.

'Well!' Betty Mitchell said. '*Well!* However will we explain to the folks back home that the most exciting thing we saw in Italy was something we hardly saw at all?'

'Let's go to *onda*,' Richard suggested, and then added to Jane, 'Or is that not allowed?'

'I'm only *torre* when it suits me,' she said, and they moved off. After a few seconds they realized Ben was not following and turned back. The big blond boy, still holding William, was rooted in the Piazza del Campo, his eyes on the tower whose belling voice was now silent. William's polite wriggles and Alex's voice brought him back from wherever he had been and he put the child down and took Alex's hand.

'Wasn't that incredible? Wasn't that the most incredible thing you've ever seen?'

'It was,' Alex said, meaning it, for like the others she had been swept into the event.

They entered *onda's* territory. Drums were beating again, and not only Giorgio's. Old men who had once led their contrada's procession at past Palios and little boys who hoped to do so in the future had run home and brought their drums into the streets and were pounding out the rhythm from every quarter while the blue and white flags swung deliriously above their heads.

'See?' Jane Patterson said to Austin. 'See how important winning is?'

A race had been won by a horse which had been drawn from a pool three days previously and ridden by a jockey from Sardinia whose conscience and loyalty were for sale, and the people were celebrating the victory more in tears than in laughter. Grown men and women were crying, young girls were sobbing in the near hysteria more usually seen during a performance by a rock star. And round another corner were Paolo and Giovanni weeping on each other's shoulders, their caps crooked, the flags they had thrown high above the Piazza del Campo trailing in the dust, their blue tunics from the Renaissance unbuttoned at the neck.

They saw Ben and extended their arms to him. He went forward and was embraced by *onda,* the wave.

Later when everyone, exhausted, had gone to bed

after eating omelettes cooked in an assembly line by Jess, Jane and Betty, Richard persuaded his wife to walk with him and a brandy on the terrace. The moon was full and hung above the hills of Tuscany, making the night a lambent blue. Nightingales shouted from the woods and below in the garden fireflies went about their business imitating the stars.

Jess sighed. 'What a country. Can we come back, Richard?'

'As often as you like.'

'And bring our grandchildren?'

He laughed. 'Certainly. But I'll have some sooner than you.'

'I suppose you will.' She took a sip of brandy from his glass.

'Are you happier about it now?' he asked, his voice low, for Alex's room was above them. 'They show no signs of doubt, do they?'

It was true. Alex had taken on board Ben's obsession with Italy with a maturity that astonished Jess. She was entirely prepared to let him do his thing in Siena, she did not assume with the greedy love of youth that Ben should pay her undivided attention and she willingly shared him with the Patterson twins, the two Sarahs and William and Annabelle.

'Happier,' Jess said. 'They aren't about to fall out of love.'

'How could they do that,' Richard said, taking hold of her, 'here of all places in the world?'

Chapter Five

THE GOLDEN COUPLE FLEW TO America and Jess began making serious preparations for the wedding reception. Georgiana Mountfield let her down badly in this. She had married off six daughters but the weddings had taken place in the morning, the guests had sat down to a wedding breakfast with 'not above Forty' in attendance and the bridal couples had entered their carriages and been driven off to one of the Channel ports. Jess supposed there were so few guests because of the difficulties of travel. Thanks to the motor car, over a hundred and fifty people would be turning up (and there would have been more, except the church would be bulging as it was) expecting food and drink. She had intense consultations with Cynthia and Sue George and they decided they could do it using the basic system of the New Year's eve parties.

'Get in caterers, for God's sake,' Richard told her.

'The food wouldn't be as good,' Jess said, and Cynthia and her daughter beamed with pride. 'You sort out the marquee and the booze and leave the rest to us.'

But it was absurd Alex wasn't there. Wedding presents began to arrive. At first they were put in Alex's bedroom but soon had to be transferred to the servants' hall, and the pile grew.

'She's got to come back and deal with it,' Jess said to Richard. 'The registered ones from your relations could be valuable.'

This brought Richard to the appalling realization that the servants' hall was not covered by the burglar alarms, and he commandeered the Patterson twins to move everything into the morning-room. In the smaller space the piles of brown paper appeared almost threatening, as though resenting not being unwrapped so they could show off their treasures. And there were, besides, several letters for Alex, some of which could well have cheques in them. It was intolerable they should not be acknowledged.

Alex, when informed of the rising tide of brown engulfing Montly, had been indifferent, but faced with the facts – a hundred and sixteen of them, according to the twins – Jess hoped she would be sensible about it. She phoned her stepdaughter and left a message with Conchita asking Alex to call, which she did the next day – and another five parcels richer – most conveniently for her at seven o'clock in the evening but when the phone rang in Montly it was midnight and the house was asleep.

'Sorry,' Alex said when this was pointed out to her. 'What's the problem?'

'Alex,' Jess said, 'you have a hundred and twenty presents to open and more than that number of thank-you letters to write. You must look at the things you have been given, decide where you want them in the States and arrange to insure them and ship them there.'

'Okay,' Alex said. 'Is that why you wanted me to ring?' She made it sound like a chore.

'I think you should come home earlier than you planned.'

'Why?'

'To sort it out.'

'I can do it when I get back.'

'Come next week. It's only a week early,' Jess pleaded.

'Can't. The girls are giving me a shower on Wednesday.'

'After that, then,' Jess said, feeling her temper rise.

Alex did not reply and Jess realized the noise in the background was not the hum of the transatlantic line but voices and music. Alex was talking to someone else, then returned to Jess.

'It'll be okay. Honestly it will.'

'Alex,' Jess said, and Richard, trying to listen in on the conversation, looked at her for her voice was formidable, 'what are you eating?'

'A hamburger. We're out by the pool having a barbeque.'

Jess slammed down the phone, got out of bed and paced around the room.

'We're all working like hell for her goddamned stupid wedding. I ask her to call and she does so in the middle of the night while eating a goddamned hamburger during a goddamned party. Well!' she stormed. 'Well, I hope she eats so many goddamned hamburgers that her goddamned wedding dress doesn't fit.'

Richard began to laugh and she whirled on him. 'What's so funny?'

'You. Dressed like that and banging on about hamburgers. I'm sorry, Jess. It is funny.'

She was so angry she could have hit him but then she saw that she was, in fact, dressed in nothing.

'Come here,' Richard said, still laughing and holding out his arms.

Deflated, she did. 'It's serious,' she said.

'Of course it is, but you know our Alex. She'll get those things unwrapped and the letters written.'

'And her darling father, no doubt, will arrange the shipping.'

'I suppose he might.'

'And her darling stepmother will be landed with the packing,' she said, a flicker of temper returning.

'Hush.'

'Goddamned hamburgers,' she murmured, ready for sleep again. 'I've a good mind to dish them up at the reception.'

*

Three thousand miles away Alex put down the phone and finished her hamburger.

'What was that about?' Nancy asked.

'Jess is fussing. You know what parents are like. She was angry, though. She hung up on me.'

'Maybe it was the connection.'

'No. She hung up on me.'

She tried to put it out of her mind, but her conscience bothered her. It was the same old thing: she was being pulled back across the Atlantic when all she wanted was to be here. She wished they were returning immediately after the wedding, except Ben was keen to go to Italy and everyone envied her a honeymoon beginning in Venice. The really fun thing was that the six people whose flights Franklin was paying for were staying on in Europe and they planned to meet up in Paris, to where Ben and Alex would fly from Rome. Ben had worked out their whole itinerary which, to Alex's secret dismay, included two days in Siena. They'd only just been there. Why did he want to go again? He had been taking intensive lessons in Italian, so Alex supposed it wouldn't be their last visit there.

But the conversation with Jess niggled and she needed Ben's assurance that her stepmother was fussing over nothing.

'If Jess was mad enough to hang up on you she has to think there's a problem,' he said.

'Couldn't I wait until we get back here and do the letters then?'

'We'll be heading south almost straight away,' he pointed out.

A brown arm snaked around Alex's neck and a voice said, 'Guess who?' into her ear.

'Clint Flanagan,' Alex said. 'Shove off. We're having a serious conversation.'

He bounded in front of her. Almost as tall as Ben, he was, but in striking contrast with his black hair and dark skin. He had flown up from his home in Florida a few days ago and was staying until he and Ben went to England. He was Ben's best man.

'Is she nagging you, Boyo?' he asked Ben. He called him that, he said, because he was Irish, and he called Alex 'milady' because her father had a title. Alex thought it silly, the names and the reasons.

'I'm not nagging,' she said. 'I'm asking his advice.'

'I'll give you advice. What do you want to know?'

'We have a whole load of presents over in England,' Ben said. 'Alex's stepmother wants her home.'

'Aw, you're not leaving us, are you, Milady?'

'I suppose I must,' Alex sighed. 'I'll go after the shower.'

Soon, *soon* and she'd never have to be bothered by any of this again.

Jess's conscience, too, was troubling her, but it could not be assuaged by changing an airline ticket, flying home and obediently writing thank-you letters. It had vexed her before, but now the day upon which

Alexandra Mountfield would become Alexandra Stanford was so close she found she was more and more disturbed. Richard said it was up to Alex, and Alex always said fiercely, 'No!', but Jess could no longer accept this. At last she went to see the wisest woman she knew: Emily Glover, the vicar's wife.

Emily made tea and they took their mugs into the garden. The vicarage cat contemplated them while Jess explained her great unease.

'I wondered about it,' Emily said. 'The invitation—'

'I know. None of the books allows for wording for a rejected mother. That's wrong too, and I should have insisted on an invitation going to her because she does care about Alex. Look at the presents she sends for her birthday and at Christmas, always arriving on time, such lovely presents which Alex ignores. She should have been given the chance to attend her daughter's wedding even if it would be embarrassing and she caused a scene.'

'Oh, she wouldn't do that,' Emily said.

'How could I have allowed it, being a mother myself? How would I feel if it were me?' She found she was crying and brushed the tears away before continuing. 'She can't have seen the engagement notice because no wedding present has come from her and she'd send one, wouldn't she, poor woman, after years and years and years of buying those other things? And if I send an invitation now with only eight days to go, wouldn't it be worse than not sending one? She's in Tokyo. I don't know how long the post takes, but she might be able to get here in time.'

'I expect,' Emily said gently, 'she would have the tact not to do so, given the circumstances.'

'She might assume Alex has relented at the last moment and wants her there. That would be the worst of all. I could phone, I suppose, but think how awkward that would be!'

Jess blew her nose. In the following silence they could hear the sound of a distant tractor as it crawled across the burnished flank of a hill, leaving behind it a swathe of brown.

'The thing is,' Jess went on, 'it's my fault. She will rightly blame me. She knows Alex will have nothing to do with her, and she left Richard so she can't expect him to bother. I was in the position to do the decent thing. It would have been easy! I could have sent the invitation with a note saying "I'm going against Alex's wishes in sending you this" – something like that, so at least she'd know someone was thinking how she'd feel.'

Emily reached out and took her hand. 'Do it now,' she said.

'It's too late,' Jess said miserably.

'It's not. Tell her what you've just told me – that you should have ignored Alex earlier and you're sorry you didn't. Write it here, while it's clear in your mind and you won't be interrupted.'

'By Alex, you mean?'

'It's the proper thing to do, Jess, and Alex's view is irrelevant. It's a matter between two mothers.'

'Yes,' Jess said. 'Between two mothers.'

Emily took her inside and settled her down with paper, pen and another cup of tea, then left her there and wandered outside again, pondering the events of all those years ago. It need not have turned out like this. It could – it should – have been different.

As if entering the stage on her cue, Nanny Mountfield unlatched the gate of the churchyard and marched up the path to the church, a trug of flowers on her arm. Emily waved (she had to, didn't she?) and the old woman raised her free hand in reply before disappearing inside. The reason for Jess's distress, for the fact that Alex had grown up motherless. The reason but not, of course, the cause.

Alex was old enough now to understand the cause – but how to go about telling her? Who would do so, and what would it do to Richard and Jess for a start? It would have been different without Nanny Mountfield. Emily remembered that difficult period, Nanny saying, 'She's been invited to the seaside/to London/to see a film, but she'd rather stay here with her old Nanny, wouldn't you, my duck?', and Alex stating firmly, 'Yes.'

Richard had been hopeless, ready to do anything anyone suggested. Emily had wanted to suggest getting rid of the nanny, but to do that amid the disruption the child was already undergoing seemed impossible, even cruel, at the time, though in retrospect the biggest disruption had been Alex mouthing everything her nanny told her. And look at the result of the woman's machinations, she who was arranging flowers in the church and genuflecting every time she passed the altar, she who was one of the very few people who had known all the facts, and had ignored them and twisted them: a marriage of which the mother of the bride was unaware and to which she was uninvited, though that was being put right now. Emily should have considered this earlier, except Elizabeth Mountfield – or Wendover – was many miles and many years away and Emily and John had been far more concerned about the effect of this marriage on their son.

She was still standing there half an hour later, gazing at the tractor labouring up the hill beyond the church spire. Why, she wondered, did they have to plough so soon after harvesting? In the old days the stubble was bright on the downs for months, black lines striping it where the straw had been fired though that was now against the law, of course. And then wondered again how she could be thinking of such things when there were a million tasks awaiting her.

Jess came out of the vicarage.

'Well!' Emily exclaimed. 'You look better.'

'I feel it,' Jess said. 'Oh God, I feel it! Emily, I don't know how to thank you.'

'It was your thought, not mine.'

Nanny Mountfield emerged from the church and stumped down the path to the gate. Jess watched her go. 'She dropped hints the size of boulders for three months before Alex came out of the clouds and asked her to do the flowers for the wedding. It drove me wild, but I wouldn't help out.'

'She drives John wild, too. It takes ages to discover what she's after.'

'Maybe it's the result of a lifetime as a servant,' Jess said, feeling charitable towards anything on two legs. 'Not asking directly for anything for herself, I mean.'

'Maybe it is,' Emily said, not believing it. In her view it was a way of getting attention. 'Henry says he's going to visit her often because it will be good practice for questioning clients. He's getting his articles transferred to a firm in Eastbourne, you know.'

'I didn't! How lovely for you.'

'And for him. He hates London.'

'Emily . . . is he all right about Alex?'

Emily smiled. 'He's my darling Henry. Like John, he is strong and full of faith in God and in the goodness of humankind. He's all right.' She shrugged. 'Not happy, but all right. Not that anyone else could tell. He seems his usual self.'

'How is Sarah getting on with Simon Patterson?'

Emily clapped her hands. 'My dear, they are so sweet and serious we dare not tease them, though

Henry has scared his father by asking how he will manage both to give Sarah away and perform the marriage service.'

Jess thanked Emily again for her help and walked towards home. They had used Henry, she, Richard and Alex. It had been most unfair of them, but who could have imagined Alex would break Henry's heart by marrying at the age of eighteen? Given time there would have been a gradual parting as their lives diverged, a slow evolution into other boy- and girlfriends.

Jess could do nothing about Henry Glover, but she had rid herself of the weight of guilt about Alex's mother. She went into the post office to find out how much it cost to send a letter airmail to Japan and was, most tediously, asked how many kilograms the said letter weighed. A birthday card approximating the invitation was put on the scales, Jess bought the appropriate stamp and walked on through the gates of Montly.

She had left William and Annabelle in the care of Richard's secretary in the office in the old coach house, but was told they were helping Albert in the vegetable garden. They weren't. Albert was among the runner beans and William and Annabelle were in an unused corner digging, so they informed her, a hole to Australia. No one had time for them. They hadn't been riding, they hadn't been to the beach, not for ages they hadn't. They had thought weddings would be fun, which was why they had agreed to this one, but they weren't. They were horrible like everything else here and so they were going to Australia. William's little spade, six inches into its journey, struck a rock, and he flung it aside and burst into tears.

'Now look!' he wailed. 'We'll never get there at this rate.'

Jess knelt and put her arms round him. 'We'll go riding, we'll go to the beach. William, please stop.'

Over ragged, chest-heaving sobs he said, 'Mummy, Alex is going away for ever and ever . . . and . . . and I don't *want* her to.'

At which Annabelle joined him. Jess held them and tried to soothe them. Albert pulled them up a carrot each, normally a high treat, but they shook their heads and urged each other on towards hysteria until Jess said sharply, 'Enough. Enough, both of you,' and they calmed down though still clung to her, their heads hard against her neck.

Alex ran into the vegetable garden and stopped in relief on seeing Jess.

'I thought they were being murdered. What's the matter?'

'They don't want you to go away and they feel neglected. They were digging a hole to Australia because they thought things would be better there.'

It should have been funny, except the children's grief was so very real. Alex looked at the hole and the discarded plastic spades and her eyes filled with tears. 'Oh,' she whispered. 'Oh no.'

Jess pushed the children away and took her handkerchief out of her bag. Her letter to Alex's mother was there, and she closed the bag before wiping William's and Annabelle's faces.

'We're going to the beach,' she said, standing up. 'And I think we might get ice creams on the way.'

'I'll come with you,' Alex said.

'No!' William yelled and muttered something under his breath.

'What?' Alex bent to take his hand and he snatched it away.

'You've got letters to write.'

'William!'

'You always have and you won't show us your presents properly, so why should you have ice cream?'

Now Alex was crying. Jess gave her the handkerchief. It had been cried into by four Mountfields in little over an hour, surely some kind of record.

She picked up her handbag and the two spades. Was it William's rejection of her that was causing Alex's tears? She didn't like it, obviously, even though William was already relenting, agreeing that perhaps Alex could come if she didn't have ice cream as a punishment for being so nasty.

Alex returned the soggy handkerchief to Jess. 'I'll get their bathers. Where are they?'

'In their rooms, I hope. It's true, we haven't used them for ages.'

Alex, fully reinstated, took the children away and
Jess followed them into the house. She found a spare
invitation in her desk, put the letter inside it and
stamped and addressed the envelope. What else?
Airmail sticker. She stuck one on, thrust the
invitation and enclosure in, sealed the flap and
rammed the incriminating evidence back into her
handbag. Why incriminating? She was doing the
right thing . . . but she couldn't face the scene if Alex
found out.

She stopped the car outside a shop in the next
village. 'You choose your ice creams,' she said and
gave Alex some money.

Without questioning what she would be doing,
the three of them tumbled out of the car and into
the shop. Jess went as far as the red pillar box
outside, opened her bag, took out the envelope and
posted it.

Done. Gone. Safe in the hands of the Royal Mail
and impossible to retrieve.

The bride's mother was not there, however, when
Alexandra took Benjamin to be her lawfully wedded
husband and Benjamin took Alexandra to be his
wife. Back down the aisle càme the golden couple
and out into a pealing of bells. There was something
that seemed stage-managed about the wedding
procession, so flawless it was, so beautiful its
members, and so symmetrical too. The blonds in
front, the glow of Alex's cheeks and the blue of her

eyes her only colours; the two children with their shining chestnut heads; the maid of honour and the best man walking behind them, both black-haired.

Jess watched as the bridal pair were photographed outside the church, first on their own and then with their attendants. The formal grouping suddenly broke up in laughter as there was a scuffle between Ben and Clint and Alex, her veil lifting in the breeze, turned her new husband to reveal one tail of his coat attached to a tail of Clint's.

'You tied a knot, Boyo,' Clint said. 'I wanted to tie one too.'

Jess laughed along with everyone else, but something was wrong. Her instinct had always told her this marriage was doomed. Had she just seen the reason? She felt strangely calm about it, however. Divorce was easy. A third of marriages ended that way and every one of them began with a version of this: the ceremony, the dress which was only worn once, the photographs, the assembled guests.

Alex and Nancy detached Ben from his best man, William and Annabelle were told to hold hands and behave themselves, and the bridal procession moved down the path and out of the churchyard. The villagers of Montly were gathered by the gate and smiled to see their squire's daughter on her wedding day as she walked on the arm of her handsome husband back to the manor house. Many of the guests followed and Jess, realizing she should be there even though only Ben and Alex would be in the receiving line, turned to go. Franklin Benjamin Stanford Senior was before her. He seemed horribly more frail than he had been last summer, but his brown eyes were as sharp as ever.

'They'll be okay, Jess,' he said. 'They love each other. They'll be okay.'

Had he been reading her mind? – or had those eyes seen what hers had done?

'Yes, they love each other,' she said. 'Come, Franklin. There's a car for you.'

'Me and the other crocks, you mean.'

They went to the gate where Henry Glover, a little white-faced but otherwise composed, was loading the crocks – mainly elderly relatives of Richard's – into cars, helped by Ben's friends who had, along with Henry, been ushers in the church. The American boys had overcome their self-consciousness at wearing tail coats and high, stiff collars and were enjoying themselves, bowing extravagantly as they opened car doors, giving the old biddies exaggerated compliments and receiving delighted reproofs in return.

Mike and Tim – the latter a friend from Ben's high school in New York who Jess had not met before – saw Franklin and came over to him, offering him their strong arms in place of Jess's weak one.

'My sister, where is she?' Franklin said, worried suddenly in the petulant way old people can be. 'Where is she? Maisie? Maisie, you come here!'

'She went earlier. Rob, Miss Stanford went, didn't she?'

Rob confirmed she had and Franklin was helped into the back of a car called up by Henry. Jess joined him.

'Silly Maisie,' the old man murmured as the car moved off. He laid his head against the seat back and closed his eyes. 'Sorry. I'm tired.' He groped for her hand and she squeezed it gently. It was a bone-filled piece of skin and nothing more. 'They love each other,' he repeated. 'They'll discover the rest. You'll see.'

'Yes,' she said, comforted. Ben was innocent, she was sure, as innocent as Alex and they would write upon each other's blank pages. Beginning, Jess imagined, with the letters of the alphabet.

But the niggle was still there: what kind of innocence had led Ben to choose Clint Flanagan as his best man?

The reception was everything receptions should be. The guests ate the food Cynthia and Sue George had prepared for them, cheered as the bride and groom cut the cake and laughed at the right moments in the speeches. When all was done, Jess went upstairs to help Alex change.

'Call us,' Jess said. 'Call us when you get to Paris.'

'I will.' Alex flung her arms around her stepmother's neck.

'Thank you, Jess. Thank you for being everything

to me. I'm . . . I'm sorry if I've been difficult these last months.'

'Oh, *you!*' Jess said. She looked into her stepdaughter's eyes. 'I'm always here. Will you remember that? On the other end of a phone, or I'll come to you if you need me.'

'All right,' Alex said, supposing this was the sort of thing mothers told their daughters at such moments.

A knock on the door signalled Ben was ready. Jess kissed Alex and left the room and a little later the golden couple, hand in hand, came down the stairs. More kisses, cries of 'good luck', Alex's bouquet was caught by Nancy and the newly married pair got into a car, suitably decorated, and drove away.

Nanny Mountfield cried to see her nursling go, Franklin Stanford cried. Inexplicably, late that night the bride's father awoke and cried.

And, when she heard about it, the bride's mother cried too.

Chapter Six

DAVID WENDOVER, COMMERCIAL COUNSELLOR AT her Britannic Majesty's embassy in Tokyo, sat at his desk and stared at the copy of the London *Times* before him. At his elbow was an envelope addressed to his wife, which evidently contained a card of some kind. It had come through the normal post and not via the diplomatic bag, so it could not be from anyone they knew well. In any case, the postmark settled it: Eastbourne. He looked back to *The Times* of Monday 18 August and the wedding announcement there. This and the envelope were obviously connected, and he could not believe that anyone, even in this world where dreadful deeds were done every day, could be so cruel.

He peered at the date on the postmark. The eighth of August. So they had made some attempt to inform her before she read it in the paper. Big of them. In fact, he supposed the intention could have been to give Elizabeth time to get there, and she might have been able to but the envelope had taken more than three weeks to arrive and David had been away while Elizabeth had stayed in the house by Chuzenji lake in the mountains. And could that be the cruellest blow of all? It might be that this was Alex's handwriting and she had, at the last minute, decided to ask her mother to the wedding. David Wendover had no idea what Alex's writing looked like, and neither did his wife.

Back to the announcement again and this interpretation seemed unlikely. 'Alexandra Victoria, daughter of Sir Richard Mountfield . . .' No mention of a mother. No mention of the woman who had carried her and given birth to her, during the process of which they had messed her around so much that she was unable to have any more children. And while that had been going on, her husband . . .

David Wendover clenched his fist and scrunched *The Times* in it as though it would prevent anyone else reading the announcement. How on earth was he going to break the news to Elizabeth when he arrived in Chuzenji tonight? He wondered what she would be doing now. Out on the lake in a hired boat with her sketchpad, perhaps, or perhaps she had driven away from there and was sitting before her easel in some silent, lonely place, contemplating her painting and his coming with no idea of the pain he would bring her.

She was the perfect diplomat's wife he thought, and had often told her so. Beautiful, gracious, witty, intelligent and discreet: what more could a man who had made his career in the Foreign Office hope for?

Children, she always replied – as though he hadn't known all along she couldn't have them, as though he didn't need her more than he needed a thousand children. And there was her art, her personal reservoir of resources. It was difficult for the wives of diplomats, moving every two or three years, often to countries they would not want to visit for two weeks, not seeing their children – nor even being within easy reach of them – except for school holidays, having to attend the endless round of parties where their behaviour could affect their husbands' careers, not being able to make permanent friends, their only permanent home (and many of them did not even have that) occupied by them during home postings and tenanted by strangers when they were abroad.

Elizabeth Wendover found none of this a problem. For her a new country meant a new light to paint. The first thing she decided when they arrived in another embassy house was which room would be made into her studio, and to this calm place, drawn by her personality, other wives would come with their troubles. Elizabeth's studio had averted many nervous breakdowns, of that David was sure. And her paintings were not cosy little scratchings or scrapings either. She'd had London exhibitions – modest ones to be sure, but even so – and the work she had been doing in Japan was spectacular. The president of a Japanese corporation had seen one of her paintings on the dining-room wall when he had come to dinner (Elizabeth had said it was vulgar to hang your own work, but David had insisted) and the next day, through a go-between, had offered an extraordinary amount of money for it.

'Christ, David,' a colleague at the embassy had said, 'sell him the contents of Elizabeth's studio and retire.'

'She thinks she'll have to give the thing to him. She thinks to say, even through a go-between, that the painting isn't for sale would insult him and make her seem impossibly conceited. She says she can't accept the money in case it ever gets out and reflects badly on me.'

'Some sort of bribe, you mean? Why would Sato-san need to bribe you?'

'She's resolute.'

'She has a point, I suppose,' Chris conceded. 'It could be made to look bad.'

Elizabeth had given her picture away without complaint and not long afterwards a present had arrived from Mr Sato, a silk-screen print which had delighted and worried Elizabeth in equal measure. Her painting, she said, was nowhere near the value of this exquisite thing; she couldn't accept it, but how could she possibly refuse it and what on earth was the next step?

'We get into one of those escalating wars of present-giving and I end up having to hand you over to Mr Sato,' David had said. 'No, it's not worth it.

Let's do as Chris suggests and retire.'

But Mr Sato wanted more of Elizabeth Wendover's work and engineered a path to acquiring it without putting an untimely end to David's career. An art dealer from Hawaii had visited Elizabeth's studio and offered to mount an exhibition of her paintings. She had at first refused, saying it was not seemly to sell her work in the country in which her husband was serving, but had – with reluctance – agreed to let Mr Watanabe hold the exhibition in Honolulu, which venue he lit upon having worked out what 'not seemly' meant.

David Wendover unclenched his fist and slapped his hand on the desk. This, *this* was the woman the people who had composed the announcement had decided did not exist, she the innocent party in the whole disgusting business, she who had suffered the most. David had never blamed Richard Mountfield for keeping Alex away from Elizabeth – it was the hag of the nanny who had done that – but it was unforgivable of him not to have informed her of their daughter's wedding. Didn't he think he owed her something? Yet wait: was this his writing on the envelope? David rather thought not. Bastards, like leopards, seldom change their spots.

And how *was* he going to tell Elizabeth? Thank God for two things, anyway: firstly that Elizabeth was away and he hadn't, as he usually did, taken their personal post home at lunchtime without sorting it through, and secondly that he'd seen the damned announcement at all. Waiting for him had been a coy postcard from his nephew in Australia telling him to keep an eye on the court circular page. David had waded through the back numbers of *The Times*, sent from London, and discovered the jammy little sod had got himself engaged to the high commissioner's daughter and this.

He couldn't let it hang over him, so he would leave for Chuzenji this afternoon. Imai-san could bring back most of the luggage and Chieko, who was with Elizabeth, this evening instead of tomorrow and David and Elizabeth would be alone tonight. The house there would be packed up after this weekend, their tenancy of it ended.

David phoned home to tell the cook and the driver the change of plan and attempted to smoothe out *The Times*. Elizabeth had to see it and he wanted to disguise the evidence of his anger.

He had an early lunch, changed out of his suit, packed his toothbrush and shaving gear, then went downstairs and selected some wine to take with him. Sighing, he added a bottle of brandy and went to the kitchen where Mariko-san was preparing a hamper. The cook bowed, packed the bottles away and offered, with a deprecating duck of the head, a taste of the salmon mousse she had prepared to delight the palates of her master and mistress.

'*Oishii desu,*' David said. 'Delicious.'

Mariko-san closed the hamper lid, fastened it and Imai-san bore it away to the car. Mariko-san took

David's overnight bag and had a brief tussle with him about who should carry his briefcase, which David won, then bowed as the car moved away through the leafy embassy compound, out of the gates and into the mad rush of Tokyo.

David looked at the back of Imai-san's neat grey head and wondered what he and his wife made of their country's economic triumph. What did they get out of it, working as they did for the embassy of a country which had failed where Japan had so spectacularly succeeded? For the past thirty years they had been employed in the British Embassy, some distant predecessor of David's having decided he needed a personal driver and everyone since, at the Imais' request and because Imai-san was prepared and willing to act as gardener as well, keeping the status quo. During those thirty years Britain had declined, its empire disbanded, its economy had faltered forward in fits and starts. The Imais, joined quite recently by Mariko's widowed sister who had quarrelled with her son's wife, were cocooned from the horrendous cost of living in Tokyo but at the same time marooned, left high and dry in the servants' quarters of the embassy house with no possibility, surely, of ever earning enough to move out. Most of the other servants were Filipino and the yen they earned here, though paltry by Japanese standards, was wealth at home. Thank God for Chieko's son. The quarrel between his mother and wife notwithstanding, he would look after his relations in their old age, and – presumably horrified and embarrassed by their lowly position as servants to the impoverished British – was urging them to retire forthwith. But the Imais and Chieko held out. Chieko's son would not retire them to a green oasis in the heart of the capital city near the Imperial Palace with a large garden they could wander in when there was no one else around. No way would he, and David suspected Chieko and Mariko had planned the quarrel. It had come most conveniently when the Wendovers' Filipino maid, isolated and miserable with the two well-entrenched Japanese, had begged to be allowed to fill a vacancy among her own kind in the first secretary's household. David smiled to himself. Perhaps, after all, the Imais got quite a lot out of working for the British.

The car stopped. The pavements of the sky-scrapered streets were a crawling mass of humanity. You could practically feel the energy that last year had increased an already burgeoning economy by a whacking six per cent. How could the West catch up with Japan now? It had dozed on the starting blocks, believing the Japanese were a nation of imitators not innovators, that their success was due to cheap labour, that it couldn't last, and had only woken up when the Japanese – and many of their Asian neighbours – were disappearing into the blue yonder, unquestionably the economic powerhouse of the world, dynamic and aggressive, ever seeking to expand. The corporation to whose president Elizabeth had given her painting was planning to build a plant in the north-east of England as a bridgehead to invade the European continent, believing – and with justification – that the Japanese could manage and motivate a British workforce better than the natives.

Imai-san swung the car off the main road into one of his favourite rat runs, and David abandoned his undiplomatic and unpatriotic musings and settled to work.

By mid-afternoon they were driving through the streets of Nikko and past the shrine which housed the three monkeys that saw, heard and spoke no evil.

'Are you sure you don't mind going back tonight?' David asked Imai-san.

'No, sir. No mind.'

He would do almost anything to avoid spending a night away from Tokyo, whose traffic jams were his life's blood, but David thought it was right to ask.

They began the ascent to Chuzenji up the series of dizzying hairpin bends. The maple trees were beginning to turn scarlet as they climbed from summer in Nikko to autumn in Chuzenji. The lake was mirror still as they went alongside it, though it could produce violent, choppy waves – the result, perhaps, of the anger of the dragon legend had it lived in its depths.

Imai-san stopped the car, got out and opened

David's door for him. David stepped into a wondrous cool silence and noted with relief the absence of another car. With luck, Imai and Chieko would be on their way before Elizabeth returned. The maid came running out of the house, exclaimed and bowed and Imai-san explained why they were here.

'She say a' ready,' he told David.

Naturally it would be. Elizabeth was in charge.

Within half an hour they were gone. David made himself a cup of tea, put on a sweater and sat on the verandah to await his wife. The envelope and the copy of *The Times* were in his briefcase. He still didn't know how he was going to tell her.

A car drew up and a door slammed. David went around the corner of the house and Elizabeth, in the act of taking a canvas from the boot of the car she had hired for her stay here, looked round and saw him.

'David!' she called, replacing the painting and running towards him. 'What a lovely surprise! How was Kobe?'

'Hot, boring, lonely.'

He put his arms around her and kissed her, but she soon pushed him away.

'Something's wrong,' she said with certainty. 'What is it?'

He should have realized he could hide nothing from her. He led her to the verandah and sat her down. 'It's about Alex,' he said.

Hope then fear crossed her face. How many women of forty, David wondered, could look beautiful without make-up?

'Alex? What about her? David, she's not dead, is she?'

'No, no . . . Elizabeth, she's married.'

'Married?' she whispered.

He showed her *The Times* and watched helplessly as the insult cut into her, the double insult that she had not been told and that Alexandra Victoria Mountfield – now Stanford – acknowledged no woman as her mother.

'I think they tried to let you know,' he said, giving her the envelope.

Her hands shook and she had trouble tearing open the thick paper of the flap. 'It's an invitation,' she said listlessly, 'but obviously I wasn't intended to be there.'

She pulled it out of the envelope, and two sheets of paper, closely written on, fell to the floor. She picked them up and looked at the signature.

'From Jess Mountfield.'

She began to read and David went into the house to get her a brandy. Her quiet acceptance frightened him. Why didn't she rage as he had done? Did it mean she had at last accepted defeat and would no longer send her daughter the carefully chosen birthday and Christmas presents?

He went back to the verandah and Elizabeth was no longer there. He had a moment of panic before he saw her sitting at the end of the wooden jetty that stretched a short way out over the water of the lake. He joined her.

'She's a good person,' Elizabeth said, staring towards the sinking sun. 'Read it.'

He gave her the brandy and took the letter.

'Dear Mrs Wendover,' Jess had written:

> I am afraid I am sending this without Alex's permission and against her express will. I wish with all my heart it were not so and have done my best to persuade her that she is wrong, but to no avail.
>
> Until this moment I had gone along with her, believing, I suppose, that it was her business and not mine. I realize now this is not the case. What Alex thinks and feels has nothing to do with what is right, and it is right her mother should know of her marriage and come to it if she so wishes. Please forgive me for coming to my senses so late. As a mother myself, I can begin to imagine what the pain your estrangement from Alex has been like and am sorry to be adding to it by giving you the news she should have told you months ago. Or perhaps you saw the notice of her engagement and were too upset to respond?

David looked up. How had Elizabeth missed that? He knew she always read that page. They must have been away. There had been a fortnight in Thailand . . . another narrow squeak, then. He read on.

If so, I apologize again for my thoughtlessness.

She is a lovely girl, your Alex. As you must do, I wish she was not getting married quite so young, but she is determined upon it and your daughter is as stubborn as she is beautiful. Ben (as he is called) is a charming young man, and she is joining him at his college in America. We will miss her greatly.

Will you be able to get to the wedding at such short notice? As I said, I haven't told Alex I am writing to ask you, but should you decide to come, I will, of course, inform her.

Regards,
Jess Mountfield.

PS. How stupid. I haven't explained. I'm Alex's stepmother.

'Your daughter,' David commented, 'is clearly quite something. This woman seems terrified of her.'

'She was agitated and worried when she wrote that. She's a good person,' Elizabeth repeated.

'She hasn't told you where Alex will be in America,' he pointed out.

'It wasn't deliberate. She will.' Elizabeth, her hands still shaking, gulped at her brandy. 'If I ask her.'

'Will you?'

Very suddenly, she began to cry. Her shoulders heaved and she bent her head and her tears flecked the paint-stained knees of her jeans. Her brandy glass fell into the lake and as David slid across to hold his wife to him he watched it sink slowly through the clear water and settle on the algae-covered stones beneath their feet. Elizabeth was trying to say something, and he held her closer, pulled off the scarf she wore around her head, and listened.

'So . . . *stupid*,' she sobbed. 'So stupid to be upset. Why, after all this time?'

'Not stupid,' he said into her hair, blonde like Alex's, though neither of them knew that, not for sure. Fair-haired six-year-olds can turn into mousy teenagers.

'Stupid to have hoped . . . hoped for a miracle.'

'There can be a miracle. Elizabeth, now she's grown up and married there could be more of a chance, especially since her stepmother – this Jess – has contacted you.'

How, David wondered, had Richard Mountfield managed to marry two special women? Elizabeth was right: Jess Mountfield was a good person. She had meant every word of what she had written and, given the circumstances, her letter was the most Elizabeth could have expected.

Elizabeth tugged a painting rag from her back pocket, and was about to use it to blow her nose until David removed it and replaced it with his handkerchief.

'At least she's away from that horrid old woman,' David said.

'Nanny? Yes, she's away from her.'

A motor boat went by, its wash splashing the jetty. As the sound faded away, Elizabeth stood up. 'We'd better go in. Chieko-san will be wondering what's happened.'

'She's on her way to Tokyo with Imai-san.'

She stared at him as he, too, stood. 'Sorry,' he added. 'It's just you and me and Mariko-san's hamper for the weekend.'

'You took the afternoon off and got rid of the servants because of this?'

'I – I was angry for you. I wanted us to be alone.'

They walked down the jetty.

'What shall I do, David?' she asked as they reached the lake shore.

'Write back, of course,' he replied at once. 'You must, to thank her.'

'Shall I ask for Alex's address?'

'Yes . . . Come on, my love. You're cold.'

For the sun had almost gone and a mist was rolling across the lake.

'My painting gear—'

'I'll get it.'

He brought it in from the car and put her latest canvas on a chair in the kitchen, where she was unpacking the hamper.

'How do you do it?' he asked. 'You make a landscape look unmistakably Japanese without using the Japanese stylization.'

'Don't you think it's because the landscape is Japanese? The old artists didn't invent it, they depicted what they saw – which is what I do.'

What she had seen today was a waterfall and a pine tree, painted in great detail, the waterfall full of movement and the pine utterly still. Somehow she had made it appear a very desirable place to be.

'What else have you been up to while I've been away?'

'They're on their way to Tokyo,' she said absently. She was studying *The Times* again. 'Franklin Benjamin Stanford the Third. Doesn't that name ring a bell?'

'Not in me it doesn't.'

'Son of Franklin et cetera Junior. I remember. *His* father was or is if he's still alive – a multimillionaire. Richard was involved with one of his companies in some minor way.'

'So your daughter's married money. That's clever of her.'

'Yes.' She put aside the newspaper and bent to remove her shoes. 'I'd better change.'

She went upstairs carrying her shoes; although the ground floor of the house was western the upstairs was Japanese and had tatami matting on the floors. A few minutes later she reappeared and they watched the dark eat up the lake.

'Strange to think we won't be coming back here,' David said.

'We might, to the house across the lake when you're the ambassador. I'll terrorize the young wives and be known as the diplomatic bag.'

'Both equally impossible.'

'I wonder where we'll be this time next year.'

'Who can tell? Elizabeth, find out where Alex is. We could go to America from England during our leave and try to see her. Her husband's family comes from New York so with luck they'll be near there. A few hours in a plane. Married and on neutral territory, surely there's a better chance.'

Elizabeth thought of her other attempts to see her daughter. Finally defeated by Alex on home ground at Montly, Elizabeth had tried to win over the headmistress of Alex's school, writing to her regularly and always receiving the same answer. The woman sympathized with Mrs Wendover and had done her best to persuade Alex to see her mother, but the child had become so disturbed at the suggestion that it was considered best to discourage a visit at this time. At every time. Right at the beginning, in desperation, Elizabeth and David had even offered to employ Nanny Mountfield but the old cow had indignantly refused. Perhaps they should have simply removed Alex – as Elizabeth was entitled by the courts to do – but the prospect of having a child who did nothing but scream that you were wicked had been fairly horrific, and Elizabeth had never dreamed that she would not see Alex again; she had never fully appreciated how thoroughly Nanny Mountfield had poisoned Alex's mind and regretted yet again the loophole created by the long convalescence required after the difficult birth through which the old woman had wriggled and taken charge of new-born Alex.

But there had to be more hope now. A married woman – even a married eighteen-year-old – could not resort to screams or shelter behind her teachers. If Elizabeth could arrange a meeting with her husband first, perhaps he could persuade her that her mother was not the ogre Alex seemed to think she was.

'Don't you agree?' David said.

'That there's a better chance? Yes!'

She wrote to Jess Mountfield when she got back to Tokyo, thanking her for her letter and asking her for Alex's new address. She added, fearing any slight inconvenience, that Jess could reply via the diplomatic bag by sending a letter to the Foreign Office in London and using an ordinary stamp. A month went by and she began to lose heart, but then one lunchtime David brought home a fat packet postmarked Eastbourne and addressed to Mrs David Wendover in the forward-sloping writing that had so mystified him before.

'I would have sent someone over with it,' he said, 'but I've been busy this morning and only just seen it.'

She opened the packet and out came a pile of photographs of Alex from the time Elizabeth had last seen her to her wedding day.

'I'm sorry not to have replied straight away,' Jess wrote, 'but I had this idea and it took more time than I thought to go through the albums and get everything copied.'

She also gave two addresses for Alex, one in Miami and one on Long Island.

'She's just like you,' David marvelled, looking at one of the recent photographs. 'Not quite as beautiful, of course, but near enough.'

Elizabeth was silent as her long fingers sorted through the pictures of her lost child. Alex as she remembered her, a little girl of six, aged eight on her pony, ten squinting into the sun as she held a puppy to her cheek, twelve and now she held a baby, each of them captioned and dated by Jess on the back until Alex, all in white, stood outside the church at Montly with a tall, blond man. 'The Golden Couple' Jess had written.

Chieko-san announced lunch and, not wanting to be without them, Elizabeth took the photographs into the dining-room with her.

'Madam!' Chieko exclaimed. 'You?'

'My daughter.'

Chieko made startled noises, and David glanced at his wife. She had never hidden the fact of Alex's existence but neither had she volunteered information before. He felt a pang of anxiety: had he been too encouraging about the prospects of a meeting between them? He couldn't bear it if she had to suffer again.

Elizabeth slid a photograph across the table and he picked it up and looked at it. Two children, a boy and a girl, both auburn-haired, gazed back at him.

'William and Annabelle, Alex's half-brother and sister – sorry, couldn't resist showing them off,' it said on the back.

Did Jess Mountfield know Alex had another half-sister? One nine months or so younger than her? David rather thought not.

'Lovely children,' he said.

'Aren't they?'

Elizabeth put the pile of photographs aside and helped herself from the serving dish Chieko-san was offering her.

'Can I borrow Imai-san this afternoon?'

'Of course. Where are you going?'

She flicked the photographs. 'I want to get some of these copied and enlarged, and I'm not sure where to go or how the parking will be.'

'You'll do a portrait from them. Is that it?'

'I'm going to try.'

'Well, you made me look very handsome.'

'You are handsome, my darling. I paint what I see.'

She went about it slowly, doing several exploratory sketches, for she didn't paint many portraits – her one of David had been informed and inspired by her love for him – and she wanted this one of her daughter to be the best she was capable of. While it simmered on the back burner she continued to paint canvases for her Honolulu exhibition, which was set for December, and throughout that autumn she and David drove out from Tokyo each weekend and into the old Japan that still miraculously survived in the mountains. They stayed at the traditional inns, the *ryokan*, and at one of these Elizabeth broke her own rule and painted Fujisan, the mountain that seems a cliché of itself, as it appeared most beguilingly between two trees, its white cap glinting in the cold, crisp air.

'Don't send it to Honolulu,' David said. 'Let's keep it.'

'We'll probably end up keeping them all,' she said. 'Who's to say they'll sell?'

David suspected they would, though. He had spoken to Sam Watanabe, the dealer, who knew his job and had told just enough people about Mr Sato's interest in the artist, and just enough people wanted to own a painting by someone Mr Sato admired. Ambitious employees would acquire a Wendover, so long as it was smaller and cheaper than those bought by their boss, as a mark of respect for his taste, and Sam hoped Mr Sato's business rivals would be keen to prove that their judgement was as discerning as his and anything he could own they could too.

But Elizabeth was being so prolific and her work so very fine that David did not want it all in secretive houses or the boardrooms of Japanese companies, and he persuaded her to hold some back.

'You choose them,' she said.

'How many am I allowed?'

'My darling, as many as you want.'

He chose ten. The one of the waterfall and the pine tree, of Fujisan, four more of the ones she had done this autumn of rural Japan when she had been so extraordinarily on song and four she had painted during their first few months here, including one of a shrine, its *torii* highlighted against a bulldozer and a crane, amid a turbulence of mud and redevelopment. How these people bashed and bullied their landscape, flattening mountains to make golf courses or to build factories and apartment blocks or even, as in Kóbe, a new island in the sea. An acquaintance of David's had been here twenty-five years ago and had sent him photographs of a village called Hayama on the coast a couple of hours' drive away from Tokyo. They'd had a weekend cottage there, he wrote, and he, his wife and children – grown up now, of course – had happy memories of the place. Emperor Hirohito had had a house there and they would often see him in a baggy pair of shorts poking around in the rock pools. Would David go and see how much it had changed?

Changed! David and Elizabeth had been to visit

the famous Daibutsu, the giant bronze statue of the meditating Buddha at nearby Kamakura, then felt like Rip van Winkles in Hayama with their photographs of little thatched houses, fishermen up to their waists in water pulling in their nets by hand, views of the sea from tree-clad hills, as they gazed at the bustling marina and the concrete buildings that filled the skyline. The photographs were greeted with incredulity by shopkeepers as the Wendovers, thinking there must be another Hayama, tried to establish that they were in the right place. These were of *here?* Laughs to prevent the *gaijin* being embarrassed by their foolish mistake. Then a man, not that old, had adjusted his glasses, peered closely at the photographs, put a forefinger on one of the fishermen and turned away.

'Kore wa watashi deshita,' he muttered. 'This was me.'

Deshita. Was, not is. Had he turned away to hide his emotions?

Well, it was only what had happened to thousands of other villages throughout the world, and the people who worked so hard needed somewhere to sail, play golf or otherwise unwind within easy distance of where they lived and worked. They travelled a great deal but couldn't sensibly go abroad at weekends. But the obliteration was so wholesale. Even the hills, it seemed, had gone, and nowhere around here remotely resembled the photographs only twenty-five years old.

Where had the fabled love of nature gone, the love of beautiful things? Oh, the Japanese bought objects at the auction houses of New York, Paris and London, but that was different. Owning a painting by Van Gogh was not the same at all . . . Yet perhaps it was. Surely the love of beauty had always, throughout Japan's long history, been minimalist, celebrated by the *haiku*, the minimal poem. There was the *bonsai*, the miniature tree, *ikebana* which used just enough flowers and no more; a cherry tree in bloom, a branch of it, a single blossom and no matter where it grew . . .

But then, but then: could it be that Mr Sato wanted Elizabeth's paintings because they reproduced with an artist's eye the beauty of his country which he could no longer – or spare the time to – see himself? David went through his wife's canvases again and realized for the first time that she had ventured some way to the minimalist approach from the very beginning of their time here. Half a landscape, a quarter, a smaller fraction, whereas before she would have attacked the whole thing. He stole an eleventh painting to contemplate in his old age while he grew vegetables in the garden of their home in Somerset.

Elizabeth was amused by his interpretation of her work. She painted what she saw, she said. It was merely a hobby. The exhibition was a joke, especially if Sam got the money he said he would. At least it would justify the riotous cost of their weekends away.

'Don't you want to keep any?' he asked.

She selected one he hadn't considered, an Impressionistic view of the Ginza, the people and the neon signs outside the bars amorphous blobs of colour yet the whole giving off the energy and the life of the street.

'You confuse and excite me,' he told her.

She shook her head at him. 'After all this time? Surely not!'

'Now more than ever.'

'What a shame we have to go to a party and you can't prove it to me now.'

'Can I later?'

She touched his hair, going grey at the temples. He would, she often said, make a very distinguished ambassador.

'Later,' she promised.

Sam Watanabe descended upon the studio and packed up the canvases to take to Hawaii. He fretted about the ones she was retaining but was defeated by her calm insistence that her husband wanted them. Two weeks later they flew to Honolulu for the opening of the exhibition. Sam was rubbing his hands in glee. Sato-san had been over, he said; Sato-san had spent a lot of money.

'How can he buy before the preview?' David asked.

'Easily. He wrote a cheque. Come on, you know why this was set up. He's a sensitive man and understood Elizabeth's dilemma. Have you been working?' he said to Elizabeth. 'We can do it again next year.'

'Give me a chance,' Elizabeth said. 'Anyway, I won't be in Japan next year.'

'I'll find you wherever you are.'

They did not know where they would be. And surely it was the Japanese content in her paintings that was causing the fuss, and that would certainly not continue.

Sam drove them to their hotel and left them to settle in, saying a car would pick them up at five and take them to the gallery. The press wanted to talk with Elizabeth before the party, he said.

'I feel like Denis Thatcher must have,' David said as they sat on the balcony of their hotel suite. 'Attached to his famous wife's handbag.'

'I'm not famous. It's a joke. I've always thought this whole thing is a joke. Thank goodness the Foreign Office doesn't mind what wives do these days. This would never have been approved of. It's what I tried to avoid. And what am I going to say to the press, for heaven's sake?'

But she coped, serenely, graciously, as she always did, while David, catalogue in hand, wandered around saying goodbye to his friends. He would not be seeing them again, even those Mr Sato had not bought, in spite of the fearsome price tags Sam had put on them, and by the end of the evening an Elizabeth Wendover was a scarce commodity indeed.

Sam took them out to dinner and handed Elizabeth a cheque. 'There's more to come,' he said. 'That's your share of the ones I've been paid for and the deposits on the rest.'

Elizabeth glanced at the cheque, blenched, and put it away.

'You sure you don't want to send over those others?'

'They are David's paintings.'

Sam bit into a huge shrimp and waved the tail at David. 'How about it?'

'Sorry, they're not for sale.'

Sam sighed and called for more champagne. 'Pity. Still, it's been great . . . Elizabeth, you keep in touch, you hear? You won't run out on me now, will you?'

'I'll tell you where I am. I can't do any more than that.'

Sam turned to the fourth person at the table, a woman journalist from Boston who was an old friend of Sam's. She was here on vacation, she said, and was thrilled to have had the opportunity to see Elizabeth's work.

'What can I do?' Sam asked her. 'I find an artist who the Japanese are willing to commit *harakiri* to buy and she's about to walk out of my life for ever.'

'I don't know, Sam,' she said. 'Commit *harakiri* yourself?'

'Hell, no,' Sam said. 'My ancestry's Japanese but my soul is all-American. I'll take the money and run.'

The Wendovers stayed for two more days before returning to Tokyo. A cleared studio was what Elizabeth had been waiting for and after Christmas she began working on her portrait of Alex. She had sent Jess photocopies of some of the sketches she had done, and Jess had written back with expressions of wonder at the likeness. Alex's two mothers had become regular correspondents and Alex, Jess wrote, was loving her life at college in Miami. Elizabeth wondered how Richard viewed this pen friendship between his wives. With extreme nervousness, she assumed, though he need not have done. Elizabeth was not going to make another woman unhappy by telling tales of long ago.

After her deliberations, the portrait came quickly to her brush. She was not copying a photograph, or even any of her own sketches, but was painting from her memory of them and from her imagination – for once, not what she saw. The result was brilliant, but it almost made David weep. It looked like a daughter lost to her mother, the face half turning towards the artist, the eyes with a dawning recognition, the lips about to say, 'Ah – so it's you!' Except the painting froze the moment before the words were said and revealed only the desperate hope that one day they would be spoken. David thought it the saddest thing he had ever seen.

Elizabeth let it dry, took it to be framed and ordered a case for it, then asked David if one of the embassy secretaries could find a courier to carry a parcel to Miami. He was relieved he didn't have to look at the painting, but was also concerned. What would Elizabeth do if Alex didn't acknowledge this?

'Please ask for me,' she said.

'If it's really what you want.'

'It is.'

When he had gone back to his office, Elizabeth wrote a letter.

> Dear Ben,
> You don't know me and I expect Alex has not mentioned me to you, but I am Alex's mother, your mother-in-law.
>
> I have not seen her for a very long time, much to my great distress, and would like you to tell her something for me. Tell her that children's views of the world of adults are not always correct, that adults can mislead and lie, that children can be misguided as well as guided. Things are not as they seem. I would like to tell her the whole truth, but I can not . . .

Could she not? Would she if it would mean a reunion between her and Alex? She had the proof, and Alex was old enough now to understand such words as 'adultery' and 'blackmail'. She thought of the nice woman who was now Lady Mountfield and her two sweet children, and, sighing, she continued.

> I can not, and neither can I even hint at why this is so, but will you tell her the rest?
>
> I have painted you a picture of your wife, Ben. My wedding present to you. I hope it is a good likeness, but of course I do not know. I did it from the photographs Lady Mountfield sent me.
>
> You both look very lovely, and I wish you every happiness in your married life.
>
> > Yours,
> > Elizabeth Wendover.

She showed the letter to David.

'Good Lord,' he said.

'Jess says he's got perfect manners.'

'So he'll have to write back, you mean?'

'It's the idea.'

'Oh darling, don't rely on it. Please.'

'Don't worry. I've been taking disappointments for twelve years. Did you find my courier?'

'He'll be here at nine thirty in the morning.'

Not long to wait before David came with a letter with an American stamp on it, the writer's name on the flap of the envelope. She took it from him, her face suddenly white.

'You open it,' she said, handing it back.

He did so.

'It's all right. Elizabeth, it's all right! Look.' He showed her the colour photographs of a golden-haired, smiling young man. 'They want you to paint him.'

She laughed, the most joyous unrestrained sound he had ever heard from her.

'Is it what you planned?'

'I hoped. Oh, how I hoped!'

She read Ben's letter.

Dear Mrs Wendover,

That picture of Alex is the most beautiful thing I've ever been given, ever in the whole of my life. Thank you for it.

I told Alex what you wrote and she's kind of confused and is thinking about it, but she is sure of one thing. Will you do a picture of me so we can have the set? I guess it's a bit much to ask, but if you want to give Alex a wedding present this is what she would like.

I didn't know about you. It's sad you haven't seen each other for so long but maybe when Alex has sorted out how she feels that can be put right. I'd really like to see Japan!

Regards,

Ben and

added to that, resentful, reluctant, uncertain but there, in the same pen but different writing: 'Alex', and a postscript, 'I'd like a painting of Ben. Thank you.'

And a month after that the Foreign Office, apparently inspired by divine providence, informed David his next posting would be to Washington, DC.

Chapter Seven

BEN SWUNG THE TROLLEY AROUND a corner and heaved it to a halt halfway up the next aisle.

'Hey, Alex, don't we need some of this?'

Alex put some packets of peanuts and what she had learned to call potato chips and not crisps in the trolley and looked at the wall of soap powders Ben was standing in front of.

'I suppose we do, but what brand?'

'How about this one? It's biodegradable.' Ben picked up a carton the size of a small suitcase.

'Do we need it that big?'

'May as well. Save us coming here too often, except it's kind of fun. What else?'

Alex consulted the list they had made. 'Eggs, milk, coffee. Things for the party.'

They were being really married, they decided. They examined the huge range of goods which promised to make their floors and furniture sparkle and their kitchen and bathroom cleaner than clean and picked out a few at random. Ben found his favourite brand of peanut butter and some light bulbs, Alex added some interesting looking eatables to the crisps and nuts they were giving their guests this evening and they both exclaimed over the discovery of paper plates. Why hadn't they thought of this before? they asked each other. Already their apartment had become the place where people stopped by in the evenings and they usually ended up eating a take-away meal. Paper plates would save the washing up. Which reminded them, and they bought some washing-up liquid as well as ten dozen paper plates to be on the safe side.

They wheeled their booty to the check-out, and it was packed up and taken to the car by one of their fellow students at the University of Miami, one less gilded than the golden couple who was having to work his way through college. The car had been driven down to Miami by another student, this one from Glasgow – Glasgow in Scotland! – for whom it had been a cheap way to get to Florida.

Ben and Alex Stanford didn't have to worry about anything being cheap. Franklin had increased the allowance he paid Ben, had paid Alex's college fees, provided her with credit cards and had opened a checking account for her.

'What's that?' she asked when she was told.

'One you write checks against,' Ben replied.

'Oh – you mean *cheques!*'

The credit cards would be essential when buying the formal dresses Nancy had told her were necessary for frat dances, whatever those were. Alex remembered how bewildered Jess had been when she had first arrived in England and was beginning to realize what she had been through. Challenges, though. Nothing more. Challenges to be met and overcome.

'Can I drive?' she said, when the other boy had finished putting their purchases into the car.

Ben mock groaned and tossed her the keys.

'Go carefully, okay? I don't want a heart attack today. Remember to look left first and that you've got a lot of car in front of you.'

She had nearly had an accident, forgetting these two things, and had edged the car forward so she could see oncoming traffic but had looked for it in the wrong direction.

'I will,' she said.

Ben kissed her briefly and yelled, 'Get her rolling then. Oh, Geronimo!'

He had found a liquor store owned by an Italian, a Tuscan furthermore, and he directed her there since he wanted to buy Italian wine for their party tonight.

'Where next?' Alex asked when this transaction had been completed (in Italian). 'How are we off for music?'

'Clint and the rest will bring some. Let's get home.'

Home! Alex loved that word. It meant their apartment in a low-level block around a courtyard containing palm trees. It was near the campus and the other apartments there were occupied by people from the university, mainly graduate students and teachers, which had worried Alex until she had discovered they weren't bristling professional types but young and friendly. One greeted them as Alex parked the car and helped them bring in the bags of groceries and the cases of wine.

'Jesus, Alex,' Ben said when the man had left. 'There's so much to do. Maybe I'd better not go to the game this afternoon.'

'Nancy's coming round. You go.'

Nancy didn't like football either. Alex had been to see the Hurricanes play once and had found it terrifying and confusing. She was glad Ben concentrated on swimming and not football, though he wasn't taking that so seriously since he had come up against the real hot shots and had learned, also, to drink wine the way the Italians did.

'Go,' she said to him again, and he put his arms around her and said, 'You're a wonderful wife, Alex. The guys thought everything would change when I got married, but it hasn't, has it?'

'I don't know what it was like before,' she said.

'Like it is now, but not nearly as nice. Say, what do we have for lunch?'

They had bought piles and piles of things but still had nothing suitable to eat, so when Clint arrived along with some other boys he was sent to get some pizzas and Alex and Ben used their new paper plates.

'Great,' Ben said afterwards, crumpling them up and throwing them away. 'Look at the hassle they save.'

'I'm not so sure, Boyo,' said Clint. 'I think you should leave the wife with a heap of dirty dishes. It's more traditional.'

'I'm leaving her. Isn't that enough?'

'Only for the afternoon, I hope.'

'Don't worry, Milady, we'll bring him back safe and sound.'

They went to the Orange Bowl and Alex wandered around the apartment in a daze of happiness. As though Ben would go off dumping her with the chores . . . not that there were any to speak of, as the janitor's wife came in three times a week to tidy the place up. Ben was the most perfect husband and theirs the most perfect life together. She could not imagine what would have happened to her back in England if she had not met Ben.

Feeling a need to do something wifely for him, Alex went into their bedroom and sorted out their washing. Her jeans, his jeans, his shirts, hers, her pants and his, though he called them shorts and to him pants were trousers. She found it moving, their clothes together like this, and was bundling them into the washing machine when Nancy arrived.

'Oh my, Mrs Stanford at work!' she exclaimed.

'That's right,' Alex said, finding the name thrilling. She picked up the suitcase of powder. 'Where does this go?'

The two girls unravelled the machine's mysteries and then unpacked the results of Ben and Alex's trip to the supermarket that morning.

'How many people are coming, for god's sake?' Nancy asked. 'Five hundred?'

'Only about thirty. Never mind. We'll have other parties.'

Every Saturday, Ben said, was a celebration since they'd been married on a Saturday, but tonight was to celebrate Alex's ownership of fifteen credit hours, these being the result of her hard work at the college in Eastbourne. She had sat five exams and had, she had been told, CLEPed out of five classes. She now had half the number of credit hours that Ben had and was determined upon pursuit of his total. She had discovered the brain her teachers said was somewhere inside her skull and was enjoying using it and Ben, while pretending to be scared that she'd graduate before him, was truly proud of her.

Nancy began making dips.

'Clint's asked me to the movies Monday,' she said. 'That's okay, isn't it?'

'Yeah, but I never thought he liked me much last year.'

Alex handed her a bowl. 'Maybe he fell for you in your bridesmaid's dress. He seemed pretty interested in you in Paris.'

Clint had not been with the other five – since, apart from Nancy, he hardly knew them – while Alex and Ben were in Italy. He had taken off for

Ireland and had met up with the rest of them at the time and place they had agreed on, the place being the only one they all knew of in Paris: the Eiffel Tower. It had seemed absurd when they had decided upon it, but it had worked out fine. Clint had greeted Nancy enthusiastically, saying she was the darlin' he had walked down the aisle with, and Nancy hadn't minded since during the past couple of weeks she and Mike had decided the two of them were going nowhere.

'So did you accept?' Alex prompted.

'Sure.'

'It'll be good if you two get together. We can go round in a foursome, can't we?'

'Yup.'

Nancy would not think about what Mike had said when he had first met Clint at Franklin Stanford's house. He'd said the guy was a fag, but that could not be. He didn't mix with the gay set here in Miami, he went around with athletes, boys like Ben, and he took out other girls. It wasn't like the old days when you had to disguise what you were, so Mike was wrong. Maybe Clint had fallen for her in her bridesmaid's dress, maybe she had imagined his dislike of her last year, maybe he wanted to take her out because, in fact, he liked her. Mike had to be wrong, because if he was right then Clint had asked her out so they could, as Alex suggested, make up a foursome, which he wanted to do so he could see more of . . . Ben! Which was ridiculous and Mike was wrong.

And so, later, when Clint held her close and said, in the accent he had acquired in the time he'd spent in Ireland, 'How about givin' me a kiss, me darlin'?', she gave him the best kiss she knew and his response was more than equal to it. He didn't look like a fag, he didn't act like one and, as she noted when they danced on, he didn't feel like one either.

He offered to drive her to her dorm and they left, with the other guests, saying thank you to the golden couple as they went.

'Now you're not to be doin' anything tonight, you hear me?' Clint added. 'No clearin' up. Me an' the lady here'll be along in the mornin' to help. Okay?'

Alex, leaning sleepily against Ben, nodded and smiled and Ben said, 'We're not doing anything tonight except going to bed.'

Clint punched him in the ribs and told him not to show off.

He wasn't gay!

Ben closed and locked the door and went to the kitchen and poured them each a glass of milk.

'I thought that went well,' Alex said, as she had heard Jess say to her father at the end of parties.

'It did. You were a proper hostess.'

They went into their bedroom, got undressed, into bed, kissed each other good night and, as they did most nights, fell immediately asleep in each other's arms.

*

They took up running in the early mornings, Ben going the length of each block, turning and looping around her until she complained it made her feel dizzy and said he should go at his own pace. He would not leave her, though. He and Nancy had told her that she must take care in Miami; that it was a dangerous place and she must never – not ever, not even on campus – go out alone at night. She was hardly likely to do so, but was impressed enough to wonder if the early morning was dangerous too. Then she discovered running mates and Ben did two circuits to their one, catching Alex as the other girls peeled away to go to their dorm and they would race the last few hundred yards, Alex, as she became fitter, gaining a head start and often beating him home. Afterwards they showered, soaping each other and kissing. She loved touching Ben's muscular body, tenderly soaping it and splashing water on the soft parts where the shower couldn't reach. Then, when they had dressed, they would have breakfast at a coffee shop nearby, where they did eggs just how Ben liked them and had the most wonderful fresh orange juice.

One morning in the shower something stirred in both of them. Ben grew huge and hard and this was exciting to her. Scarcely bothering to dry themselves, they went to bed and, instead of making the most of his erection while it was there as he had done the few times they had managed this before, he waited for a while, stroking her before going inside her.

This time there was no pain or discomfort but another, very different feeling and she wondered if it was an orgasm, but decided it could not be as it didn't seem as though she had been sucked into a whirlpool or stars had exploded in her head (or elsewhere), which was how the novels she bought at airports said she should feel. Still, it was nicer than it had been before, more interesting, and she was disappointed it was over so soon but when Ben raised his head and said, 'Wow, that was good!', she hugged him and smiled and agreed it was, and they ran to their classes late, pleased with each other.

It didn't happen the next day or the day after that. Alex didn't mind. She liked holding Ben naked in bed, he holding her; she liked the shared showers and the gentle, loving touching. This was sex: kissing and holding hands but a bit more so. This and the paper plates, the pizzas and the parties was marriage.

They flew to New York to spend Thanksgiving with Franklin and Ben's parents on Long Island. Franklin was resting when they arrived and the nurse/valet who he had, most worryingly, employed refused to disturb him. He was predictably furious and positively ran into the drawing-room to greet his golden couple, ignoring the valet's strictures and Maisie's anxious twittering. Alex waited so Ben could greet his grandfather alone, but Franklin motioned her forward.

'Where's my kiss?' he barked. 'Don't I get a kiss?'
She gave him two, one on each cheek.

'Stand back,' he ordered. 'Stand back so I can see
you both.'

They did, laughing at each other and at him. He
nodded, satisfied, and they helped him to his chair.
Maisie muttered to her friend that there wouldn't
be room for them near the fire tonight and went and
sat by the windows, now curtained and not open to
the light as they were the first evening Alex had been
here. Ben talked quietly to his grandfather and Alex
sat on a sofa between her mother- and father-in-law.
They hardly knew her, they said, and it was too bad.
Would she and Ben come and stay a night or two
with them in New York after Christmas? Maybe
they could go to the theatre.

Alex said she'd look forward to it, but her heart
gave a little lurch at the thought of everything going
on at Montly at Christmas as it had done for
centuries, and she not there. It was her first touch of
homesickness and it was compounded by the meal
they ate now for Thanksgiving – the traditional
English Christmas fare of roast turkey but the
whole jerked out of kilter by the addition of
pumpkin pie and the fact it was happening in the
wrong month.

'My lovely girl is sad,' Franklin said, putting his
thin hand on hers. 'What's the matter?'

She couldn't tell him about Christmas. She and
Ben had decided they would spend it here with him,

and it would be dreadful if he felt she was doing so unwillingly.

'I was thinking' – and she had been, in a sense – 'of what it must be like for Jess, away from her family at Thanksgiving. I hadn't realized how it's a time to be together.'

'Why don't we give her a call?' Franklin said.

'It's too late,' Alex said. 'It's after midnight there.'

'When did you last call home?'

Alex looked at Ben. He shrugged.

One phone call, in fact, and two brief but ecstatic letters. They had phoned her last week, she remembered in a surge of guilt. Maria, the janitor's wife, had taken the call and left a message, but since it had said 'no worry' Alex hadn't and the note had vanished amid the debris of a meal.

'We'll call tomorrow,' Ben said.

Franklin was escorted to bed soon after the meal was over and Ben and Alex chatted to Maisie (and her friend) and to Frank and Joan Stanford until they, too, went upstairs. Ben took off his black tie, undid the collar of his shirt and pulled Alex down to sit beside him on the hearthrug in front of the fire.

'I like your dress,' he said. He put his hand inside it and stroked her breast. He often did it. It felt good.

'It's odd having to be smart after so long being like slobs.'

'You've never been like a slob,' he said, kissing her. 'And how about the frat dance? You were a knock-out.'

Conchita came in to clear way the coffee cups and, on seeing them, exclaimed an apology.

Ben took his hand from Alex's breast and they both stood up, said good night to Conchita and went towards the stairs. They had agreed it was too much of a bother for Maisie and Conchita to open their wing of the house for the three nights they would be here and had also thought, but had not expressed aloud, it would be even less bother if Ben slept in his old room and Alex in the one she had used in the summer. It was the first tiniest inkling either had that perhaps there was something wrong in their perfect marriage. It may have been this, or Conchita's affectionate but knowing smile, or being caught with his hand on his wife's breast, but by the time they had closed the door of the bedroom assigned to them Ben was well and truly roused. And like that other time after the shower he took it slowly, confident that his erection would stay with him as he undressed his wife, exposing her body bit by bit to his eyes and lips and hands until she was naked in front of him. He led her to the bed and laid her on it, watched her all the time as he undressed himself. Yet even then he waited as he lay beside her, his head propped on one hand while his other played over Alex's body. She gasped and reached for him. Their lips met in an explosion and she opened to him, eager to have him there, and felt that thing the novels describe though their words were inadequate.

Ben, still inside her but softer and smaller now,

touched her cheek. A lock of crinkly gold hair had fallen forward on his wide, smooth brow and she brushed it back lovingly.

'I think we're learning, Alex,' he said.

'Maybe we could do a course at college and learn more.'

They both giggled and hoped they hadn't awoken the household.

'Did we make a lot of noise?' he asked.

'You could have screamed and I wouldn't have known.'

'Serves them right for going to bed so early. How else are we to pass the time?'

He rolled off her and cuddled her close to him. She felt drowsy and infinitely relaxed. He kissed her hair. 'Okay?'

She tipped her head so she could kiss his chin. 'More than okay, except you've taken my bones away.'

He laughed softly and they slept.

The memory of the night before was in Ben almost before he was awake the next morning. He awoke Alex by touching her in the places he had discovered and they made love again, showered, dressed and went to join Frank and Joan in the dining-room.

'Boy, am I hungry!' Ben said, holding out a chair for Alex, his hand brushing her neck as she sat down. 'Tell Juan two dozen eggs and a pigful of bacon, Conchita.'

Everyone smiled. It was obvious what they had been up to and their happiness was a joy to behold. Frank made a mental note to phone Richard when he got back to New York and tell him to stop fussing, though why he should worry about Richard Frank didn't know.

Alex and Ben went to say good morning to Franklin before driving to Austin and Betty Mitchell's house. It was Ben's idea they should go. Their glow held off cold November, radiated it away.

'Whatever you saw or thought you saw or didn't see at all,' Betty wrote to her daughter, 'don't worry about it. They couldn't keep their hands or eyes off each other.'

It was exactly what Frank had reported to Richard and Jess, greatly relieved, wrote to her stepdaughter giving her the name and address of the gynaecologist on Long Island she had asked Betty to recommend and telling her to go and visit him during the Christmas vacation. She would have to switch from a British to an American brand of pills, she told her, and wasn't to leave it to the last moment in case the doctor had to check on a match.

Jess had no idea if this was true, although it made sense, but the purpose of the letter was to remind Alex to take the pills. Jess supposed she must have been or she would be pregnant already, but on the evidence of their Thanksgiving visit to Long Island Jess thought it worth making the point.

It was a good point, for Alex hadn't been bothering about the pills though she began to after they got back to Miami, beginning on the one marked Sunday and hoping for the best. When Jess's letter arrived and Ben asked what news there was from home, she tried to say it was personal but that seemed silly. It was personal between her and her husband and, anyway, she couldn't hide the letter from him. They had picked it up from their mail box after their run, had their shower and were now waiting for the coffee to percolate while Ben crushed oranges in the machine they had bought and Alex attempted to cook eggs over easy as Ben liked. Since the revelations of Thanksgiving this was much more preferable to the coffee shop.

'Jesus, Alex, have you been taking the pills?' Ben said.

'Sort of.'

'Sort of!' Ben poured orange juice into two glasses and looked at the letter again.

She felt a spurt of anger. This was the late twentieth century, for heaven's sake, and birth control was as much the men's responsibility as the women's. And how could she be expected to remember to swallow something every night when the chances were, until recently, it would be needed about once a month?

But then he was her darling Ben again, saying he was sorry, he should have thought about it and why hadn't she told him?

How could she have done? Oh, now she could, now that they made love so often and with such pleasure in each other . . . but then? She was just under eighteen and a half years old, but thousands of generations of women were in her genes as she answered, lying to make her man feel better about his sexual strength, 'I was embarrassed, Ben.'

Which was half true.

'I'm an only child,' he said as he started into his eggs, 'and I always wanted brothers and sisters. I want us to have lots of babies, Alex. Lots of 'em.'

'So do I, Ben, but not yet.'

'No. Not yet.'

He pushed his plate away, held out a hand and tugged her round the table on to his lap. They were both wearing their bathrobes. He kissed her.

'My beautiful wife. *Wife*,' he said, loving the word and her. 'Are you safe now?'

'I don't know. I suppose I'd better go to one of these gynaewhatsits and see.'

'Soon, Alex. Don't wait until Christmas.'

'Soon.'

'Today, okay?' He set her aside and began to eat again. 'Go to the best, Alex. Only the best for you.'

He did not suggest how she go about finding a gynaecologist in Miami, let alone the best, but Alex summoned up courage and asked one of their neighbours. There was a list in the Yellow Pages, she was told, but the good people would not be able to see Alex for months. She should go to a women's health care clinic, and was found the telephone number and address of the nearest one. Ben insisted on driving her there and coming in with her. The gynaecologist was a woman and was very tactful and understanding. Having listened to stammered and evasive explanations of why Alex had only recently begun to take her pills regularly, she sent Ben out of the room saying she wanted to examine his wife. Relieved, Alex told her the whole story.

'Do you think you need sex counselling?' she asked. 'I can recommend someone.'

'No, oh no,' Alex assured her. 'It's fine now.'

The woman then asked when in her cycle Alex had started taking the pills; Alex did not know and was told to stop taking them and to wait for her first natural period and begin again properly.

'You should be okay in five or six weeks. In the meantime you and your husband must use another form of contraception.' She went on to explain what these could be and Alex, recoiling from having to put anything inside her, said they would manage. The woman worked out dates, said she'd like to see her at the start of next semester to check on how things were going and, to Alex's horror, told her what symptoms to look out for if she was pregnant.

'You mean I might be?'

'Of course you might!' Didn't they teach them about the birds and bees in England?

She prescribed a different brand of pill and then invited Ben back in and gave him an edited account of what she had told Alex, and she added, because she meant it and could see the boy needed it, 'I'm truly impressed at the support you're giving your wife today. I have patients with husbands twice, three times your age who don't get this kind of care and understanding.'

It did help. He paid the bill for the consultation with a kind of swagger and went and bought some condoms. It wasn't as good, though. His erections fainted under the onslaught of the thin rubber – in sexy colours though it claimed to be – and amid the nervousness that Alex may be pregnant, though that was more on her part than on his. After a while they went back to kissing and cuddling in the shower, and back to the coffee shop for breakfast.

It would soon be Christmas. Alex had become used to the oddity, as it seemed to her, of Santa Clauses strolling around the shopping malls of Miami and the piped music in the department stores dreaming of a white Christmas. She and Ben went downtown and bought wonderful presents for everyone at home. Shopping for William and Annabelle meant they could spend hours in the toy departments and two small English children were going to have the time of their lives. Nancy and Clint came along too sometimes, and the four of them decided to give themselves a Christmas treat by having a weekend at Disneyworld in Orlando. Nancy and Clint were going steady but they didn't sleep together, so Ben shared a room with Clint and Alex with Nancy.

'Sorry to be taking you away from your wife, Boyo,' Clint said on the first night as they got undressed.

He hoped Ben slept naked. Just to look at him and think of him in the next bed gave him a rush.

'It's okay right now,' Ben replied. 'We got into a muddle over Alex's birth-control pills and until it's sorted out we have to be careful. She may even be pregnant.'

Clint was stunned. The use of the word 'we', the casual admission that Alex and Ben had a healthy sex life, the proprietorial way Ben spoke of Alex's body . . . Oh, Clint assumed they had tried sex, but he had been sure Ben could not enjoy it. What kind of a marriage was this anyway, with people around at their apartment most nights, Alex working like it was going out of business, Ben keeping up with his training – though not as seriously as before – coming to football games, any movie or meal out inevitably in a foursome with him and Nancy? They were hardly ever alone, and Clint had been certain that was because Ben was Alex's friend rather than her lover. He had fallen for Ben the moment he saw him, the day the freshmen had their first try-out at the pool. He had been surprised at the news of the British girlfriend, shocked at the engagement, but when he'd seen Alex and Ben together he had known the marriage couldn't last and had been prepared to wait. Ben would understand what he was, as Clint had done when he was sixteen, and his glorious innocence – so appealing, this – would be gone. Ben was the reason Clint hadn't come out at college knowing, until he realized, Ben would not have a friend who was gay. It was why Clint had taken up with Nancy, since a guy alone could not attach himself to a married couple, however strange and temporary that marriage was, and Nancy was happy to have an easy-going relationship after her break-up with Mike. Had she noticed he was passionate only when Ben was near? He thought not. After that first time he had been careful to keep it light.

Alex might be pregnant, though! Jesus H. Christ! They *were* alone. They were alone in their bed every night. Yet Clint kept his cool as he said, 'Wow, Boyo, I guess you don't need that, right?'

'Right,' Ben said, getting into bed wearing just his boxer shorts. Clint had to force himself not to stare, not to let disappointment show. 'We want kids, of course,' Ben went on, 'but now would be a tad soon.' He shrugged his beautiful brown muscled shoulders, looked at Clint from out of his beautiful blue eyes and smiled.

'Still, if it's happened, it's happened, hasn't it?'

There was pride in his voice, pride and a kind of satisfaction. Clint reached to turn off his bedside light, needing the dark to swallow up further confidences.

*

214

Back to Long Island for Christmas, and the young Stanfords took up residence in their wing of Franklin's mansion. Franklin presented Alex with a Nissan sports car, a little thing, he said, for her to run around in, a reward for the As and Bs on her semester report.

'All mine?' Alex said, dancing around the red car which Ben, on his grandfather's orders, had driven from its hiding place somewhere on the property. 'Really?'

'Really all yours,' Franklin said.

Alex bounded up the steps to where Franklin was standing outside the front door, swathed against the cold in overcoat and scarves.

'Thank you. You shouldn't have, but thank you very much indeed.'

He accepted her hug and kiss. 'Don't you want to go have a drive in it?'

'Yeah!' She ran back down the steps to the car. 'Out!' she said to Ben, who was in the driver's seat testing the gadgets. 'These holidays you have to ask me for permission to drive.'

His big white car was still in Florida. There were others here he could use but he got out of the Nissan and went on one knee before his wife, down on the gravel while his parents and grandfather looked on.

'Can I have a go?' he pleaded.

'Only after I've had one.'

The others watched as Alex, after a couple of

bucking starts, drove the car around the corner of the house and away.

'They're okay,' Franklin said softly to himself. 'They're okay.'

'Sure they are, Dad,' his son said, taking his arm to help him inside.

Later that morning, Franklin sat between his golden couple in church and leant on them as they stood to sing the carols, adding his feeble quaver to their strong young voices and, after the service, showing them off to his neighbours. Many of them Alex knew, for several members of the gang were there with their families and so were Betty and Austin Mitchell, who were coming to the mansion for lunch. They called Montly when they got back from church. William answered the phone, his voice sounding so English as he said, 'Montly three eight five,' and then Alex's ears were assaulted as he yelled, 'Alex? Is that you?' Everyone spoke to everyone and Alex had a weep afterwards, but she enjoyed her first American Christmas. That night Ben overcame his distaste for the rubber and they made love for the first time in nearly three weeks. It was over too quickly and not very good for either of them but they wished each other happy Christmas and promised it would be like it was before – better even – when they could be rid of the damned condoms.

She learned she was not pregnant a few days later, on the morning they went to New York to stay with

Frank and Joan. The elder Stanfords gave a party to introduce Alex to their friends and to Ben's friends from his high school. One of these, Timothy, had come to their wedding and he kissed Alex, claiming old acquaintance, and said marriage suited them both.

'Over four months of it and we're not bored yet,' Ben said.

This was the first time Alex had been to New York since those few boiling days on her first visit to America when all they had wanted to do was get off the sizzling streets and into the air conditioning. It was different in winter, and Alex loved the avenues lined with towering, shining steel and glass.

'It's so beautiful,' she said to Ben as they stood near Central Park and looked down Sixth Avenue.

'Is it?' he said, he who dreamed of a walled city of warm brick, a palace-ringed, scallop-shaped space at its heart.

She kept her appointment at the clinic at the start of the next term. Ben offered to come with her but she preferred to go alone and Ben could not refuse her the car since she had been so generous with the Nissan, left in Franklin's garage since Alex's latent British puritanism could not justify them having two cars in Florida.

The woman smiled at Alex's earnest assurances that she was taking the pills each night, at the way she had written the relevant dates down on a piece of paper and showed her diary as further proof.

'Okay,' she said, 'keep taking the pills according to the directions, but use further protection until you start the next pack.'

'Oh no. Must we?' Alex said, deflated and distressed.

'Is there a problem?'

'No – no.'

'There is,' the doctor said and added, although it was not part of her job, 'You want to tell me about it?'

Haltingly, Alex explained about Ben's aversion to rubber.

'Do you help him?'

Alex stared at her. 'Help him? How?'

Why had this pair of children got married if not for sex?

'Do you initiate sex? Try to get him going?'

'No. It – it just happens when he's ready.'

'And you never try to make him ready? There's two people there, you know, making love to each other.'

Alex didn't reply, and the woman nearly laughed aloud as interest, speculation and then avid anticipation showed on the young girl's face.

'Are we really not safe just with the pills?' she asked at last.

'It would be safer with something else.' She checked back on the dates Alex had given her. 'You were dead on time and I guess I shouldn't say it, but I reckon you'll be okay.'

218

'Thank you,' Alex said.

She drifted to the car and drove home, stopping on the way at an Italian deli to buy stuff for the recipe they were cooking tonight, then stopped again to pick up things for breakfast. She thought about what the doctor had said. How would she go about initiating sex? Maybe she wouldn't need to now, but it offered intriguing possibilities.

Ben came in soon after she got home, but Clint was with him and soon other people would be arriving.

'Okay?' Ben asked, giving her a kiss.

'Okay.'

'What's okay, Milady?'

'The universe.'

Later the phone rang. Clint answered it as Alex and Ben were in the kitchen attempting to make spaghetti carbonara from the Italian cookbook Ben had given Alex for Christmas.

'It's for you, Boyo,' Clint said and, to the rest of the room, 'Hey, shut up and let the man hear.'

Ben spoke for a short time, put the phone down and rejoined Alex.

'Who was it?' she asked.

'Some courier joint. They've got a package for me and have been trying to deliver it all day. The guy said he'd bring it round now.'

'Why didn't he leave it with the janitor?'

'Didn't know there was one, maybe. Maybe he's supposed to give it to the person it's addressed to. I wonder what's in it . . . Okay, how are we doing?'

Alex consulted the cookbook. 'Is the spaghetti done?'

'Yup.' Ben said, fishing out a piece, tasting it and feeding it to her for confirmation.

'Then we drain it, put it back in the pan, mix in the sauce and *pancetta* and serve with parmesan cheese.'

'*Parmigiano*.' Ben drained the pasta. 'Sauce, *pancetta*, Alex.'

'Here you are.'

'Big spoon and fork, Alex.'

'Shouldn't we chop it up?' she said as Ben struggled to get the strings of spaghetti properly coated with sauce.

'It would be cheating. Big bowl, Alex.'

'Here.'

The spaghetti slithered in.

'Plates, forks, spoons, salad, Alex.'

'On the table.'

Ben lifted the bowl and carried it into their main room. '*Signori e signorini* . . . oh and *signora*,' he added, winking at Alex. '*Ecco spaghetti alla carbonara*. Shit, I've forgotten the word for cooked, but cooked *per mia bella sposa anche per me*.'

Everyone clapped and cheered and, when they began eating, judged the pasta delicious. The package for Ben arrived when people were beginning on second helpings, but they put their plates aside and crowded around speculating on what it might be.

'It's from Mrs David Wendover,' Ben said, reading the docket.

Alex, beside him and as interested as everyone else, gasped and said quickly, 'It must be for me.'

Ben showed her the labels. 'Franklin Benjamin Stanford the Third.'

'No "Mrs" in front of it? There must be!'

'It's written twice – three times including the docket. It's my parcel and you're not having it.'

'It's a fine big one, Boyo. Open it up,' Clint said.

'Don't, Ben,' Alex said. 'Please.'

'Why not?'

'It's from my mother.'

'Your *mother?*'

'My real mother. Jess isn't, you know.'

'Sure I know, but—' Ben noticed everyone had fallen silent and this wasn't a conversation that could continue in front of them. He would talk it over with her later and in the meantime find out what this newly acquired mother-in-law of his had sent him. He couldn't not open it now and Alex, presumably realizing this, nodded slightly and sighed. Someone went to the kitchen to fetch a sharp knife which Ben used to cut the strings, then tore away the Sellotape on the brown paper. Beneath it was a slim wooden crate with a hasp at the top fastening down the lid. Ben flicked it open and pulled out an object wrapped in corrugated cardboard. The cardboard was held together by masking tape and attached to it, also by masking

tape, was an envelope marked 'for Ben Stanford'.
No possible lingering doubt about who this was
meant for. Ben glanced at Alex as he balanced the
package against his legs, removed the envelope and
tore it open.

'We can't take the tension,' a voice called as Ben
scanned the letter. He tucked it into the back pocket
of his jeans, bent down, undid the masking tape and
pulled away the cardboard and then some layers of
tissue paper. He held the picture up and gazed at it
as people jogged his elbows so they could see too.
There was silence and then cries of wonder, but still
not everyone could see. Ben carried the painting over
to a chest of drawers and put it on top, leaning it
against the wall. Carefully he cleared the other
things off the chest so the painting was alone and
then stood back.

'Alex's mother painted it,' he said. 'It's her
wedding present to me.'

'It's beautiful,' Nancy breathed. '*Beautiful!* Alex,
why didn't you say your mother is a great artist?'

They had to turn to find her. She was by the case
the painting had arrived in and was in a turmoil of
confused emotions. The major one was anger, pure
fury that her mother had invaded her new life in this
back-door way by sending the picture to Ben, but
under that were other less definable feelings: the
shock when Ben had held the painting and she had
looked at her own face; a certain . . . shame? . . . as
she had recognized something in that other, canvas

self although she could not determine exactly why it should be so; bewilderment as she was congratulated for having such a talented mother. How should she react to that? And then Ben. She had never told him her mother was alive, had let him assume she was dead and her reluctance to talk about her was because it pained her too much. The letter from Jess telling her she had felt obliged to inform her mother, about her marriage had been waiting when they had arrived here and had been read, thrown away and forgotten, easily concealed from Ben amid the excitement of moving in. What had the woman written to him? She wished everyone would go away so she could explain things to him, but instead they were picking up their discarded plates and beginning to eat again, standing around the portrait, admiring it and now insisting she ask her mother to do one of Ben.

'It seems to me,' a girl called Maggie said, waving her fork at the painting, 'that you're waiting for someone or something, and I reckon it's Ben next to you on the wall.'

'That's right!' the boy, Abe, standing next to her said. 'It's only half a painting, isn't it? It's waiting for more to happen.'

Of course she had to say she would ask for one of Ben!

'She hasn't signed it. What's her name?' Abe wanted to know.

'Elizabeth Wendover.'

'Does she exhibit?' He did classes in art history, as did Ben. He obviously fancied himself as an expert – except so did everyone else tonight.

'I don't know,' she said. 'I – I haven't seen her for some time. She divorced my father.'

'Well, she can't be an amateur. Not when she paints like that.'

At last they went. Ben stopped Alex from beginning to clear up, poured them each a glass of wine and took her to sit on the sofa opposite the portrait.

'Okay, so what's the story?' he asked.

'Nothing special. She left Daddy and me when I was six years old. She deserted us.'

Ben twisted himself round so he could get the letter from his back pocket and handed it to her. He read it again as she did so for the first time.

'What does it mean?' she said. 'All this about lies and misleading?'

'I don't know. Looks like you have to do some thinking.'

'I was six years old, Ben!'

'Didn't she try to see you?'

'Yes, but I refused.'

'It's terrible, Alex. Terrible you haven't seen your mother.'

'She deserted us,' Alex repeated stubbornly.

'Her letter indicates that maybe it wasn't so straightforward.'

'I don't believe it.'

'This isn't the first present she's sent you, is it?'

'She sent it to you.'

'You know what I mean.'

'No, it isn't.'

'Will you write and ask her for a picture of me?'

She was cornered and furiously silent.

'Or don't you want one?' he said.

'She's manipulating us,' Alex burst out. 'Don't you see?'

'Maybe she is, but who can blame her? Okay, I'll write, shall I? I have to anyway, to thank her. It's really great,' he went on, leaning back and stretching his legs in front of him. 'Now I have two Alexes. One who'll always look the same and seems about to say something beautiful to me, and the other who can be in any sort of mood.'

She laughed then, turned and buried her face in his chest. 'You write.'

'And you get photographs.'

Ben found paper and pen and cleared space on the table. By the time he had a letter he was satisfied with, Alex had selected photographs to send with it.

'Come on,' he said. 'You've got to sign too.'

'No.'

'Yes.'

She dragged herself across the room, took the pen he held out to her and signed her name.

'Put something else. It's your mother, for God's sake.'

She scribbled a few words at the bottom of the

225

page. Ben folded the letter, the photographs in it, and said he'd mail it tomorrow. They stood before the portrait on their way to their bedroom.

'It's the best present I ever had. I told your mother that and it's true.'

He kissed her. Things were happening inside his jeans and he felt about ten feet high. He'd done something right, something to correct a wrong – or begun to, at least – and he'd ordered his wife around and she had obeyed.

'Did the doctor say it was okay?'

'Yes.'

He picked her up, carried her to the bedroom and laid her down on the bed. 'Then we can make love all tonight and all tomorrow.'

He undressed her top half and, remembering what the doctor had said, she tugged at his belt.

'I want to see you too.'

He watched her unbuckle his belt and undo the top button of his jeans.

'Hold on,' he whispered as she was about to attack the zip. 'Something's keen to get out of there and it doesn't want to be hurt on the way.' He eased the zip around his erection. Tentatively she stroked him.

'No, Alex,' he said into her ear. 'It's wonderful but it'll make me too quick. It's got to be slow to make it good for you.'

That must mean he didn't need help, then; and it was very good for her.

'It's always going to be like that,' he said, after they had cleaned their teeth, Alex had taken her pill and they were back in bed. 'I was getting worried. I mean, a guy should have a hard-on when he gets naked into bed with a girl like you. A bit of rubber shouldn't put him off. I was wondering if there was something the matter with me.'

'There's nothing the matter with you.'

She felt him. Instead of touching him gently, impersonally almost, as she did in the shower, she was purposeful about it, deliberately seeing if she could rouse him as the doctor had said. He lay and enjoyed it and soon he was hard again. So it worked! This was fascinating. She bent and kissed him, and soon the fascination was lost in excitement as she made love to him, not letting him do anything until he couldn't stop himself and pulled her on top of him.

'Wow!' he breathed afterwards. 'Where did you learn to do that?'

She couldn't tell him about the doctor. 'Where,' she countered, 'did you learn how to make it good for me?'

'From a book.'

'A book? Ben, really? Where is it?'

'In the store. I only got to read a little of it, but there were pictures.'

She began to laugh. 'Why didn't you buy it?'

He was laughing too. 'I was embarrassed. I had to buy something, though, and that's how you got that book of poetry.'

'Ben, how I love you! How very much I love you!'

It was raining the next day, and Saturday. They didn't go for a run and had breakfast in their apartment. At Alex's insistence, they went and bought the book Ben had seen, saying they were married, they both wore wedding rings and shop assistants were used to selling such things. Ben posted the letter to Alex's mother and they went home, put a note on the door saying 'gone fishing' and nearly made true Ben's promise that they would make love all day.

'I reckon it's done for, Alex,' Ben said, when they got to bed for real that night and Alex started playing with her new toy.

She kissed it. 'I don't think so,' she said. 'Not quite.'

On Sunday, as they always did, they met up with Nancy, Clint and a crowd of others for brunch.

'Well, and where were you yesterday?' Clint asked.

'Fishing. Didn't you see the note?' Ben pulled out a chair for Alex and sat next to her.

'What did you catch?' There was an edge to Clint's voice. Nancy looked sharply at him and he added a grin to his face, but Ben and Alex didn't notice as they smiled at each other.

'Trout, wasn't it?' Alex said.

'Yeah. Some of them and a couple of sharks.'

Alex's hand was on his thigh, practically touching him up, and now Ben's hand was on hers, squeezing it and tucking it even closer. Had Clint been wrong?

There was a chemistry between them today he hadn't seen before, not even when he had been looking closely for it after that time in Orlando when Ben had made the startling revelation that Alex might be pregnant. They'd locked themselves away in their apartment for twenty-four hours for Christ's sake, Clint's brain told him, behind a note that may as well have said, 'Go away, we're fucking.' Ben had missed the game yesterday afternoon and they hadn't turned up at a party in the evening. What should Clint do now? Drop Nancy, find himself a nice boy and shut himself off from Ben for ever? Shut himself off from this whole group, he supposed, as there were no other gays here. There were no Hispanics, Blacks or Jews either. The real city of Miami – the one Clint came from – may as well not have existed as far as this bunch of WASPs seeking suntans was concerned: no gangs, no kids pushing drugs, no shootings, no poverty. An enclave of white, down-the-middle privilege and he knew what they would do if he brought along a boy to Sunday brunch, both of them basking in the afterglow of sex as Ben and Alex were now. Get up and go, that's what, most of them. Anyway, he didn't want another boy. He wanted Ben, and he had to stay Ben's friend and pretend to be straight if there was ever any chance of getting him. In spite of the evidence in front of him – Ben ordering food from the waiter 'for my wife', as though he couldn't do enough for her, as though she couldn't speak for herself in her plummy English voice – he couldn't stop loving Ben. It was a habit, and so were Nancy and this crowd, and habits were hard to break. He turned to Nancy and her dark eyes met his. Was that suspicion, calculation in them? Christ, that wouldn't do. He kissed her cheek.

'How is me darlin' this fine day?'

'It's raining,' she said. 'It's been raining for two days.'

'Let's sue the state of Florida,' someone said.

'Have you hung your painting, Ben?' Abe asked.

'We thought we'd wait for the one of me.'

The conversation roved over the miracle of Alex's mother's painting and then to things more general. The Stanfords, as usual, asked everyone back to their apartment after brunch but people soon began drifting away, realizing, perhaps, that things had changed.

'Oh, you're not going too?' Ben said as Clint hauled Nancy to her feet and made ready to leave. But he was only being polite.

'Yep. I'm taking my girl to the movies.'

How long had he gazed besottedly at Ben and how long had Nancy seen him doing it? He had to make up lost ground. He took Nancy's hand as they walked through the continuing rain to his car.

'I feel kind of jealous, I guess.'

'Of Alex, Clint?'

Jesus, she had seen something then!

'Of them both. They have something special. Who

wouldn't feel jealous?' He stopped, turned her to him and kissed her. She was tense at first, then relaxed and kissed him back. He opened her raincoat and felt her breasts through her shirt. Was this supposed to be exciting? He sighed into her ear. 'Nancy—' he began.

'No, Clint. I didn't with Mike and I won't with you.'

He adopted a minor sulk. It seemed to impress her. 'I'm sorry,' she added.

'Hell, Nance, you have to admit it's hard on a guy when his best friend is getting as much as he wants – getting more right now by the look of them when we left – and I have to make do with an occasional kiss.'

She laughed. 'How about more frequent ones, then?'

He sighed again. 'If I have to, Nance. If I have to.'

Nancy was impressed and thought what she had seen were wild imaginings, some odd legacy of her time with Mike and the way regret and loss ambushed her at unexpected moments as she remembered Mike, his arm around her shoulders as Clint's was now, saying with certainty, 'The guy's a fag.' It was nonsense. And the other reason it was nonsense was that Clint always lost his bogus Irish accent when he was being serious.

Case proven.

Abe grabbed Ben as their lecture on history of art ended.

'I got something to show you,' he said. 'Time for a coffee?'

'What is it?'

'You'll be excited and so will Alex.'

He brought two styrofoam cups over to the table where he had parked Ben.

'Elizabeth Wendover, right?' he said, sitting down. 'Alex's mother?'

'Are there two of 'em?' He pulled a magazine out from the pile of stuff he had dumped on the table, flicked through it until he found the pages he wanted, then turned it towards Ben.

'British artist causes stir in Honolulu,' the headline read over a double-page spread.

'It's her all right,' Ben said, after reading the first paragraph of the article.

'Go on and you'll see your wedding present from her is worth no small bucks.'

Ben read the whole article. There was a picture of the artist with her husband and some other guy, but it was so small he couldn't see what she looked like, and black-and-white reproductions of a couple of paintings. The woman who had written the text was high in praise. Ben turned to the cover of the magazine.

'How come a Boston arts mag covers an exhibition in Hawaii?'

'Unusual, I guess,' Abe said. 'But who knows how these things happen?'

'Can I take it and show it to Alex?'

'Sure you can.'

Alex was working on an assignment for her English professor. She read the piece and, as Ben had done, peered closely at the photograph of the artist then she set the magazine aside and returned to her books.

'Aren't you interested?' Ben asked.

'I read it, didn't I?'

'Or proud. Abe was for you.'

'I don't know the woman. I told you.'

'It's bad you don't, and I'm going to make sure you do.'

'She's in Japan.'

'I'd like to see Japan. Wouldn't you?'

'Suppose so.'

Ben turned to the portrait, still on the chest of drawers. 'There are times,' he told it, 'I wish I just lived with you. You don't sulk. All you do is look at me and whatever you're about to say is exactly what I want to hear.'

Alex laughed reluctantly and put down her pen. 'I got us steak for supper,' she said.

'The portrait speaks! Exactly what I want to hear.'

'Is anyone coming over?'

'Later, maybe . . . Alex, don't you think you should write to your mother?'

'Why?'

'It's been over a month and maybe it was a bit much to expect her to do a painting of me, now we know she's a successful artist. Did you see the prices they paid in Honolulu? I only wrote her a short note.'

'Write her a longer one, then.'

Ben had kept the letter Elizabeth Wendover had sent him and he brought it out and showed it to her again. ' "Adults can mislead and lie," ' he quoted. ' "Children can be misguided." '

'Daddy's a liar and misguided me. Is that what I'm to believe?'

'Talk to him about it when he's here. Will you?'

'I might.'

The portrait of Ben arrived two days later, by courier as before.

'You have to write now,' Ben said. 'You must! You have to answer this. It's so sad it almost makes me cry.'

He held up the letter Elizabeth had attached to the painting of Ben.

'Nine words,' it said.

> Nine words from you, Alex. Not even one for each of the years since I've seen you, but they gave me such pleasure and joy. I hope you like the painting of your husband. However often you look upon it, though, it will not be more often than I look upon those nine words from you. Do I dare send you my love? It's here, Alex, and it's yours – all of it whenever you want it.

'You must,' Ben repeated. 'How can you not?'

'Maybe I will. Don't hassle me, Ben.'

When Clint saw the painting of Ben, he stared at it for a long time. Elizabeth Wendover had made them a pair and they were meant to be hung side by side. To match the one of Alex, there was a half smile on the lips but it was obvious here what the confident, canvas face of Ben was about to say as it gazed at the same spot Alex was. 'I'm here beside you and I love you,' was what.

'Your mother's a genius, Alex,' Nancy said, and then to Clint: 'Hasn't she captured him perfectly?'

'Sure has,' he said, but his heart screamed *No*.

Sir Richard Mountfield came to visit them and Alex went to meet him at the airport.

'Mrs Stanford,' he said, folding her in his arms. 'Don't you look beautiful and well!'

'How is everyone at home?'

'They send you loads of love and I've promised to take a million photographs.'

He was first scared and then impressed by Alex's handling of the big white car.

'We're driving it up to Long Island after finals and will use the Nissan here next semester. This car uses so much gas! We went to a meeting. Do you realize half of Florida will be under water in forty or fifty years unless we do something about carbon dioxide? No one here seems to mind. They think it'll just go away.'

'Have you been talking to William? It's his latest thing.'

'His last letter mentioned it.'

'Won't driving to Long Island use a lot of fuel?'

'Yes, but Ben can't bear to get rid of this. He says it'll only be bought by some kid and go on guzzling gas. I'm looking forward to the journey north. I've hardly seen anything of America. We're going to the Keys for spring break. It's party time, you know.' She swept the car into another lane and went on: 'Daddy, you must be careful here. You must never go out alone at night. Miami's a dangerous place.'

'We read about that in the English newspapers. And about the drugs.'

'Yeah. A lot of the kids smoke pot. Ben threw someone out of one of our parties when he caught him doing it. He can't stand people smoking ordinary cigarettes, let alone anything else. Clint – that's Nancy's boyfriend—'

'Ben's best man.'

'Him. He's on the swim team and he gets drug tested regularly. They're really fierce about it.'

She chatted on, talking about her work, how she was aiming for straight As and taking extra classes so she could begin her major and graduate at the same time as Ben. Or something like that. Her conversation was larded with Americanisms, her accent if not mid-Atlantic then edging in that direction. And now she was showing him the entrance to the campus. On a bit and she turned another corner.

'It's so geometrical,' he said. 'Don't you ever long for an unexpected English curve?'

'Sometimes, maybe. And a hill. Florida is *flat*. Here's home.'

Ben came forward as Alex opened the door.

'Great to see you, sir,' he said, shaking Richard's hand and taking his luggage. 'We've put you in the den. I hope you'll be comfortable,' he added anxiously.

Richard glanced around the room, the bed made up and everything tidied away. They had made an effort, and Richard was touched.

'I would have been happy in a hotel,' he said.

'Oh no. We want you here with us.'

They showed him the bathroom and left him to wash. It was off their bedroom and when he came out he had a quick snoop. A double bed, two pillows on each side, on one bedside table a book. Richard's eyes stood out on stalks as he opened it, registering that it was well thumbed. He put it down, not wanting to be caught with it, and resolved to buy a copy to take home to Jess. It would prove to her that this marriage was whole and real, and it might – he hoped it would – interest her in other ways.

He went and joined his daughter and son-in-law in their sitting-room. Ben offered him a drink. Didn't he like Scotch? They'd bought some specially for him. Richard accepted the whisky and looked around.

'Oh I say!' he said, going up to the paintings on the wall. 'Who did these? Aren't they lovely!'

Alex had forgotten their significance for her father and was totally unprepared. Ben put his arm around her.

'Alex's mother sent me the one of Alex as a wedding present and we asked for the one of me.'

'Elizabeth? *Elizabeth* did them?'

'The first one came completely out of the blue,' Alex said defensively, assuring him of where her loyalties lay.

'Sweetheart,' he said, 'I never stopped you seeing her. I wanted you to, but you were such a stubborn little thing and wouldn't.'

'She still is stubborn,' Ben said. 'I keep telling her it's right she should know her mother.'

'Of course it is,' Richard said, turning to the portraits again. 'She used to paint, but I never realized she'd be this good.'

He was disturbed, but hiding it well. The past, the woman he had fallen in love with, married and deceived suddenly appearing in the present like this was bound to be disturbing.

'How did she get such likenesses, though?' he said, having to say something.

'From photographs. Your wife sent her some of Alex and we sent ones of me.'

That rocked him and he couldn't hide it. He gulped at his whisky.

'Didn't she tell you?'

'She mentioned it, I believe,' he managed. Why hadn't Jess told him? How could she have kept him in ignorance and allowed him to come here and be made a fool of? 'They are beautiful,' he said, attempting to paper over all kinds of cracks. 'Do you think she'd do ones for Jess and me to have?'

Alex was also furious with Jess and she ached for her father as he tried to redeem the situation.

'They'd be most dreadfully expensive,' she said, and told him about the Honolulu exhibition.

'So I've got a famous ex-wife and you have a famous mother.'

Alex hugged him. 'I'm glad you've come.'

Richard laughed and hugged her back. 'Is he taking proper care of you?'

'The best. Can't you see?'

'Yes. Yes, I can.'

Ben also laughed, but his blue eyes were stern on Richard.

'Sir, I can't make her thank her mother. She must! You make her.'

Richard shook his daughter's shoulders. 'Alex, I'm ashamed of you. Naturally you must write to her.'

He had never insisted before, after the Christmas and birthday presents, but she didn't notice as she submitted to the wills of the two men in her life. The tension vanished and Richard sat and watched entranced as the golden couple did domestic things together.

'I was going to take you two out to dinner,' he said.

'We've got everything here. We thought you'd like a quiet night after your journey.'

So old and infirm, he was, that the flight from New York had exhausted him. 'Tomorrow, then.'

'That'd be most kind, sir.'

'Richard, Ben!'

'Richard.' Ben brought two bottles of wine for his inspection. 'There's a Barolo and a Brunello. Which would you prefer?'

'The Brunello?' Richard said, having no clue.

'Excellent choice,' Ben said, and reverently opened the bottle.

Richard stayed only a few days and after he had left Ben sat Alex down with paper and pen.

'You promised your dad. I understand you couldn't do it while he was here, but you will now. I'm off to the gym and I want it finished when I get back.'

'What do I write about?'

'You, your life here. Me! Anything!'

Alex wrote their address on the top right of the page, then 'Dear—'

'What do I call her?'

'Mother, Mum, Mom. For Christ's sake, Alex!'

'Dear Mother,' she began.

Chapter Eight

'I THINK YOU SHOULD HAVE told me, that's all.'

'I'm sorry,' Jess said for the hundredth time on the journey from the airport. 'I knew she was painting Alex but had no idea she would send it to them. And I will not admit I've done anything wrong. Why shouldn't the poor woman have photographs of her daughter?'

'I didn't say it was wrong. I only said you should have told me.'

'Okay, I should have told you.'

'Why didn't you?'

'I don't know why. I didn't do it in secret. You just didn't notice. We've never talked about Elizabeth—'

'Elizabeth! Are you on first-name terms, then?'

'I suppose we are. She thanked me for the photographs and sent copies of some sketches of Alex asking for my comments.'

'Why didn't you show me those?'

'I hid them from you,' Jess confessed miserably. 'By that time there seemed too much explaining to do.' That and somehow Alex's mother and Richard's first wife were completely separate in her mind.

'How many letters have you had from her? I haven't seen any Japanese stamps.'

'Quite a few. They don't have Japanese stamps. They come in the diplomatic bag.'

'I see,' Richard said. 'What has she said about me?'

'We haven't mentioned you. How could we? It's Alex who is the reason for our correspondence.'

Jess stopped the car in a layby. In the distance the Long Man of Wilmington stood on his hill. 'Have you finished?' she asked. 'We're nearly home and have to pick up the children from Emily. They are longing to see you and I don't want them to hear us quarrelling.'

She waited, her hands in her lap, for further interrogation from her husband.

'Yes, I've finished,' Richard said.

'Good.' Jess reached to turn on the engine, but he stopped her, turned her face to him and kissed her. 'Not much of a homecoming, is it? My turn to apologize.'

'I feel so guilty about her,' Jess whispered. 'She hasn't any other children. It's as though I've stolen her daughter from her.'

'What rubbish!' he said, then hesitated. 'It wasn't me who stopped her seeing Alex, Jess. It was Alex herself and – well – I don't think Nanny helped.'

'I know it wasn't you, but it doesn't change anything.'

'Will it,' he said, 'make you feel better if I tell you that both Ben and I agreed she should write to Elizabeth?'

'Did she agree though?'

'Yes. Ben's determined to make her do so and I'll weigh in again if she reneges.'

'Then I feel very much better.'

'Elizabeth also did a painting of Ben, from photographs they sent her. She gave the one of Alex to Ben, you see, and the one of Ben to Alex. He's desperate for Alex to thank her.'

'What a clever way to winkle her out!' Jess exclaimed.

'Yes . . . the portraits are brilliant, Jess. Brilliant. I found it rather odd seeing them.'

'That and then finding out I'd—'

'Hush. We won't talk about it again. Listen, I bought you a very exciting present.'

'Did you?' She smiled for the first time since Richard had come out of the customs hall and immediately confronted her with what she had done. 'I hope you have for the children too. I'm afraid it accounts for around fifty per cent of their desire to see you.'

'From me, and from Ben and Alex.'

'Are they really happy, Richard?'

'Deliriously. No exaggeration. My present will prove it.'

He showed it to her after supper, when the children were safely in bed and they were sitting by the fire. He was enchanted to see colour rise in her cheeks as she looked through it.

'This beside their bed?'

'A copy of it, well read. This one's for us.'

'How brave of you to buy it.'

'Wasn't it? I dreaded the customs men going through my luggage, but luckily they didn't.'

'I was wrong, then. Thank the Lord for that.'

'They had to discover each other, Jess.'

'Evidently,' Jess said, her eyes glued to the book, 'they have discovered a great deal.'

He moved closer to her. 'Do you suppose we could do that?'

Jess turned the book upside down and regarded the picture thoughtfully. 'Are you feeling athletic?'

'Very.'

'Well then,' Jess said, 'let's give it a whirl.'

Two weeks after Richard returned to England, Jess received another letter from Elizabeth Wendover. She showed it to Richard after lunch.

'It's the nearest she's ever come to mentioning you,' she said.

She had offered to show him the other ones but he said it would be like checking up on her. Checking up on precisely what she had no clue, but she could understand why he was bewildered by the friendship – on paper at least – between his two wives.

'Go on, read it,' she said as he sat at the kitchen table, the letter in his hand. 'Or,' she added falteringly, for it suddenly occurred to her that the reason for his anger when he came back from visiting Ben and Alex and his refusal to read the other letters might be because he was frightened of opening old wounds. 'Or only if you want to.'

'I will if you want me to.'

'Don't if it would upset you.'

'Upset me? Why?'

She tried to explain and he laughed and said softly, 'Jess, really!' They'd been making frequent use of the book he had bought in America and agreed that Alex and Ben were wise to keep their copy by their bed. His and Jess's was rather less on display but becoming as well thumbed.

Richard unfolded the letter and began to read.

My dear Jess,

I've had a letter from Alex! A proper one, long and full of news about her and Ben. I can't believe it. I can't believe it and have to take it everywhere with me so I can touch it and know it's true. Oh, there's no fairy-tale ending. She doesn't, literally speaking (literally here meaning on paper and not the proper definition. Am I making sense? I'm too happy to know), rush into my arms and say, 'Mummy darling, I love you,' like they do in those mawkish films. She calls me, most formally, 'Mother' and signs it 'yours sincerely' and it begins most stiffly (having thanked me for a painting of Ben I gave her) as though the whole thing was an essay she'd been ordered to write for her homework – 'My Life in Miami', write on both sides of the paper, use the top line and watch the spelling. It soon loosens up, though. She is having a wonderful time and adores Ben. I do too, for she does not neglect to inform me that it was he who insisted she write to me.

Sorry to rattle on so, but I must, and to someone who understands as I know you do. David does, of course, and is as thrilled as I am, but he is not always here and I am scared of boring him. And I have to wait before I reply to Alex, don't I? And be calm and sensible when I do so I don't push her too hard. I hope she'll agree to see me, or Ben will make her, and I'll have to be calm and sensible about that as well. We are leaving here next month, will have some time at home in Somerset and then David is posted to Washington. I'll be within easy reach of Alex then.

Jess, thank you, thank you. It was the photographs you sent that brought this about, and what you told me of Ben. And, I suppose, my devious mind. Is there anything – anything – I can do in return? I could paint your children, but I expect that would be awkward as I think I would need to see them first.

Though my pictures of Alex and Ben were done from photos, there was something in the mind's eye, and in the heart, which fleshed them out. Good heavens! How arrogant I sound and I don't even know if the paintings are recognizably them.

I attach our address in Somerset. I suppose convention decrees we do not meet, but I have come to regard you as a friend and, to be brutally frank, I may need more support from you in the future. Everything happened a long time ago, didn't it? Past history.

With love,
Elizabeth.

Richard gave the letter back.

'I'll talk to Ben. Between us we'll make Alex see her.'

'Thank you.'

'Will you reply to that?' He nodded at the letter.

'I think I must. To tell her what you just said and to share her pleasure in it.'

'What about meeting her when she's in England?'

'I guess,' she said cautiously, 'it depends on you.'

He fiddled with his coffee cup. 'I think I'd find it difficult.'

'Then I won't. But,' she warned, 'I shall certainly offer my support if she needs it, as she said she might, in the future.'

He took her hand. 'My dear crusader, I'm dazzled

by your shining armour. Of the services you have performed for Alex this is the noblest by far.' He bent and kissed the hand he held.

'Richard!'

He looked into her eyes. 'It's true. Don't you think the injustice has worried me all these years?'

Injustice? This was a new word.

'I must go,' he said, before she could explore it further. 'I want to look at the sheep. It's Jeff's day off and Matt is spraying the wheat.'

'Oh Lord, don't tell William.'

'People need their daily bread and that comes from well-grown, disease-free wheat.'

Richard was being a farmer at the moment. He switched from that to being a business man and back with a logic that defied Jess and infuriated the farm manager. He liked it this way, he said; it was the Yin and Yang of him. Jess suspected that it was more the Yin and Yang of the business, but since he did not discuss it with her she had to go along with it. Silas and Marner saw him putting on wellingtons, recognized the Yin (or was it the Yang?) and bounced around excitedly.

'Do you want to come?' Richard asked.

'To look at sheep?'

'For you it would be a walk with me.'

'I'll come,' she said. Annabelle was at school now and Jess was still adjusting to the amount of free time there was. Jane Patterson had told her of ominous mutterings about inviting Lady Mountfield to join various committees and Jess supposed she should do her bit for the local community, but there was something else at the back of her mind. She would have to discuss it with Richard when she was sure, though she was already as certain as she could be. The fact was she missed the patter of tiny feet. With the children at school and Alex gone, the big house seemed empty. Jane had roared with laughter, asked Jess if she would want another baby every time the youngest child went to school and suggested she join Jane doing upholstery classes at college in Eastbourne. Perhaps she would do that, or perhaps the time should be used to look at sheep with her husband. Jess donned wellingtons and Barbour and they set off up the track edged with primroses and violets while the dogs sniffed out spring on the wind.

Richard stopped and leaned on a gate. Jess did so too. There were sheep, lots of them, and even more lambs.

'What are we looking for?' she asked.

Richard ordered the dogs to sit and stay. 'Anything wrong.' He climbed over the gate and held Jess as she landed on the other side. It was the gate where, fifteen months or so ago, he had put the idea of marrying Alex into Ben's head. 'And perhaps,' he added, 'you'd like to select some lambs for the deep freeze.'

'Right,' she said briskly. 'I'll have that one, with the black legs and face. Yup. And the one over there who's staring at us so endearingly.'

'Banned. They're both ewe-lambs.'

'Do we only eat the boys?'

'We don't need many boys, but the girls make more lambs. That's how it works. Didn't you know?'

It was the perfect opening to a discussion about another little lamb of their own, but Richard said, 'I've been thinking, Jess, about Elizabeth's offer to paint William and Annabelle. It would be a lovely thing to have, wouldn't it?'

'But she said she'd need to see them.'

'We could all meet. Elizabeth, David, you, me and the children.'

A tickle of dread ran from Jess's stomach to her heart. 'Because you want to see her. Is that it?'

'As she said, it's past history. Gone, vanished for ever into whatever hole such mistakes go.'

'Then why did you say you'd find it difficult if she and I met?'

'I don't want you comparing notes on me. Bloody hell, surely you can understand that?'

She could, easily. She hadn't thought that part of it through.

'And if,' he said, 'you continue to doubt my love for you, I shall take you home and up to bed and have a go at page fifty-six.'

'You almost make me want to doubt you.'

He caught her flying hair and trapped it against her neck. 'You,' he said. 'Only you who brought me out of the cold and lonely dark.'

'What would we say to people who asked who the artist was?'

He thought about it. He didn't much want the picture – well, he did but there were plenty of other artists on the planet – but he was terrified of Jess and Elizabeth meeting alone. If they were all together, perhaps he could take Elizabeth aside and persuade her not to reveal everything to Jess. He couldn't write to her (what if she showed Jess the letter?) and it wasn't the kind of thing you could say over the phone. He wished Jess had not begun this, but it was done now; and he'd meant what he'd said to Jess earlier about the injustice. Who knew Alex's mother was Elizabeth Wendover? Emily and John Glover, but they wouldn't say anything. Jane and Ralph Patterson might, but they didn't know the whole story. Nanny knew it, and who Elizabeth Wendover was, but she had told a different tale for so long that Richard could not imagine anyone believing a new version. Christ, what a muddle though!

'As Elizabeth wrote,' Jess said, misinterpreting his silence, 'it could be awkward.'

'Wouldn't you like a painting of the children? The ones of Alex and Ben are stunning.'

'I would, but only if it won't cause difficulties. Let's agree it will and forget about it.'

She had corresponded with Elizabeth without him knowing. Would she meet her?

'Why not say Elizabeth Wendover did it? Why not

say Alex's mother, for God's sake?'

That would shut up any gossip. Gossip starved on the truth.

'Would you really feel okay about it?'

'Really. Now let's look at these sheep.'

They found one entangled in a briar, her twin lambs hovering anxiously. The more the ewe had struggled the more she had become entwined, and she began to struggle again as Richard and Jess approached.

'Hey up, girl,' Richard cooed, taking his penknife from his pocket. 'Hey up, we're here to save you. Get her head,' he instructed Jess. Jess nervously placed a hand on the thick wool of the ewe's neck and the animal jerked away. 'She's not going to break, Jess. Shove her head between your legs and squeeze hard.' He grinned at her as she complied, straddled the ewe's back end and began to cut the bramble from the fleece. It took some time to pull the stuff from the wool and Jess's knees and thighs were aching when Richard told her she could release the ewe. They both watched as she ran from them, called to her lambs and they began sucking from her distended udder, their tails twirling madly.

'We've achieved something,' Jess said. 'How very satisfactory.'

'We shouldn't have needed to. I told Jeff not to use those cowboy contractors to cut the hedges. It might have been a bit cheaper, but we could have lost that ewe and her two lambs.' He pointed. 'They missed about twenty yards. We'll have a repeat of today unless something's done about it, which means taking Matt off the spraying and up here tomorrow.' He stared balefully at the offending hedge. 'And what's even more worrying,' he went on, 'is that someone – pray it was young Matt and not Jeff – inspected these fields before the sheep were put in here and didn't notice.' His wife's grey eyes were on him. 'What's the matter?' he asked.

'I always thought you were a businessman who played at being a farmer. That isn't true, is it?'

'You've been too much indoors and children-bound,' he told her. He felt her jeans where she had held the sheep's neck. 'Lanolin. The real thing. See?'

There was a patch of shiny grey on each leg.

'Have I? Have I been children-bound?'

'Sure to have been.'

'But you go to the office, the office in the coach house each day.'

'It's the farm office, Jess. These acres need a bit of managing.'

She had always taken the children to the sheds to see the newborn lambs and listened vaguely as Richard spoke of the various jobs on the farm, but since she had met him as the British end of Charman Trading and she had been part of the American she had assumed his real interest was in business.

'And anyway,' he said, 'farming is business.'

'Don't confuse me.'

They completed their inspection of the flock and

then Jess, noticing the time, flew down the hill, into her car and off to collect the children.

'You smell funny,' her daughter said.

'Sheep.' Jess related what had happened.

'Lambs are nice but sheep are boring,' Annabelle commented from the back of the car.

'Were they all right?' William asked.

'Who?'

'The lambs.'

'Fine.'

'Good.' There was satisfaction in his voice. No emotion, just satisfaction. Was farming in his blood? Jess wondered.

She went about with Richard most days after that. He was endlessly patient with her, answering her stupid questions and seeming to delight in her ignorance.

'Not bulls, Jess,' he said of the cattle grazing the low land around the river. 'Bullocks. Bullocks is bulls without bollocks.'

'You seem to do one hell of a lot of castrating.'

'We have 'em off at the first opportunity. Everyone's except our own.'

Another baby could wait, for this closeness with Richard filled the holes in the house.

'So what are you?' she asked one day. 'A farmer who plays at being a businessman?'

'Yes,' he said. 'Play. I suppose that's what I do.'

*

In April they met Elizabeth and David Wendover, on neutral territory at a hotel in the New Forest. William and Annabelle, mystified by the idea of being painted, waited with their parents in the lounge of the hotel and watched as the wild ponies of the New Forest approached the fence surrounding the hotel's gardens.

'They're giving them crisps,' William said. 'Why do people do that when there are notices everywhere saying not to feed the ponies?'

'Because they're silly, silly,' Annabelle said.

'I'm not silly. You wouldn't like Pickles to be fed crisps, would you? Oh no! Now they've thrown the crisp packet away. Who do they think'll clear it up?'

William was just seven and he worried morbidly about everything. After the Easter weekend he had nearly wept at the mess people had left behind in the countryside they came, presumably, to admire, at the drink cans and fast-food containers which had been tossed out of cars into the lanes around Montly. He worried about the dirty sea, about seals and whales and global warming, about the destruction of the rain forests in South America. Helped only a little by Jess, he had written to the Prime Minister and to the President of the United States (scrupulously informing the latter that he was half American and thus entitled to be heard) asking them why they went on using words when what the Brazilians and the rest wanted was money. Why not buy the forest from them and pay them to take care of it? He was desperate to grow up so he could read long words, pay taxes and demand that something be done or, better still, do it himself. With his own money (though Jess had reimbursed him) he had bought a copy of *The Young Green Consumer Guide* and under his influence Montly had turned the colour of grass – or rather, as Jess had said to Richard, the colour of the nitrate-laden wheat fields, for having converted Jess William was in ruthless pursuit of Richard and his farm manager.

'Oh good!' he exclaimed now, disproportionally relieved as the crisp packet was picked up. He turned away from the window, a grin spread across his face, and froze, staring across the lounge to the entrance.

There was no doubt who the blonde woman was, for she had given her beauty to her daughter. Yet Alex's beauty still owed much to youth and this woman's was ageless. It had been lived and earned and would stay with her for ever. She seemed to have about her an aura of calm and certainty as she scanned the room until the man beside her said something to her, gestured towards the Mountfields and took her arm. They were a dignified couple and exuded such authority that as they walked across the lounge everyone else watched them pass and a waiter ignored other demands for his attention and followed. Jess and Richard stood up and William, not knowing why, grasped his sister's hand.

It could have been a sticky moment, this. It should have been, but when Elizabeth Wendover reached the man she had once loved and who had deceived her so shamefully she smiled, took his hesitantly offered hand, brushed her lips against his cheek and said, 'Richard, my dear, how are you?'

The tension vanished, though no one was relaxed. David Wendover shook Richard's hand and Elizabeth looked at Jess.

'How lovely to meet you at last. How lovely to be able to thank you in person for everything you've done.'

'It was nothing,' Jess stammered. 'I just hope it works out okay.'

'But you're American! You never told me that.'

'Didn't I? I can't have thought it was important.' Jess drew William and Annabelle forward and introduced them. They greeted Elizabeth and David Wendover politely, but their eyes kept straying back to Elizabeth. She told Richard what she would like to drink, for the waiter was still hovering, and she and Jess sat down together on a sofa.

'You've silenced them,' Jess said, indicating the children. 'It's because you look like Alex. Isn't that so, darlings?'

'Sort of Alex,' Annabelle said, and William nodded solemnly.

The two men sat in chairs opposite and David Wendover watched his wife for the signs of strain or unease which only he knew, for if he saw them he would remove her and sod the stupid painting. He didn't have to be a diplomat now. The waiter brought their drinks and, satisfied, David engaged Richard in something which, were Richard more perceptive and less preoccupied as he tried to listen to what Jess and Elizabeth were saying, he would have realized was expert small talk.

His guilt had made Elizabeth into a monster and he really believed she might tell Jess the whole sordid truth as she sat a few feet away from him in the public lounge of a hotel. It did not enter her head, of course, as she spoke to the children, trying to discover something in them to paint, and she and Jess compared the latest photographs from Miami.

'She'll see me,' Elizabeth said. 'Ben has made her promise. Between him and you and Richard she has been worn down. I've had three letters from her. Three!' She paused and smiled wryly. 'Oh, I know Ben makes her write them and it's he who sends me the photographs, calling me most charmingly mother-in-law, but they are such a joy to me and it's all because of you.'

'I should have done something years ago, but I'm glad,' Jess said, 'very glad for you. She'll have to love you, you know, because if she doesn't she won't be able to look at herself in the mirror.'

'Are we really that alike?'

'Yes, you are. Even more than the photographs show.'

Who in any case could not love this woman, her low, slightly husky voice, the sense of calm she had which made you want to be near her? William was using the photographs in her lap as an excuse to lean against her, though his attention was far more often on her than on them, and Annabelle for once seemed overawed. Richard was constantly darting glances at her, and Jess thought she understood and felt no jealousy. Apart from anything else, the bond between Elizabeth and David Wendover was so strong it was almost tangible, the looks that passed between them so intimate that it seemed an invasion to intercept them. Not that these were obvious or indiscreet, but Jess was hyper-alert.

Their entrance into the dining-room for lunch had the head waiter scurrying up to them and he conducted them to their table with maximum ceremony. Richard was in theory host, but David was offered the wine list and even after Richard had ordered the wine the bottle was presented to David for inspection. He dealt with the potential embarrassment so skilfully that it was hardly noticed, and was helped out of the way by Annabelle. She had been doing some hard thinking, but remembered her manners and waited for adult silence before she spoke.

'Are you,' she asked, fixing her eyes on Elizabeth, 'me and William's mother-in-law?'

'Why should you think that?' Elizabeth said.

'Ben's our brother-in-law and you said you're his mother-in-law. It's sense!'

'So it is,' David murmured, and William stared longingly at Elizabeth hoping for a marvellous new relative.

'It doesn't work like that,' Richard said to Annabelle, and then to Elizabeth: 'We tried to explain, but we can't have got through.'

'You did get through,' Annabelle said, her attention momentarily diverted by the waiter placing her food before her. 'You said she's Alex's mother and even though we're Alex's brother and sister it didn't mean she's our mother. That'd be silly because Mummy's our mother, but you didn't explain about in-laws, except for Ben and he's been our brother-in-law for ages.'

'I'm his mother-in-law but not yours, I'm afraid.'

'Oh.' Annabelle picked up her fork. 'What a pity,' she said.

After lunch Elizabeth went to the car to fetch her sketchpad. Richard followed her and caught up with her in the car park. 'I must talk to you,' he said urgently.

Elizabeth unlocked the car door and reached inside. 'Must you, Richard?'

'Please.'

She collected her pad and pencils. 'Very well.'

No one caught the signal, but as they set out for a walk a short while later David engaged Jess in conversation so Richard was able to be beside Elizabeth.

William gazed around. 'It's a forest, but there aren't any trees. Did they burn them down?'

'There are trees, but the ponies need the clearings to graze on,' David said. 'Did you know an English king was killed in the New Forest?'

'No. What was his name?'

'William, like you. He had red hair, and that is why he was called Rufus.'

David began telling the children and Jess about William Rufus and they fell behind as Elizabeth and Richard walked on.

'They are delightful,' she said. 'Annabelle's the leader in spite of being younger, isn't she? William is more thoughtful.'

'He cares so much. He's trying to tell me how to run Montly. He'll probably ask you if you use lead-free paint.'

'Good Lord, I haven't checked. Still, it's right he should care. It's his world.'

'Yes, except he's over-anxious. He gets nightmares about it.'

'Poor little chap.'

There was silence, then: 'Well, what is it you want to say to me?'

'Elizabeth, I – I haven't told Jess everything.'

Elizabeth stopped and looked back. David had the others enthralled in the story of William Rufus's fateful day's hunting.

'What does she know?' she asked Richard as they walked on.

'Nothing, really. Only that I'm divorced.'

'I see.'

'You won't tell her, will you?' he blurted out.

'She's delightful, too. Your wife.'

'I – I don't deserve them, do I?'

'I expect that depends.'

He understood. 'No, Elizabeth. Never that. I was young and foolish then. I've learned to cherish what I have.'

'And what of the other child? The one who—'

'The mother married and her husband adopted her. They went to Australia.'

As though it was impossible to come back, as though Montly and Sir Richard Mountfield were impossible to find. Still, that was none of Elizabeth's business. Jess might be shocked but the offence had not been committed against her. Jess would, however, most certainly have been shocked if she had come across the package Elizabeth had found – in an innocent search for a piece of string, for heaven's sake! – for it proved Sir Richard Mountfield to be a deceptive, scheming, lying, callous cheat and not the loving husband and father he presented to the world. It was all there in the package: photocopies of Richard's letters written throughout Elizabeth's pregnancy with Alex and for two years afterwards, promising marriage, accepting another daughter as his own and since then attempting denials, of his cheques, substantial ones, made out to the woman he called 'my own darling Nellie', of bills from hotels where they had stayed, including one dated the night of Alex's birth; and a covering note demanding a huge sum of money for the originals. Elizabeth had left the evidence there, fatally, as it turned out, for Nanny Mountfield to discover, and fled to Emily Glover. Richard's abject apologies and his remorse hadn't touched her heart. The betrayal was too total and then, when she had met David, she had realized there had never been any real love between them. But she could not regret their marriage for it had produced two precious legacies: her extraordinary, cosmically ordained meeting with David at the hotel in Eastbourne to where she had gone to contemplate her bruised and confused future and where he was staying after attending the funeral of some retired Foreign Office official; and Alex.

Alex.

Alex was near to her now, and she would need all the means at her disposal to win her.

A herd of ponies was cropping the grass ahead of them. The stallion raised his head and, upon detecting no hope of a picnic, led his in-foal mares away.

'There was,' Elizabeth said, 'no need to set up this elaborate charade so you could ask me not to tell Jess. I won't.'

'Thank you. Elizabeth, thank you. And it isn't a charade, honestly. We would love to have a painting of William and Annabelle.'

She didn't seem to hear him. 'But I think you should tell her, Richard, for when I meet Alex I will say what I must.'

'Everything?' he faltered.

Again she looked back. David and Jess were talking and William and Annabelle were, possibly, acting out the story of English history they had just heard.

'The minimum,' Elizabeth said to Richard. 'Adultery. The seventh commandment. It's not a lot to confess, is it?'

'No, I suppose it isn't.' He felt the old inadequacy before her calm certainty; amazement, too, that he had once dared ask this woman to marry him. He knew why he had done what he had done to her. She had never been his the way Jess was his, the way she was David Wendover's. When she had curled herself around her pregnancy, excluding him, he had gone in search of Nellie, though it didn't matter what her name was, who she was. She had made him feel like a man and not a boy and for a while he had thought he would prefer to be married to her than to Elizabeth. She had then made a complete fool of him, since it had turned out he was not – not by a long chalk – the only man in her life, that the child may well not be his, that all the time she had kept the evidence against the moment he would change his mind and had used it to blackmail him. As one of his own lambs to the slaughter he had been, and the prospect of his wife and daughter hearing the whole story was too awful to contemplate. Telling them about a casual affair, a bit of honest, everyday adultery would not be particularly easy, but he had a bit of time to think about it. Would Elizabeth keep her word, though? He had no right to expect it.

They reached a stream. Elizabeth sat down on a convenient boulder, opened her sketchbook and tore out two sheets of paper. 'Would you give these to David? He will fold them into splendid boats for your children to sail on the stream, and while they do that I'll make some rough drawings of them.'

He took the pieces of paper and stood irresolute. William and Annabelle were running towards them and David and Jess, now walking briskly, were not far behind.

'No more than the minimum, I promise,' Elizabeth said. 'It's not a lot for a share in my only child.'

'I've had some peculiar meetings in my life,' David said, steering the car out of the hotel gates and pointing it westwards and home, 'but that beats the lot.'

'Was it awful? I never dreamed such a thing might happen when I offered to paint Jess's children. I only offered, anyway, amid the euphoria of the letter from Alex.'

'Not awful for me, not really. For you, perhaps.'

'No. I'm glad to have met Jess. I owe her a lot.'

'And Richard? No nerve ends twitching?'

'Not one,' she said, and touched his cheek.

He took a hand from the wheel and put it on her knee. 'I couldn't help feeling a bit jealous.'

'Fool!'

'Not jealous now or in the future. Jealous about the past.'

'It's gone, David.'

'I know, I know. So what was today about?'

'Richard was worried I might tell Jess the ghastly truth.'

'Ah.'

'Understandable. He's told her nothing of it.'

'It would be a trifle difficult to explain to the woman you were planning to marry that not only were you an utter bastard but a stupid bastard to boot,' David said, replacing his hand on the steering wheel. 'Imagine paying a blackmailer by cheque!'

'You always give yours cash, do you?'

'Used tenners every time. What an amazing thing the civilized human is,' David went on. 'I never believed I could be in the same room as Richard Mountfield and resist ramming his teeth into his gizzards, and yet look at us today.'

'It's your diplomatic training,' Elizabeth said. 'In any case, what satisfaction would a toothless Richard give you?'

'That. Satisfaction. Don't you ever feel a need for vengeance?'

'How can I? How can I possibly when out of what he did there came you?'

He was silent as he overtook a horsebox. 'It's the facer,' he admitted then. 'So perhaps I should thank him for keeping you safe and ignorant until I could meet you in a hotel in Eastbourne.'

'Just at the moment I could save your career.'

'Just then.'

It was an old joke: David, ex-Cambridge, in his thirties and unmarried, had been nicknamed 'the Seventh Man' by his friends in the Foreign Office.

'Cosmically ordained,' Elizabeth murmured.

'What's that, my love?'

'It's what I thought today about the way we met.'

He chuckled. 'It was indeed.'

Elizabeth closed her eyes. The day had been more of a strain than she had realized. How strange to think Richard Mountfield had taken her virginity, on the night he had proposed and she had said yes; that the two men at the table at lunch a few hours ago were the only ones in the world she had slept with; that she had once loved Richard Mountfield. She had met him at a party in London and she was twenty when they married, he twenty-one. He had recently begun running Montly and they thought they had a lot in common, she remembered, because they were both orphans. It was all they had in common, but before that truth was evident Elizabeth was pregnant and Richard was bedding another woman. How long would their marriage have lasted if she had not found that package? Had he meant her to discover it?

She yawned. None of it mattered now. She and David were blissfully – cosmically, indeed! – happy together and soon she would see Alex; Richard was happy with Jess and his two children. Elizabeth had liked Jess. She had believed Richard when he had said he was behaving himself, but she hoped he wasn't up to any of his other tricks. He had always been a schemer, always planning some new wheeze. He was going to make a fortune growing . . . what had it been? Carnations? Chrysanthemums? No, something more exotic, totally inappropriate, and field upon field of them had rotted where they stood. What had it been? Trying to remember, Elizabeth fell asleep.

She awoke when David parked the car in the driveway of their house. 'Gosh, I'm sorry,' she said, registering where she was.

'You've been like a dormouse since we got back. Falling asleep everywhere.'

'It's because I'm relaxed. Those last few weeks in Tokyo were hectic.'

'Elizabeth, you're not ill, are you?' he asked anxiously. 'Are you feeling well?'

'Never better. It's aeroplanes, I'm sure.'

'*Aeroplanes?*'

'In the old days we would have come home by sea, wouldn't we? A five or six-week journey to unwind.'

'We could have come back by sea.'

'If we had we wouldn't be here yet, and that would be a shame. We have so little time as it is.'

More than usual, though. Some cog had slipped or stuck and they had been granted an unprecedented three months.

They got out of the car. Elizabeth had loved this place from the moment she had first seen it, when David had brought her here for their honeymoon. It had belonged to his parents, who had moved to a more convenient cottage in the village. Elizabeth and David let out the London flat when they were abroad but could not bring themselves to allow anyone else to live here, the one place they called home. It was not big – compared to Montly Manor it was tiny – but for two people who never wanted to be far away from each other it was perfect. Elizabeth had given it a present out of her earnings from the Honolulu exhibition: a conservatory leading off the sitting-room and facing west to catch the last of the sun. They had chosen it from catalogues sent to them in Tokyo and Bryn, who looked after the house and garden while they were away, and his son, who was a builder, had performed miracles so it was there when they had arrived back. David, despite his talk of dormice, needed at least as much unwinding as she and had formed the habit of having a snooze there each afternoon.

They went up to their bedroom. Elizabeth removed her dress and put on jeans and a sweater and David exchanged his flannels and sports jacket for his official Somerset uniform: a pair of ancient cricketing whites discarded by his father and held up by his exalted old school tie, a shirt from the same source and a cardigan with patches at the elbows.

'It's no good, you know,' Elizabeth told him. 'You still appear utterly distinguished.'

'I never considered for a second that I could appear anything else.'

'Forgive me. I thought you were dressing to make a point.'

'I'd undress and make another one, except I desperately need a drink and I want to examine my peas and broad beans. And,' he added as they went downstairs, 'you didn't tell me your reply to the brave Sir Richard's request.'

He poured them both drinks and they went out into the evening. Beyond their garden were two hummocky hills pretending to be mountains. How they did it was a mystery, but often their subterfuge worked and Elizabeth found herself surprised yet again that the creatures grazing on them were sheep and not abnormally large cattle. It was doubly frustrating because she could not capture the mystery on canvas.

The broad beans and peas were behaving themselves and the progress of the potatoes, courgettes and carrots was also deemed satisfactory. They would feast on their own vegetables before they had to leave.

'So what did you say to the brave Sir Richard?' David asked as they ate cold chicken and salad in the conservatory.

Elizabeth told him.

'Your generosity is extraordinary,' he said when she had finished. His voice had a brittle edge to it and she raised her eyes to his.

'It was for Jess, not him.'

'It's still extraordinary.'

'I've forced him to confess to something. Isn't that enough?'

'I could write the letter for him. Easy! "Dearest Alex. I should have told you this a long time ago, but now I am being forced to. When you meet your mother, as you will do shortly and ought to have done years ago, you should know that the reason for our divorce was entirely of my own making. Even while she was giving birth to you (a birth, by the way, that ensured she could have no more children) I was screwing—"'

'David, stop!'

'Why? Why aren't you as angry as I am?'

'Because you can't be angry about something that can't be changed.'

'We can change the future.'

'Yes. Yes, we can.'

'Tell Alex *everything* if it will help.'

'Maybe,' she said slowly. 'But I'll need to see her often, won't I? I can't sit her down and say, "Okay, here's the evidence. Love me, not your father." Can I?'

'Do what you must how you must.'

'Will you be with me?'

'Wicked Uncle David will be there watching over you, but he won't show himself until he's invited – by both parties. He'll be there, though, and don't you forget it.'

'How I love you,' she said.

David cleared away their supper things, returned to the conservatory and held out his hand.

'Come.'

'Where to?'

'Where do you think when you say such a thing and look at me in such a way?'

'It's not yet dark,' she protested, laughing at him.

'What law says it must be?'

This was the other thing about their house in Somerset. Here they were alone. No servants, no near neighbours, no parties to go to wearing polite smiles. They had never stopped having a honeymoon here.

Up in their bedroom, blue twilight now outside the windows, she unknotted David's old school tie. Each time they made love it seemed to be the first, as though their discovery of each other would go on for ever. Surely his hand had never been there before, not exactly there, not quite like that, and his lips never like this before. She came, flooded with love for him, and when he too was still she was astonished to feel tears on his cheek where it was pressed against hers.

'I hated today,' he whispered. 'Elizabeth, I *hated* it.'

'Hush, my love.' She held his head against her breasts. 'Hush. No more words.'

'No more words except I love you.'

Chapter Nine

Alex and Ben Stanford were having an argument, and since it was the first time such a thing had happened it quickly became twenty-four carat. They were crossing the Atlantic for part of the summer, that much was agreed. They would go to Montly, naturally, and yes – all right (from Alex) they would visit Elizabeth and David Wendover. Jess had written to say how they had met up, that Elizabeth Wendover was a beautiful woman, one Alex would be proud to claim as a mother. She had bewitched William and Annabelle, Jess wrote, and secretly Alex was intrigued, though she could scarcely admit such a thing, even to herself. She allowed Ben to steamroller her into consenting and yes – *all right* – she would ask her mother if they could come and whether the dates proposed would suit her. Fresh from this triumph, Ben again presented her with the itinerary for the rest of their European tour.

Italy, of course, including a whole week in Siena.

'But what will we do? We've seen everything.'

'We walk around, we sit in the cafés, we watch

the place live and breathe. We'll be there for the Palio. You liked that last year, Alex.'

'Why a week, though? And why Urbino again? We've been there.'

'So we've been there, ticked it off on the list of places to see. We've been, but we don't know the place.' Ben got up from the table spread with maps and guide books. 'Maybe you don't want to go to Italy at all. Is that it?'

It was, partly. If she had to go she would prefer it to be somewhere they hadn't been before, but mostly she would like to fly straight back to Long Island from England and have a summer of fun there.

'I'll go on my own,' Ben added. 'You stay at Montly and I'll go on my own.'

'Ben – no!'

She went over to him and, to distract him, she undid the zipper on his jeans. It hadn't failed before, not once since the doctor had told her about it, but it failed her now. Ben brushed her hand aside, zipped himself up and turned away.

'Not now, Alex. Jesus, sometimes I wonder if you think of anything else.'

This was breathtakingly unfair.

'Well,' she said, having to lash out, 'one of us has got to think about it and both of us enjoy it. Maybe you want a break from me – from it.'

'Alex, that is bullshit. It's got to be the stupidest remark I ever heard.'

275

'Go ahead. Trail around boring old Siena on your own. I don't care.'

'Maybe I will, if that's how you feel.' The bell rang and, 'Oh *shit!*' he said, walking over to open the door.

Clint stepped into the room. 'Lovers' quarrel?' he said softly, smiling into Alex's stormy face.

'Yes, and if you had any tact you'd leave right now.'

'Whoa, whoa,' he said, laughing and backing off. 'Boyo, you look like you need rescuing. Let me take you out of this.'

Ben picked up his wallet and rammed it into the back pocket of his jeans.

'Ben, you can't leave like this. You can't!'

'If you think Siena's boring I can do what I goddamned well please.'

'Where are you going?'

'You want to come to boring old Siena?' Ben asked Clint.

'Sure, Boyo. Name the date.'

The door slammed behind them.

Anger fuelled Alex as she raged around the apartment. Ben was a selfish, mean pig. How dared he leave in the middle of that? How dared he say she only thought of sex? She wanted to get out of here, not be home when he came back, but there was no-where to hide. Nancy was with some study group and there wasn't anyone else she could talk this through with. Miami was brassily hot, the sky too blue, the wide streets too straight. Alex suddenly longed for the cool of home, the downs, the unexpected English curve. She thought of the narrow, shaded streets of Siena. Ben was being selfish to expect her to spend a week there, wasn't he? Or was she being selfish to want him to forego time in the place he loved so much? Anger went and was replaced by anxiety. Where was Ben? Had he meant what he said to Clint? Perhaps they were arranging flights even now. Self-pity fell upon her like a shroud and she was close to tears when, twenty minutes later, she heard the door unlock and Ben rushed in.

'We won't go to Siena,' he said.

'We will. For as long as you like.'

'I was horrible to you. I'm sorry.'

They hugged each other. Ben's character did not contain temper and the little spurt of fire had vanished as soon as he had entered Clint's car, though he was still disappointed and upset. Then what Clint was saying had got through to him. The guy was assuming Ben had been serious, was saying what a gas Siena and Italy would be. It was wrong, Ben realized. Wrong for many reasons but mainly because a man should not attempt to drive a wedge between another man and his wife, which was what Clint was trying to do. A true friend would have told Ben not to be so crazy and to get back to Alex. Soon guilt about what he had said to her was marching an army through him.

'Take me home,' he had said. 'I shouldn't have walked out on her.'

Clint slowed the car and stared at him. 'No, Boyo, I guess you shouldn't. I was only kidding. She'll go to Italy with you, no worry.'

Ben, being Ben, had taken the words at face value and now, as he held his wife even closer, he forgot the implications of what Clint had done and Clint's real motives, anyway, would never have occurred to him.

'As long as you like,' Alex repeated.

'No, as you like.'

'A week, then.'

'Honest?'

'Honest.'

'I'll give you a week in return. Anywhere in Europe.'

'Scotland,' she said, the first cool place that came to mind. 'Where we didn't go last year.'

'Scotland, then.' His hand travelled up her bare leg, under her dress. 'And that other thing I said,' he whispered. 'I didn't mean it.'

'We both said silly things.'

'Will you come to bed with me, wife of mine?'

The way to end all quarrels, a 'gone fishing' notice on their door to greet Clint when he came creeping back, unable to stay away, unable to forsake the habit of hope.

'I'll write to my mother, shall I?' Alex said later, wanting to please Ben and volunteering contact with her mother always did that.

'And I'll go buy something special for dinner.

Lobster,' he said, wanting to please her. 'Your favourite.'

He kissed her lovingly and left, their marriage back in sweet accord, and Alex swept the maps aside and sat down to write and ask her mother if she and Ben could visit them.

A letter which was received with astonishment and delight in Somerset. Elizabeth handed it over the breakfast table to David.

'Tell me. Tell me I'm not dreaming.'

He read the letter and looked into her shining eyes. 'You're not dreaming.'

'Alex and Ben are coming here? *Here* in a few weeks' time?'

'If you write and tell them they are welcome,' he said, teasing her.

'I'll do that.' She took the letter back and reread it. 'Will they stay the night, do you suppose?'

'Suggest it, my love. Gently.'

'Gently. Yes.'

She could not sit still. She dragged David up to the best spare bedroom, made him test the springs of the bed. Would Alex and Ben be comfortable? she asked. Weren't the curtains shabby? How about new wallpaper?

'If you want. But Elizabeth, calm down.'

'I can't. How can I? Alex here!' And sleeping in this room, not the one that had been assigned to her years ago. Strange, how strange.

David put his hands on her shoulders to anchor her to him, fearful for an absurd moment that her exuberance would float her away.

'I'm very happy for you,' he said.

'How clever of Alex to have married such a good man as Ben. It's bound to be him, but for once' – again she read the letter, for she had not let it go – 'she doesn't say so. I can't wait to meet him, to see them both.'

'Brave Sir Richard will have to do his confessing sooner than he thought, won't he?'

'Yes. Yes, he will.'

Brave Sir Richard, though, would have more time. Alex and Ben would never sleep under the roof of the house in Somerset and Elizabeth Wendover would never meet her golden son-in-law.

The trip to Europe was cancelled within twenty-four hours of Alex and Ben arriving at the mansion on Long Island, for Franklin was dying.

'Why wasn't I told?' Ben demanded of his father.

'He wouldn't let me. He's been hanging on for you.'

'That close?' Ben asked, his face going grey beneath the tan.

Alex squeezed his hand. 'Go and see him. I'll start unpacking the car.'

Ben began to walk up the stairs while Frank and Juan helped Alex take their luggage into the wing. The maids had been in and the furniture shone in the

May sun. Outside the open windows, beyond the smooth lawns, Long Island Sound sparkled. Could Franklin be leaving this for the last long dark? How awful to think of him lying here so ill while she and Ben had made their carefree way north.

Alex was putting a pile of Ben's shirts away when he appeared in the doorway of their bedroom. He was crying.

'He wants to see you, then both of us together.'

Franklin was going into the dark from light. As in the wing, the windows of the huge room were open and looked out over the same view. Flowers were everywhere, the scent of roses heavy on the warm air. Maisie went out as Alex entered and a nurse, at a gesture from the figure on the bed, followed.

'Come to me, Alex. Let me see you.'

His voice sounded frail, quavering, but not near death. Then Alex bent to kiss his cheek and saw that the brown eyes were dull. She sat by the bed and he took her hand.

'They want to put me in hospital, stick tubes in me, just for a few more weeks of life. Told 'em it wasn't worth it . . . undignified.'

The words faded away and the eyelids fluttered closed. Alex half rose, wondering if she should call the nurse, but his fingers tightened on hers.

'Mrs Franklin Benjamin Stanford the Third. That's you.'

'It's me, Franklin.'

'He'll need you.'

'I'll be there.'

'Don't let him be sad.' His voice faded again and she bent closer to hear. 'Give parties. Lots of your parties. You hear?' There was a strange sound and again she wondered about calling for help. Then she realized he was laughing. 'I beat the doctors by nigh on two years,' he said. 'Lousy bunch of pessimists. I fired the lot except for my friend Joe.'

'Couldn't you,' she said, her own voice quavering now, 'beat them for a little while longer?'

'It's the end, Alex. It's been good. Listen — one last thing . . . You help him. You're strong and sure. I already told him to lean on you. Will you let him do that?'

'Yes, I will.'

There was a box of Kleenex among the medical paraphernalia on the trolley by his bed. She took a tissue and blew her nose.

'None of that, I told you,' Franklin said. 'Those paintings you talked of. Did you bring them home?'

Alex nodded. 'Do you want to see them?'

Ben and Alex propped the paintings up on tables at the foot of Franklin's bed then sat with him until he dismissed them, saying he had to have his medication and they should swim or sail.

'We'll come back later,' Ben said.

'Mind you do. I'll be here.' He wheezed a chuckle. 'I'll be here in body if not in spirit.'

He confounded everyone for another ten days. On the third day he threw a bedpan at the doctor for

282

suggesting he'd be more comfortable in hospital, but by the fifth he was begging for ever higher doses of drugs to control the pain. On the ninth he came out of his near coma and thanked his sister for bringing fresh flowers to his room.

'I'm being a nuisance,' he said. 'I'm sorry, but I want to die here.'

He had never thanked her or apologized for anything before, and poor Maisie's fragile reason was quite overset. Franklin clicked his tongue at her, and asked the nurse on duty to call the rest of his family to him.

'Maybe I was wrong,' he said to his son. 'If I was it's too late now.'

'Dad, I was wrong. I—'

'It's over. Forgotten.' He kissed Maisie and Joan and then he held his golden couple's hands. 'Remember what I said? Lots of parties and don't be sad. I've had a rich life. You live yours half as good and you'll be doing well.' He grinned at all of them, his eyes with the old sharpness in them. 'See you in heaven.' The eyes came to rest on the doctor and dulled suddenly. 'Sorry about the bedpan, Joe.'

'Revenge for catching you with that bucket of water. Remember that?'

'Twelve, weren't we? Thirteen?'

'Something 'round there.'

'Can you get me out of this, Joe?'

'I can't do that, Franklin, but I can make it easier to bear.'

'Do it for me, Joe. Do it.'

Twenty-four hours later, he opened his eyes for the last time, said, 'Mary, is it you?', and died.

'I know what he said,' Ben wept, 'but I can't help it.'

'Of course you can't. My darling Ben, how could you?'

He fell to his knees before her chair, buried his head in her lap and cried. She held his heaving shoulders, stroked his golden head and she felt old, old, old.

Jess, Richard and the children arrived, and as soon as they were settled in Austin and Betty's house Jess borrowed her mother's car and drove over to see Alex.

'Are you coping?' she said as her stepdaughter ran towards her.

She held Alex away and gazed at her. 'Yes you are, just.'

'Am I glad to see you!'

'I would have come earlier. You only had to ask.'

'You're here now. That's the important thing.'

'How is Ben?'

'He's okay, sort of. He's sailing with Rob. Franklin kept saying don't be sad, but it's difficult.'

Alex led Jess to the wing and offered her tea, coffee or wine. Jess's body clock was way into the alcohol phase of the day, so Alex opened a bottle of white wine which they took through the sitting-room and out on to the terrace. Jess stopped to admire Elizabeth Wendover's portraits, now hanging on the sitting-room wall.

'They are beautiful. I can't wait to see the one of William and Annabelle.'

'Did you tell her we weren't coming?'

'I did. She was disappointed but she understood.' Jess paused and then said, 'Alex, she'd understand anything. She's a truly special woman.'

'I'll see her when she gets here,' Alex said, and was astounded to find something inside her that she could identify as anticipation.

'Yes, or you may still go to Europe this summer, mayn't you?'

'I suppose so.' They sat on the terrace and sipped their wine. 'Where's Daddy?'

'With the kids. They turned shy on Mom and Dad and we couldn't both leave them in case they panicked.'

'How long can you stay?'

'As long as you need us. Montly's under control. Jeff's moved in.'

'What about William and Annabelle's school?'

'A while away won't harm them. Alex, do you want to talk about Franklin?'

'He was,' Alex said, her voice shaking, 'a tyrant and a bully, but he was kind to me, kind to anyone he loved or respected. I think he was in great pain at the end, but he could still make jokes.'

She told Jess about Franklin's last days. They laughed over the incident with the bedpan and cried a little at the irascible yet lovable spirit gone.

'How is Maisie taking it?' Jess asked when they had dried their tears and Alex had poured more wine.

'Hard to say. She and her friend rabbit on about how he thanked them and said sorry. Joan found her in the linen cupboard yesterday whispering about a scheme.'

'I must say hello to Joan and Frank before I leave.'

'Don't go yet. Here's Ben.'

A sail had skimmed into view. It tacked away, then swooped back towards the jetty, dropped, and the boat came neatly alongside. Ben waved, stared, waved again, said something to Rob and, leaving him to make the boat shipshape, he jogged across the lawn and bounded up the steps to the terrace two at a time. There were lines of strain around his eyes and perhaps he had lost a bit of weight, but apart from that he seemed to Jess to be his normal healthy self. She rose to greet him.

'What can I say, Ben? I'm so sorry.'

His brow clouded. He muttered, 'Yeah, okay,' and touched Alex's shoulder.

She felt his denim cut-offs and smiled up at him. 'You'd better change. How did you get so wet? It's not rough out there.'

'Rob's steering. He hit a wash broadside. Can you find us a beer, Alex, while I put on dry clothes?'

'Sounds as though he doesn't deserve one.'

'He didn't mean it. He's just a lousy helmsman.'

'As bad as me?'

'Worse.'

He tugged her to her feet.

'But you're cold!' she exclaimed, pushing him towards the door. 'Have a hot shower, Ben.'

Like any other married couple, though younger and more beautiful. Exactly as Richard, Frank and Austin and Betty had reported. What Jess had seen outside the church at Montly was gone, if it had ever been there at all.

The funeral. The church packed with those who wanted to pay their last respects to Franklin Benjamin Stanford Senior. Ben composed, though holding Alex's hand tightly until the coffin went through the curtains to the flames when he had to bring out his handkerchief, but so did others there. After the funeral and after the guests had departed, the will.

To Franklin (Frank) Benjamin Stanford Junior, two million dollars and an item of furniture of his choice from the mansion.

To Joan Martha Stanford, *née* Butler, two hundred and fifty thousand dollars and an item of jewellery of her choice.

To Margaret (Maisie) Agnes Stanford, one hundred thousand dollars, an income for life and a great deal of legalese which, as the lawyer droned on, Alex worked out meant provision for her to be kept in a private institution should her brain entirely fail her.

To Conchita and Juan Sanchez, twenty-five thousand dollars.

To various charities various amounts.

In a codicil dated the first of September the previous year, To Alexandra Victoria Stanford, *née* Mountfield, one million dollars and the jewellery that had belonged to the testator's late wives.

More legalese as Alex, who had wondered why the grave-faced lawyer had invited her into Franklin's study for the reading of the will, gasped and grabbed Ben's arm, but the lawyer, impervious, read on.

The residue of the estate, after taxes et cetera et cetera had been paid, to Franklin Benjamin (Ben) Stanford III.

Residue! It sounded like nothing. What remained. The dregs in a coffee cup. Alex felt sorry for Ben, thinking he had been left out, until it became apparent that this included the mansion and everything it contained (less one piece of furniture), the land on which it stood, other bits of real estate, and an income from a trust which would be set up along lines ordered by the testator.

'There are other instructions,' the lawyer said, 'which I am to carry out in one month's time. If you have any queries in the meanwhile, please do not hesitate to contact me.'

He placed a small pile of business cards on the

desk in front of him, stood up, bowed to them and left the room. Maisie and Conchita and Juan, amid a babble of excited Spanish, followed him and Ben stared at his father in bewilderment.

'What does it mean?' he asked.

'It means, Ben, that you're a millionaire.'

'Two million dollars means you are. And a million makes Alex one too.'

Frank shrugged his shoulders. 'Then you're probably closer to being a billionaire.'

'Mom?' Ben said.

'I didn't hear any bad news.' She went to them and, bending, kissed their cheeks. 'Now go change out of those sombre clothes and get some air and exercise. Off with you!'

Where, indeed, was the bad news? They smiled at her in relief.

'Tennis?' Ben asked Alex.

'I can't beat you at tennis. It's no fun for either of us.'

'A sail, then.'

Millionaire, billionaire. Just words. Joan waited until the door closed behind them. 'Thank God for Alex,' she said softly.

Frank took her hands. 'I'm sorry, Joan,' he said.

'Sorry about what? Two million dollars to you, and a quarter-million to me is . . . well. Generous!'

'He could have afforded to be a lot more generous. A whole lot more.'

She released one hand and poked him in the chest.

'You always were greedy, Frank. Listen, can we leave here tomorrow? There's a committee meeting I should get to and Ben seems okay.'

'Sure,' he said heavily. 'You never did like this place, did you?'

'But neither did you! You always said you'd sell it at the earliest opportunity. That's why Franklin left it to Ben – to him it's been a second home.'

Let her believe that.

Joan had asked Richard, Jess, Austin and Betty for dinner. While the children swam with Ben in the pool before their early supper, and Austin and Betty tactfully wandered around the gardens, Alex told Jess and her father about Franklin's will. Jess's surprise caused her not to notice Richard's lack of it – and he did not, anyway, have to feign anything about Alex's legacy.

'A million dollars!' He whistled. 'I'll know where to come for a loan, won't I?'

'We all will,' Jess said.

They gathered in the drawing-room before dinner, on time out of habit, the men wearing dinner jackets as Franklin had always insisted. Maisie twittered in and they turned, almost expecting her – in spite of the incontrovertible evidence of the day – to be preceded by Franklin. Conchita served Maisie her two drinks and soon afterwards announced that dinner was ready. She had laid a place at the head of the table, Franklin's place.

'You sit there,' Frank said to his son. 'You're the head of the household now.'

'No!' Ben said fiercely, and to his mother: 'It's your party. You say where we should go, but don't put me there.'

She soothed him while simultaneously issuing a chiding glance at her husband, and directed people to their places – putting Frank, correctly, in his father's seat – except for Maisie, who had parked herself at the other end of the table where she always sat. Conchita brought in the first course and accepted compliments on it on Juan's behalf. Everyone talked determinedly of everything but the will until Conchita brought in the dessert, Juan's mango ice cream decorated with a variety of tropical fruit. Maisie helped herself to a large portion, picked up her spoon and waved it at Frank to gain his attention.

'Yes, Aunt Maisie?' he said.

'The hundred thousand dollars that nice man mentioned. Is it for us?'

'For you. Yes, it is.'

Maisie ducked her head to her left. Austin, sitting there, gave a nervous start.

'So, my dear, we can put our little scheme into motion, can't we?'

'What scheme is that, Maisie?' Joan asked.

Maisie plunged her spoon into the ice cream. 'We'll tell you when we're good and ready,' she said.

Ben's eyes met Alex's and he grinned at her. After

the past two weeks she had thought she'd never see such an expression on his face again. She almost melted with love for him and wished her mother-in-law had not followed the convention that said husbands and wives should not sit next to each other.

After dinner Joan tried to persuade the two young people to go out. 'Roscoe's,' she said. 'Isn't that your usual haunt? Franklin told you to have fun, remember? You tell them,' she said, appealing to Jess. 'They've been like hermits since they got home.'

'Then they most certainly should go out.' Jess took their arms. 'Come and say good night to the children first.'

They were watching a video in the den. Conchita had found time to check on them between serving courses, and Juan had made them a bowl of popcorn. They weren't sleepy, they said; they thought America was great and why couldn't they spend every evening like this?

Jess left them to it and they went back into the hall.

'Be off with you,' she said to Ben and Alex. 'Enjoy yourselves.'

'We have to change first.'

'So change!'

Alex reached up and pulled Ben's black tie undone, as if that would force him into action. 'You can drive,' she said.

'Okay.'

They hadn't quite been like hermits. They had seen their friends, inviting them over for tennis or a sail, but it had been very subdued – as it had to be with a dying man in the house – and they hadn't been to any parties or met up with the gang *en masse*, those members of it who were on Long Island for the summer. The big crowd at Roscoe's that night was a bunch of eighteen- and nineteen-year-olds, living hard and high before they dispersed to their colleges in the fall. Alex and Ben knew many of them and greeted them as they looked around, finally locating their special friends at a corner table. In the moment before they were noticed, Alex saw that Nancy's and Mike's heads were close together as they talked intently. They sprang apart and joined the others in welcoming Ben and Alex and finding chairs and drinks for them. They took tender care of Ben, surrounding him with their love and support – many had come to the funeral earlier that day – and, having quickly realized that he did not want to talk about his grandfather, chatted cheerfully until Ben almost seemed his usual self. Alex wangled Nancy aside.

'What's going on?'

'What do you mean?'

'You and Mike.'

'We're friends,' Nancy said.

'More than friends, Nance. Talking about the good old days, were you?'

She laughed. 'That's right.'

'And Clint's a long way away.'

'He is.'

Alex was glad, glad Mike and Nancy were together again and Clint was far away.

They arrived home and went to their bedroom. Ben flopped, still dressed, on the bed and closed his eyes.

'It's been one hell of a long day,' he said. 'But it's true what they say about funerals. It's the final goodbye, the real end.'

'My poor Ben.'

'It's okay. I feel better. I won't stop missing him, but I can imagine life without him.'

She sat on the bed. He opened his eyes. 'What about his will, Alex?'

'We go out and spend a million dollars. We give parties as he told us to.'

He smiled faintly. 'Give parties, yeah. And maybe we could buy a rain forest. William was telling me about them in the pool.'

'We could go to Europe. Your week in Siena, mine in Scotland.'

'Later, maybe. We'll stay here for now.'

He yawned. Alex hoped he would sleep peacefully and not thrash around in nightmares. She coaxed him up, made him undress and wash and put him into bed. He was asleep by the time she joined him there, and she lay awake in the dark for a while.

Let him lean on you, Franklin had said. She

thought she was doing that and felt more like a mother than a wife. They hadn't made love once since coming from Miami. Ben hadn't been interested and it seemed inappropriate for her to try to make him. Why were women stronger than men? she wondered. Or was that unfair? She would lean on Ben if something dreadful happened to her family, and he would be strong for her. How much rain forest would a million dollars buy? She would have to ask William. She snuggled up to her husband and slept.

They waved goodbye to Frank and Joan the next morning. As their car disappeared around the corner of the house, Maisie turned briskly towards the door.

'Come on, dear,' she said. 'We'd better start making those calls.'

She disappeared inside and Ben held out his arm, bent at the elbow, to Alex. 'Come on, dear,' he said. 'Tell me what you'd care to do today.'

He was smiling, no shadow on him. After the funeral a new beginning. She touched the dimple in his cheek and took the proffered arm. They ambled towards their end of the house.

'I'd like to go shopping,' she said, after a while to think about it, 'and buy ingredients for the pasta dish I'll cook for you tonight. I'd like us to eat alone.'

They had been having their meals with Frank,

Joan and Maisie and she felt they needed time to themselves.

'Sounds great,' he said, hugging her.

'And let's give a barbeque by the pool tomorrow, if the crowd can make it. We'll buy things for that as well.'

'Sounds greater. You start calling people and I'll tell Conchita we won't be eating there tonight.'

'Ask Juan to make some of his barbeque marinade.'

'Sure will.'

She completed his rehabilitation after supper, though for a while she had doubts about whether it was going to work and was relieved more than satisfied afterwards. Then moved, so moved, as Ben gazed into her eyes and said, 'I don't know how I would have gotten through this without you, Alex. Marrying you was the best thing I ever did.'

Maisie delivered her bombshell while they were beside the pool preparing for the barbeque. She strode over to them, almost unrecognizable because of the beam that lit her face.

'They've got us a cancellation,' she announced.

'What cancellation, aunt?'

'For a round-the-world cruise, of course.'

Ben sat down and gaped at her, and Alex dropped the packet of napkins she was holding.

'You're going round the *world*?'

'At the end of next week.'

'Jesus!'

'I spoke to the nice lawyer man and he said he'd arrange for the fare to be advanced from the hundred thousand dollars.'

'Do you have a passport, Maisie? And you'll need injections.'

Maisie glared at Alex contemptuously.

'I have a passport. How do you think I got to your wedding last year? And I spoke with Joe and he's checking out what I need. He said he'd write a letter for the ship's doctor. In case,' Maisie explained guilelessly, though no one seeing her now would guess she had a disordered brain, 'I get a problem.'

'Well, have a good time,' Ben stuttered.

'We've always wanted to travel.'

She marched back to the house. Alex fell on to Ben's lap and they laughed and laughed.

'Oh boy,' Ben gasped. 'How many cancellations do you think she asked for?'

'Seriously, Ben, do you think she'll be okay?'

'Why not? Hell, she runs this place. She's not insane, exactly, just a bit—'

'Eccentric?'

'A lot eccentric,' Ben admitted.

Eccentric or not, Maisie left on her world cruise. The mansion seemed bewilderingly empty without her. How had she and a frail old man filled the place? Ben and Alex gave parties, barbeques, ate take-out meals late at night after an evening at Roscoe's or elsewhere, everyone sitting around in the kitchen of the wing, music playing loudly, some dancing perhaps. Yet when the guests went home even the wing seemed empty, as though the rest of the enormous house was leaning on it, leaking its loneliness through the interconnecting door.

'How is it all?' Jess asked her stepdaughter after ten days of this.

'What all? It's fine.' Alex applauded as William managed to go a width of the pool doing the overarm crawl Ben was teaching him.

Not fine by everyone, however. Conchita and Juan appeared at the back door of the wing the following morning.

'We come for order,' Conchita said stubbornly.

Alex invited them into the kitchen. They refused to sit down, but stood stiffly, their hands at their sides.

'What's the matter, Conchita?' Ben asked.

Lots was the matter. The señor and señora had many people over and they only ever asked Juan to make his barbeque sauce or some sandwiches. Okay if the señora liked to cook, but they buy in food already cooked (furious and frustrated expletives in Spanish from Juan as punctuation); did Meesta Ben and Meesus Alex no longer need them? Juan said something to his wife and Conchita translated for Alex.

'You once say Juan is most best chef. Why you no like his cooking now?'

Alex was horrified at the prospect of them leaving. They were loyal and totally trustworthy, and what would Maisie do if she returned to find them gone?

'You are most best chef,' she said to Juan. 'Silly of us. Aren't we silly, Ben?'

'We are,' Ben said, as worried as she. 'Tell him we'll eat his cooking, Conchita.'

Conchita translated and Juan, grinning, drew a notebook and pen out of his white overall pocket.

'One time week we talk menu,' Conchita explained to Alex. 'Today lunch?'

'Salad,' Alex said, glancing at Ben for confirmation. He nodded.

'Salads every day by the pool.'

'Most best salad,' Juan promised.

'Today dinner?' Conchita continued.

They struggled through a week's menu and agreed, like a pair of recalcitrant children, that they would in future eat dinner in the main house. Juan volleyed Spanish at his wife.

'He say you give parties. He want to cook for them. He say he give guest ver' special thing.'

'Okay, thanks,' Ben said, and Conchita and Juan departed satisfied.

'Wow,' Alex said, and Ben brushed the air in front of his face, pretending to dry the sweat.

That evening Ben put on a tie and jacket and Alex a dress and they made their way through the interconnecting door and into the drawing-room. There was an unused, musty feel to it, in spite of the open windows. Conchita appeared with a beer for Ben and a dry white wine for Alex, and Ben delivered to her the bottle of wine they would have with their dinner. She took it and told him that when they had guests Meesta Stanford and Juan used to go to the cellar in the morning and select the wines needed. Meesta Ben, she indicated, would do the same.

'I didn't know there were cellars here,' Alex said.

'I haven't been to them in years. Let's go have a quick look.'

'Dinner ready twen' minutes,' Conchita said firmly. She met them at the door leading to the cellar steps and handed Alex a bunch of keys. 'Mees Stanford leave these. You have now.'

Alex took them, found the right one, unlocked the door and they went down the stairs. It was a vast cellar, stretching away under the mansion, and appeared to be filled with rack upon rack of wine, each carefully labelled with a number.

'Shit!' Ben breathed. 'Holy shit! I'd forgotten this.'

They wandered around, switching on lights as they went. Alex pulled out a dust-covered bottle at random.

'Château Lafite.' She giggled, feeling somewhat light-headed. 'Shall we have this instead of the Chianti?'

He took it from her, handling the bottle carefully. 'Jeez, Alex, do you think we should?'

'Why not?' she said. 'It belongs to you.'

He was silent as they retraced their steps.

At the foot of the stairs was a small table on which there lay a leather-bound book, a corkscrew and some decanters. Alex picked the book up. It went back years, detailing the wine bought, when, the quantity and cost, the number assigned to it in the cellar and remarks upon it written in Franklin's handwriting. Still silent, Ben decanted the wine, took the book and they returned to the drawing-room, having locked the cellar door behind them.

They were called into dinner. Conchita had taken as many leaves as she could from the table, but Ben and Alex were a long way from each other as they sat at the places at each end. Ben was too preoccupied to baulk at taking his grandfather's chair and they ate their first course in continuing silence.

'I say, you up there,' Alex said at last. 'Could you slide down the salt?'

There was some in front of her, but she had to get through to Ben somehow. It wasn't, she knew, the fact that he owned several thousand bottles of wine that was weighing on him; he was realizing for the first time that he owned the whole mansion – as, to be honest, was she. It had most probably been the purpose behind Conchita and Juan's visit to them this morning, why Conchita had handed over Maisie's keys. Alex had a second of panic. Was she supposed to run this place? Surely not! She'd be back in Miami in the autumn, a student. Maisie would come home. Even so Alex was daunted, and to prove she was not she told Conchita to move her setting so she was sitting at Ben's right side. The Puerto Rican woman had made her point but her bullying had gone far enough.

Alex's minor triumph produced a slight smile from Ben. She winked at him. 'Why don't we ask people over for a formal dinner like this? It would be different.'

'Start a fashion?' he said, making an effort to rally. 'Yeah, let's.' He poured them each more wine. 'What do you think of it?'

'An unpretentious little number,' she said, swilling it affectedly around her tongue. He did the same and then made as if he was going to spit it out on the carpet.

'Don't!' Alex said. 'It's your carpet, remember?'

'Yours too. I shared my worldly goods with you, remember?'

The wine, the good food, the lack of an expanse of table between them restored both their spirits. Instead of going to Roscoe's that night they discussed who to invite to dinner, watched some television and then took each other to bed, Ben, for once, as eager as Alex and in need of no seduction or coaxing.

The next morning, Ben sat by the pool with Franklin's wine book and his own reference books while Alex gathered up Conchita and took her into the mansion's kitchen to face Juan. On hearing that the señor and señora would like to give a dinner party for fourteen in three days' time, he rolled up his sleeves, raised his hands and eyes to heaven, muttered something and began writing furiously.

'He pleased. Most very happy,' Conchita informed Alex. 'Like old day, he say.'

'Will you manage?'

Alex was given to understand no problem. The two daily maids would help out. Juan would, Conchita went on, present a menu for the señora's approval and so the señor could decide on the wine. The señor, when told about this, appreciated the confidence in him but considered it misplaced. He was newly converted to wine, he said, and that Italian. Franklin's were largely French.

'His remarks are pretty useful, though,' he said, staring at the neat columns. 'I guess I'll manage.' He turned the book towards her. 'Is that what we drank last night?'

She looked. 'Yes. Wasn't it?'

'I think so. Château Lafite nineteen seventy-five. It shouldn't be drunk until the year two thousand, Grandad says. And you called it unpretentious!' He closed the books, put them in the poolhouse and advanced upon her. 'Want to go for a swim, you unpretentious little number?' he invited.

She backed away. 'Not just now, Ben.'

He chased her, caught her and jumped with her into the pool. She screamed at him about her T-shirt and shorts, but even as he shut her up with a kiss she was conscious of relief as they put another trial behind them.

It was Nancy's idea to make the party an overnight affair. It would be a let-down for them to return to their parents' houses after such a grand evening, she said. Conchita, when asked, had no objections and Juan was in seventh heaven.

It became known as Stanford Revisited. Ben greeted their guests in the afternoon wearing a pair of plus fours they had found in the attic and gripping an unlit pipe between his teeth. The rest of him was bare, apart from a tweed peaked hat.

'Too demned hot for anything else, what?' he said, allowed by Alex to mimic a British accent and anyway she was doing the same. She stood beside her husband outside the main doors wearing a flared miniskirt, a bikini top, a long rope of fake pearls knotted in flapper fashion and a band around her head with a feather sticking out of it. To match Ben's pipe she had a cigarette holder.

'So naice to see you,' she cooed. 'Do find yourselves a bedroom – empty mind you, darlings. No hanky-panky here – leave your things and come to the pool for tea.'

'With crumpets?' Rob asked. They had made great efforts in the short time they'd had to prepare. Rob was unmistakably the Great Gatsby, but Mike upstaged everyone by doing a striptease on the diving board and revealing a knee-to-shoulder swimming costume. He pretended to be frightened of jumping into the water until Nancy, similarly attired but her costume grotesquely frilled, edged along the diving board and gave him a push.

'Ditched the bastard, what?' Ben yelled, chewing on his pipe. 'Demned fine thing too!'

After their English tea – cucumber and paste sandwiches, exquisitely prepared by Juan, sponge cakes so light they melted on the tongue – everyone dispersed to their rooms to change into evening clothes before meeting for cocktails on the terrace outside the drawing-room.

'You could have lots of themes,' Christine said to her host and hostess. 'How about *Gone with the Wind* next?'

'Yes, how about it?' Alex said to Ben.

'Frankly, my dear,' he replied, 'I think it's a demned good idea.'

This was the way to cut the house down to size.

Jess, Richard, Austin, Betty and the children came to dinner one night and Richard invited his daughter to stroll with him in the rose garden while William and Annabelle had their swimming lesson with Ben.

'I've hardly spoken to you alone,' he said. 'Are you all right?'

'That's what Jess keeps asking. Of course I am.'

'A million dollars . . . Alex, what will you do with it?'

'No idea. Buy a rain forest, perhaps.'

'Seriously, though, you should invest it.'

'In what? Ben's lawyer will advise me, I suppose.'

'How about taking advice from your father and investing in poor old England?'

'Okay,' Alex said indifferently.

Richard peered at a rose. 'Shall I, then, ask Jack Robinson,' he said, naming his accountant, 'to write to Ben's lawyer?'

'Okay,' Alex said again.

Richard straightened up and curled an arm around his daughter's shoulders.

'No greenfly,' he said. 'A bloody miracle.'

Jess and her mother talked for a while later that night.

'They're okay,' Betty insisted, having listened to Jess's fears about Alex and Ben. 'They're sweet. They are playing at being adult in that house. There were times I thought I'd laugh out loud.'

Jess paced about. 'They're too brittle, too glittery. It's not like them.'

And all that glitters . . .

Poor golden boy, poor golden girl. Their trial was yet to begin.

Chapter Ten

A MONTH AFTER FRANKLIN'S FUNERAL his lawyer
called Ben and asked him to visit him at his
office in New York City.

'Do you want me to come?' Alex asked.

'No way. Why should two of us swelter?'

He put on his smart cream-coloured suit, kissed
her goodbye and drove off to the station.

His appointment was for ten thirty so Alex did
not expect him back for lunch which he said he
might have, anyway, with his friend Tim. She began
to be concerned when he had not returned by six
o'clock and ran to greet him when she heard the car
in the drive. He parked it in the garage and got out.
She gasped. He looked terrible – worse, even, than
he had when his grandfather was dying.

'Well, hi,' she said. He seemed too unapproach-
able to kiss.

'Hi.'

'Ben, what is it?'

He brushed past her. 'I need a swim.'

He swam up and down the blue pool, up and
down, lap after lap. Alex hovered behind the

poolhouse listening to the rhythmical splashing that went on and on and on. What on earth could have happened? At last the splashing stopped and Alex dashed away and sat on their part of the terrace, somehow not wanting Ben to know how anxious she was about him. He appeared a short time later, back in his suit but wearing a clean shirt.

'Ben, what's the matter?'

He shook his wet head. 'It's nearly time for dinner. You want to change?'

She put on a dress and they moved along to the terrace of the main part of the house.

'Anyone else tonight?'

'Just us.'

'Good.'

Dinner and they made small talk – small talk! She enquired about the weather in New York, he about what she had been up to today. Jess had brought the children over for a swim, she said. William nearly managed a length doing the front crawl and was longing to show Ben. The rest of the day had been spent waiting for him, though this she did not say.

After dinner – the dining-room seeming more huge and empty than ever – Ben drained his glass and stood up.

'Come for a walk?'

'Okay.'

They were supposed to be going to a party, but that could wait.

Ben led her across the lawn to the Sound. He bent, picked up a stone and lobbed it into the water.

'We thought a million dollars was a lot of money. Right?'

'Right.'

'It's peanuts, Alex. A lump of shit compared to how much the old man had.' He threw another stone. 'And I now have. Or will do when I'm twenty-one, but we're not going to lack anything between now and then.' Another stone splashed into the Sound. 'Not one goddamned thing.'

'Is that so very bad?' she asked hesitantly.

He took her hand and they walked along the water's edge. 'I finished with the lawyer and other people around midday,' he said, 'and I walked in Central Park all afternoon. I did a lot of thinking, and one thing I worked out was this: okay, so many people don't have enough money, and that's sad. Some people don't know when they have enough and go on wanting more and more, and that's kind of sad too. There's enough, Alex and there's too much. Enough money is freedom, but too much is a great motherfucking millstone around your neck.'

She stopped and turned him to her.

'We share the millstone. We share everything.'

'It gets worse.'

'How? How does it get worse?'

'Granddad owned fifty-one per cent of Charman Trading. I saw the bottom line of their figures today. I don't understand much about it, but it doesn't look good. There have been some bad decisions. After Granddad retired, he kept putting money in there to keep them going until he blew a fuse and said no more, not if they didn't listen to him. That's when he changed his will.'

Alex didn't need an afternoon walking around Central Park to understand how this was worse than the millstone of dollars. Franklin had changed his will to . . . what? The precise motive was irrelevant, but to annoy, destroy or exact revenge upon his son rather than benefit his grandson. Let him lean on you, the old man had said. He'll need you. Had he been having second thoughts as he lay dying? Alex hoped he had, for what he had done was appalling. See you in heaven, he had said.

Then she realized something else.

'So—' she began.

'You've got it, Alex. I – we – own a majority of our fathers' company, though your dad is a pretty small chicken in there. He only has ten per cent.'

'But fifty per cent of the bad decisions,' she insisted, not believing it but wanting to share *everything*.

'Maybe. I don't know.'

She stroked his brow, trying to wipe away his distress. 'Why not give your father the rest of his company, then at least you won't have to worry about that?'

'I'm not allowed to. Not until I'm twenty-one.' It was almost dark now. She couldn't see his tears but she could hear them in his voice. 'He shouldn't have left me the money – so much money, Alex! – just to get at Dad.' He swallowed a sob. 'And that's the worst thing of all . . . Alex, in Central Park today I despised my dad and I almost hated Granddad for what he's done.'

'You mustn't say that.'

'It's the truth.'

He bent and felt for another stone. He handed it to her instead of throwing it into the Sound. 'You can have a diamond as big as that,' he said. 'Would you like one?'

'No. No, I wouldn't.'

'Why not?'

'It's not – it's not my kind of thing.'

'You get a choice. I don't.'

They started back towards the vast mansion, black against the sky with only a few lights showing in it. Too much money, too much space. Another trial. She would not let him mope.

'Let's go to the party,' she said.

'I don't think I want to.'

'We must, Ben. If we don't it might seem as though the only parties we care to attend are those we give ourselves.'

'Would it?' he asked, concerned.

'It might.' It was the sort of thing Nanny used to say when Alex made a fuss about going out to tea. 'And,' she added, 'Donna would want to know why we didn't turn up.'

311

'Don't say, Alex. Don't say about the money.'

'Of course I won't. I can't anyway, since you haven't told me the amount.'

'The amount?' he said. 'They estimate, after taxes and the minor bequests – yours is a minor bequest, Alex – between two and four hundred million dollars.'

She lurched against him in the dark, heaved out of her stride by the millstone, perhaps.

'He was an ace businessman,' Ben went on in the same monotone. 'He only set up Charman Trading to keep him interested as he grew older and he called it that in memory of his first wife. He'd made a fortune by the time he was forty and invested it, making other fortunes. He had his fingers on the pulse of western economy. It was incredible. He bought and sold as though he could see into the future . . . oil, gold, silver, coffee. You name it, he traded in it, always buying and selling at the right time. An ace businessman, which is why it was so goddamned fucking *stupid* of my dad not to take his advice.' His voice had risen. He paused and then said more quietly, 'Well, he's paid for it, hasn't he?'

'Yes,' said Alex, still dazed. 'He has.'

They went to the party and talked and laughed and danced. Two to four hundred million dollars, the music seemed to roar. With that many millions you don't need more. Four hundred million is twice of two. With that many millions there's nothing you can't do.

They sang 'Four hundred million bottles hanging on the wall' on the way home. A hundred million bottles fell each verse. They soon had it down to nothing and, because it scanned better, they began again with a hundred million bottles and a million accidentally falling. They had sore throats and sixty-six million bottles remaining when they turned into the drive, and their singing faded.

'Okay,' Alex said. 'It's a lot of money, but we'll handle it.'

Ben operated the signal to open the garage doors. He parked the car and they got out. There was a door leading from here into their wing and Alex waited as Ben unlocked it and deactivated the burglar alarm. He was whistling 'Ten Green Bottles' under his breath and the irritating jingle was trapped in her head too.

Four hundred million bottles hanging on the wall . . .

Just words. Only a number.

'If you say so, Alex,' Ben said when she told him this. 'If you say so.'

They undressed, washed and climbed into bed. He kissed her and, hopefully, she touched him. Nothing there. She went on until he turned over in bed, his back to her.

'Not now,' he said.

Not at any time recently, what with the late hours they had been keeping and the inflexible schedule of the maids in the morning.

Alex listened to Ben's breathing. She knew he wasn't asleep. They had to get over this as they had surmounted everything else. She longed for them to be in Miami, in their apartment which was the right size for them. They should sell this place and find somewhere smaller here on Long Island, but how would Ben react to that? Was it another thing he wasn't allowed to do until he was twenty-one? She would have to find out, go with him to see the lawyer, share the burden.

'It'll be all right,' she said aloud, and Ben rolled over and wrapped his arms around her.

'I'm sorry,' he whispered.

'It'll be all right,' she repeated.

She shared the burden with her father and Jess. Richard was speechless, but Jess went straight to the heart and soul of it.

'The old bastard!' she exclaimed. 'Oh, that dreadful old man!'

'It's what worries Ben most,' Alex said.

'Of course it would! Poor Ben.' Poor both of them, she thought, even if it was absurd in the light of that amount of money. Or was it? No. There were many precedents that proved it was not. The two million dollars left to Frank was now revealed for the insult it was evidently intended to be and Jess glanced at Richard, wondering how he would react to this gigantic slap in the face to his business partner. It could be deemed to include, she supposed, a rap over the knuckles to him. He was looking, as she must do, incredulous, but there was something else. A light of excitement in his eyes?

'Did you say at least two hundred million dollars?' he asked at last.

Alex laughed shakily. 'Anything up to four hundred million.'

Richard shook his head in amazement and again Jess looked at him. When had Franklin changed his will? Suddenly Jess remembered that afternoon at Montly. The children playing croquet and Richard reading his files. The handwritten letter from Frank which Richard had not let her read and had then suggested they came to the States. What had the letter said? That there had been one quarrel too many and the old man had changed his will? Was that why Richard had encouraged the affair between Alex and Ben? Surely not! Why, anyway? Alex marrying a rich man wouldn't help Richard.

She challenged him later that night when they were preparing for bed in their room at her parents' house.

'Yes, I knew about the will,' he responded casually, having anticipated her question.

'And did you plan for your daughter to marry Franklin's money?'

'Whenever could I plan anything for Alex? Come on, Jess! They are having a hard time at the moment, but they are happy together. You've seen how he relies on her, how supportive she is. Just consider how it would be for him without her.'

She thought of Ben alone in that great mansion, alone with his grief and hundreds of millions of dollars. Not alone, though. Joan would have stayed with him and Frank too, commuting into New York – except how uncomfortable that would have been for them, living in their son's house and having to help him cope with the money that was rightfully theirs, Frank travelling into New York to work in a company of which Ben was the major shareholder.

How could Franklin have done this thing? How *could* he? He had known what a blow the facts about his will would deal his grandson, for he had instructed his lawyer to wait before giving him the details; he must have thought it would help Ben, but Jess wondered if it wouldn't have been better for Ben to have been delivered both blows in one huge dose so one could be an antidote to the other. And, considering this, it was no surprise that Franklin had encouraged Ben's and Alex's marriage. A girl like Alex, as the old man had said on the day they had become engaged, was exactly what Ben needed.

Richard was saying something and she asked him to repeat it. 'I said I'm proud of her. Really proud. She's being almost as good a wife to Ben as you are to me.'

She gazed at him, her grey eyes still sceptical. 'Did you,' she asked again, 'plan for Alex to marry Franklin's money?'

He took off his shirt and threw it over a chair. 'I hoped.'

'Richard, why?'

He shrugged. 'Dynastic ambitions, perhaps? You're my however many greats it is grandmother's biggest fan. Georgiana had clear ideas about what was desirable in a son-in-law. You told me that.'

'When you were objecting to Alex marrying Ben,' she reminded him.

'Last-ditch nerves. No man gives his daughter away lightly.' He went to her. 'Jess, there was no pressure. They fell in love and are still in love. Ben is handsome, kind and rich – Georgiana's dream.'

She moved away. 'You'd better not try the same thing with Annabelle. As God is my witness, Richard, don't try it.'

'Listen, Jess,' he said, catching her arm and forcing her to face him. 'If Annabelle comes to us hand in hand with a boy like Ben we'll reach for the champagne—'

'Alex came to us hand in hand with Ben and you refused to open champagne.'

'If she comes with a boy with hair down to his waist, no hair at all or a bit of hair in a crest on the top of his head coloured bright orange, fifty safety pins in his nose the better to sniff glue – or worse – and no money and no job, we'd have to accept him. Accept him or lose her. Isn't that true?'

She had to agree it was. Put that way, Ben was indeed a dream and so distracted was she by the ghastly picture he'd painted of Annabelle's future suitors that she did not delve into the implications of what Richard had said. In any case, her mind was on what could be done now and not what had happened in the irretrievable past.

'Richard,' she said, 'I know you have to get home but would you mind – if Alex wants it, that is – if the kids and I stayed on? Their school term's been shot to ruins anyway and I think Alex needs someone on her side.'

'My darling, darling Jess, how very good you are!'

He gave her a long deep kiss and was relieved to feel her responding, but even as she did he felt a deeper satisfaction.

At least two hundred million dollars!

And every single one of them married to his daughter!

He might be a small chicken in Charman Trading, but he was in a big chicken's worth of shit elsewhere. The stockmarket had failed him along with thousands of others, and then John King had come up with his gold-plated scheme. He hardly knew the man. Why had he become so involved with him? No risk in property, he had said. The property market had failed as spectacularly – though over an agonizingly longer time – as had the stockmarket. But Alex wouldn't fail him. She would intervene with her husband's money to save Montly . . . Well, save was a slight exaggeration, but even so. Good God! Her million dollars would almost do the trick!

Oh Lord, though. If Jess stayed on . . . When was Elizabeth arriving? July, wasn't it? Should he talk to Alex before he left? No, she had enough on her plate. He'd do it later, over the phone.

Alex longed to yell 'Yes, please stay!' to Jess but somehow she didn't. She gabbled instead about their parties. The one for her birthday – Jess and Daddy would be here for that, wouldn't they? Frank and Joan were coming because Joan was soon going to Maine; the *Gone with the Wind* one which everyone had wanted more time to prepare for, the one for the Fourth of July. Alex had said couldn't the two be combined but had been told it was not appropriate to celebrate Independence Day with a Civil War theme. And Jess, not wishing to flog the issue, and Richard reprieved again, packed their bags and flew away on the day after Alex became nineteen years old.

Friends from Ben's and Alex's life in Miami came for the *Gone with the Wind* party. Abe came, and Maggie, and Terry and Rick. And Clint, of course.

'Won't it be embarrassing for him and Nancy?' Alex had asked Ben.

'Do you think? I don't reckon it was ever that serious. She hit Clint on the rebound from Mike and has re-rebounded. Isn't that right?'

Nancy, when consulted, agreed this was true. She had written to Clint, she said, and had to face him sooner or later. On the whole she'd prefer to do so sooner and with Mike at her side.

Clint arrived the day before the party along with the other out-of-state house guests. That evening, reverting to the old life, they ate take-away pizzas in the wing as Juan was busy preparing for the next day and Alex, some vague instinct instilled into her by Nanny surfacing, remembered that one must consider the servants. Since Juan and Conchita had complained when they were underemployed she supposed they could not do so now, and the two daily maids were on extra hours to deal with the mansion's occupied twenty-odd bedrooms and to help out with the party. Conchita and Juan's son and daughter were assisting their father in the kitchen with the two meals that would be served tomorrow and Juan had assured the senor and senora these would have a suitable Southern touch to them. Alex thought she had detected a faintly disapproving look in Conchita's eyes even as she was assuring Alex that Juan was most very happy since he loved to cook.

'Why so pensive, Milady? And you're not eating.'

Clint Flanagan's voice.

'I was worrying about the servants,' she said, without thinking.

'Worrying about the servants!' he mimicked. 'What a bore!'

'No, listen you,' she said, as he began to orchestrate the others. 'I'm worried that they're okay. This party is giving them a lot of work.'

320

'Jesus, Alex, are they okay?' Ben said. He was still lost, adrift among his millions of dollars, but seemed briefly anchored by this potential crisis.

'Yes, it's fine. I'm sorry. I shouldn't have brought it up, but Clint asked and I answered. Forget it, all of you.'

'We understand,' Maggie said. 'We'll be considerate and appreciative and keep our rooms neat and tidy like the well-raised boys and girls we are. Won't we, you guys?'

They murmured agreement and Alex, now embarrassed, said, 'As though you wouldn't!'

'You're right to be concerned,' Maggie said, and to Ben: 'Isn't she?'

He gave Alex a smile, the anchor continuing to hold. 'She's my Alex,' he said tenderly, as though there was no one else in the room. 'She's always right.'

But later, when the others had dispersed to their rooms in the main house, the millstone was weighing on him. It was like it had been when they were first married – worse, since she knew the pleasure sex gave them both. She dared not attempt seduction for it was even more difficult if – when – it did not work. After the Fourth of July, she thought as she lay beside him, they should go away, away from the oppressively big house and the bloody money. A week in Scotland, perhaps. A week in Siena.

*

New York dress hire shops had been plundered for costumes for the party. The girls had agreed between them that no one was to aspire to Scarlett O'Hara's seventeen-inch waist, but there was a secret war over their hairstyles. Some were taking the easy way out and hiring wigs, but others had consulted their mothers' hair stylists (Alex had consulted Betty's) and went off to have their heads fancy-dressed in time for the eleven-thirty start – mint juleps in the rose garden – of the party. Having established that his other guests were happy lounging beside the pool, Ben took Clint sailing.

A squall took them out from the jetty and then died. The mainsail flapped, undecided on which side it belonged, and the jib hung lifeless.

'Looks like a paddle home, Boyo,' Clint said.

Ben worked the tiller. 'Better not get too far away or we'll be late for the party.'

'It's sure going to be hot in those costumes.'

'Yeah.'

Clint looked at him. 'You seem depressed, Boyo. You want to talk about it?'

'I guess I do,' Ben said after a pause. 'Let's get the mainsail down. We don't want to be caught napping by another squall.'

Clint dropped the mainsail and lashed it to the boom. The boat, turned towards the shore, inched through the water under the jib and a glaring blue sky. 'So talk,' Clint said.

Apart from Alex, Ben hadn't spoken to anyone

about the millstone, the burden. Everyone knew
something had happened. The fact that he and Alex
and not Frank and Joan were in residence at the
mansion had not gone unremarked, but no one
knew about the amount of money. How could Ben
talk this over with Mike, Rob or anyone else he had
known since he was a kid? How could he ask them
not to repeat the conversation to their parents, for
example, who were avid for information? Or decide
who was to be the recipient of his confidences? The
news couldn't remain private for ever but Ben
wanted time, time to come to terms with it so that
when it did come out he could turn the comments
away with a casual shrug.

Clint was different. He lived down in Florida and
somehow it was easier to confide in someone you
hadn't known for long.

Over the gentle flapping of the jib, Ben told Clint
about the fortune he had inherited. Clint's whole
body jerked and the boat bobbed in the water.

'That's one big load of dough, Boyo,' he said.

'It's too much, don't you see?' Ben worked the
tiller again to row the boat back on course and use
the whisper of wind that had arisen. 'Too goddamn
fucking much.'

Could there be too much money? Clint wondered.
He was on a swimming scholarship to the University
of Miami and if he lost that scholarship it was the
end of school for him. Soon after he had first met
Ben he'd had to make some excuse for not going

out with him and a group of others. Ben had not believed him and finally Clint had admitted he could not afford to keep up with the rich mob. After that, Ben had always paid whenever it had been steep, always unobtrusively, yet letting Clint buy the minor treats so his pride was kept intact. It was another of the reasons Clint loved him, another reason he believed Ben loved him.

Apparently you could have too much money, for Ben was looking as miserable as if he had lost a fortune instead of finding one.

'Yeah, Boyo,' he said at last. 'Too goddamn fucking much.'

'That's right.'

They went about in slow motion, and when they were on their sluggish way again Ben told Clint of the dreadful thoughts he'd had about his grandfather, how guilty he felt about them.

'No one can blame you for those,' Clint said.

'That's what Alex says.'

'How's she taking it?'

'She's fantastic!' Ben said, showing some animation for the first time. 'Really great. Jesus, Clint, I'm lucky to have her.'

Not what Clint wanted to hear, not at all. But then Ben, having bestowed upon Clint the role of confidant, continued to pour out his troubles. What was the matter with him? he asked. He couldn't get it up. He was in bed every night with the most beautiful girl, a girl who was every man's fantasy.

Wasn't she? he demanded.

Clint agreed she was since it was impossible to do anything else.

'So what's wrong with me?' Ben concluded.

Oh, how Clint's heart leapt at those words! He reached out compulsively and put a hand on Ben's knee where his cut-offs ended.

'Don't you know, Ben?' he whispered. 'Oh my Boyo, don't you know?'

Ben looked down at Clint's hand and Clint swiftly withdrew it. Steady now. He had to be slow and careful.

'No, I don't know,' Ben said. 'If I did I wouldn't be asking you. What's wrong?'

Those blue eyes full of innocent, anxious enquiry.

'Maybe,' Clint said cautiously, 'you need some time apart.'

'Apart! What good would that do?'

'So you can sort one thing out at a time. Here your problems about the money, your grandfather and Alex are all on top of you. Away from here, and from her, maybe you could shake them down.'

Ben gazed over Clint's shoulder at the mansion, the boat's creeping progress having at last brought them to within three hundred yards of the shore. The huge place had always been home to him; now it seemed almost malevolent, its windows glaring at him, challenging him to own it. You think these parties are going to do the trick? it was saying. Have another try, boy!

'Maybe Alex and I should take our trip to Europe,' Ben said, now seeing a building some dared to call a town hall dominating a space where the soul might be at peace.

Clint knew what Ben was dreaming of. 'Alex,' he reminded him softly, 'doesn't like Siena.'

Something flared in those blue eyes, but still they were fixed on the shore. Clint turned to see what it could be, but there was nothing there but the house.

They came alongside the jetty, tied up the boat and stowed the sails.

'Well?' Clint asked as they walked across the lawn and were about to separate, Clint to go to his room in the mansion and Ben to the wing.

'I'll think about it. And thanks for listening.'

'Any time, Boyo. Any old time.'

Many versions of Rhett Butler came to the party, but only one of them – with gleaming black hair and a Gable moustache painted on his upper lip – was as dangerous and predatory as the original. He really felt as though he had been blockade-running and had returned with treasures and trifles. Okay, so they weren't yet in the palm of his hand, but they were there within his reach. In his elation he forgot he was Nancy's discarded boyfriend and, worse than ignoring her, he engaged her in friendly conversation as they sipped their mint juleps without making any reference to their past relationship. Nancy, whose colouring made her a perfect Scarlett, became more and more flustered by each impersonal smile until another Rhett – this one Mike – came to escort her to the lunch tables set out under the shade of the trees beyond the rose garden.

'Flirting again, my dear?' he said lazily.

'Mike, no! It was *weird!*'

He raised an eyebrow and she hastily reconstituted herself into a Southern belle.

'Fiddle-de-dee, it was mighty strange,' she said. 'Shit Mike, it *was* weird. And we can't do this for the rest of the day.'

No one else was attempting to. Rick, dressed in uniform of confederate grey – he had already joined the army, he informed everyone loftily – was discussing the Middle East with Christine, and Rob was at the centre of a group of belles who were angrily disputing his assertion that Clark Gable had false teeth and bad breath, which was why Vivien Leigh had not wanted to kiss him when they were making *Gone with the Wind*. Donna had removed her wig and was using it to fan her face as she listened, green eyes intent, to whatever it was that a very smitten Abe was saying to her.

A man – a pompous, humourless pedant who had been in Roscoe's one night and somehow had been given an invitation to this – told Alex that her guests should discuss matters more suitable to the historic nature of the occasion they were supposed to be recreating.

Alex, her ringlets flicking her shoulders, tapped

him on the knuckles with her fan. 'You mean everyone should be talking about the justness of a war to defend the right to keep slaves?'

He opened his mouth, closed it and said finally, 'So why are we dressed up in these clothes, then?'

'To have fun.'

He turned away and for an instant she saw how empty it was, how silly. Then the feeling vanished as she registered how everyone was enjoying themselves. And what was wrong with that? She urged them towards the lunch tables and, a few yards away, more tables laden with food presided over by Juan and his son and daughter. Alex raised her voice.

'It's Southern manners we're having here, which means the gentlemen collect the ladies' food – and would they get on with it, please!'

A most unliberated female cheer greeted this, but the men went forward eagerly enough.

'Them with those trim little waists of theirs,' Tim remarked, 'I don't reckon they'll be wanting too much of this here magnificent spread.'

'Cut that out,' Maggie roared. 'Some of our waists ain't so little.'

Juan grinned broadly as the first plate was held out to him and said something to his daughter.

'He says not to worry,' she translated. 'He wants everyone to taste his cooking.'

'Reprieved,' Ben called to the girls, who were searching for their places and sitting themselves on alternate chairs at the tables. Conchita and the other two maids began distributing wine, beer and mineral water.

'Girls drinking!' one of the men said, shocked. 'Land sakes, what's the world coming to?'

Ben caught his wife around her trim but not that little waist. 'You go sit down. I'll bring your food.'

He kissed her cheek. She kissed his ear and ran her hand over his crinkly hair. He looked gorgeous in his costume and she told him so. He held her closer and the crinoline in her petticoat caused her long skirt to bounce out behind her.

'Jesus, Alex,' he said, 'how are we going to dance with you in that gear?'

She laughed up at him. He seemed less haunted today.

'The gear will be the least of our problems,' she said.

He laughed back. 'I guess that's right.'

An orchestra would be providing the music for tonight, playing waltzes, polkas, quadrilles. Those on Long Island had had some hilarious dancing lessons from a woman who had come to the United States in 1938 but still retained a strong Viennese accent.

'*Von*-two-three, *von*-two-three,' she had shouted at them. 'It's no *goot*!'

And the waltz was simple compared to some of the other dances.

Ben gave her another kiss and a gentle push in

the direction of the belles. 'Go sit down. I'll bring your food,' he repeated. She fluttered her fan, curtseyed to him and obeyed.

Rhett Butler, lingering in the rose garden, saw the kisses and the possessive hands and his pirate's heart decided they were irrelevant.

The next step, though. The next step. How to board the ship and take it.

The *Gone with the Wind* party was too much of a success, too much fun, and no one could think how to follow it. The house guests stayed on for the Fourth of July celebrations, but there was a sense of lassitude, of anticlimax. Ben went to New York to see the lawyer again – 'to sign something. Just a formality,' he said when Alex demanded to go with him. He went off after breakfast, wearing jeans to show how informal the formality was. Alex discovered that her guests would like to play tennis and, taking her post from the table in the hall, she went into the wing to change. There was a postcard from Maisie, a letter from Nanny and another with the handwriting on the envelope she had come to recognize as belonging to her mother. Alex opened it with the faintly apprehensive feeling she always had since they had begun their spasmodic correspondence a few months ago, still having the idea she was being disloyal in spite of what her father had said.

She read the letter quickly while groping for her

tennis shoes and socks, then sat down on the bed
and read it again.

She went barefoot to the kitchen, made herself a
cup of instant coffee and read the letter yet again.
She could feel the love for her in it. That wasn't so
surprising since she had known it was there, but
what was surprising was her acceptance of it,
something in her that she could diagnose as a desire
to return it. She was called 'my darling Alex' and
didn't resent or reject it. Why? Because she was
feeling soft and weakened by what had happened to
her and Ben, which Elizabeth Wendover – having
been told of it by Jess – knew about and had
responded with three pages of understanding?

She'd understand anything, Jess had said. She's a
truly special woman.

Annabelle and William had also talked about her.
'You felt like snuggling up to her,' William had
told her, shrugging his shoulders, unable to explain.

And she had no other children. No child but Alex
had ever snuggled up to her by right.

Alex was supposed to be playing tennis, but she
had to answer this letter, to thank her mother for it
and to say how disappointed she and Ben were that
they had been unable to go to England, that she
looked forward to seeing her here in the States.
Perhaps she could come and stay. They had, she
said, for the first time, been able to joke about it,
about twenty spare bedrooms. When were they due
to arrive in America?

It didn't take her long, and she ran to the tennis courts afterwards with rare enthusiasm and energy. Ben returned in time for lunch. No anxious wait, no bombshell news. But she did not show him the letter from her mother: that was hers to draw upon secretly for strength to share the millstone.

Ben wanted to make love with her that night, and willingly she turned to him.

Failure.

'It's okay,' she said. 'Ben, really.'

'It's not okay. Nothing is.'

'It will be,' she insisted.

He was silent for a while, and then he said, 'Alex, I need to get away.'

'Yes,' she said eagerly. 'Let's do that.'

'I meant alone.'

'Alone?' she faltered. She tried to look into his eyes, but his forearm was over them. 'Why alone?'

'I have to sort myself out. I know you'll think I'm crazy, but Siena will help me—'

'We'll both go.'

'I'd worry about you, Alex. Worry you wouldn't be enjoying yourself.' He took his arm from his face. There was desperation in his eyes, and desperate sincerity. 'Can't you see? Siena will put it in perspective. It'll piss on four hundred million dollars, the pain one man recently dead is causing, and tell me so what? The Piccolominis, the Chigis and the Medicis were among the richest men on earth, and the most powerful, and they are dust along with the menials who licked their boots. Dust, and I'm still here. What does a few million dollars matter? That's what Siena will tell me, but I have to be there and listen.'

'Let me come with you,' she pleaded, fearful for him on his own. What if Siena didn't say it, what if he didn't hear? She cursed herself for that stupid argument when she had said the place was boring.

'I'm sorry, Alex. I have to feel free.'

'Free? I don't keep you trapped, Ben.'

'I didn't mean that. I don't want to be free of you. I love you. It's because I love you that I'd worry about you if you came with me.'

She was crying now, and he held her to his broad brown chest. 'Only for a little while. I have to get away from here and I must go there. When I come back it'll be okay. Okay for always, I promise. I'll be able to love you properly.'

'But what will I do when you're gone?' she sobbed.

'You could go to Montly, maybe. We'll fly over together and I'll pick you up from there when I'm through.' He kissed the top of her head.

Her tears eased and she lay quietly in Ben's arms, the hair on his chest tickling her cheek. Montly. Her mother, even? A great tug at her heart. But how could she? How could she explain that her husband of less than a year preferred to be without her? Her father and Jess would accept the reasons, but what would she say to her old friends, to Henry, for example, and to Nanny and those others who had disapproved of her marriage? They would assume it was in crisis and she would have to cope with that as well as the concern about Ben. And for all the understanding in her mother's letter, she could not dump herself on someone who was, in effect, a complete stranger for an unspecified period of time. No. She would stay here, among people who knew her married and knew she and Ben loved each other.

Ben stroked her back. 'Please don't cry,' he whispered. 'I've thought it through and this is the only way.'

She raised her head and tried once more. 'Can't I come with you?'

'You've got me over the rest,' he said, wiping a tear away with his thumb. 'This last I must do on my own. It's selfish, maybe, but I can't see another way through the fog.'

'Then go,' she said. 'Go, and I'll try not to mind.'

The desperation, the anxiety and misery vanished from his eyes. He shifted in the bed so he could take her face in his hands. 'Oh wife of mine, you are some special girl,' he said. 'What did I ever do to deserve you?'

And out of a surging sea of sentiment, the weight eased and they made the most glorious love.

She wondered if this would change his mind, but it did not. It was a brief lifting of the fog, a glimpse of the light on the shore which had to be reached, apparently, via Siena. But what if it didn't provide the comfort and perspective he was so convinced it would? What would he do there, alone, then?

He went to book his air ticket the next morning. He had not talked of his journey at breakfast (thinking of her? Not wanting their guests, who were leaving tomorrow, to speculate about why he should want to leave his wife?), but he had confided in Clint during their morning work-out in the pool, and Clint found Alex as she wandered in the rose garden.

'Milady among the flowers,' he said, approaching her.

She whirled around. Ben's best friend – apart from herself; and the stupid things she'd said about Siena which were now excluding her from the place gone from her mind.

'Did he tell you?'

'He did.' He draped an arm about her shoulder. 'Would you like me to go with him?'

She looked up at him in relief.

'He wouldn't worry about you, would he? . . . Could you, if he wanted you to?'

'Sure I could. I just have to call my folks and get them to send my passport to me.'

'Do it,' she said, pulling free of his arm and pushing him towards the house. 'Do it *now!*'

He was glad she forced him to turn away so she couldn't see his grin.

And Ben was glad of neutral company, as he put it, and he arranged for Nancy to stay with Alex so she would not be too lonely.

At the airport Alex thanked Clint. Actually thanked him.

'I'll take care of him,' he promised, kissing her.

Ben kissed her, in a very different way. 'I'll be home soon,' he said. 'I won't be long.'

'Call me. You know what the post from there is like.'

'I'll call you, and write every day.'

Another kiss. He walked towards the barrier.

'Ben!' she yelled.

He looked back and she went to him. 'Buy a villa there. A castle. We can afford it.'

His blue eyes blazed. 'Do you mean it?'

'Near Siena. With a pool for me to laze by while you fetch the bread.'

He kissed her one last time.

'Home soon,' he murmured, 'with or without a castle.'

He went through passport control and was out of sight.

He called her from Rome the following afternoon – evening for him. They'd had a good flight, and had hired a car. They'd be driving north tomorrow. She told him to go carefully on those mad roads; he loved her, he said, and she told him she loved him too then went outside to join the others gathered around the pool.

Mike's voice reached her with devastating clarity, freezing her where she stood. 'At least I got my girl back from that fag,' he said.

There was laughter, then Rob's voice. 'Oh come on, Mike. That's bullshit.'

'Ben had better not turn his back on him, that's all. The guy is a goddamned fag, for Christ's sake.'

'Then why does he want to be with Ben?'

'Why does Ben want to be with him?'

More laughter and something Alex could not hear, then Nancy. 'Will you button it?' The sound of a yell and a splash.

Someone had got a ducking, but no one had denied Mike's accusation about Clint or answered his question about Ben.

Nancy came out of the poolhouse and saw Alex standing there. 'Was that Ben?' she asked. 'How is he?'

'Fine,' Alex said mechanically.

'Oh shit, you heard, didn't you?' Nancy took her hand. 'Pay no attention. It's Mike being crazy.'

'Of course it is.'

'Don't even think about it.'

'Why should I? It's crazy, as you say.'

She had to think about it, though. Mike's over-attentiveness throughout dinner – five of them at the vast table, Ben's chair at the head of it empty – was a form of apology and his assertions that he had only been kidding made it worse. Roscoe's, and she the only married person there, the only one not in a pair and having to explain Ben's absence. Home and a talk with Nancy in the kitchen before they went to bed, and Nancy wearily admitting at last, 'Okay, so I sort of suspected Clint but it was only because of what Mike had said. And hell, Alex, it doesn't mean Ben is gay. He's married to you, for God's sake.'

Some comfort there. Ben was her husband and loved her, had told her so again a few hours ago. Bed thus comforted, but a spinning brain that would not rest and spawned little beasts she did not want to meet.

Was Clint gay? In spite of his attempts at apology, Mike obviously thought he was and so did Nancy. Alex had always sensed Clint was not quite easy in her company and now, suddenly, the word came to her which precisely defined what he felt: jealousy. That was it.

But it didn't mean Ben was gay. The idea was absurd.

Why did Clint want to be with Ben? What did he want to . . . do with him? Was he trying it at this moment in their hotel in Rome? How would Ben react?

Stupid thoughts, yet others chased them like hounds hunting a fox.

This bed and the failure it had witnessed these past weeks, the failures through their married life. How often would they have had sex if the doctor in

Miami hadn't told Alex what to do? Until Alex turned up Ben had never had a regular girlfriend.

More thoughts, the hounds hot on the scent and giving belling tongue.

Had Ben's grandfather suspected something in Ben, and was it why he had encouraged their relationship and early marriage? He had known he was dying and wanted Ben to be settled and not at the mercy of every fortune-hunting . . . man? Or woman. Why not woman?

Alex loved being married to Ben and could not contemplate being anything other than Alexandra Stanford, but looking at it objectively it was unusual. There were few other students among the thousands of them at Suntan U who were married. Had the old man made it easy for them so Alex could keep Ben from himself?

He was not gay. She did not believe it. But if Clint was – *if* Clint was – then he must believe that Ben was too.

Round and round, sleep eluding her, the other side of the bed so utterly empty.

The hounds changed foxes, ran in a different direction. Alex sat up, her eyes wide open, and stared into the dark.

Franklin had changed his will. When? There was a copy of it in their desk. Alex crept downstairs so as not to wake Nancy, found the will and tried to recall when her father had announced they were coming here. Before the Pony Club dance, and they had left afterwards. She rummaged around in her side of the desk and found the notebook in which she had written her articles for Henry. 'New York. First Impressions' dated nineteen days after the will.

Coincidence, surely. If not, *why*?

It was three thirty, eight thirty in England. She picked up the phone. Jess answered and, on hearing Alex's voice, exclaimed about the time. Alex cut in on her and asked to speak to her father.

'He's out on the farm,' Jess said. 'Alex, what—?'

'Please answer two questions. First, did you ever think Ben was gay?'

'Alex, what is this?'

'Did you?'

'But he's not, is he? What nonsense.'

She had not denied thinking it, though, and there was a revealing lack of shocked reaction.

'Second, did Daddy know about Franklin's will before we came to America?'

Silence, then, 'You'd better ask him about that.'

Alex gave vague replies to Jess's anxious enquiries and replaced the phone.

So it seemed her marriage had been arranged by, each for their different reasons, her father and Ben's grandfather. She could not think what Richard's motives were, but she had tracked down Franklin's.

It was nonsense, as Jess had said. She would not allow it to be anything else. Sleep now, and plan a campaign later.

The maids awoke her at ten thirty with their

perplexed Spanish chattering outside her door, and then Nancy came in with a cup of coffee.

'Your stepmother called. Alex, she said you were up until nearly four.' She put the coffee on the bedside table. 'She's worried silly. You – you haven't told them at home about Ben going off to Italy with Clint.'

'No, I haven't.'

Alex rolled out of bed, washed, dressed and took the coffee on to the terrace. She told Nancy the conclusions she had reached in the night.

'Jesus!' Nancy said when she had finished. 'You've taken one tiny piece of yarn and knitted a whole garment with it, and that one piece is that maybe – *maybe* – Clint is gay. Where did the rest come from?'

'Logic.'

'You've freaked out, Alex. Ben loves you. Even if you don't know it anyone seeing you together does.'

It was the most central fact, and one she had lost sight of in the dark hours.

'She smiles!' Nancy said. 'Boy, it's good to see.'

Amid the relief, though, Alex still had a niggle. Men and women who loved each other should be able to express that love physically. This was not something she could talk over with Nancy for Nancy, although under heavy siege from Mike and maybe about to surrender, was a virgin. Before the niggle could take over, a car appeared and screeched to a halt on the gravel outside the house. Betty

Mitchell emerged from it and marched over to the foot of the terrace steps.

'I hear you've gone crazy,' she said to Alex. 'The men in white coats are waiting by the front gates. Come along.'

She smiled reassuringly at Nancy, bundled Alex into the car and drove her away. 'I've sent Austin off to play golf – as many rounds as he wants. We've got all day and you're going to tell me *everything* on your mind. Okay?'

'Okay,' said Alex, but feeling her defences go up at this head-on attack.

They didn't have a prayer, however, before Jess's suddenly formidable mother. Betty mixed them each a Martini and ordered Alex to a chair on the verandah.

'Now tell me why you've come up with the idea that your husband might be gay,' she demanded.

'Jess thought so,' Alex muttered.

'She did not,' Betty said. 'She thought both of you were young, ignorant and innocent, and was concerned about the sex side of your marriage.'

Sex. The word was out, and as though it had been a plug holding in a cascade of doubts and worries Alex found herself relating the intimate details about her and Ben.

'Oh sweetheart,' Betty said. 'Why didn't you talk to Jess about this? It's perfectly normal, you know.'

'*Is* it?' Alex asked. They were on their second Martini, and alcohol and the luxury of sharing her troubles had made her so relaxed she was prepared to believe anything.

'Sure it is,' Betty said. 'You have to learn sex, like you have to learn everything else.'

'That's what Ben said,' Alex interrupted eagerly. 'And learn how to be married.'

'Right. And you've managed pretty well, haven't you? These past two months have been dreadful for you, but worse for Ben. It was his grandfather and, however much you try to share the burden, it is his inheritance. If he was older, more experienced, less sensitive, maybe he could have coped without something giving up on him – but only maybe, I'd say.' She poured Alex another drink. 'It's difficult for men, you see. When they've failed once they get twice as worried the next time and twice as likely to fail again.'

'I think it got like that.'

'Okay. And it was good again before he left and it'll be even better when he gets back . . . Oh come on,' she said as Alex started to cry. She held out her arms and Alex flung herself from her chair and – as Ben had done when his grandfather died – wept unrestrainedly, her head buried in Betty's lap. 'You get it out. Ben will soon be home and it will be fine.' Alex was sobbing, but Betty could tell she was listening. 'He was right to get away,' she went on, unknowingly repeating Clint's advice to Ben. 'He has a lot on his mind and it's best he sorts it out bit by bit.'

'But what about Clint?' Alex said, sitting back and blowing her nose. 'He's with him and I'm not.'

Betty began to prepare lunch. 'So what about Clint?' she said. 'If you can't seduce Ben do you think Clint can?'

Put like that it seemed ridiculous. Alex and the third Martini had a little giggle over it and obediently went to ring Montly to allay the alarm her call this morning had raised.

Her father, his voice high with anxiety, said his only desire had been to see Alex happy, and she was happy with Ben, wasn't she?

Alex and the third Martini agreed and forgot to enquire after his knowledge of Franklin's will.

Jess asked why, for heaven's sake, hadn't Alex told them Ben had gone to Italy? Alex launched into an explanation, in the middle of which Jess demanded to talk to her mother. Alex took over the mixing of the potato salad while Betty received what sounded remarkably like a dressing down for getting young girls drunk.

'Let me do this my way,' Betty said. 'I'll talk to you later.' She put down the phone and looked at Alex. 'Step-granddaughter – is that what you are?'

Alex nodded uncertainly.

'A bit older than the grandchildren I'd been counting on at this time of my life – William and Annabelle are more what I'd had in mind – but I'll have you if you'll have me. Austin will weigh in too if you want.'

Tears leaked down Alex's cheeks again.

'Now stop that,' Betty said, hugging her. 'Is it a deal? Any more trouble and you come to me, agreed?'

'Yes. Thank you.'

'You don't need to thank grandmothers, honey. Even step ones.'

Lunch and a sleep on the verandah dispelled the effects of the medicinal Martinis and Betty returned Alex to the mansion. Nancy ran to the car with news that brought a sparkle to join the peace in Alex's eyes. Ben had called from Siena. The line had been terrible, but he said to tell Alex he loved her and missed her and would phone tomorrow, Italian systems permitting. It had taken him half an hour to get through today.

'Well, and what more do you want?' Betty said.

'Nothing! Thank you, dearest Step-grandmother, even if you say you don't need thanks.'

Betty kissed her. 'Remember, you come to me with any more nonsense – at least until your mother gets here.'

'Yes. Until she gets here.'

That jolt in the guts again, overcoming the relief and elation: the strange, and strangely familiar and thrilling, feeling of anticipation she had when she thought of meeting her mother, the woman whose love was unconditionally hers.

Nancy held her hand as they waved Betty goodbye and then turned her, carefully, as though she were an invalid, towards the house. 'There's a barbeque over at Ella's tonight,' she said, 'but we won't go if you don't want to.'

'We'll go. You want to, don't you?'

'Only if you do.'

'I do,' Alex said.

Ben, who had gone away so he could be everything to her when he got back; Jess, with loving concern, galvanizing her mother into action; Betty listening to her, letting her cry and adopting her as a granddaughter; Nancy prepared to give up an evening with Mike for her; and that other love awaiting her . . .

I'm spoilt, she thought. Nanny was right.

Ben called the next afternoon on another static-laden line and most of their conversation consisted of shouted requests to repeat what had just been said. But three calls in three days . . .

'There's a guy who cares,' Nancy said.

No word during the next three days, but Alex felt a calm certainty and confidence about the future. She believed what Betty had told her not because she wanted to believe it but because it gave off the generous ring of truth. And she did some thinking for herself and reached positive conclusions. Whatever Clint was and whatever he thought about Ben was irrelevant. Ben was above all things honourable, and for that reason alone he would return to her. He might – *might* – return with revelations about himself, but his sense of honour would not allow him to take even a first step on a new path without telling her, and she wouldn't give him up without a fight. But the more she thought about it the more preposterous such a notion seemed and the more likely Betty's diagnosis became. Franklin's death, the awesome legacy he had left Ben, the betrayal of him it represented: these were logical causes of Ben's difficulty with sex. And it had been good, in spite of the problem of two ignorant people trying to teach and learn from each other.

A call from Ben on the fourth day. A miraculously clear line which ever after Alex would believe was an intervention from God. She asked if she could join him, she could house-hunt, she said, while he wandered around Siena, but he interrupted her.

'I'm coming home, Alex,' he said.

'But – you haven't even had your week,' she said, managing to register with a vague sense of surprise that hearts could feel as though they were exploding with joy.

'I don't need it. I'm cured. I just want us to get on with our lives. We took a day in Florence. Alex, did you know the Medicis left the works of art in the Uffizi to the people of Florence in perpetuity? The Germans took some away in the war but they had to return them because of some old will. Isn't that fantastic?'

'Yes,' she said. 'Yes.' And then, realizing what he was getting at, added, 'Is that what cured you?

Knowing there are things you can't buy?'

'Maybe. Sort of.'

'Have you found us a castle?'

A soft laugh arrived on Long Island. 'There are some of those for sale but we'll find one together later. Listen, Alex, my mind's been jumping skyscrapers. We have this money and we need to learn how to handle it. Let's change majors and get into the business school so we're ready for whatever it throws at us.'

'We'll do that. We will!'

How had seven days in Italy effected this change in him? Alex curled up in the big leather chair behind Franklin's desk – she took the calls here because it was completely private – and they talked and planned on. They would do good with the money, they decided. Buy a few rain forests, save the whales and the ozone layer and feed starving Ethiopians – save the planet, goddamnit!

'How is Clint?' Alex asked eventually, needing to lay the last ghost.

'Kind of pissed off I want to leave so soon. I said he could stay on, but he's sticking with me. We'll do a loop along the coast and get a flight from Pisa, Genoa maybe, to Paris or London and then to JFK. And you. Two, three days perhaps. Do you mind?'

'Horribly much.'

Another laugh. 'I'll make it up to you, Alex.'

She told him, once more, to drive carefully on those maniac-infested roads and to make sure he didn't get on a plane targeted by terrorists. He joked about how he'd hire an army of sniffer dogs and pay with his gold credit cards.

He loved her, he said.

She loved him, she said.

A miraculously clear line, surely arranged by God.

Chapter Eleven

FRANK HAD TEARS RUNNING DOWN his cheeks, which was absurd because grown-ups didn't cry, especially not grown men.

'Ben missing believed drowned?' Alex shouted. 'How can Ben have drowned?'

Frank muttered something that Alex couldn't understand and suddenly Betty Mitchell was there. Alex stared at her.

'What does he mean "missing believed drowned"? It's a silly thing to say.'

There was a horrible sound like a dozen chain saws trying to bite steel, and Alex did not know it was her own screaming.

Austin Mitchell was there too. He tried to hold her in brown arms covered in thick iron-grey hairs, but she wasn't having it. The old doctor who had advanced upon Franklin with a syringe containing peaceful death appeared and seemed to want to do the same thing to Alex. She wasn't having that either, and backed away from him until he offered her pills.

'They'll make you feel better,' he promised, his

ruddy face tempting her away from the lip of hell.

She swallowed two pills. They seemed to make a difference and she could watch with detached interest as Betty and Nancy packed a suitcase for her. Apparently she was going away. She could hear telephones all over the house being used. No bells were ringing to signal a call from Ben, but she could feel the lines tingling.

'I want to take that skirt,' she stated, pointing, and Nancy stuffed a navy-blue wool skirt into the suitcase for Alex to wear in Italy in July. Betty came and knelt before Alex, took her hands.

'Why is Nancy crying?' Alex asked. 'It's only believed, isn't it? Ben can't drown.'

A rachet seemed to move over in Alex's brain. She could sense it changing gear, shifting direction.

'Ah,' she said. 'I understand now. He couldn't carry the millstone and decided to get rid of it. The baby and the bathwater.' Her woozy eyes met Betty's. 'He phoned me, you know. He said he was cured. Lying to make me feel better, my darling Ben.'

'Not so, Alex.'

'I was worried about the roads and the planes. What a fool I was.'

Mike was there when Betty took her to the waiting car – a big gas guzzler, but not Ben's white one.

'Take care of Nancy,' she said to him. 'She'll probably want to go home.'

Mike was crying too, which was odd, and so was

Joan Stanford when they met at the Alitalia desk at the airport, her friend from Maine with her.

'He was such a strong swimmer,' she sobbed. 'How could he drown?'

Alex had solved this. 'Didn't you know,' she said briskly, 'he had a millstone around his neck? Anyone would drown trying to swim with one of those.'

Another rachet shifted. She raised her voice and Frank – dealing with the tickets at the check-in – half turned to her. So did other passengers, scenting tragedy and wanting to report something different about a routine transatlantic flight.

'You should have listened to your father, Frank. You would have got the money if you had. If you had listened, Ben wouldn't be believed drowned because of the millstone. Between you and your father, he's missing. Gone!'

'You mustn't say such things,' Betty chided her.

'Why not, if they're true?'

They were in first class and were offered champagne. Someone – Alex didn't know who – fed her more pills. She was flying above the plane and could see the winged silver tube way below her; below it was the Atlantic, night advancing on it from the east. Then she was in the sea, deep under its surface, searching for Ben.

'He's missing believed drowned,' she told the passing fish, but they swam on by with vacant eyes.

She may have eaten, she may have slept. She was

352

back in the real world when they landed at Rome and were hurried off the plane through customs and immigration and were delivered into the care of an official from the American consulate. A whispered conversation with Frank, who put an arm around Joan and reached for his daughter-in-law.

'He's found known drowned,' Alex said before he could speak, and Frank nodded.

Why the hurry, then? Why this frantic haste as they were hustled through the crowds?

'Alexa! Hey Alexa!' someone called in an Italian accent, and as she looked a flashbulb popped light into her eyes. The consular official hugged her to his crisp laundered shirt, hiding her under his open jacket. She could smell his deodorant.

'Why do they want pictures?' she asked as more light exploded.

'Pay no attention. We're doing fine.'

'Why?' she persisted.

'In here,' the man said, pushing her through a door and amputating the bedlam as the door closed behind them.

She did not ask again and Gene Parry thanked God for that. How could he explain that the beautiful widow of a multimillionaire was exactly what the press needed to fill the pages of its newspaper in the dog days of summer? More of the vampires would be waiting in Piombino, presumably. How in hell had they gotten on to it so soon? They must be able to scent blood from hundreds of miles away. Still, Piombino was the pigeon of the guy from Florence.

He looked at the bereaved group. The mother was crying softly and her husband was holding her. The girl – the wife, the widow, for God's sake! – was standing alone, staring at nothing. Her composure chilled him. Obviously what had happened hadn't hit her yet. She seemed the same age as his sixteen-year-old niece, and it crossed Gene's mind that he might have misread the fax and it had said 'sister' and not 'wife'. Then the girl lifted her left hand and ran it through her hair. There was a gold wedding band and an engagement ring on the fourth finger. Gene found the sight almost unbearably moving.

Another door opened and a woman in Alitalia uniform came in followed by two men. 'The plane is ready,' she said. 'These are the pilots.'

The younger of the two men muttered something to the other, and they both smiled and gazed at Alex. It was as reflexive as breathing to a Roman when faced with a beautiful woman, but it filled Gene with fury.

'Her husband is dead,' he said sharply in Italian. 'Show some respect.'

Immediately they assumed a tragic mein. Gene turned from them and was horrified to see Frank Stanford handing out pills to the two women.

'Sir!' he exclaimed, frightened for a surreal moment that he was witnessing a triple suicide.

'They need them,' Frank said. He took a notebook from his pocket, opened it and looked at his watch. His pen hesitated over the page and his brow furrowed. He seemed about to cry. 'I put down the times,' he said. 'Joe said I must, but they don't work.'

Gene took the book from him and figured out they were taking these things every four hours. No wonder the girl didn't know where she was. Gene wrote down the time, adding in capital letters 'Italian', and the Alitalia woman produced *acqua minerale* in plastic cups so the two Mrs Stanfords could swallow their pills. Frank Stanford, Gene noted, had palmed one and swallowed it dry.

Gene gave Frank an envelope containing the money wired from his office in New York and went with them in the courtesy car to the plane he had hired.

'Is there enough here to pay?' Frank asked, holding out the envelope.

'It's been dealt with,' Gene said gently. 'Go, now. You'll be met at the other end.'

Frank Stanford helped his wife up the steps while the pilot and his assistant loaded the luggage.

Gene took Alex's arm. 'You too.'

'Where are we going?' she said, not moving.

'You'll be landing at an airstrip near Piombino.'

'Where's that?'

'On the Tuscan coast. It's where the ferries to Elba leave from.'

'Elba.'

'They kept Napoleon there.'

'I know. Thank you for your help,' she said, as Nanny would have expected her to, and to the Italian woman added, '*Grazie. Tante grazie.*'

The plane took off and, once again, Alex was floating high above. How strange. Italy looked exactly like the map she and Ben had, the one open on the table in their apartment in Miami when they had quarrelled. There was Siena among the green and brown of the interior, there was Florence. She panicked because she could not find Elba. Out to sea, you fool! she told herself and a blob appeared in the sea off a place on the coast she had designated as Piombino. She felt comfortable then.

Jess and Richard were waiting at the airstrip when the plane landed. They put their arms around her, but she shrugged them away and was about to speak when Frank, emerging from his drug-filled haze, noticed the presence of his old friend.

'What happened?' he said. 'Richard, for Christ's sake what happened?'

Richard waved his hands helplessly. Tears were running down his cheeks. 'It was so bloody stupid. Apparently they tried to swim to Elba, to see if Napoleon could have escaped. A wind blew up waves, and it was those, or cramp, or maybe he hit a log or something . . . and that was that.'

'That was that,' Alex repeated. 'Stupid. Quite right.' She began walking away from the group standing by the plane under a searing Tuscan sky, then whipped round to face them. 'Napoleon had a ship. He had a ship and he *did* escape.' She shook her head at them. 'No. Ben couldn't have been that stupid. It was the millstone and I was right . . . I don't resent you arranging my marriage,' she told her father. 'I can't, because we were so very happy, Ben and I, but I have a horrible fear that if it hadn't happened then neither would this. No, listen,' she went on, overriding sounds of protest and concern. 'I can't work everything out because it doesn't quite balance. He had to get away from me because he was married to me, you see, which is why he came here. But he needed me to share the millstone. And it got him. Got him and sunk him when I wasn't there.'

'Oh honey,' Jess said softly, approaching her as though she were a nervous foal, 'how could he have managed the millstone if you hadn't married him? What would have happened then?'

Alex gazed at her blearily. 'It's that I can't work out. Anyway, he didn't manage, did he? It got him.'

'It was an accident, Alex. Accidents happen. They are always tragic, but they happen – even to expert swimmers.'

They took her to the cars parked in the shade of the airstrip's single building. She sat in the back of one, Jess and Richard on either side of her, and Joan and Frank went in the other with the man from the US consulate in Florence. They drove off along one of those roads that resemble a mini rollercoaster. *Strada deformata*. The warning sign was a pair of graphic humps in a red triangle.

'Here comes a camel!' Ben had called whenever they had encountered them on their honeymoon trip.

There were lots of camels in Italy. This one had its usual complement of insane drivers. Mad drivers on camels. Just like New York, Ben had said.

How could he have done this dreadful thing and left her behind?

The pain was gathering at the edges of the fuzz in her brain. She knew she'd have to face it, embrace it and learn to live with it, but she wanted another pill so she could hold it off for a while longer – hold off the knowledge that it was there waiting for her.

Why was the driver speeding over the camels? A dead body would wait for them. Wait for ever.

'Are we going to a hotel?' she asked.

'Yes, sweetheart.'

'The one Ben was staying in?'

'Yes. We managed to get rooms.'

'I can sleep in Ben's, can't I?'

She thought they both stiffened.

'Sweetheart—' her father said.

'Why not?'

'No reason why not,' Jess said soothingly.

'He left something for me. I know he did and I know where it will be. He didn't try to swim to Elba with his luggage, did he?'

'Of course not. We'll find it for you.'

They seemed to be heading towards battlements of rusty iron studded by towers belching filthy smoke.

'Is that Piombino?' she asked.

'Yes.'

It had to be a mistake, all a mistake. Ben couldn't have wanted to come here. The smell from the chimneys invaded the car, then they were beyond the nightmare landscape and the sky widened. Alex couldn't see the sea, but she knew it was there. The driver said something in Italian, stopped the car and a moment later the consular official's head appeared in the open window.

'What do we do about the paparazzi?'

'If they get their photographs will they go away?' Jess asked.

'It's the best chance, I guess.'

'They are sick.'

'Maybe, but knowing that doesn't help us right now.'

'Alex—' Jess began.

'They want photographs. It's okay. I just want to get there.'

Men called her name and cameras clicked as she went into the hotel. It wasn't important. She waited while Frank and Joan checked in and allowed Jess to search her handbag for her passport.

'I want the key to Ben's room,' she said.

'We'll get it later. Have a shower and change your

clothes first. You must long to after your journey.'

A question squiggled through the fuzz in her head. 'Clint!' she exclaimed. 'Clint! Did he drown too?'

Richard took keys from the receptionist and picked up Alex's suitcase.

'He was rescued by a fishing boat, we understand. He's in hospital, but he's all right.'

The fuzz became a thousand writhing worms. 'Why can't I see Ben's room? Is it because – oh God, it must have been! – Clint's room too?'

She was aware she was making a noise, and they were no longer in the foyer but somewhere which seemed to be an office.

Richard held her and kept telling her what she was thinking was nonsense. 'You know it,' he said firmly. 'Don't you?' He was crying again, but still she had no tears to shed.

Jess came in and waved a key under Alex's nose. 'Okay?' she said. 'They couldn't let anyone into a room hired to someone else, but Tony Devlin explained, they checked your passport and here you are.'

Alex grabbed the key and went out of the door, followed by Richard with her suitcase. Jess crossed the foyer behind them and gestured thanks to Tony Devlin, who had indeed explained matters to the hotel staff but had first told Jess he had taken Clint's bags to the hospital and there was no clue that he had ever been in the room. Tony was now waiting while Frank settled Joan in and would then take him to perform the ghastly task of formally identifying Ben's body.

'Here,' he said, handing Jess the bottle of pills and notebook. 'Mr Stanford gave them to me. You'd better be in charge.'

Jess took them and hurried to catch up with Alex and Richard. They should have anticipated Alex would want to see Ben's room but the reason they were here – first rumour, then mind-numbing fact – had blasted common sense away. That and the hideous, insistent ringing of their phone, people introducing themselves smoothly by name, gliding over that of the newspaper they worked for, and asking dreadful questions.

Jess watched as her stepdaughter fitted the key into the lock, turned it and flung open the door. She seemed almost animated as she went to the nearest bed, heaved the bag on the rack at the end of it over the low board and undid the zipper.

'He hadn't unpacked,' she said. 'He can't have expected to stay long. Well, I knew that, didn't I?' Her eyes wandered around the room. 'There are his jeans,' she said, nodding at a chair. 'I expect he arrived and was very hot and wanted to have a swim as soon as possible. Dragged out his swimming trunks and couldn't wait to get wet. That was my Ben.' She looked around again, and then lunged towards the beside table. 'He unpacked something else, though, didn't he?' She laughed and held up a framed montage of photographs. The golden boy, the golden girl, all smiles and love and happiness.

Beside Jess, standing in the doorway, Richard swallowed a sob. Jess gripped his hand and tried to stop herself giving in. One of them, apart from Alex, had to stay strong.

She was pulling Ben's clothes out of the bag. 'It's hidden,' she explained. She emptied the bag and drew out a notebook concealed in a pocket at the bottom. 'Not really hidden, only a bit more difficult for anyone to find.' She opened the book and showed them the first page.

'Alex's letter from Italy,' it said in large letters surrounded by crude drawings of towers, churches and palaces.

'Now I'll know what he was really thinking about, won't I? About the millstone, about Clint ... About me.'

She began to read, watched fearfully by Richard and Jess.

'What if it's a confession he was gay?' Richard whispered. 'It could be a suicide note, for God's sake.'

'Then she has to know. But look at her,' Jess whispered back. 'It's a love letter from her husband.'

Alex was not sitting on a bed in a hotel room in Piombino surrounded by the clothes Ben would never wear again. She was somewhere else, somewhere there was no millstone.

He would write to her every day, he said, as he promised he would. A continuous letter which she could read when he got back. It wasn't that he couldn't be bothered to mail one every day, it was because they would reach her after he did and it would be odd. He'd give her this and go sailing, he said.

Rome. Hot. He'd called her earlier. They'd had dinner near the Coliseum – the place, the actual, real, no-fake place where the Christians were sent to the lions – and then seen St Peter's by night. He was writing this in bed and missing her. He hoped he didn't reach for her and fall out. It was a goddamned narrow bed.

To Siena. He remembered the camels.

The Piazza del Campo, the Palazzo Pubblico and the Torre del Mangia. The July Palio over, the August one ahead. He'd seen Giorgio, Paolo and Giovanni and they sent her love – and, hey, Giorgio was engaged to Anita, the girl he'd brought along that night they'd met up for dinner. Ben and Alex were invited to an *onda* wedding, though no date had been fixed yet. Ben felt his feet grow roots, he said, and Siena was pissing on his dollars as he knew it would. Had she meant it about buying a place in the country near here?

'Yes,' she said out loud. 'Yes, I did.' And she didn't notice how Richard and Jess moved slightly, as if their puppeteer had twitched his fingers.

The trip to Florence, and Ben's dollars further

363

pissed on. He was coming home. He wanted to be with Alex because they had lots to talk about, and anyway he wanted to be with her.

'Hell,' he wrote, 'I've read this over and seen I haven't told you I love you. Wife of mine, I love you, and even though I'm coming home soon I have to write this down because it's clear in my head now, and when I see you other things will get in the way.

'Alex, we have the money and we can't run away from it. It doesn't need to be bad, does it, not if we do good with it? We must learn how to handle it, that's all. How about us changing majors at college so we can learn together?'

Alex closed her eyes, hearing him speak more or less those same words in her last conversation with him. The pain was closing in on the fuzz and in a strange way she was ready to welcome it. She read on.

'And I've been thinking more. The crazy way we've been living this summer. I know Granddad said to have parties but it's gotten out of hand. It's like life is a party if you can afford to make it one. That's wrong. I'm not saying we shouldn't have fun, Alex. Sure we should, but we must think of other things. Be more responsible, I guess. Yeah. Responsible is a good word for it. Take hold of our lives and live them, and not let those fucking dollars lead the way. We keep them in order. Agreed, my Alex?'

'Yes,' Alex said again. She picked up one of Ben's T-shirts and hugged it to her as she continued reading. It was a later entry.

'I've just spoken to you. I wish we could drive straight to Rome and home, but I feel kind of guilty about Clint. He's hardly seen anything of Italy. He's been a bit strange. Nervous, almost. Maybe he doesn't like Siena and can't conceal it as well as you. Whoops. Joke, Alex. Joke, joke, joke. It's hot here and we both need to cool down in the sea. I'd like to see Elba where Napoleon ended up, having seen where he crowned himself at Reims. We were there on your birthday, remember?

'Okay, so he really ended up on St Helena, but we'll never get there.

'Two, three days until I see you, wife of mine. Listen, why did we always want to have parties when it was so great with just the two of us?'

Hopefully, Alex turned the pages in the rest of the book, but there was nothing there. She flipped back through her letter from Italy looking for dark parts, but there was only light. Ben had loved her and was leaving Siena and Italy only a few days after he had arrived so he and Alex could get on with their life together. The most marginal mention of Clint and the guilt of the most innocent kind. His elation at overcoming the millstone must have led him to attempt the mad swim to Elba. He was used to the smooth blue waters of a pool, not unfriendly seas with ambushing winds and waves. Wind, weather, cramp, a piece of flotsam – the cruellest of accidents had overcome him.

'How far is it to Elba?' she asked.

'Seven miles. More maybe,' Richard replied.

'Stupid. *Stupid!*'

And at last she cried for her beloved golden boy.

She welcomed the oblivion more pills brought and did not know how long she was in it. When she awoke her traitorous body told her it was hungry. The others were in the restaurant downstairs, Jess told her, and did she feel up to eating there? Alex showered and climbed into the dress Jess selected from her suitcase. Somehow during her sleep she had reached conclusions.

She and Jess arrived at the table in the corner of the hotel restaurant. Richard, Frank and Tony Devlin stood to welcome them.

Alex kissed Joan and then Frank. 'I'm sorry about what I said at the airport. It was terrible of me and I didn't mean it.'

'Oh Alex, honey,' he said, taking one hand while Joan grasped the other, 'I know. Don't think of it again.'

Alex had a strange vision. It was not like those times on the way here when she seemed to be out of her own body, but concrete, certain. She had five – maybe even six – parents. She was Jess and Richard's daughter, of course, but she would be one to Frank and Joan, too. She was their daughter-in-law and nothing would ever change that, but she was also a memorial to their lost son, their surety he had once lived. In their old age, she resolved in the fractions of seconds this blazed through her mind, she would be there to remind them of him.

And there was the woman who was the fifth parent. To her Alex was a lost daughter, as lost as Ben was, and whatever she had done when Alex was a child she did not deserve the bereavement Alex, Frank and Joan were suffering now. In the confused emotion since Elizabeth Wendover had sent Ben the painting the sure centre of the whirlpool had been Alex herself, what she wanted, how she felt. She had come round to thinking she would like to see her mother with no real consideration – though Ben had considered it, darling Ben – of what her mother had gone through. Those presents, year after year . . .

Alex's mind flipped and jerked the picture into another configuration. Instead of being at the centre of everyone's love she saw herself earning it, returning it with the dividends it deserved. She had known – had known even when she had written that spontaneous letter to her mother in reply to the one after Franklin's death – she was conferring happiness like an absolute monarch upon a serf. It had had a lot to do with how she had felt afterwards.

So. There was Alex, still at the centre but radiating outwards instead of greedily grabbing everything in. There were Frank and Joan upon whom she would bestow the love of a daughter, there were Jess and Richard who had no doubt of it, there behind them were Austin and Betty Mitchell, self-appointed step-grandparents. And there were shadowy Elizabeth Wendover and her husband David, the Wicked Uncle David who Alex could not help but consider was the cause of what had happened. Alex would not mind, though. She would give her mother love as freely as she had learned to accept it from her.

But before that there was something to be done, another conclusion – like her apology to Frank – which had emerged from her drug-induced sleep. She squeezed her parents-in-law's hands and sat down between them. A waiter presented her with a menu which Jess, seeing Alex's appetite disappearing as she looked at the variety of dishes on offer, swiftly removed and asked Tony Devlin to order grilled fish. He did so and the waiter wrote on his pad, sighing loudly in sympathy for the beautiful girl widow. A short time later he returned with *acqua minerale* and the bottle of wine Richard had ordered. Frank reached for it but Jess beat him there.

'No, Frank.'

'One glass won't harm.'

'No.'

She was not Frank's keeper, but she had checked the notebook and worked out the discrepancy between the pills Alex and Joan had taken and what was left in the bottle. He had come to her on his return from identifying Ben, handed her a plastic bag containing his son's wedding ring and watch and, abandoning the pretence, had begged for a pill for himself. She had given him one and was certain he should drink no alcohol. Firmly she poured him, Alex and Joan mineral water.

Alex picked up her glass, drank deeply, put it down and again took her parents-in-law's hands. 'You might not like this,' she said, 'but please think about it before you say anything. Ben will be cremated, like his grandfather, and we could have the funeral here.'

'Okay, Alex,' Frank said wearily. 'I don't see what difference it makes.'

'It's not that,' Alex paused, wondering how to go on. The old Alex would have demanded, informed without consultation, but the new one could not do that and yet was not quite comfortable in the unfamiliar skin. 'Ben would want his ashes in Siena,' she went on at last. 'It's where he felt he really belonged, you see.' Again she paused and then added, 'His letter to me proves it. I'll let you see it, if you like. It will show you.'

It was an incredibly generous offer and even the new Alex regretted it had been made, for her letter from Italy was the most precious thing she owned. But Joan and Frank Stanford seemed disinclined to take her up on it as they stared at her in shock.

'Nothing of him back home?' Joan whispered. 'Nothing?'

Alex knew she could insist, but she needed to

persuade. 'He longed to be a part of Siena. It's the last thing I can do for him.'

Their food was served and Jess, anxious Alex should eat, searched frantically for another topic of conversation, but there was none. The cold body in the morgue was centre stage and Alex was intent on keeping it there, though discussing it over a meal seemed rather gruesome. Except why should it be? Jess chided herself. Alex would never think of such a word in connection with Ben. She was eating her fish and telling her parents-in-law over and over again how she did not mean to upset them, it was for Ben and not for herself. She was talking too much, becoming almost hysterical, but her tongue dried up suddenly as she looked down at her plate. She seemed shocked to see it was scraped clean, apart from a tidy clump of bones. Chatter from other people in the restaurant encroached upon the table in the corner, kept at bay until now by Alex's voice. A group near by broke into loud laughter and they could have been on a different planet.

Tony Devlin cleared his throat to gain their attention. 'You could divide the ashes,' he said. 'Take some to Siena and bury the rest back home.'

'Is that possible?' Jess asked.

'I don't see why not. It would be better to have the service in Florence though. I know the system and there are English-speaking Protestant priests available.'

'Thank you,' the three women said simultaneously.

Tony remembered the unseemly rush when the fax had arrived at the consulate asking, as a favour, that someone go to Piombino. Everyone had wanted a couple of days at the coast, away from the heat and the procession of lost passports and stolen credit cards, assisting the family of the 'frigging millionaire stiff' as it came to be called, and Tony had been envied when he had landed the assignment. Would the rest of them in Florence envy him this, though? A stiff was impersonal, unattached to people who cared for it, and it did not have a nineteen-year-old widow whose bravery was terrifying.

'I'll arrange it,' Tony Devlin said. 'Leave it with me.'

He had another problem, though, and he fixed on Jess to share it with when they went for a walk after dinner. It was only ten o'clock, four in the afternoon for those who had flown from America, and everyone feared what kind of sleep lay ahead. The photographers had, mercifully, gone and the night was warm. Light and cheerful noise spilled out of the cafés and *bar-ristorante* and the Italians were on their streets where they loved to be. Tony touched Jess on the elbow and she fell in beside him, allowing the others to go on ahead.

'Clint Flanagan?' she said, in response to his remark. 'What's he got to do with us?'

'Does Alex want to see him?'

'I shouldn't think so.'

A girl and a boy were walking in front of them.

Her T-shirt said 'Hollywood Hot!' on it and his hand was in the back pocket of her jeans. They stopped and kissed. How odd that this was going on while Clint Flanagan, around whom Jess's fears for Alex's marriage had crystallized, was lying in hospital – the same one which housed the morgue Ben was in, perhaps.

'How is he?' she asked reluctantly.

'He's okay. Depressed, but okay. I've got to get him home and, well, the thing is he has little money. Ben was paying for everything, and since they had no fixed itinerary they hadn't reserved return air tickets. Kind of expensive,' he commented, 'for a pair of college juniors.'

'Ben could afford it.' And, oh Christ, did that mean Alex could do so now? In someone else's voice, with someone else's cold logic, Jess said, 'I'll talk to the others and we'll pay to get him away and charge it to the estate, but we'll need a deposition from Clint to say it was Ben's debt.'

'Thank you, Lady Mountfield.'

'Jess, for heaven's sake,' she said automatically. She had found a thick wad of dollars when she'd repacked Ben's bag while Alex was asleep. Could that be used to get Clint home? They might need it themselves for there were unknown expenses to deal with, ones where credit cards might not be accepted. 'Does Clint want to see Alex?' she said.

'He hasn't said so, but he knows you're all here.'

'And he's alone. Depressed.' Jess sighed. 'You

think one of us should see him, don't you? If not Alex then Frank or Joan, or even Richard and me. See him and tell him – what? That it wasn't his fault and he's to stop feeling depressed?' She rummaged in her handbag, found a tissue and blew her nose. 'All right, all *right*,' she said violently. 'You find out if he wants to see Alex, and if he does I'll raise the subject with her. Not otherwise.'

'I didn't mean to upset you.'

'You're doing your job. You're doing it brilliantly and truly we're grateful. It's just so . . .'

'Yeah,' he said. 'It is.'

They went down a darker street and on to a paved area. Young people were entwined on seats set into the balustrades or sat at tables under garish umbrellas made of plastic straw listening to rock music sung in Italian-accented American. The thump of the synthesizer faded as Jess and Tony caught up with the other four and they walked out along a finger of land pointing across the sea towards Elba. They could hear the hiss and gurgle of water on rocks. At the end of the promontory a lighthouse winked and one on Elba replied. Further along, at the base of the humps of hills, shone a string of lights. A ferry garlanded in yellow moved from left to right, harvesting a band of moonlight as it went, and in the opposite direction travelled a less decorated ship taking supplies to the metal works, Jess assumed. Nearer to shore small boats hunted squid. It was altogether a very occupied sea. And harmless, friendly, unthreatening.

Someone, Joan perhaps, had spoken Jess's thoughts aloud, for Frank said, 'Maybe there are currents, undertows, and there's no wind tonight.'

Alex's voice, barely above a whisper as she gazed at the island Napoleon had been given in exchange for his empire: 'It doesn't seem very far away. It looks like quite an easy swim,' and Richard, in a sudden fear that she might try it, led her away.

Alex went to sleep that night, with the help of more pills, but Jess was woken in the early hours of the morning by sobbing which seemed to come from a tortured soul in hell. Jess put on the light, got out of bed and knelt by her stepdaughter. Alex was still half asleep, but her eyes opened as Jess took her heaving shoulders. For a moment they showed hope, then quickly clouded over.

'I thought it was a nightmare, but it wasn't, was it?'

'No, I'm afraid not.'

'A big, whole, wide world and no Ben anywhere in it.'

Jess held her and let her cry until she insisted upon getting up and exchanging her nightdress for the T-shirt of Ben's she had held as she slept earlier.

'That's better,' she said. She climbed back into bed and lay on her side so her blue eyes were on a level with Jess's grey ones. 'We never quite learned to be married, Ben and I,' she said, 'but we were getting there. It's sad we weren't given time.'

'It is.'

'And the worry about him being gay—'

'Crazy.'

'I know. I thought for a while he might have committed suicide because of that and the millstone. Nonsense. The letter proves it.'

'Nonsense, of course.'

'I'd like to read it again.'

Jess found the notebook and, seeing Alex absorbed, returned to bed. When she awoke next it was day, the light was still on and Alex was asleep with her letter from Italy clasped to Ben's T-shirt at her breast.

To the others time seemed interminable, the little town wedged between the metal works and the bright blue of the Mediterranean soon explored and bored with, but Tony Devlin was working hard and moving things on at speed. There was a post mortem and an inquest, neither of which was mentioned to Alex, but Frank had to attend the latter. Clint had been there, he reported, and afterwards had been driven away.

To Rome, Tony Devlin said. He had not wanted to see them, but he had sent them a scrawled note, the signature barely legible. 'I'm sorry. What else can I say?' it read. Jess would not show it to Alex.

At least they could now go to Florence.

'Are you sleeping with me or Alex tonight?'

Richard asked Jess as they arrived in their hotel room.

'Alex. I must if she wants me to.' Jess sat on the bed and reached for the phone. 'I'm going to call the children. Will you see if Alex wants to talk to them?'

He made for the door and then was arrested by his wife speaking his name. She had put the phone down and was staring out of the window over the red roofs of Florence.

'What is it?' he said.

'I've been wondering about it and haven't dared suggest it to either you or Alex but . . . Richard, should Elizabeth Wendover be here?'

'Elizabeth,' Richard said, standing very still. 'Hasn't she left for America?'

Jess struggled to remember dates. 'Next week, I think. She may not know what's happened, or have read it in the newspapers. That's dreadful. I don't have her phone number with me, but Jane could ring Jeff at Montly and get it.'

'What about Alex, though?' Richard said, seeking and finding inspiration. 'Isn't Ben's funeral enough to cope with? Let her meet Elizabeth when she's had a chance to get over that.'

Jess's troubled, honest eyes met his, and for a moment he was tempted to make his confession then and there. Sense, however, prevailed. He would have to talk to Alex too, and this was not the time for it. He crossed the room and sat beside Jess. 'I hope they get on together – truly I do – but to put extra strain on Alex now seems appalling.'

'I suppose so.'

'Ask Jane to get the number and ring Elizabeth. You're right, she should know.'

Jess smiled at him and reached for the phone again. 'Give me five minutes.'

William and Annabelle were riding under the supervision of the two Sarahs. Jane was about to yell for one of the twins to fetch them when Jess stopped her.

'How are they?' she asked longingly. She'd spoken to them every day, but had not been able to have a proper conversation with Jane.

'They are fine. They miss you, of course, and are upset and confused about Ben, but Emily Glover has talked to them a lot about it.'

'Did they pick their flowers for him?'

'This morning from your garden. And arranged them in a vase all by themselves. Then we went to the church and put the vase in the lady chapel. John let Silas and Marner come too because William and Annabelle insisted they were Ben's friends, and we said some prayers.'

Jess tried to imagine the scene, the two Labradors, her two children, before the altar of the side chapel in the church at Montly on which was a vase of flowers arranged by inexpert but loving little hands.

'Don't let Nanny tidy it up,' she warned.

Jane laughed. 'She was there and about to, but

Emily made her promise to leave it alone.'

They chatted more. Jess gave Jane the number of their new hotel and said they would be going to Siena, and why.

'Poor you,' Jane said.

'Poor me? Poor Alex, you mean.'

'Well, naturally, but she's getting the sympathy. I'm sure you need some too.'

Jess had a vision of Jane coming to Florence with William and Annabelle, her fluent Italian and earthy common sense smoothing paths, but instantly dismissed it. Small children should not be part of this and, in any case, Alex required all her attention. Jess thanked Jane, said they would call the children at the usual time, and rang off.

Not Jane, but Emily Glover. Much the best person. And why the subterfuge?

She went to the next room, reported that the children were out and Alex, confounding her utterly, preempted her by saying, 'My mother will want to know . . . about Ben. I should have thought sooner.'

'I was going to ask Emily Glover to tell her.'

'I'll ask her. Later, after we've talked to William and Annabelle. Frank and Joan haven't been to Florence before and I promised' – said Alex, the old Italian hand – 'we'd go for a stroll.'

'Can we come too?' Richard said, almost jealously.

'Oh Daddy!' she exclaimed, taking his arm, assuring him of her love.

She seemed to be older than any of them.

She cried as she listened to Annabelle and William's account of how they had prayed for Ben, but she hid her tears from them.

'Silas and Marner too?' she whispered. 'How sweet!'

'We're going to change the flowers and keep them fresh for ever and ever and ever,' Annabelle said.

'Ben would be pleased.'

'He knows. John and Henry told us. He's with Jesus.'

'He is, isn't he?'

Such a clear line, and Alex remembered the difficulty Ben had telephoning her, an enormous ocean between them. She rang the vicarage at Montly, and Emily Glover agreed at once to contact Elizabeth Wendover.

'Please tell her I asked you to. Please make it clear and say I'll see her in America when this is over. The number,' Alex said in a relay from Jess, 'is in the book by the hall phone . . . Thank you very much.' Emily spoke more and Alex listened, smiling.

'John and Henry are coming,' she told Richard and Jess afterwards. 'They are absolutely determined, Emily says. John may be able to take the service, or at least assist, and Henry wants to give the address.' Alex's eyes were sparkling, as they did whenever there was something that would make Ben's disposal more worthy of him, but the light soon went from her and she covered her face with her hands. 'But how can they afford it? Jess, Daddy, persuade them to let me pay. I've got my million dollars, for heaven's sake. Credit cards. They have nothing. Please persuade them . . . no, I will.'

She rang the vicarage again and, her voice breaking but utterly determined, she told the Reverend John Glover she was grateful for his and Henry's offer but could not accept it unless she paid for their flights. The Reverend John had quite a lot to say in reply, allowing Alex no room for argument.

'Well?' Richard said, when at last he had finished.

'He says it wasn't an offer to be accepted or rejected. I could reject their roles, he said, but not their attendance. They'll drive here, leaving tonight. He told me to get off the line so he can arrange for someone to cover him on Sunday.' She was crying. 'How good people are, and I have been so bad.'

'Nonsense!'

'It's true. If I hadn't been selfish about Ben going to Siena he would have wanted me on this trip. I wouldn't have let him swim to Elba.'

Richard rocked her and made soothing noises. There were no words that could be of any use.

People are good. Ralph Patterson, worried about the vicar's car making the sixteen-hundred-mile round trip and wanting to represent his family, drove Henry and John Glover to Italy. With consummate sensitivity, having consulted Frank and Joan, Tony

Devlin had arranged for the funeral to be held in the Anglican church rather than the Episcopalian one Americans used in Florence, believing, as he told Jess, it would comfort Alex to hear the service said in a British accent. Unbelievably, John Glover knew the priest and was invited both to assist at the service and to stay with him. Henry moved into the spare bed in Richard's room and Alex's conscience and the Glovers' pride and pocket were thus preserved.

A skeleton of a congregation gathered in the Anglican church of St Mark, but a skeleton with rather more flesh upon it than might have been. Tony Devlin was there with his wife; people from the British consulate turned up and so did a party of six Americans staying at the hotel who had been moved by the tragedy of Ben's young life; there were three or four reporters. Flowers, there were, from Elizabeth Wendover, from the villagers of Montly, from several places in America. Henry spoke most beautifully of Ben and the Reverend John and his friend conducted the service with pure faith in their voices. The hearse and its cortege drove through the chaotic streets to the crematorium, where the last words were said and the coffin moved forward into the incinerator. Joan fell against Frank and Alex screamed it was a mistake and he should go into the ground. John and Henry Glover held her, whispered to her about Jesus's promises and heaven and she was quiet.

*

That afternoon the adults, exhausted, retired to their rooms for a siesta.

'Don't you want to sleep?' Henry asked Alex.

She shook her head. She couldn't sleep without pills, and even they didn't prevent the nightmares. She needed to be as tired as possible when she went to bed.

'Will you show me some of Florence, then?'

'Henry – yes!'

They walked through shaded side streets and squares to the *duomo*. In the cool, dark interior Alex put money in a box and lit a candle for Ben.

'It's the wrong religion. Does it matter?'

'God won't mind,' Henry said, and he lit one as well.

They left the cathedral and stood among a sweating crowd of tourists admiring Ghibert's east door of the baptistry.

'Michelangelo called it the gates of paradise,' Alex said. 'Is Ben really there, Henry?'

'Yes. Beyond the gates.'

'Do you honestly believe that?'

'I do.' He walked her away.

'With Jesus?'

'Yes.'

'Then is it wrong of me to want his ashes in Siena?'

'No, it's not wrong.' He steered her to one of the tables of an outdoor café and sat her down. 'Not at all. What would you like? I'm parched.'

He ordered her Coca-Cola and his beer in passable Italian, nice comfortable Henry with his curly brown hair and pale skin already turning pink on his forearms and in the V of his open-necked shirt.

'Thank you for coming,' Alex said, when the waiter had gone. 'And for what you said this morning.'

'I hope it helped.'

'It did.' Their drinks arrived and she sipped her Coke. 'Are you still going to be a priest?' she asked.

'Afraid so.'

'You'll be a very good one. Henry, do you remember what you said about dentists?'

'*Dentists?*' he repeated, raising a startled eyebrow at her.

'You said it was lucky for the rest of us that people wanted to become dentists. Well, I think it's lucky for us – or for whoever your parishioners are – that you want to be a priest. Priests are needed just as much as dentists, aren't they?'

'They are,' he said.

They finished their drinks and strolled down to the Arno and across the Ponte Vecchio.

'The Boboli Gardens are a bit further on. They're peaceful. Joan and Frank like going there. Do you want to see them or should you do some serious sightseeing?'

Henry said it was too hot and crowded for sightseeing and he would prefer to walk in the gardens. He knew Alex needed to talk. She was worried about how she would scatter the ashes. It had to be in Siena and not the country around it, she said, because Ben had so wanted to belong to the city, but its people might not like her pouring ashes on their streets. She wondered about releasing them from the top of the Torre del Mangia (the high tower above the Piazza del Campo, she explained, the names summoned from Ben; how else could she have remembered them?), but what if someone saw her and stopped her?

'We'll be there,' Henry said. 'We'll guard you.'

'You're coming to Siena?'

'If you want us to.'

'Yes. Yes, please. That's all right then.'

She went on to talk about the memorial service she would arrange, when the second urn would be buried. It had to be perfect. She needed to study the hymn book carefully. The ones they'd sung this morning were hurriedly selected. And did Henry know of a reading to suit Ben? Henry said he would think about it and Alex chattered on.

Was she being impossibly brave? Henry wondered. Or had it not sunk in yet? A bit of both, perhaps. Alexandra Stanford, nineteen years old and a widow.

Was it possible that God sometimes makes mistakes?

To Siena with one of the two urns. Alex walked

between her parents-in-law from the parked cars to the Piazza del Campo, wanting them to understand why their son's ashes should be scattered here, and was pleased to hear an indrawn breath from one side and a faint 'Wow' from the other as they entered the great space.

'Ben loved it,' Alex said. 'He'd sit here for hours and watch it.'

She left them and went to John Glover. 'See?' she said, gesturing to the Torre del Mangia. 'See how high it is? And there's a wind.'

John had been alarmed on hearing Alex's plans, had asked if there was a river, a wild garden maybe, and on hearing there was not he had reserved judgement. The tower was high, there was indeed a wind. The people wouldn't know what was being scattered over them and surely they breathed in far more noxious things every time they walked down a road. Wondering what the headlines would read, what his bishop would say if they were found out, he smiled his agreement at Alex and she bounded across the square to the Palazzo Pubblico to buy their tickets, the shoulder bag containing the urn banging at her hip.

Fifteen minutes later, at the top parapet of the Torre del Mangia, the wind blowing the Reverend John's conscience away whipped their hair across their faces. They moved so it was blowing from their backs and waited for some German tourists to leave, then, slickly, as though it had been rehearsed, Ralph,

Richard and Henry blocked the entrance to the parapet, Frank and Joan flanked Alex as she took out the urn, unstoppered it and John spoke a prayer in a strong voice that defied bishops and the wind.

The dust that had been Ben swirled and vanished over the Piazza del Campo and among the palaces, churches and streets of the city where he had felt his feet grow roots.

Gently Jess took the empty urn, slid the bag from Alex's shoulder and replaced the urn in it. They went down the steep steps, the two bereaved women sandwiched between men.

'Thank you,' Alex kept saying. 'Thank you.'

She seemed drained and utterly blank and bereft when they arrived once more in the piazza, but did not want to sit at one of the cafés around its rim.

'You wait here,' she said to Frank and Joan.

'I won't be long.'

Henry went with her as she strode to the *duomo*, lit candles there and then, in some kind of trance apparently, wandered around the city, taking – at random, Henry thought, hoping they were not lost – abrupt turns down narrow roads.

'How does an expert swimmer drown?' she asked him once.

'By accident, Alex. Accident.'

'There's something else.'

She turned another corner and stopped. This was the place. She remembered a time last summer, when she had been happy. She was here and over there

Ben had been embraced by two boys in blue velvet costumes, silver-netted caps on their heads, their flags trailing in the dust.

The solution.

Ben had been claimed by *onda,* the wave.

Chapter Twelve

B EN'S LAWYER ARRIVED AT MONTLY from New
York. There would be no unseemly court case,
he assured Alex, for Ben had made a will and
left all he owned to her. He talked on, saying she'd
have a substantial income, explaining how the
constraints upon Franklin's legacy devolved upon
Alex and the trustees would run the estate until she
was twenty-one; then he became aware that his new
client was gazing at him in horror and panic.

'But why did he make a will?' she said, the dark
fears about Ben's death resurfacing.

The lawyer, catching Jess's agonized glance, said
hastily it had been on his powerful recommendation
and Ben had agreed. Alex, as Ben's wife, was his
legal heir but the size of the fortune, the fact it was
held in trust for Ben and that Franklin's affairs had
not yet been sorted out, as well as the controversial
(he said, a question mark in his voice) nature of his
will made the clear-cut disposition of Ben's legacy
of paramount importance. For the same reasons he
advised Alex to make a will now. He had other
things to discuss with her, but she needed time to

recover from the surprise and think over what he had told her. He would return tomorrow, he said, and took himself and his hired car and driver to the best hotel in Eastbourne.

'Charging it to Ben's estate, no doubt,' Richard said when he heard.

'And why not?' Jess countered. 'It will also pay for our expenses connected with going to Italy for the funeral. He asked me for a reckoning.'

'Oh,' Richard said. 'That's something, then.'

The lawyer reappeared the following morning and this time Richard sat in on the meeting, which had not proceeded very far before Alex stopped the man.

'Why can't we discuss this in New York?' she said.

He seemed surprised. 'You mean you'll be in the States?'

'Of course I will. I have to finish college. I must arrange Ben's service.'

What had she been doing these last weeks since Ben's funeral? Everything had been a daze. She had played with the children, helped them change the flowers in Ben's vase in the church, met Henry in the pub some evenings, had eaten and slept, had cried in the early mornings as the sun rose and when she turned the light out at night, but at no other time. The world switched to a sharper focus now.

'Of course I'm coming back,' she said, and for the first time she looked directly at the lawyer. He smiled at her. He had friendly lines in his face and she saw he was someone she could trust.

'I've forgotten your name,' she said.

'Marcus Grimaldi.' He held out a hand. 'Welcome aboard, Mrs Stanford.'

She took his hand, shook it and smiled back at him. She was supposed to have the weight of a millstone around her neck, but she couldn't feel it – not at all – and she knew it was because Ben had rid himself of it before he died. He hadn't bequeathed it to her.

'Mr Grimaldi—'

'Marcus.'

'Marcus, then. Ben was – we both were – going to change major, do business studies or whatever and learn how to deal with this money . . .'

She paused, wondering if he would laugh at the idea of subduing the dollars and making them do good, but he prompted her on with an infinitely sympathetic, 'What a great idea. I knew Ben would come through.'

'He did, didn't he? But . . . but I can't go back to Miami. I don't know how to change colleges or where to go or anything. I can't go back to Miami. I *can't*, but isn't it too late to transfer?'

Marcus Grimaldi surveyed her and scraped a palm across his chin. 'Under normal circumstances, perhaps, but one of your trustees can help, I believe. How does Columbia sound to you?'

'Columbia?'

'In New York City.'

'New York!' she exclaimed. 'Then I could commute from Long Island.'

'Are you planning to live there?'

'I think so,' she said uncertainly. 'For the time being, at least. I'm allowed to, aren't I?'

'Sure. It's your house.'

A tug at her neck, which she ignored.

'Can everything else wait until I get back?'

Marcus Grimaldi glanced at Richard, who had remained silent throughout.

'Sir—' he began.

'You want me to go?'

'I'd like to talk with your daughter alone.'

Richard left the room.

'Alex, did you think about what I said yesterday?' Marcus Grimaldi asked.

'About a will?' she said, sighing.

'Right.'

'What happens if I don't make one?'

'It would go to your next of kin, but it could be very messy.'

'My parents? Why should they have Ben's money?'

'We hope they won't,' he pointed out. 'It's only a precaution.'

'You probably said that to Ben.'

'Probably I did.' He remembered the day Ben had visited him, the way he had wilted when he'd discovered why he'd been ordered there. Franklin should have told him to order Alex along too. He was impressed by her grasp of things, and even more when she said, evidently hating the whole business – and who could blame her? – 'I'll leave it to Frank and Joan. It's only fair.'

'Good girl.' He opened his laptop computer and after some tapping produced a document for her to sign and summoned his driver to witness it along with himself. 'There. Painless,' he said. 'That will do for now. See you in New York. When will you be arriving?'

'Soon, I suppose.'

'Let me know, okay? I'm your friend, Alex. Don't take a step without me.'

'I won't,' she said, comforted.

He refused Jess's invitation to lunch, saying he wanted to catch the earliest flight home, and Richard escorted him to his car. He returned to find Alex replacing the hall telephone, a disconsolate look on her face.

'I was trying to ring my mother,' she said, 'but she's gone. The phone's switched through to someone else.'

'She left some time ago. There was a letter, remember?'

'I'd better book my air ticket.'

'Not just now, surely,' Richard said, responsibilities, guilts and worries piling around him.

'It was my promise to you that I'd go through with college in America.'

'I won't hold you to it.'

392

'I have to do it anyway. For Ben.'

'Alex, I must talk to you.'

He guided her into the morning-room and they both sat down. Alex, her mind full of a future life dedicated to the way Ben had decreed in his last phone call and letter, scarcely heard her father at first but her attention was caught when he mentioned her mother.

'What did you say?' she asked, sitting forward and staring at him.

'It was my fault she left us. Mine. You – you got hold of the wrong end of the stick and how could I explain that?'

'What did you do?'

He attempted a light shrug. 'Had a casual affair and she found out.'

Silence, except for the sound of Albert mowing the lawn; they could hear when he wrestled the machine round at the end of each run.

'What about Wicked Uncle David?' Alex said.

'She met him afterwards.'

He watched her anxiously as she tried to work things out. 'It must be true,' she whispered, it seemed to herself. 'It has to be. He's had to tell me because I'm going to meet her.'

'It is true, Alex, to my shame. I should have told you before, but you were so determined to believe your version – and, well it's hard for a man to confess such a thing to his young daughter. Can you understand that?'

'I suppose I can,' she said slowly. She had picked up the diversionary scent and was following it.

'I didn't lie to you. You simply wouldn't listen to anything your mother and I said.'

Adults can mislead and lie, children misguided as well as guided.

'Nanny!' she shouted, pouncing on her prey. 'Then did Nanny lie?'

He did not reply. Another silence lengthened.

'Daddy,' she said at last, and he looked up and met her gaze. Shocked, he could not tear his eyes from hers. They were calm, confident, demanding more truths, making him feel inadequate: Elizabeth's eyes.

'Why did you want me to marry Ben? You knew about Franklin's will, didn't you?'

He couldn't help himself. 'I need money,' he blurted out.

'Ah!'

'As an investment.'

She stood and went to the window, apparently finding Albert and the mowing machine fascinating. 'How inconvenient for you,' she said, 'that Ben died. He would have been twenty-one before me. As it is you'll have to apply through the trustees. You heard what Mr Grimaldi said. Had you realized my million dollars isn't mine to dispose of as I please?'

'I – I'm sorry, Alex.'

'What for? I will never regret marrying Ben.

Never. We loved each other, you see, so your motives don't matter. Is Montly safe?'

'Yes. More or less. I've had to put it up – a bit of it – as surety against a loan I've taken out on these properties in London. It should have been all right, Alex. It should have been profitable, and will be in the long run, but what with the interest rates and the fall in prices—'

'I'll talk to Mr Grimaldi. Maybe the trust can put up money, be the surety or whatever it's called. I don't want Montly threatened.'

'Thank you, Alex,' Too, too humble, but Alex didn't seem to notice or care.

That direct gaze again. 'Have you told Jess?'

'What?' Playing for time, he was, and not doing it very well.

'Any or all of this.'

'No. Nothing.'

'I won't, but don't you think you should?'

'Yes,' he said. 'Yes.' Cowered and humiliated before Elizabeth's daughter.

An early evening in August on top of Wilmington Hill. The Long Man below her, his great staffs threatening dire consequences to anyone daring to challenge him, the graves of people who had lived here in a far distant past – old they were when the Romans had come and seen and conquered – behind her. Old when the Piccolominis and Chigis had built Siena.

What did a few lives in the late twentieth century matter?

She sat on the grass, out of the wind on a high hill by a barrow which contained the dust of someone honoured in a time before history was recorded in writing. What was the point of it? All of life?

It was there to be lived, though, by everything that breathed.

'And that includes you, doesn't it?' she said to Silas and Marner and they wagged their tails at her, their tawny eyes asking permission to chase the rabbits they scented.

There was a shout on the wind and the dogs bounded towards it. Henry Glover, his suit jacket over his shoulder, walked across the springy grass. She stood up.

'They were worried about you,' Henry said. 'I thought you'd be here.' He sat in the dip she had been occupying and invited her to sit beside him. She hesitated.

'I don't want them to worry.'

'I rang when I found your car. Jess's car, rather. They know I'm with you.'

She sat and he put a reassuring arm around her.

'They told me about Ben's will. So you're a rich girl now.'

'Did they tell you anything else?'

'No. What else?'

She related her father's revelations of the morning – only this morning? It seemed light years away –

and Nanny's tearful, defiant response. 'I can't blame Daddy. At least not for that, but Nanny! The dreadful injustice done to my mother . . . Nanny telling me and I believed her, of course I did, that my mother had run away with Wicked Uncle David, leaving us. Henry, how could she have done such a thing?'

Wise Henry was, for once, at a loss for words, overwhelmed by the old woman's ruthless manipulation of a young life. 'It must have been because she loved you and didn't want to lose you,' he said finally.

'It must, but how unforgivable! I can understand Daddy couldn't tell me the truth, really I can when I'd been so brainwashed . . . Well, maybe he should have done later, when I'd grown up a bit, but I suppose it was difficult because of Jess. We've been in touch, you know, my mother and I. Ben made me. Because of it I think I love her already, but this – this! I feel so guilty. Henry, my poor mother. How can I ever make it up to her?'

'You must try. I'm sure she'll understand.'

'Oh, she'll understand,' she said. 'She'll understand.'

Silas, followed by Marner, came up to check on them and dashed away again.

'There's more, Henry,' Alex said. 'Tell your parents about Nanny if you want, but please not this. I have to talk to someone. I'm sorry it's you and I hope it won't make you feel awkward.'

He tightened his arm around her. 'What is it?'

'Daddy. He's been very foolish, I think.' And she told him of that other revelation.

Henry, still punch drunk from what he had heard about Nanny Mountfield, reeled under this new onslaught. 'You're saying your father arranged your marriage because he wanted access to the fortune he knew was being left to Ben? Alex, that's dreadful. It can't be true!'

'It doesn't matter,' she said impatiently. 'Ben and I wanted to be married, but it's . . . embarrassing having to deal with Daddy about the money.'

'How much is it?'

'I don't know.' She laughed shakily. 'However much it can't make a dent in what Ben had. He'd want to save Montly.'

Henry was outraged, and tried to hide it under his legal hat. 'You mustn't let your father treat you like a milch cow. You should start by making him fire his accountant and lawyer and employ ones appointed by you and this Grimaldi fellow. There must be a proper business agreement.'

'Perhaps,' she said, 'but don't ask me to criticize Daddy, Henry. It's hard enough having to take in what Nanny did.'

'No criticisms then,' he soothed. He felt her relax and said after a while: 'I've found a poem for Ben's service.'

'Have you, Henry? What?'

'It's by Shelley. He was drowned off Italy not far

398

from where Ben was. He wrote it for Keats, who died in Rome. I photocopied it at the office.' He reached for his jacket. 'It's called "Adonais". Appropriate, I thought.' He handed her some sheets. 'It's very long, but I've marked four or five verses.'

She read in silence. Three horses padded past them, their riders gigantic against the sky. 'Say this verse out loud,' she said, pointing. 'Please.'

He took the sheets back and began:

> To that high Capital, where kingly Death
> Keeps his high court in beauty and decay,
> He came; and bought with price of purest breath,
> A grave among the eternal. – Come away!
> Haste, while the vault of blue Italian day
> Is yet his fitting charnel-roof! while still
> He lies, as if in dewy sleep he lay;
> Awake him not! surely he takes his fill
> Of deep and liquid rest, forgetful of all ill.

'Thank you. It's lovely,' she said.

'They were both young when they died, Shelley and Keats. Not as young as Ben, though.'

She lolled against him, reading the poem as he held it. 'Yes,' she murmured. 'It's perfect . . . But Henry, it's not what you're going to read. I want you to do the bit from Ecclesiastes about how there is a time to every purpose under the heaven. It fits, especially now when I've discovered that everything in my life – even those bits I thought I'd done myself

– has been arranged by other people. Except for Ben's death. The only accident. Do you know Ecclesiastes?'

'"A time to be born, and a time to die; a time to plant, and a time to pluck up that which is planted." Alex—'

'We'd better get home.' She jumped to her feet and whistled the way he'd taught her when they were children, two fingers in her mouth, and Silas and Marner appeared with pink tongues hanging from their black muzzles. Henry rose and they began walking towards the path (no thought of sliding madly down the steep slope upon which the Long Man stood) until Alex stopped and turned, holding her hair out of her eyes so she could look directly up at Henry.

'You will be at Ben's service, won't you?'

'Alex—'

'I'll pay for the flight. Please.'

'You mustn't squander this money. Even though you think it's limitless you mustn't squander it.'

'I won't, but can't I be allowed one little indulgence? I want you there, Henry, you and your voice to symbolize Ben's love of the Old World. Please come.'

Henry, by a sheer act of will, had taught himself to consider her lost to him, but he was more devastated by her now than he had ever been.

'Are you going to America to live?'

'Yes, to finish college, anyway. What would I do

here? I've been a wife, you see. I can't go back to being a daughter . . . a daughter to Daddy,' she added, the words lost in the wind.

She ran down the path, the woman reverting to the familiar girl, the dogs giving chase liking this game. Henry followed more circumspectly, the smooth soles of his shoes making his footing precarious. He caught up with her at the bottom of the hill and they walked together to the car park.

'I suppose you're about to say I should forgive Nanny,' she said. 'Maybe I should but I can't – not yet. Not until I've met my mother. I'll forgive Nanny if she will.' She directed the dogs into Jess's car and closed the back door. 'And she will. I bet she will. Drink at the pub later?'

'All right.'

He drove home behind her, shepherding her along even though she didn't need it. It had not occurred to him to tell her to forgive the horrible old woman who had infected her with vicious lies, and he felt more anger over the way her father had behaved than she did.

'It means I'm not ready for the priesthood,' he said to his mother, having rushed into the vicarage kitchen and related the story of Nanny Mountfield's perfidy to her.

'No one thinks you are,' she said, inwardly alarmed because she recognized other resurging emotions behind his display. 'You'll be a lawyer first.'

'Yes.' Not listening.

'And what of your father and me? We knew and didn't tell Alex. We should have done.'

'How could you? Alex accepts Richard couldn't. She's – Mum! She's a saint!'

'Henry—'

'Ben forced her to contact her mother. Ben, who I took to be no more than a muscle-bound hunk of America. Oh, I liked him – what I saw of him. Who couldn't? – but he did that. Put a mother and daughter unjustly separated together. It's something, isn't it? So sad he can't reap the outcome.'

'Henry,' Emily began again, trying to find words to comfort and support him.

Her son, twenty-one years old and ageless since he was fourteen, was crying.

Henry, his usual composed self when he met Alex later that night at the pub in the village, learned she had booked a flight and had agreed with her father that he would tell Jess what he had to after Alex had left.

'I shouldn't think Jess will mind much, but it would be best if I'm not here,' she said. 'It wasn't her Daddy deceived, was it? Lots of people have affairs.'

Which was true, but Henry thought Jess would find Richard's admission of his financial troubles and the way he had proposed to solve them much more difficult to accept. He did not say anything, however, and a diversion was created as his sister, Sarah Patterson and her brothers together with a clatter of friends came into the pub. Sarah Glover was holding Simon Patterson's hand and was not altogether pleased to see Henry. She manoeuvred her party round the corner after greeting him and Alex, and Henry craned his neck trying to see more. It was no good. Sarah had hidden herself well and as Henry sat back defeated Alex's eyes met his. Those . . . what? mature *married woman's* eyes, full of amusement and – yes! – affection.

'Henry the mother hen,' she said. 'So what if she holds his hand? She's old enough.'

'She's seventeen.'

'You held my hand when I was sixteen,' she reminded him. 'I met Ben when I was seventeen. I wish it could have been sooner so we'd had more time together.'

'It's not that,' he muttered, trying to forget the implications. 'Sarah and Simon have been holding hands for ages. I was trying to see what Sarah's drinking. Mother worries.'

'Henry worries.' Alex picked up their empty glasses and went to the bar. She returned a short time later and put Henry's beer in front of him. 'Orange juice,' she reported. 'I was drinking wine at her age – at pubs I wasn't known at – and you bought it for me, you horrible hypocrite.'

He grinned at her, loving her teasing and her acknowledgement of their shared past.

'Wasn't I wicked?' he said.

'Dreadfully,' replied this peacefully contained, tragic, brave woman aged nineteen.

She reverted to the subject of Ben's service, wanting his confirmation he would be there. She would send him a ticket, she said, as soon as a date had been arranged.

'Will there be any difficulty getting time off work? You've already rushed to Italy and back.'

'No difficulty, but you mustn't pay, Alex.' It would have put him on a par with Richard, he considered, though he wondered how he'd afford a transatlantic flight.

'I can't let you come unless I pay,' she said. 'Henry, I'll need you there. It's selfish of me, but I will.'

Put that way, could he refuse?

They left, a relieved chorus of good nights from the youthful contingent following them, and Henry escorted Alex home through a light mist.

'Will I see you tomorrow?' she asked as they reached Montly Manor's front door.

'Possibly. If you haven't flown away by then, and if you make an appointment with my secretary.'

'Dear Henry,' she said, and kissed him warmly on the cheek. 'Dearest Henry.'

He walked back to the vicarage, his feet treading on all kinds of impossible clouds.

Alex went to Nanny Mountfield's cottage to say goodbye, and no one knew what else she said except for the Reverend John Glover to whom the old woman ran for confessional comfort, which the Reverend John was disinclined to give since he was Low Church and, in any case, could not tell Nanny Mountfield what she wanted to hear: that the lies she had told were the truth.

Alex hugged her half brother and sister and stepmother, and her father who did not deserve it. And she hugged Henry and made him promise again he would fly to America and read from Ecclesiastes about how there was a time to every purpose under the heaven.

And Henry, having said goodbye, went home and seemed in such serene spirits that his mother fretted over him, her wise and lovely Henry, but his father smiled a knowing, secretive smile.

'Ecclesiastes was right,' he said. 'There's a time to every purpose.'

Alex's step-grandparents were at JFK to meet her, but only after she had endured a shattering time in customs. An official wanted to open Ben's urn to ensure it did not contain cocaine or heroine, and Alex had to spill out her dead husband's passport, his wedding ring, the wallet she had given him which contained his credit cards, his death certificate and the documentation from the crematorium in Florence – which she had to scrabble in her suitcase to find – as well as her own unmistakably genuine tears before the man relented, wished her a nice day and went in search of more profitable victims. He was not entirely heartless, however, for he sent a female colleague to Alex to calm her down and help her with her suitcase which, as suitcases do at such times, was pretending it had never contained the things she had just taken out of it.

'They'd do anything, these drug traffickers,' the woman said, effortlessly repacking the case.

'Even that?' Alex said, gesturing towards the urn.

'I'm afraid so. We have to be tough.'

'Do I look like a drug trafficker?'

'Oh honey, you'd be surprised. You okay now?'

'Yes.' Alex found her strength. In spite of everything the American accent was welcoming.

The woman gathered up Ben's possessions and put them in Alex's handbag and then, ignoring Alex's feeble protests, ordered a security guard to wheel the luggage trolley out of customs.

'What happened?' Betty said as the security man touched his cap and departed.

Alex told them. Austin bristled in fury and was about to go and demand explanations when Alex stopped him.

'It's no one's fault. It's just so depressing that any-one could consider using such a way to smuggle drugs.'

Betty had been warned by Jess that a new Alex would arrive in New York, but even so she was startled. She stepped aside and witnessed further revelations.

'Oh, I didn't see you.' Alex flung her arms around her parents-in-law with total generosity.

'We wanted to make sure you were home safe,' Joan said.

'Home,' Alex said. 'Yes. Safe.' Marcus Grimaldi was there and a strange man had taken charge of her luggage.

'Alex—' Austin warned, but she had seen the photographers.

'What do you want me to say?' she asked generally. 'What do you expect of me?'

There was a clicking and Marcus Grimaldi spoke to the reporters. Then a car door was open in front of her and she found herself through it and inside, Frank and Joan next to her and Austin and Betty in seats facing them. Marcus joined them and the car moved off.

'Alex?' Marcus said to get her attention. He indicated the man sitting beside the driver, the one who had carried the luggage. 'This is Ed Turner.'

The man gave her an encouraging grin. White teeth below a huge pair of sunglasses. 'Here to protect you.'

'*Protect* me?'

'It's a wicked world, Mrs Stanford.'

Marcus leaned forward and touched Alex's hand. 'Your trustees insist, and so do I. You'll need protection at least until the fuss dies down.'

The limo swooped around a corner and stopped. Joan and Frank kissed her again and prepared to get out, explaining that their car was here.

'Listen to Marcus,' Joan said. 'He's right.'

'I will,' Alex said, dazed.

'You wouldn't prefer to stay with us in the city? Or we could go to Maine. My friends there will welcome you.'

'No. I must go and face that place. Are you going to Maine? Ben's service—'

'I'll stay in New York until then. Can we come and see you soon?'

'Oh, please. Please do that.'

'Take care of her,' Joan said to Austin and Betty and, to Alex, 'I'll call you this evening.'

The limo pulled away, and Betty sat beside Alex.

'This car is insane,' Alex stated, and Austin glanced at Marcus.

'It wasn't our idea.'

Alex leaned back in the luxurious seat and closed her eyes, trying to ignore the drag she felt around her neck. Marcus Grimaldi was kind and friendly, but had he scared Ben that day when he had summoned him to New York and told him the extent of his inheritance? Had he hinted at a lifestyle dictated by Ben's money, a lifestyle Ben would not have wanted? Had he, in fact, handed Ben the millstone? Ben had put a rock in Alex's hand and said she could have a diamond as big as it, Alex remembered. Alex had wanted no such thing, and neither did she want to go around in cars that were equally conspicuous of wealth. Well, she wouldn't in future. Think what William would say for a start!

In the meantime, she had to admit this limo was comfortable and astounded herself by falling asleep, waking only when they were driven through the gates of the mansion. There were two uniformed guards manning a barrier and as the limo slid round the side of the house another man pacing along the waterfront came into view.

'You're going to be a good girl about this, aren't you?' Marcus said. 'It's the way it's got to be.'

Alex, still half asleep, agreed numbly.

Conchita and Juan came running down the steps and, amid tears, embraced her as she got out of the car. They escorted her into the drawing-room of the mansion and a few minutes later Conchita served tea, including little cucumber and paste sandwiches.

'Like in England?' she said anxiously.

'Just like,' Alex reassured, though no such things had ever appeared at Montly.

Marcus brought her a file containing letters, opened, their envelopes efficiently stapled to them. 'You don't want to read all the mail you've been receiving,' the lawyer said. 'Alex, I promise you don't.'

'Okay,' Alex said. Jess had been opening her post at Montly because some of it was from cranks and upset her. These letters were of shocked sympathy and she put them aside, preferring to read them in private, and picked out a postcard, colourful among the rest, and turned it over. 'Oh, for heaven's sake,' she exclaimed between laughter and tears. 'Betty, Austin, you won't believe it.'

The postcard was from Maisie. She had discovered love and peace on an ashram in India. Marcus had told her the news about Ben but Alex was not to be sad: a baby boy had been born in their community on the day Ben had died and her guru had assured her it was Ben in a new karma. She would stay and watch over him and would not, therefore, be returning to the USA in the foreseeable future.

'She jumped ship,' Marcus said. 'Cunard contacted me and then Maisie did about money.'

'Wanted it for her guru, did she?' Austin growled.

'She's happy,' Alex said. 'Isn't that the most important thing?'

Betty returned the postcard to Alex. 'I think it's great. She hasn't had a lot of pleasure in her life and if she finds it there then good for her.'

Marcus got up and prepared to go. 'Now listen,' he told Alex, 'you're to be sensible about this security business. Ed Turner's in charge and you must do as he says.' He presented her with his enchanting smile and she realized he wasn't giving her a millstone, even if Ben had taken one from him. 'Don't make us worry about you. There's been a lot of publicity about Ben and the money and people out there are thinking there's an easy way to get hold of some of it.'

For the first time she understood and felt a touch of fear.

'I'll be sensible.'

'Atta girl. Come – with Ed – and see me soon. Oh, I'd almost forgotten,' he said. 'Columbia want to talk to you.'

'They do? Wonderful!'

Marcus took out a card. 'Call her, and mention him.' He scribbled a name on the back. 'Let me know how it goes.'

He was driven away in the limo and they rang Montly to report Alex's safe arrival and deliver the extraordinary news about Maisie. Soon afterwards Nancy, Mike, Christine and Rob turned up, asked to dinner by Betty.

'You'll want to be with your friends,' she said. 'We'll drop by tomorrow. Call if you need anything. *Anything.*'

'Thank you, Step-grandmamma, papa.' She kissed them, waved them goodbye and went into the drawing-room.

'Wow! Trying to break into Fort Knox is nothing on getting in here,' Nancy said. 'How are you?'

'Surviving, I think. Oh, Nance, don't cry. You'll set me off.'

'Sorry.' Nancy gulped and Alex was engulfed by Mike. His cheeks were wet, too, and Christine brought out a Kleenex.

'Why no cry?' Conchita demanded as she handed round drinks. 'Why no? It's no shame.'

So they did a bit, Conchita too until she fled muttering she had to see about dinner.

'Great to see you,' Rob said, the first to recover. 'We thought maybe you'd stay home.'

'No. I have to finish college for a start.' She looked at Nancy. 'But not at Suntan. I couldn't—'

'No,' Nancy said quickly, 'I guess you couldn't.'

Alex told them about Marcus Grimaldi and how she might go to Columbia.

'You mean you'd commute to the city and live here? Alone?' Christine said, aghast.

'I must. I must, you see. Now, when it's too late, I have to behave like a responsible married woman.'

Responsible. Ben's word.

'I think I can see that,' Nancy said into the silence that followed.

The phone rang, clicked off and rang again – Joan, as she had promised – and then Conchita called them into dinner. She had not laid a place at the head of the table and it seemed to intimidate the others, who were suddenly searching for words. They had not yet mentioned Ben's name and in here his absence was somehow more palpable. Alex – the new Alex – who missed Ben every minute of every hour of every day sought to put them at their ease by bringing him into the conversation in the most natural way she could. Practical, anyway.

'There'll be a service for Ben,' she said, 'and I want you all to read at it.'

'Read what?' Christine said nervously.

'It's a poem by Shelley.'

'He . . .' Mike's voice trailed away.

'Drowned off Italy. That's right.' Alex helped herself to some of Juan's special fish pâté and smiled thanks at Conchita.

'Is it "Adonais"?' Mike asked, making the most of the breaking ice.

'Four verses of it, one for each of you.'

'It's perfect!' Mike said.

'Are you sure?' Christine said. 'I never was much good at reciting poetry.'

'We'll put in a load of practice. It's a beautiful idea, Alex.'

'It wasn't mine, it was Henry's,' she said, pleased his choice of poem was approved of by Mike who was majoring in English literature at Harvard, no less.

'Who's he?'

Alex thought of Henry and his calm strength. 'He's my friend,' she said.

'I remember. He was at your wedding, right?'

The broken ice melted and over the rest of the meal they spoke of Ben freely and his oldest friends remembered him without embarrassment before his widow, and with much love and quite a few tears. They repaired to the drawing-room. Alex found the photocopy of 'Adonais' and Mike read Henry's selected verses to them.

'All those werts and thys,' Nancy marvelled. 'Will we really be able to do it?'

'Sure we will,' Mike said.

They talked on and Rob was about to pour

another round of drinks when Conchita put a stop to it. 'The señora tired,' she said, indicating Alex whose eyelids were sinking irresistibly. 'She have long journey and time wrong for her.'

'Never bothered me before,' Alex mumbled.

She'd only had one glass of wine, but she heard her words slurring, felt her legs not working. Something was wrong and yet seemed contrarily quite right as she was helped upstairs by Conchita, Christine and Nancy. She undressed and fell into bed.

'See you tomorrow,' Christine said, and Nancy kissed her.

She awoke early, the sun low over the Sound. Jet lag working in the other direction. She was wide awake and, as she always did in the early morning, cried for Ben, beating the pillows with her fists and demanding of God why He had taken him from her. She heard soft sounds and Conchita was holding her, murmuring comfort.

'Oh,' Alex said. 'You haven't been here all night, have you?'

'I watch over you. That Turner-man think he most important. I take care most important things.'

'Yes.' Alex looked around the room. It was familiar, yet not. 'Franklin's room,' she said.

'Is right you be here.'

'Yes,' Alex said again. It's what she and Ben should have done. Moved into the main house and

414

overpowered it. Having lived at Montly, where every bed had a history, it didn't bother her to be lying in the one Franklin had died in.

'You wan' breakfast?' Conchita asked.

'What time is it?'

'Six, almos'.'

'Conchita, it's too early! You sleep, I'll sleep. Breakfast at the proper time.'

Alex turned over and, amazingly, slept again. When she reawoke Conchita had gone. Alex showered and dressed and went downstairs. Conchita brought orange juice and coffee into the dining-room and her heart nearly broke at the sight of Alex alone at a table which could have seated twelve; she wondered if, after all, she would not be happier in the wing.

Alex, however, startled her with a smile. 'This is silly, isn't it?'

Conchita tried to shrug, but nodded instead.

'I've been thinking,' Alex went on. 'The room called the boudoir isn't far from the kitchen, is it?'

'No far,' Conchita said, seeing what her young mistress was getting at.

'We could bring the table and chairs from our dining-room in the wing and put them there. Yes?'

'I arrange,' Conchita promised. 'What egg you want? You mus' eat,' she said, as Alex began a refusal. 'I saw you last night. You push food around, play with it.'

Alex, to please her, agreed she would like a poached egg. Two arrived surrounded by crisp curls of bacon and, amazed for the second time that day, Alex ate the lot then took a cup of coffee into Franklin's study, found the priest's number and phoned him for an appointment. He was able to see her later that morning and she thanked him, put the phone down, thought for a moment, took a grip of herself, picked the phone up again and punched out the number Marcus had given her. Maria Goldberg answered about half a second into the first ring and cut through Alex's explanations, saying she knew who she was.

'How were your grades at Miami?' she asked.

'As and Bs. Mostly As. I have sixty credit hours.' She had caught up with Ben but it had gone almost unnoticed; there had been no celebrations while Franklin was dying.

'Shit!' Maria Goldberg yelled and Alex reckoned goodbye Columbia. 'Excuse me,' the woman added, 'I just dropped my doughnut. How'm I gonna get sugar outta the computer keyboard?'

'I – I don't know.'

'Someone better,' the woman snarled. 'Okay, Alex. Those grades sound pretty good.'

'You mean I'm in?' Three times amazed.

'There's the bureaucratic shit to deal with, but yes. You've got some powerful guys at your back and you're obviously not stupid.' Her voice changed suddenly, rocking Alex back on mental heels. 'You're having a tough time, I hear,' she said gently, and when Alex could not reply, 'Yeah, well let Columbia help. Come and see me and we'll discuss your courses.'

'I'll work hard, I promise. Thank you—'

But Maria Goldberg had put the phone down. After a pause for a breather, Alex rang Betty.

'Are you okay?' Betty asked.

'Fine. I seem to be into Columbia.'

'Terrific!'

'Come to lunch, Step-grandmamma.'

Brittle, Betty decided. 'If it won't be any trouble.'

'No trouble.'

'Then we'd love to.'

Alex sat in Franklin's big chair. No trouble. How could it be? She'd tell Conchita and Conchita would tell Juan, who loved to prepare good meals. But there was an awful feeling in the pit of Alex's stomach. She went into the hall of the mansion across which two men in the security guards' uniform, under Conchita's direction, were heaving a sofa. Reluctantly Conchita left them to it and went with Alex to the kitchen.

'You translate everything for Juan,' Alex told her. 'Listen, when were you last paid? For your work here?' she added as they gazed back at her without speaking.

They gesticulated wildly with their hands and insisted it was okay, but Alex finally discovered they hadn't been paid a single cent since Maisie had left.

'But what of the parties? How did you pay for them?' Those silly parties.

'Meesta Ben give money,' they explained. '*Okay.*' 'Enough?'

They muttered some more and Juan produced a notebook in which, most neatly, his expenditure was recorded. Ben had given him a few hundred dollars at intervals, these also recorded, but the two columns in no way balanced and further questioning elicited the information that much of this money had been used to pay the daily maids. Alex had asked Conchita to get them to do extra hours and the idea of paying them had never crossed her mind. What children they had been two months, a lifetime, ago!

Still Conchita and Juan kept insisting it was okay, okay, Meesta Franklin Stanford had left them money, and it became more embarrassing and precarious until Alex said, 'It's my fault, see? Not Ben's. He didn't understand about these things, but as his wife I should have done.'

(Although he had: at least he'd thought to give them money. Alex forced herself not to think of their simple life in Miami, their shopping together.)

'I'm sorry,' she said, and could see their resistance crumbling, 'I have to go out, but when I get back I want to know how much I owe you – for this and your wages.'

She told Juan there would be two extra for lunch and was on her way back to the study when Ed Turner waylaid her. He wanted her to meet the security staff, he said, and led her into a space which she recalled had been used as a storage area. There was now a television screen presided over by a man in uniform.

'There's a lot of sophisticated equipment out there,' Ed said, 'or there will be when we get it all in place. But it's still operated by humans. Look at the faces of these guys and not the uniforms. This here is Bernie.'

'Hi,' Bernie said, taking his eyes away from the screen for a second or two.

'Am I really in danger?' Alex asked as Ed Turner took her to the man guarding the waterfront.

'Ma'am, I have no idea, but you ain't going to spoil my good record by getting anything nasty happening to you.'

Half an hour later he delivered her back to the mansion. She felt humbled by the hard work and the good will of the men who were protecting her and, although she did not know it, they were being that much more alert having met her.

'Are we going out?' Ed asked.

'Yes. To see the priest and I want to buy a plane ticket.' Henry's presence, in spite of the friendliness, absolutely imperative.

'Which motor are we going in?'

'The Nissan.'

'I'll bring it round.'

'I'm driving,' Alex warned. 'I know the way.'

'Ma'am,' Ed Turner said, patting a bulge under his jacket, 'you're welcome to drive. I need hands and eyes for other things.'

She was not a prisoner, Alex told herself. She would be sensible. She went into the study and called Marcus Grimaldi to make sure she could withdraw a substantial amount of cash from either her own or Ben's and her joint account and why. He said she could and she didn't need to ask about every minor thing.

'I only wanted to know if the money was there,' she said. 'And it's not minor to Conchita and Juan.'

'I stand reproved,' he responded, a laugh in his voice, and she remembered what she had to ask him on her father's behalf. Time for that later, though. She told him about her conversation with Maria Goldberg and he promised to deal with the bureaucratic side.

She rang off and gazed around the room. The desk was a good size and the view over the Sound nice, but the decor was unappealing. She'd be spending a lot of time in here, doing her course work and running the house; she would redecorate it, she decided.

Out in the hall an armchair was being borne one way and dining chairs were arguing passage through the door into the wing with the two daily maids bearing Alex's clothes.

Conchita bustled her out of the front door. 'You go. Fixed when you back.'

Ed Turner opened the driver's door of the red Nissan.

Sensible, responsible, Alex told herself, getting in.

The priest had known Ben well and they had a long, satisfying talk. It would be a memorial service followed by an interment, he said, and they arranged a date and time. He would visit her before then to discuss details. She thanked him and drove Ed to the printers the priest had recommended and Alex found the decisions she had to make about everything – from the typeface to be used on the service sheet to the number she should order and whether Ben should be Ben Stanford or Franklin Benjamin Stanford III altogether too much. She took samples of print and wording away with her. Joan and Frank would want consulting, and Betty and Austin might know about numbers. And should she, as the woman at the printers suggested, send out cards announcing the service? The USA wasn't like Britain where the same newspapers were read all over the country.

'Are you okay to drive, ma'am?' Ed said quietly, putting a large hand on hers.

'Yes.' She shook away the tears and started the car. 'And please call me Alex.'

'Then, little lady, you can call me Ed.'

The mansion seemed to welcome her when she arrived back. It was alive and sparkling and flowers were everywhere. There was a gardener, Alex realized, more than one maybe. Had he or they been paid by Juan and Conchita too?

She admired the way the boudoir had been converted into a charming dining-room then, an idea taking hold, went into the great drawing-room. Yes, it would do.

Followed by a mystified Conchita, Alex led the way into the wing. No ghost awaited her: she and Ben had hardly lived here. She would have to get their things sent up from where they were in store in Miami. That was one place she did not want to return to; perhaps Nancy would arrange it.

'Here,' she said, stopping before the portraits of her and Ben. She climbed on to a chair and took them off the wall, handing them carefully down to Conchita. She carried Ben's and Conchita hers. As they manoeuvred them through the connecting door Conchita called loudly and Juan and Ed came running. Conchita babbled at Juan, who hustled Ed into the drawing-room. After much effort they removed the huge painting above the fireplace, and it was hard to judge which of the three of them was the most disappointed on seeing the pale oblong revealed. Ed Turner gazed at them, at the portraits propped against a table's legs and then at the wall.

'Hell, it's only paint,' he said. 'I got a cousin who's a genius with the stuff. He'll mix the colour so you'll never notice the difference.'

'When could he come?' Alex asked.

'Right now. You met him this morning. He's a security man like me.' He grinned at her, unhooked his radio, spoke into it and listened to the crackly voice on the other end. 'All set,' he said. 'Mr and

Mrs Mitchell are at the gate and he's hitching a ride with them.'

He and Juan went out and Alex grabbed Conchita before she could escape.

'Has Juan added up the money I owe you?'

He had, Alex could tell. She held out her hand and Conchita plunged her own into her apron pocket, thrust a piece of paper at Alex and ran to open the door to Betty and Austin. Alex glanced at the paper. Meticulously itemized, it revealed that Conchita and Juan had spent nearly two thousand dollars of their own money; their wages were on top of that. Austin and Betty had lots of advice to offer about the service sheet and, yes, Alex should certainly order cards. Austin sketched a plan to show how Ben's proper names and the one he had been known by could both be accommodated and Alex, liking it, said she would show it to Joan and Frank tomorrow.

'There's something else wrong,' Betty said. 'You promised you'd tell me. What is it?'

They had finished lunch and Conchita was out of earshot. Alex told them about the awful debt and showed them Juan's paper. 'I feel so guilty,' she whispered.

'Think how much worse it would have been if they'd had to ask you,' Betty said prosaically. 'You've taken hold of the issue on your first day in charge. I'd guess they're pretty impressed. No way is it your fault, Alex. Maisie should have told you what to do before she went away.'

Alex's spirits rose. It was true, and until yesterday it had been assumed that Maisie would be coming back.

Nancy, Donna and Christine appeared in the afternoon; they had brought their tennis things and how about a game? They played and swam, then went to the drawing-room to see how Ed Turner's cousin was getting on. Alex gasped in delight for the oblong was hardly visible. Duane Turner was on a stepladder holding a hair drier. He switched it off, backed down the ladder and examined his work.

'Unconventional,' he commented, 'but it'll do, hey?'

'It's brilliant,' Alex said. 'Can we hang the pictures now?'

Duane Turner had Donna and Nancy hold the pictures up, demanding they move them an inch one way and then another. When he was satisfied he hammered hooks into the tiny marks he had asked them to make and hung the portraits himself. Nancy and Donna rubbed their sore arm muscles while Duane Turner cleared away his paraphernalia and came to join them.

'Now if I could paint like that,' he said softly, gazing at Alex and Ben as they gazed back at him, 'I wouldn't need no job as a security man, would I?'

The portraits had been at home in the apartment in Miami but seemed to have grown to fit this room. It was extraordinary.

'Who did 'em?' Duane asked, still gazing.
'My mother,' Alex said.

Chapter Thirteen

FOR THE FOURTH TIME THE taxi driver stopped to ask the way. This time he grunted with satisfaction, gunned the motor of his ancient yellow cab, then slowed down and indicated right.

'No more'n a mile,' he said over his shoulder.

She had rejected two drivers at La Guardia airport since they had insisted the place she wanted to go was in New York City, and two others had rejected her before she had come to an arrangement with this man. He had, early on in their journey, drawn back the screen between him and his passenger and they'd had conversations ranging from Winston Churchill's policies during the Second World War to the number of Hispanics in the States these days. Now, though, he was silent, and Elizabeth Wendover was glad of it.

Was she right to appear unannounced? She had vacillated all morning, half hoping for an invitation, trying to dare herself to pick up the phone, dial the number she had already memorized and ask for one. Then after lunch she had come to a decision. Her daughter had returned to America alone, so the newspapers said. She had sent that unequivocal message from Italy via Emily Glover. Of course Elizabeth should go to her! She phoned David and explained.

'But I can't get away today,' he'd said, miserably anxious for her.

'It will be all right.'

'What if it isn't? Elizabeth, what will you do?'

'Come back. David, I'll ring Meredith but will you make more profound apologies for my absence tonight?'

He had said he would, returned from his office, made sure she had plenty of money and had driven her to the airport and kissed her and held her as though she was going away for years.

'Phone me,' he murmured into her ear. 'I'll be frantic until you do.'

'It'll be all right,' she insisted.

That optimism had sustained her until this moment, when the cab swung left into a gateway and was halted at a barrier. Two uniformed men came forward and Elizabeth and the cab driver wound down their windows.

'I'm here to see Alexandra Stanford,' Elizabeth said.

'You expected?'

'No. No, I'm not.'

The man bent and looked at her closely. A slow grin spread across his face.

'Ma'am,' he said, 'do you paint pictures?'

Startled she admitted she did.

'Tell me who you are so my boss'll let you through.'

'Elizabeth Wendover.'

'More.'

'Alex's mother.'

He grinned again, stood upright and spoke into his radio.

'Taxi,' he said, in response to some query. 'Yeah, yeah, okay . . . Jeez, Ed, there's no doubt about it. Hey, why don't we give the little lady a surprise?'

Elizabeth sat there in a state of bemused, excited shock. Alex must have spoken of her then. She was right to have come. How happy David would be for her! Her friendly cab driver had his licence checked and his photograph compared to the real thing, and the man who had known who she was got into the front seat, told the driver to follow the road and slewed round to face her.

'Your painting and mine are on the same wall,' he said.

'Are they?' she managed. She was wondering whether she should pay the driver off. But what if it was disastrous and she had to hang around while another cab was called? That would be dreadful. She asked her driver to wait.

'You want a coffee and a sandwich, man?' the guard asked him.

'Okay,' the driver said, overwhelmed by the size of the place – as, indeed, Elizabeth was as she stepped out of the cab. A cool breeze blew off the water beyond the lawns, a blessed relief after the humidity of Washington. The guard ran up the steps of the house and rang the doorbell, touched his cap, wished her a nice evening and got back into the cab.

The door opened and Elizabeth walked forward. The dark-skinned woman in maid's uniform gaped at her, then raised her hands to her mouth to cover an incredulous, delighted laugh. Another security man in the hall simply stood and gazed at her.

'I'm Mrs Wendover. I would like to see Alex, if that's possible.'

The maid, her eyes still round, took Elizabeth's overnight bag and led her towards a great pair of doors. She opened one and ushered Elizabeth in.

'Señora—' she began.

A blonde girl stood up and turned around. Behind her was her own portrait, the one in which she seemed about to recognize someone and speak. She hesitated for a moment, her blue eyes widening as the maid's brown ones had done, then 'It's you,' she said. 'It's you, isn't it?'

Conchita closed the door and Alex stared at her mother.

'But you're beautiful,' she said.

'So are you,' said Elizabeth, but thinking: with shadows under her eyes and too thin; no wonder after what she had been through. And: how quickly a long-undisturbed maternal spirit awakens and wants to go into action. And again: how instant and committed the love.

She crossed the vast room and stopped about three feet from where Alex, still staring, was standing. None of her experience as a diplomat's wife could help her here. What was the next move?

It came from Alex, and from a most unexpected angle. 'I'm sorry,' she said.

'*Sorry?* What for?'

'I got everything wrong. Daddy only told me the other day how he – then I discovered what Nanny had done. The lies she had told me. I believed her. I believed—'

'Oh darling, what does it matter now?'

And her daughter was in her arms.

'I rang you in England after I found out, but you'd already left.'

'That was a shame.'

'I was writing to you.' One of Alex's arms jerked backwards, and over her shoulder Elizabeth could see paper strewn around where she had been sitting. 'I don't have your phone number in Washington. Would the letter have reached you if I'd addressed it to the British Embassy?'

'It would, but you don't have to bother about that any more, do you?'

'No.'

Elizabeth carefully pushed her away. 'Let me look at you.'

Shyly, Alex met her mother's eyes. 'Ben wanted

this so much. I wish you could have met him.'

'So do I, Alex.' She glanced up at her portrait of her son-in-law and silently she thanked him. He had made this moment and was so horribly not here. A shadow clouded her happiness, except happiness was too small a word for what she was feeling. There was a tug at her arm and Elizabeth, allowing her daughter to turn her, saw their joint reflections in a large, ornate mirror. It is hard to recognize yourself in another face but side by side in the mirror the resemblance was striking. No longer did Elizabeth marvel at the reaction of the man at the gate and the maid who had let her in.

She told Alex about it and out of a kind of nervousness, needing conversation, asked what kind of painting the man on the gate did. Alex was explaining when the maid entered bearing a tray of drinks.

'This is Conchita,' Alex said, and, 'Conchita, this is my mother.'

'I can tell.' Conchita put the tray down. 'Your taxi-man still here,' she told Elizabeth. 'Want to know what he do.'

A moment of tension, Conchita feeling it most of all since she had precipitated the decision that now had to be made.

'Do you have to go?' Alex stammered. 'Please stay the night if you would like to.'

'I would, Alex. Thank you. I'd better pay the driver.'

'I take you,' Conchita said, unable to keep a smile from her face.

Elizabeth followed the maid from the room and Alex's voice followed them both. 'You won't go, will you? You really will stay?'

Elizabeth stopped and looked back. Her daughter so tiny in a vast room.

'I won't be long.'

Alex gestured to the tray. 'I'll make you a drink. What would you like?'

'Is there a dry white wine?'

'Yes! Yes, there *is!*' For some reason Alex laughed.

She is lonely, Elizabeth fretted to herself. Naturally, newly widowed. But what was she doing in this ridiculous house? It was even bigger than Elizabeth had first thought, she realized, as Conchita conducted her across the hall, through another door and into a corridor which led to the kitchen where the taxi driver was waiting. Elizabeth paid him, adding a generous tip, and the man thanked her and was escorted out by a guard. Conchita then introduced Elizabeth to her husband – the real reason, she knew immediately, for her being brought here; the driver could easily have been summoned to the drawing-room. As his wife had done he threw up his hands and exclaimed at the likeness between her and Alex; he invited Conchita to remark upon how even more beautiful their young senora would be as she grew older and enquired eagerly how long this senora would be staying as he could see at a glance that here was a woman who would appreciate the best he could cook.

'He say it is good you come here to be with our Alex,' Conchita translated, not for a moment considering that Elizabeth might speak Spanish.

She found her way back to the drawing-room. Alex was on the phone, apparently putting off an engagement for later that night. Elizabeth felt some concern but Alex smiled at her, put down the phone and said, with much less shyness in her voice, 'That was Nancy. She's longing to meet you.'

'Were you supposed to be going out with her? Alex—'

'I didn't want to. It was only for a drink where a crowd of us meet up. I'd forgotten to tell Ed Turner anyway, and' – a dreadful lost look – 'I wouldn't have enjoyed it.' She braced herself. 'Here's your wine. It's what I drink. Do you suppose it's in the genes?'

'I'm sure it is,' Elizabeth replied gravely. She sipped the wine and raised her eyebrows. 'Our genes have excellent taste. It's a white Burgundy, isn't it?'

'I've no idea,' Alex confessed, and went to the bottle to check. 'It *is!*' she said. 'How did you know?'

Elizabeth laughed at her. 'Come here.'

Her daughter sat beside her, a vital six inches of space between them. Elizabeth picked up her right hand. 'It's the ring I sent you from Japan. And the matching bracelet.'

'I found everything you gave me and brought them here.' With her free hand Alex showed Elizabeth the chain she was wearing around her neck. 'It was Ben's very first present to me.'

'They all match!'

'Something moves in mysterious ways, doesn't it?'

There were other more palpable miracles for Elizabeth to savour as she listened to Alex's chatter, Ben's name in every sentence, jumping from subject to subject. She wasn't relaxed – nowhere near it – but she was trying terribly hard. And soon Elizabeth had other worries.

'Alex,' she said into a momentary silence, 'may I use the phone? I have to ring Dav – my husband.'

'Yes, of course.' Alex stood up so abruptly that she spilled her drink. 'There's one here, or in the study. You'll want to be private. I must go and change so you'll be as private as you want. Use this one. It'll be more comfortable.'

Elizabeth stood too and took Alex's hands in hers. 'It's sure to be a bit awkward at first. How could it be anything else? Alex, I have a husband and his name is David.'

'Wicked Uncle David,' Alex whispered, attempting a joke.

'He still calls himself that.'

'Does he?'

'He'll be so thrilled I'm here with you. He made me promise to ring him. He's at a party and he'll be waiting for my call.'

'Then call him.' Alex twisted away. She was crying, and suddenly Elizabeth realized what an appalling gaff she had made. Alex had had a husband who had cared for her – possibly – as much as David, anxious in Washington, cared for Elizabeth.

'I understand,' she said. 'I'm sorry. You cry, darling. Cry away.'

Eventually Alex's sobs subsided. She began to apologize, saying she really must go and change and Elizabeth was to ring David.

'Why change?' Elizabeth said, holding her tighter.

'For dinner. It was Franklin's law.'

'I have nothing to change into. I didn't dare, you see, bring extra clothes.'

'Didn't dare? That's silly.'

'It might seem so now, but it didn't then.'

'You can wear my clothes,' Alex said. 'Easily you could.'

'If we really have to change for dinner then I suppose I must.'

Was this how mothers of teenage girls were supposed to behave? Elizabeth didn't have a clue.

Alex said she would go and look something out while her mother made her phone call. She hesitated and then added, 'Would David like to come here for the weekend?'

'I suspect he'd like to a lot. I'll ask him.'

Which meant she'd be spending more than one night here. This was unreal. Alex went out and

Elizabeth dialled the number of the minister's house in Washington. The dinner party tonight was a 'fun' one, but even so she did not want to cause too much disruption. She gave her name to a servant and no many seconds later Meredith Duke was on the line as apparently scatty as she had been any time these past twelve years in spite of her current status as wife of the British chargé d'affaires. She and her husband had overlapped with the Wendovers at the embassy in Madrid, soon after David and Elizabeth had been married when Elizabeth had been commuting to England in the hope of winning over her daughter. It was appropriate they should be in at the end of the story whose beginnings they had witnessed.

'Darling!' Meredith screamed down the phone. 'Tell me, tell me! David has this moment arrived. He's been at the Saudi Embassy, poor love, and is sprinting to the phone with a huge gin and tonic. Quick, tell me! Is it all right?'

'Yes!'

'Oh wonderful,' Meredith breathed, then David was on the line.

'Elizabeth?'

'David, she's lovely. Lovely but so very sad. She's asked me to stay—'

'Then you must. Elizabeth, don't cry about it.'

'Sorry. Reaction. I didn't bring enough clothes and she's upstairs finding things of hers. She wants you to come for the weekend.'

436

'*She* wants me to come?'

'So do I, of course, but it was her idea.'

He was silent.

'David?'

'I'm pinching myself. Aren't you?'

'It isn't a dream.'

'Then would you accept her kind invitation?'

'I will. I must go to her now. You'll explain my absence in Washington, won't you? People will understand.'

'They will. Already I hear Meredith spreading our splendid news.'

'Talk to you tomorrow. See you on Friday.'

Elizabeth put the phone down. 'See you on Friday.' So easy to say. Again she looked at her portrait of Ben. He, presumably, had said something similar and Alex had never seen him again. How carefully one must live one's life.

Conchita was hovering in the hall, waiting to show Elizabeth to her room. Elizabeth thanked her in Spanish and made some comment about the house. It was intolerable she and Juan should talk across her again without knowing she understood.

'You speak our language,' Conchita said. 'That will please Juan. I've put you in a room next to the little señora's. She screams in her sleep. She has nightmares, I think.' She sighed. 'It is hardly surprising.'

The room was enormous, had a bathroom attached and was connected to Alex's. Alex came in carrying a dress, two skirts and a selection of tops. They would all suit Elizabeth, if they fit her – and they did.

They ate a delicious dinner in a reassuringly cosy room. Elizabeth learned how Alex was going to change colleges and her major and longed to ask her daughter why she planned to live in this great house, as she evidently did. Ben in every sentence, who had left his wife a path to follow, had laid down the path Elizabeth had trod this momentous day. Ben who had been the best husband anyone could have wanted, though there was a hint at difficulties which had something to do with why he had gone to Italy without Alex.

'He had to tame the millstone,' Alex said.

Elizabeth would find out what it meant when Alex felt like telling her. And she understood why Alex had to live here. To dispose of the responsibility would be easy, and Elizabeth's daughter was not someone who would run away.

They finished dinner and returned to the drawing-room.

'Mummy,' Alex began. 'Mummy—' tasting the word.

'Yes?' Elizabeth, suffering a sudden attack of vertigo, sat down in the nearest chair. It wasn't a dream, but she needed something solid beneath her to convince her.

'Would you do a painting of me and Ben

together? There are lots of photographs.'

'Please, may I? I want to.' Both standing, Ben slightly behind, perhaps, showing Alex the way ahead . . . no, that would involve boring details about clothes and differing heights. Head and shoulders would produce the same effect anyway. 'I want to,' she said again.

'I can't draw. That isn't in the genes.'

'Who can tell where it comes from? No one else in my family ever drew or painted.'

'Your family? Mine too, then. Who is there?'

'A few second cousins, you have a great aunt and uncle and there are more distant cousins.'

'I'd like to meet them. Are they in England?'

'At the last count they were.'

Conchita brought in coffee. She was exhausted, Elizabeth noticed, could scarcely suppress a yawn. Elizabeth's astonishing daughter noticed it too.

'Go to bed, Conchita,' she said. '*You* can't have had much sleep last night and you've been rushing around all day.'

'I'm okay.'

'You're not. You're out on your feet.' Alex touched the woman's arm. 'Bed. Good night, Conchita, and thank you.'

'And please thank Juan for the dinner,' Elizabeth added. 'It was excellent.'

'He was embarrassed tonight because it was short notice. Tomorrow he'll show you what he can really do.'

'*Madre de Dios!* Then I look forward to to-morrow.'

Conchita gestured. 'Our little one is also tired. Excited and happy, as much as she can be in the circumstances, but under it she is tired.'

'I'll take care of her. Good night, Conchita.'

'Good night, señora.'

Alex stared at her mother as Conchita went out. 'You speak Spanish?' she said, impressed. 'What else can you do?'

'Not a lot. Except suggest that you too might be ready for bed.'

'Soon.' Alex stood up, her coffee cup in her hand, and paced around. 'I don't remember, you see. Since Daddy told me I've been trying to work it out. I don't remember you not being at Montly before you went away with . . . David.'

'I lived in Eastbourne for a while, and saw you every day. We went on lots of expeditions together. Don't you remember those?'

'No.'

'Then I left you at Montly. I didn't want to disrupt you too much. I didn't have anywhere to take you and thought you'd be safe until I'd sorted myself out. It never occurred to me . . . Alex, I can blame your father for many things, but I've always known who to blame for what went wrong with you. It was my fault too. I had met David and perhaps I wasn't concentrating properly. I thought you would be safe,' she repeated.

'Did Nanny know what Daddy had done?'

'She knew.'

Silence, then: 'I told Henry I'd forgive her if you would.'

'Henry?' Elizabeth interpolated quickly, to forestall the question she did not want to answer.

'Henry Glover.'

'Small and serious Henry. You used to play with him.'

'He's not small now.'

'Is he serious?'

'Sometimes. With Ben gone he's my best friend.'

'It's good to have one of those.'

'Yes . . . Can you ever forgive her? Nanny, I mean?'

'Since I doubt she will ask me to,' Elizabeth said carefully, 'I don't think the problem arises. I suspect you should, though. What's the point of not?'

'It can't be the same.'

'No. That is true.'

Alex stopped her pacing and sat on the arm of Elizabeth's chair. Elizabeth edged over and Alex slid in beside her.

'Were you very upset about Daddy's affair?'

'I was at the time, but marriages can go wrong and your father's and mine already had. He and Jess are happy with their children, and I can't imagine being married to anyone but David.' She stroked Alex's hair. 'You met him, Alex. You met him and you liked him. At first.'

'I simply don't remember.'

'Then you began screaming. My God, how you screamed!'

Elizabeth was smiling and Alex did too. 'I remember that.'

Her eyelids began to droop and Elizabeth was able to exert the maternal authority unused for so many years. 'Bed,' she said.

Her daughter came quietly, undressed herself with the charming modesty of the very young child – but only because of her sleepiness, Elizabeth thought – and even had to be reminded to clean her teeth. She climbed into bed. 'I've forgotten my pills,' she said.

'Pills? What pills?'

'In the bathroom cabinet. Or my wash bag, maybe. To help me sleep. I don't need to take the other sort any more, do I?'

'Do you need these, though?'

'I don't expect so. I don't think I did last night.'

Like a young child she held out her arms. Elizabeth bent, felt them about her and kissed her daughter good night.

'I'm glad you're here,' Alex said. And: 'I'm sorry.'

Elizabeth waited until she was sure Alex was asleep, then crept into the bathroom to find the bottle of pills and took charge of it. She left the door between their rooms open, but Alex did not cry out in the night.

*

A flurry of visitors the next day: Nancy, Alex's friend, too overwhelmed to comment on the likeness between Alex and Elizabeth but her constant wondering glances were speaking; Frank and Joan Stanford came for lunch and there were sober discussions about the service for Ben as the wording for the sheets and the cards was finalized; more friends of Alex's turned up in the afternoon, Alex's loving friends who wanted her to go for a sail, play tennis, swim. Whatever she liked.

Sailing was forbidden, though. Ed Turner had taken Elizabeth aside and reported that they'd caught a man trying to get into grounds the previous night. The guy, he said, was a harmless crackpot well known to the police – just the kind, in fact, they could have ordered to test the systems – but it proved Marcus Grimaldi hadn't over-reacted by taking all these precautions. Elizabeth agreed fervently and was then invited into the kitchen to talk over menus with Juan. She demurred at first but Juan said – and again Elizabeth could only agree – that the little señora needed time before she could deal with such important matters and went on to describe dishes of such delicacy that Elizabeth, who had only just finished breakfast, began to feel hungry. When she told Juan that her husband would be coming for the weekend the chef's eyes glowed with a fanatic fire that boded ill for David's waistline. She escaped from the kitchen and Duane Turner was lying in wait for her: could he bring some of his paintings to show her? They were lousy, but he'd appreciate her honest comments. She had to agree to that as well. She was, she realized, being knitted into the fabric of this establishment and one part of her could only find it a joy beyond words or thought – as she went to where Alex and Nancy were lazing by the pool and Alex ran to greet her and settled her in the chair she had arranged for her – while another part worried about Washington, her duties there and Alex rattling around here on her own. David would have ideas about that, she knew; and so she gave herself to the joy that only twenty-four hours ago had seemed the remotest of possibilities.

Joy, except for the dreadful shadow of Ben's death, his parents so dazed and sad and Alex's care of them so moving. She took them to see the portraits in their new surroundings and when they emerged it was obvious Joan Stanford had been crying. Nancy melted tactfully away, saying she would be back this afternoon, and Elizabeth instinctively put an arm around her daughter's mother-in-law.

'Alex says you're going to do one of them together,' the woman said. 'Would it be too much to ask if you'd do one for us?'

'Of course not.' How could anything be too much?

'She tried to explain why you're here. I didn't get it all but she said it's because of Ben. Is that true?'

'He made her write to me. It's . . . it's a long story

but, yes, I'm here because of Ben. I'm awfully sorry,' she went on awkwardly. 'He was a most special young man. I have everything to thank him for and I'm so sad I never met him.'

'He was special.'

After lunch Elizabeth scotched Alex's plan to rush off to the printers, saying the designs were completed, Alex would have to take a guard so the guard may as well go on his own. Alex consented, her friends arrived and Elizabeth forbade any idea of sailing with such finality that no one questioned her as to why.

'Tennis, then,' the boy who was obviously attached to Nancy said. 'Alex, we'll take 'em on.'

'No. You play with Nancy.' She turned to her mother. 'You partner me. You can play tennis.'

'Can I?'

'You can do anything!'

She tried to persuade Joan and Frank to join in but Frank, feeling the effects of the wine he had drunk on top of Conchita's Martinis, said he would stay where he was and maybe take a nap and Joan that she hadn't the energy to play but would watch.

'Aren't Ben's friends wonderful?' Joan said as she and Elizabeth followed the young people towards the courts. 'Aren't they just wonderful?'

Ben's friends, Elizabeth reflected as, obedient to a call from Alex to change, she left Joan and went into the house. It was odd how the round world was full of different angles.

She and Alex, in spite of the best efforts of their opponents, lost their match after a tiebreak in the third set and came off the court to find two more spectators sitting beside Joan on the wooden bench beyond the fence. They stood when Alex ran to greet them.

'Austin and Betty Mitchell,' Alex said as Elizabeth approached. 'Jess's parents.'

'Well!' Betty said. 'We don't need to be told who you are.'

Elizabeth pushed her hair off her sweaty forehead. She was glad she was wearing a knee-length skirt and not the shorts Alex had proposed.

'I've met your grandchildren, I believe,' she said.

'It was a beautiful painting you did,' Austin Mitchell said. 'Jess sent us a photograph of it.'

'Could we,' Elizabeth asked Alex, 'go to the house and ask Conchita for a cup of tea?'

Alex nodded, bewildered by why her mother should need permission. Behind them another game of tennis had started.

'You stay with your guests,' Elizabeth said gently.

'All right.'

Elizabeth looked back as she walked away with Austin, Betty and Joan. The red-haired girl had her arm around Alex and her tennis partner was handing her a Coke.

Ben's friends, Alex's friends. They were wonderful, no doubt about it.

*

446

Conchita would bring tea out to the terrace, she informed Elizabeth. Joan went to collect Frank and a silence descended upon the other three as the peculiarity of their situation hit them simultaneously. Elizabeth had once been married to the man who was now their son-in-law; their daughter had been more of a mother to Alex than Elizabeth had ever been; Elizabeth could tell, though they did nothing to show it, that they considered her a deserting mother. The severity of her punishment undeserved, perhaps, but a deserting mother nonetheless. If Richard had made his confession to Jess she had not shared it with her parents. And if he hadn't, why the bloody hell not? She had thought her anger with Richard was long past and was astounded at its resurgent strength.

'Alex is a whole lot better today,' Betty said finally. 'A different girl from the one we met at JFK.'

'You've been very kind to her, I gather,' Elizabeth said, pleased her voice sounded normal.

'She was alone and in trouble. We tried to help.'

'What trouble?' And this time the voice was sharp.

'She – she had got hold of a strange notion about Ben. It was nonsense,' Betty said hurriedly as Joan and Frank appeared and Conchita arrived with the tea.

'Why did Ben live with his grandfather?' Elizabeth asked Alex later. 'Didn't he get on with his parents?'

'Oh, he did, but he didn't like New York. He liked the outdoor life so he spent most of his time here. The people who didn't get on were Frank and his father. Frank quarrelled with Franklin or vice versa and that's why Franklin left everything to Ben, why I've got it. It's a bit embarrassing when you think it should belong to Frank and Joan – this place, the money – but there's nothing I can do about it. Not until I'm twenty-one, anyway.'

'What will you do then?'

'Give Frank his and Daddy's stupid company, for a start. It's not very healthy, Ben said.' Alex shrugged. 'You may as well know: Daddy's not very healthy either, financially.'

Elizabeth had to suppress a gasp of shock, astonishment and dismay when she heard about the other things Richard had divulged along with his pathetic affair with Nellie and Nanny Mountfield's lies, but Alex – a woman tonight and not a child – exclaimed impatiently, as she had to Henry, 'It doesn't matter. Ben and I wanted to be married. Daddy helped it happen. So what?'

All right, but as Henry had done Elizabeth thought of Jess. Richard hadn't changed at all! Still manipulating, still chasing rainbows . . .

'Mummy,' Alex said, and again Elizabeth's stomach lurched at the word.

'Darling?'

'Did Betty and Austin tell you about' – she gave a wry grimace – 'about my silly imaginings?'.

'No. They hinted at something, though. They said you were in trouble. Were you?'

'I thought so. Have you wondered why Ben went to Italy with Clint and not with me?'

'Yes.' Elizabeth, at least, was going to be truthful with Alex. They were in her room, selecting a dress for Elizabeth to wear to honour the extraordinary meal Juan had promised for tonight. Alex sat on the bed, pulled her mother down beside her and related the events of her night of crisis and doubt.

'It was nonsense,' she said when she had finished.

'That's how Betty and Austin described it.'

'They don't quite believe that, and neither does Jess. We had problems, Ben and I. We were young and ignorant' – Alex as though she was neither of those things now. 'And then the millstone. Mummy, I want you to read Ben's letter to me. I want you to be sure.'

Alex got up, opened a drawer in the dressing table and brought out a spiral-bound notebook. 'Read it,' she said.

She went into her bathroom to shower and Elizabeth opened Alex's letter from Italy. Ten minutes later Alex appeared, her hair wet and wrapped in a towel. The notebook was closed on her mother's lap.

'It was only the way you described him to me last night,' Elizabeth said, close to tears. 'It was how I was going to paint him.'

'Tell the others.' Alex put the book back in the

drawer. 'Tell them how he grew up before I did, how if I have any strength it comes from him . . . how they were *wrong*. Grew up,' she added, 'disposed of the millstone and then died, as though there was nothing left on earth for him to do. Henry says he is with Jesus. Do you believe that?'

'Yes,' Elizabeth said firmly.

A soul like Ben's could only be in the best place.

David arrived amid a thunderstorm the next evening. He would, he said, hire a car at La Guardia and, yes, he would bring her clothes and with Elizabeth's directions and a bit of ingenuity he reckoned he could get to where she was, provided the security men were briefed to let him in.

Because of the storm Elizabeth and Alex heard neither the car nor the doorbell, and two blondes stood and turned to him as Conchita showed him into the drawing-room. He hesitated a moment, wonder dawning in his eyes, and then walked rapidly towards them.

'Well,' he said. 'Well! One is my wife and the other my stepdaughter, and I think I can tell – just about – which is which.' He kissed Elizabeth and then, as though it was entirely natural, kissed Alex too.

'Hello,' he said.

'Hello.'

He put a finger under her chin and gently tilted her face up. 'It's Wicked Uncle David in the flesh,' he said, smiling teasingly down at her and Elizabeth stiffened, worried he was pushing too hard too soon. 'How about a good scream, for old time's sake?'

But Alex smiled back, took the hand that was under her chin and retained it. 'You know I don't think that any more, and I'm too old to scream.'

'You're a lovely girl. Your mother still has the edge on you, mind, but in another twenty years or so you might beat her in a beauty competition.'

Alex glanced at Elizabeth.

'I doubt it.' She squeezed his hand. 'Thank you for coming, David.'

The last hurdle cleared, simply stepped over. As though to provide punctuation, a gigantic exclamation mark to end the years of separation and misjustice, an almighty clap of thunder sounded above their heads and a streak of lightning seemed to zizz around the room. Rain powered on to the gravel on the drive.

David, having been notified by Elizabeth of Franklin's law, changed into a black tie for dinner. It was superb, and at its conclusion he asked – in response to one of those telepathic signals between him and Elizabeth which always worked and neither could understand why – if he could congratulate the chef in person. Conchita rushed to fetch Juan, who entered bearing a bottle of brandy, the label of which made David catch his breath.

'You have one too,' David told him as Juan

reverently opened it. 'It's the least a man who cooked such a meal deserves.'

Juan poured brandy into the glasses Conchita produced. 'I knew,' he remarked, 'the husband of such a señora would appreciate this.'

'So would the señora herself. Sit down. Let's all have some.'

They spoke in a mixture of Spanish and English so as not to exclude Alex, but Juan manoeuvred it so he could have a man-to-man conversation with David, enticing him with an invitation to tour the wine cellars in the morning.

'Señor Stanford was a difficult old man,' Juan announced, 'but he was knowledgeable about wine and, until he became ill, he appreciated good food. A worthy man to cook for. A chef needs that, for his pride.'

Oh Lord, David thought, seeing what was coming. 'Alex is young,' he ventured cautiously, 'but I'm sure you can educate her. What would she do without you?'

'But is she going to live here?' Juan said, abandoning his high horse. 'We hear rumours, but are told nothing.'

'Yes, she's going to live here. She'll be studying at Columbia. She should have spoken to you—'

'She's had more important things on her mind,' Juan interrupted. 'We will stay then, naturally. You have no need to be concerned. We will look after our little señora for as long as she needs us.'

'Thank you,' David said, grateful for Elizabeth's sake and, he was surprised to discover, on his own behalf as well. When he had kissed Alex she had kissed him back, which was why he had dared to tease her. Meeting him can't have been easy but she had coped with enormous dignity, the poor child. He had programmed himself to like her and found it took no effort. He felt protective.

'Señor Stanford was good to us,' Juan continued, 'and we saw Ben grow from a boy to a big, strong man.' He crossed himself. 'So very sad, and our little señora so brave. Be assured, señor, we will look after her.'

'Thank you,' David said again, knitted in.

Conchita and not Elizabeth had escorted David to their room earlier because Elizabeth had feared another backlash of emotion from Alex and had stayed with her. Now she surveyed the luggage he had brought with him from Washington.

'It must be my entire wardrobe,' she said. 'And my painting gear. David, what can you have been thinking of?'

'You.' They were both speaking in low voices. The door to Alex's room was closed and Elizabeth had been with her until she slept, but they did not want to wake her. David took his wife in his arms, kissed her properly, then set her aside and undid his bow tie.

'You're going to stay here until Alex begins

453

college, and probably for a little while after that,' he said. And, 'No,' as she began to protest, 'Meredith and I talked it over and there's no question about it. Everyone knows what has happened – it's been in the papers, for God's sake; I didn't bring the British tabloids because it's best Alex doesn't see them – and everyone understands . . . Christ, this bathroom is something, isn't it? I scarcely noticed it before,' he said, vaguely wandering in and out of it again. 'But for Alex's sake, and for no other reason (because it strikes me she could become too reliant on you), I think you should put yourself on to the shuttle and make an appearance in Washington for a couple of nights a week. That's up to you, of course.' He smiled at her and removed his jacket. 'All right?'

'Oh, David,' she said.

'You've two paintings to do, which will keep you out of mischief, and I'm pretty sure you're going to offer to do one of William and Annabelle for their grandparents—'

'They've been so good to Alex.'

'Three. Lots to keep you busy. I would suggest,' he went on, 'that you bring Alex to Washington, but she can't let go of this place now when she's taking charge of it. We shouldn't encourage her to abandon ship when she's trying so hard to get everything together.' Shoes, socks and trousers off.

How she loved his 'we'.

'And furthermore – Elizabeth, are you going to

get undressed or will I have to do it for you? – you have found for us, as you so often do, a weekend retreat, though you have rather gone over the top as far as size is concerned.'

He went to shower and Elizabeth stood in the middle of the room, thought about her daughter asleep a few yards away and about miracles in general. David had come up with the perfect solution, one that would absolve Elizabeth from guilt, was endorsed by Meredith – who was, in the absence of the ambassador's wife, loosely speaking Elizabeth's boss – and balanced most exactly Elizabeth's two duties . . . Except would Alex want her to stay here, want her and David for weekends?

Not for ever, to be sure, but certainly for the foreseeable future. It wasn't wishful thinking: Alex's 'You can do everything!' when she had urged her to play tennis (though she must have been quickly persuaded it was not true), her reluctance to be far away from Elizabeth (again last night she had refused to go out with her friends) and the total commitment of her good-night embraces (this traditional time of closeness between mother and child apparently recognized as an excuse for lack of inhibition) – all these showed not only that Elizabeth was, indeed, not indulging in wishful thinking but also, as David had noted, there were signs of incipient over-reliance which Elizabeth, however much she may relish, should not foster for both their sakes. So, again, David's solution was perfect.

The noise of the shower stopped. The storm had passed over and there was utter silence. Elizabeth removed her clothes – Alex's clothes – and found a nightie in one of the suitcases David had brought. She was about to put it on when David emerged from the bathroom.

'Do you need that?' he said, taking the nightie from her.

'David, we can't! What if Alex hears us?'

'We'll be quiet.' His eyes danced. 'If I don't get my oats from my wife consider what I might do in Washington. It's a hotbed. Temptation around every corner.'

'Offering you oats?'

'Buckets of them.'

'Help,' she said. 'Would a handful tonight satisfy you?'

'A handful of you would,' he said, then added, suddenly serious, 'Your daughter is amazing. You two together is the most beautiful thing I've ever seen.'

Elizabeth told Alex about David's scheme before they went down to breakfast the next morning. Alex's face turned pink.

'His idea?'

'His. What do you say?'

'Yes. Oh yes, please. Just for a few weeks. After that I'll be fine.'

She ran to the cosy dining-room where David,

orange juice and coffee on the table in front of him, was unfolding the *New York Times*. Before she could lose her nerve Alex gave him a hug.

'Thank you. Thank you very much indeed.'

'Settled, is it?'

'Yes. And you're to come here any weekend you can. Every, if possible.'

He ruffled her hair as he had done when she'd been tiny. 'Some, I hope, you'll stay with us in Washington.'

'I'd like to . . . I'm not being selfish, am I, wanting Mummy here?' She seemed genuinely anxious. David put his newspaper aside.

'You aren't being selfish,' he said. 'How can you be when you have made your mother so happy?'

'Wicked Uncle David.'

'That's me, horns and all.'

Yet she was everywhere in her moods, becoming excited and upset about the wrong things and at other times extraordinarily adult. She asked David to check with Juan that the financial arrangements between her, him and Conchita were on a proper footing because there had been 'a muddle' and she wasn't sure if it had been sorted out. Then she told David, quite sharply, that of course Juan could take him round the cellars; he was to choose whatever bottle or bottles he wanted to drink. Her attitude explained when Elizabeth asked if she could set up her painting gear somewhere and Alex, half crying, said anywhere.

Anywhere! She didn't need permission.

'Darling, I can't take your house over.'

'I wish you would. I hate you asking the whole time. It – it distances you both.'

'We'll try to stop then.' Ah, but how Elizabeth triumphed in that 'both'.

The next day, Sunday, Alex was in her bedroom amid devastating tears. It was her wedding anniversary.

David returned to Washington. There had been no more security scares and again Elizabeth tried to persuade Alex to go out in the evenings, but without success. She made and then cancelled an appointment with her lawyer in New York, saying she could not think beyond Ben's service. Attended by both Ed and Duane Turner they went to buy canvases and stock up on Elizabeth's supply of paint. Alex found peace in the room Elizabeth had designated as her studio, and when she was not sitting for her mother she replied to the letters of condolence she had received. Duane brought some of his paintings to show Elizabeth, who was relieved to be able to praise them.

'Have you ever exhibited?' she asked.

'No, ma'am. Or only in my mom's kitchen. Some of her friends buy 'em.'

'They deserve a wider public. You should try to interest a gallery.'

'You mean walk in off the street and plonk 'em down?'

'It's one way of doing it.'

Alex had been flicking through the canvases and she pulled one out. 'I like this,' she said. 'Can I buy it, Duane?'

His paintings were very urban. Here in the background were vibrant yellow cabs, trucks belching out carbon dioxide, but centre stage was a tree in flower. People, blurred, streamed along the pavement and in focus was a little girl, one hand held by her mother pulling her forward, the other stretched upward and back towards the blossom.

'It's yours,' Duane said.

'I must buy it. How much?'

'Thirty dollars,' he muttered.

'It's not nearly enough!' Elizabeth exclaimed.

Duane shuffled his feet. 'Mom won't let me charge more.'

Elizabeth and Alex started laughing and Duane reluctantly joined in.

'You find a gallery,' Elizabeth said, 'and see what they'd charge. Alex will pay that. Okay?'

'Okay, ma'am.'

A few hours' peace in the studio, but was overexcited about Ben's service. Her – Ben's – friends were rehearsing in private and they came to her and said Christine couldn't cope with Percy Bysshe Shelley, but Donna could and did Alex mind? No, she did not. And they wanted a poem by an American, from them to Ben, and said Tim should read it. Alex agreed frantically. She should have thought of it, she said; she hadn't meant to take Ben's nationality away.

Nancy and Donna helped her address the envelopes for the cards. They reached the letter F in Ben's address book.

'Flanagan,' Donna said, and there was a suspension of motion and sound.

'Send him one,' Alex said, and the moment passed.

The priest came to discuss what he would say at the service and Alex gave him her letter from Italy, explaining that only she and her mother had set eyes on it. Only four eyes before his two.

'Thank you for sharing this with me,' he said quietly when he had finished. 'I feel truly privileged. What a fine young man.' He paused and then said: 'I don't think I could do any better than his own words, his own testimony. Would you mind if I made notes?'

Alex could not, did not mind and she cried a bit after he had left.

Yet she took Elizabeth upstairs and showed her another bedroom further along the corridor.

'Yours and David's. You don't want to worry about me walking in on you, do you? You want privacy.' And arranged for Conchita and the daily maids to move Elizabeth's things.

Elizabeth abandoned any plans to go to Washington this first week and Alex's almost hysterical insistence that she should was punctured entirely when Elizabeth said, with perfect truth, 'David won't let me.'

Already David's personality, his authority, permeated this house and Alex found it even more irresistible than Conchita and Juan.

Then Henry Glover arrived. Alex went with Ed to the airport to meet him and she brought him into the studio and introduced him to Elizabeth.

'Small and serious Henry!' Elizabeth extended a painty hand and surveyed Alex's best friend.

Not a golden boy by any means, not judged by the photographs of Ben, but handsome enough and with an intelligence, understanding and a *goodness* in his eyes that would last him the rest of his life and make his face beautiful always. He took her hand and gave it a firm shake while Alex whirled out of the room calling to Conchita for tea.

'She's happy to see you,' Elizabeth said as she began to clean her brushes. 'She talks about you a lot.'

'Does she?'

'She does. How are your parents, Henry?'

'Very well. They send you their love. They are pleased you and Alex are together and feel rather guilty they didn't do anything to make it happen sooner.'

'What could they have done? Tell them that.'

'I will. Thank you.'

'How long are you staying?'

'I don't know. Alex sent me an open-ended ticket.

She – she paid for it,' he added, obviously finding the admission difficult.

Elizabeth removed her painting smock and smiled at him. 'One must learn to receive as well as give, don't you think? It is, under certain circumstances, a form of generosity. How long can you stay?'

'I've got two weeks off work.'

'That,' she said, taking his arm and leading him from the room, 'seems to me to be extremely generous of you.'

And Alex consented to go to Roscoe's with Henry but only, for heaven's sake, if her mother accompanied them.

'You can't stay here alone,' Alex said.

'I can. Easily. You young things don't want me.'

'We do.'

'Very well,' she said, 'if you insist. But not for long. Henry's probably jet-lagged.'

There was a great whoop as they went into the bar, Henry greeted as though he was an old friend and Elizabeth's presence as though it was normal. Ed sat at a table by the door, his constant flickering glances causing Roscoe some alarm until Mike explained who he was.

'Donna thinks you're cute,' Alex told Henry as they drove away.

'Does she?' he said placidly. 'Good. I think she's cute too.'

'Oh?' Elizabeth, sitting in the front passenger seat, was amused to hear how suspicion had replaced the teasing note in Alex's voice.

'Or I would do,' Henry went on, 'if I knew what cute really meant. Can men be it? And which was Donna anyway?'

'Henry, *honestly*,' Alex said, giving him a friendly punch and laughing in the way nineteen-year-olds ought to laugh.

She laughed the next afternoon, too, when Jess phoned with the totally unexpected news that she was here on Long Island. At her parents. Yes, the children were with her, but not Richard. He'd spent enough time away this summer.

She arrived at the mansion a short time later, agreed with Alex that she'd changed her mind and decided at the very last moment to be at Ben's service and, as Elizabeth saw with concern, avoided Henry's startled gaze. For he, who had left England a bare twenty-four hours before Jess had, knew exactly how last-minute the decision had been.

But they had to play along. Henry realized it and revamped his face into an expression of delight and Jess turned to Elizabeth, lines of strain around her eyes (caused by a transatlantic flight with two children? Elizabeth wished she could believe it).

'I thought,' Jess said, striving for lightness. 'I suddenly thought I'd like to hand your daughter over in person.'

And Alex looked on in innocent delight as two of her three mothers embraced.

Chapter Fourteen

JESS HAD LISTENED TO RICHARD'S confession with mounting confusion, hurt and then an appalling feeling of vertigo as everything upon which she had stood for the past eight years vanished from beneath her feet. She could accept the reason for the break-up of Richard's previous marriage and even the existence of an illegitimate child – she had never asked and had always assumed Elizabeth was the culprit – but was shocked to the core that Richard had allowed Alex to believe Nanny Mountfield's lies.

'Alex understands I couldn't have told her,' Richard said.

'I could have,' Jess snapped. 'Did you ever consider that? I could have as soon as I'd gained her trust. You didn't need to inform me of your silly affair for my sake, Richard, but you should have done so for Alex's.'

'I didn't think of that.'

'Evidently not.'

'At least Alex and Elizabeth are united now,' he said, hoping to placate her. 'Thanks to you.'

'Yes, and you were angry with me. Angry because

I wrote to Elizabeth.' That interrogation on the way back from the airport! 'My God, how hypocritical can you get?'

'I was frightened, Jess. Frightened she'd tell you before I did.'

She stared at him. 'But that was months ago. Why wait until now? Oh no, don't say it . . .' Jess looked at the painting of William and Annabelle. 'That business in the New Forest was so you could find out if she'd rat on you. And you have to tell me now because Elizabeth will have told Alex.'

'I told Alex before she left.'

'So you implied. And that absolved you, did it, for those years of deception? Well,' she said wearily, 'nothing can be done about those. As you say, Elizabeth and Alex are together.' She stood up. 'I must cook the vegetables. It's only stew for supper, I'm afraid.'

'There's more.'

'More what?'

He told her, attempting justification in every sentence, blaming John King's lack of business sense, about his financial difficulties.

'How much?' Jess whispered, sinking down into her chair. Her legs would not hold her.

He mentioned the figure and she closed her eyes.

'That's only the principal. We'll retrieve it – or most of it when the property market starts moving again. It's the interest that's crippling.'

'John King,' Jess said, backtracking. 'He came to

lunch and Annabelle was sick over him. She was two.'

'A pity she didn't put him off, isn't it?'

'Can't you get some money out of Charman Trading?'

'It hasn't been doing very well either. Frank isn't as clever as his father. That's why—'

'I can add two and two.'

Jess buried her face in her hands. Not simple arithmetics. A crazy algebraic formula was burning in her brain and she knew it meant x equals y. She had suspected it all along but it had seemed outrageous, incredible, until now when she realized the full components of x.

'Have you asked Alex for money?'

'Yes.' Relieved, apparently, his wife was seeing the practical side. 'My idea is that she comes in as another partner. It will be legal and above board. She could make a good profit.'

The last thing Alex needed!

'Have you,' Jess said, some demon in her wanting to know, 'been keeping creditors off for the past' – she counted carefully; it seemed important – 'the past twenty months by informing them of your daughter's engagement, her brilliant marriage, her husband's huge inheritance?'

'I wouldn't put it that crudely.'

'Crudely? Crudely!' Jess sobbed. 'Have you sent them the newspaper clippings? "Drowning tragedy of young millionaire: Wife gets all"? "Millionairess goes home. Beautiful Alex's sorrow"? Have you?'

'No, I haven't. Jess—'

'And if Ben had lived, what then?'

'I would have talked to him. It's perfectly sound business.'

'So perfectly sound that you had to sell your daughter to prop it up. Supper's in the oven. I'm going out.'

'Jess—'

And for the second time in recent years a Lady Mountfield ran from Montly Manor in distress over her husband.

Jess stumbled along the track behind the house, going upwards instinctively as though that would clear her feet of mire. She paused, wondering whether to make for the comfort of Emily and John Glover, but saw it would not do. Her brain was brilliant at arithmetic tonight: Emily and John lived on something like a fifth of the sum Richard and his partner were due to pay annually in interest. They would pretend to understand but be shocked, and rightly. It was outrageous. *Outrageous.* Her feet stamped out the word, sending up scutts of chalk as she climbed on, panting. It was hot. Global warming. Richard could have used the money to dig the swimming pool William begged for. Swimming pools were ecologically sound, he said, so long as you made sure hedgehogs didn't fall in. How did you do that? Have an anti-hedgehog fence?

Outrageous.

She paused again. Somewhere machinery was working, carting straw, perhaps, or ploughing, or reaping a last field. Richard was supposed to relieve Matt, she remembered. It was why she had cooked an unseasonal stew: something to stick to the ribs and give energy and stamina to last out these long harvest days. Yes, and what had happened to those two years ago? A farmer had gone abroad, leaving his harvest to be gathered in by others. The significance hadn't occurred to Jess then.

She climbed over a gate and dropped into the field beyond. No sheep were in it. The brambles that had so offended Richard were rampant, bobbled with reddening blackberries, a harvest for the children later in the year. She wandered down the field and forced herself to face the facts. Richard had engineered Alex's marriage to Ben so he could get access to Franklin's money, and if that was not bad enough, the worst thing, the very, very worst – and as Jess thought about it she knew it was true – was that Franklin would have changed his will again if Ben hadn't been married to Alex. He wasn't cruel. He wouldn't have left Ben alone with all that money. And now Alex was.

The fact was that Richard had deceived Jess as profoundly as he had deceived his first wife. He had presented motherless Alex to her and she had indeed mothered her, ignorant of the real reasons for her motherlessness; he had, without telling Jess, got himself into a financial hole and had hit upon a scheme to extricate himself not only by using Alex but by exploiting his wife, her parents and his two other children as well. Without a word, a sign of consultation. Appearing, on the contrary, to be an indulgent husband and father, taking them to Jess's homeland for a family holiday when it had really been as a kind of investment. Jess had believed their marriage was a partnership, a democracy, and was having to come to terms with the reality that she had been living under a dictatorship. Benign, paternalistic, but a dictatorship nonetheless.

She turned back up the hill, decisions on her shoulders whispering in her ears.

She considered Jane Patterson and rejected her. She was a good friend but when – if – this was over she did not want Jane knowing her marriage was built on a foundation of shifting sand.

Women in their thirties with children of their own can need their mothers, and Jess needed hers now.

And, most bizarrely, she needed to talk to that other woman Richard had deceived.

They were both within a few miles of each other. What could be better (apart from none of this happening in the first place)?

She met Richard halfway up the track, out of breath and frantic between finding her and not wanting to leave his sleeping children unattended. She liked him for that.

'I'm going to Ben's service,' she said. 'I know what we decided, but one of us should be there.'

'Of course, Jess, if you feel you must.'

'We'll have to leave tomorrow to get there in time.'

'We?'

'I'm taking the children, naturally. Do you imagine I'd leave them here after what happened last time?'

She had the dubious satisfaction of seeing him wince. Pickles and Alex's old pony raised their heads and walked hopefully towards them through their dusk-filled paddock.

'Shouldn't we talk?' Richard said as Jess stopped to greet the ponies.

'I must pack. Book the tickets.'

'I'll book the tickets.'

'I have to get away, Richard. Sort things out.'

The trouble was he was not the ogre of her imaginings of this past hour. He was the husband of the past eight years, the father who only a few days ago had told William he could have fifty acres of the farm to be run organically. Annabelle had demanded fifty acres too, been granted it and generously appointed William her farm manager.

'Shall we call it Ben's Acres?' Richard had said. 'Don't you think he'd prefer it to flowers dying in the church in his name?'

Ecstatically they had agreed and rushed off to consult William's copies of the *Organic Farmer* to see what the next step was.

'What brought that on?' Jess had asked Richard.

'We have to consider the Green side of things,' he had replied. 'And don't you find their obsession with Ben's flowers rather morbid?'

'Where is the land?'

'On the other side of the main road. Actually it's about two hundred acres. I knew Annabelle would demand parity and thought William would negotiate up.'

She had loved him intensely then and even more when, to William's orders, he agreed to have the fields ploughed leaving broad bands around the headlands for the wildlife and apologized to his small son because, since he kept no dairy cattle, he had no natural manure to feed the land. He had solemnly promised to make enquiries of neighbouring farmers.

How could Jess cease, upon an order from her head, loving this man? Yet had he not remained true to the one she had discovered this evening – the benevolent dictator? He had planned his treat for the children but had not shared the anticipation of bestowing it with their mother. And what was the real motive behind Ben's Acres anyway? A Green experiment, a treat for William . . . or a sweetner for Alex? The thought sharpened her anger.

'Will you arrange the tickets?' she asked as they went indoors.

'I'll try for Gatwick, but it's most likely to be Heathrow.'

'Wherever. Then I must call Mom and Dad.'

'What will we tell the children?'

'I decided to go and you can't get away, which is just about the truth.'

'Organizing William's shit, am I?'

'Richard, you have to live with what you've done. Everyone has to.'

'Nemesis. I always hated Greek at school and now I know why. You must go, I suppose, but will you come back?'

Of course she would come back, she nearly cried, shocked at his quantum leap forward. Then she remembered he had been here before. To him it must be *déjà vu*, and that other wife had gone for good.

'Please, Jess. I need you.'

'You're a good farmer. Why couldn't you be satisfied with that?'

'From now on I will be, I promise.'

'Until,' she could not help herself saying, the anger and hurt exploding again, 'Annabelle is older and you have another daughter to sell.'

'No!'

'Have you ever been unfaithful to me?'

'No!' Even more emphatically.

But he had not apologized, had not realized the basis of her pain about the secrecy, the lack of partnership.

The next morning at the airport, when the children – seasoned travellers that they were and only marginally surprised to be awoken and told they were flying to see Grandma and Grandpa begged to go through passport control and into the duty-free area as soon as they had checked in, Jess parted from Richard with some relief.

But what happiness to see Alex and her mother together; how even more astonishing the likeness between them now they were side by side. How delightful to note the care Alex took to divide her attention equally between her two mothers, recognizing perhaps – was it possible? Jess had this minute recognized it in herself – that Jess might feel a twinge of jealousy at being so abruptly and totally superseded.

Ben's service the following day, five of Alex's six parents there and the church full. The congregation sang the hymns Alex had chosen and heard that there was a time to every purpose under the heaven, heard the priest talk about Ben, weaving in his own words about money not dictating lives, his plans to do good with the wealth he had inherited. Heaven was enriched, the priest said, and Ben's family and friends should not grieve that they had lost him so much as celebrate the fact they had known him. Some of those friends read from 'Adonais', Christine first explaining why Alex had wanted this poem, taking a stanza each and speaking the difficult lines with an authority and feeling which showed the love and work they had put in. Then Christine said that although half of Ben had wanted to belong to the

Old World the other half was all-American and Tim read Robert Frost with a tremor in his voice the others had not had in theirs. Since Alex's return they had been living Ben's loss alongside her and, like Alex and as the priest had said, were seeing this service and their participation in it as a celebration of Ben's life rather than a mourning for his death. Many people were crying freely, but Alex was smiling and seemed on the verge of applauding as Ben's six friends returned to their seats.

But there was a time to mourn, as Henry had read. Ben's urn was placed in the ground next to those containing the ashes of his grandfather and of the old man's two wives. Alex shed tears then, standing between her mother and father-in-law, but when she turned away there was Henry being a rock for her. A porous rock, in fact, as he had a handkerchief ready and she could not find hers. Cameras clicked, the vultures here for what must be the last picking-over of the bones of this dreadful story.

Elizabeth went to where Betty and Austin Mitchell were standing, each with a grandchild, looking emotionally wobbly, attached to one hand. Jess's lines of worry were now on her mother's face.

'There's lunch at the mansion, remember?' Elizabeth said before Betty could speak.

'Yes,' Austin said briskly. 'We're waiting for Jess and were thinking it's more than warm enough for a swim.'

'Not in the pool, Grandpa,' William said. 'Not there.'

'In the Sound. I can't swim in pools. I sink. You know that.'

William kicked feebly at his grandfather's shoes in acknowledgement of the joke and Annabelle stared up at Elizabeth.

'You're Alex's mother. You painted us. It's at home.'

'I'm going to paint you again so there'll be one here.'

'Aren't Grandpa and I lucky?' Betty said.

William nodded his chestnut-coloured head and his free hand groped for Elizabeth. She took it in hers and bent down.

'Could we,' William whispered, 'have our own special picture of Ben? On his acres?'

'His acres?' Elizabeth repeated, puzzled.

William explained, first making Elizabeth promise not to tell Alex for they had been saving the news for their weekly phone call. Elizabeth exclaimed at how thrilled she would be and soon William was crying and Annabelle about to. Their soft bodies leant against her and she assured them they would have their painting; perhaps they could do drawings so she could see how they imagined Ben on his acres. Richard's children's tears on her cheeks, his son sobbing thanks . . . Elizabeth carefully disentangled herself and stood up. Richard's wife was coming towards them and William transferred himself to her.

She s going to paint Ben for us, but we've got to do drawings.'

'Swim first,' Austin said, picking up Annabelle and moving off with Betty. William, restored, ran after them.

'You are very kind,' Jess said. 'Painting pictures for my children as well as of them.'

'It's no trouble.' She seemed to be becoming a portrait specialist, but never mind.

'Elizabeth, do you know why I'm here?'

'I've guessed. I'm sorry, Jess, but it's different. Really it is.'

'Is it? Have you met Marcus Grimaldi? He's around somewhere. I could hardly greet him. All I could think of was how he'll despise us when he hears Alex's request.' She tried to laugh. 'I'm half expecting the ground there to shake as Franklin starts spinning. Hoodwinked! By Richard! Do ashes spin in their grave like bodies?'

'Figuratively, perhaps, as bodies are supposed to do.'

'Franklin, mind, did a bit of hoodwinking too. Quite a lot, in fact.'

'We can't talk properly now. How about lunch tomorrow? Would you like that?'

'More than anything,' Jess said, flushing.

'It is different, honestly it is.'

'Maybe,' she said. 'Maybe,' and turned and hurried to catch up with her parents and children.

Then David was at Elizabeth's side. 'What was

that about? No, tell me later. We should get Alex away. Ed is about to combust in his desire to be in two places at once.'

People were still around Alex, Frank and Joan offering condolences and Henry, in a system he and Ed had devised, was writing down the names of those invited back to the mansion who were not on the list already with the guards at the gate and politely requesting them to wait before attempting to gain admission.

'Take charge, then,' Elizabeth said and watched as David went forward and cut Alex and her parents-in-law out, making sure he walked between Alex and Henry as they made for the gate. The photographers had snapped Alex in Henry's arms and any more pictures of them together would not be wise. Ed Turner was there, ever alert, and his cousin too. How long would Alex have to continue to live with this security, accompanied wherever she went, knowing her phone calls and letters were screened? Surely after today the interest would wane – yet who was to decide to relax the protection? Not Elizabeth, certainly.

'Mummy?' Alex asked, stopping.

'Here, darling.'

'I thought you'd gone.'

'Would I do that?'

'No.'

They could take as many photographs of this as they liked.

A buffet lunch laid out in the main dining-room, Donna attempting to show Henry how very cute she found him, he charming but indifferent; Nancy suffering a reaction from the occasion as the adrenalin drained away and having to be comforted by Mike; a touch at Elizabeth's elbow and an earnest young man introducing himself as Abe something or other and saying how much he admired her painting.

He had been there, he said, when Ben had opened the parcel containing the portrait of Alex, beginning to talk about that and his eyes filling with tears. 'Excuse me,' he said, vigorously wiping his glasses as though they were to blame. 'It's so hard to believe Ben's gone.'

To distract him she entered into a discussion about art, of which he knew a great deal more than she, and then realized he would know the person she was keen to meet.

'Clint Flanagan?' Abe said, polishing his glasses again, replacing them and surveying the room. 'Maybe he's outside. Except I didn't see him in church, or after.'

Jess confirmed that Clint Flanagan – the man who had been with Ben when he had died – was not present and agreed this was odd, though added he had not wanted to see Alex in Italy in the aftermath of the tragedy. She made Elizabeth known to Alex's lawyer and then disappeared among the throng of people.

Marcus Grimaldi: iron-grey hair, a lined, tanned face and eyes as sharp as diamonds until Elizabeth thanked him warmly for organizing Ed Turner and his colleagues, when they softened slightly.

'I hear Alex is being terrific. Causing no trouble.'

'Why should she?'

'No reason, but you ask Ed about the last teenager he had charge of. He still wakes up screaming at the memory. I had a job to persuade him to take Alex on. Luckily he was free. He isn't often.'

'It's good of you to take such care of Alex.'

'Until she turns twenty-one, ma'am, you can be sure I will. And after that, if she wants me.'

'Until then she has no choice?'

'That's right.'

'So,' Elizabeth commented to David later, 'Richard has met his Waterloo. There is no way Marcus Grimaldi will allow Alex to be exploited, not by anyone. I had the distinct impression he was suspicious of me.'

'Long-lost mother turns up the moment her daughter inherits millions?'

'It's an interpretation.'

David knotted his tie. Not a black one: he was taking them out to a restaurant to give Juan and Conchita a night off and to begin, as he put it, the rest of Alex's life. 'Did Richard imagine he would get the money just by asking?'

'God knows what he imagined.'

'At the very least he should have presented Alex with a proper business strategy to put to Grimaldi.'

'Have you been talking to Henry? It's what he says.'

'He's a smashing chap, isn't he? I pried him away from the redhead and we had a long chat. I look forward, in due course, to him being my step son-in-law.' David put on his jacket and smiled at her. 'What a lovely dress. I haven't seen it before, have I?'

'I bought it the other day . . . David, what did you say?'

'You heard. He's in love with her, but it's more than that. There's a deep affection and friendship, too, which is without question returned. Her marriage to Ben will always be idealized and she won't fall in love like that again – or won't believe she can. She'll marry Henry eventually.'

'But he's going to be a vicar!'

'They're allowed to marry, Elizabeth.'

'Alex a vicar's wife?'

'Well, yes,' he conceded, 'but not for long. A bishop's wife, I'd say.'

'You're insane.'

But was it so very daft? There was no doubt of Henry's love for Alex, concealed though it was beneath banter, gentle teasing, his unobtrusive support and even the occasional ticking off. Alex had given herself to her newly discovered mother to an extraordinary extent but she talked to Henry much more openly, Elizabeth was sure, and she listened when he talked back. Look how she had calmed down since he had arrived! And she hadn't liked Donna paying him so much attention, not at all she hadn't, though she had shown it only through a few questioning glances and most probably had not diagnosed the reason for her unease. She would miss him horribly when he went home and after that there would be an enormous ocean between them, to say nothing of the gulf Alex's money represented. But if David was right Alex wouldn't fall in love with anyone else, certainly not in the next two years while she finished college, and the Atlantic wasn't an insuperable barrier. And the money? Alex might change but at the moment she was planning to follow Ben's path, and who better to co-administer such a fortune for charitable purposes than a priest who had trained as a lawyer?

All in the future, though. Now they were in the restaurant being settled at their table while Ed Turner and his fiancée seated themselves at an adjoining one. It had been Alex's idea. She had invited Ed to eat with them and when he had refused, saying they didn't want him there, she had suggested he might have a girlfriend he could bring along so he could have a nice night out too. Sure he had a girlfriend, he'd said. A fiancée, in fact, called Diane. An attorney-at-law, in fact, who worked in Marcus Grimaldi's office.

'Then bring her,' Alex insisted. 'You can hardly have seen her recently,' and she called the restaurant to arrange the reservation for them.

Alex a vicar's wife, a bishop's wife? Why not, since she would be Henry's wife? And here was Henry beginning the rest of her life, concentrating on their forthcoming visit to New York. He had spoken to Joan, who had confessed it had been years since she had seen the sights of her own city and would show Alex and him around, if they could stand the heat. She had said they should spend the night – two even – with her and Frank. They had plenty of room and would like it very much if Alex would agree to that.

He hit the right buttons and Alex began looking forward. She would see Marcus and also Maria Goldberg at Columbia. She'd probably need Henry's protection, she joked, and told them about her conversation with the fearsome woman.

'You'll defend me, won't you?' she asked.

'Must I?' he complained. 'I was hoping to have time off to go to one of those places on Forty-second Street.'

'We can do that as well.'

Henry laughed. 'No. I want to see where you'll be studying so I can imagine you there.'

'It will be comfortable knowing you're doing that,' she said.

David invited Ed and Diane to join them for coffee and brandy and they shifted their chairs around and asked for coffee: Ed because he was on duty and Diane because she had a long drive home.

'To New York at this time of night?' Alex said. 'Why? It's Saturday tomorrow. Stay! Ed, you have a bedroom in the mansion, don't you?'

He muttered that he did.

'Well then . . . or,' Alex fumbled on realizing her *faux pas,* 'there are plenty of others.'

There was general laughter and Diane accepted Alex's offer and asked for brandy. She told them she had met Ed in law school. He had flunked out because he hated sitting and listening, always wanted to be doing. He was bad at delegating responsibility, she said, which was at once why his business could not expand and why he was greatly in demand. And why they never found time to get married.

'You should find time,' Alex told them. 'If you don't it could be taken away from you. Taken away without any warning. Time can play horrible tricks.'

'We should listen to the lady,' Ed said after a short pause. 'She could be right.'

Conchita was shaking Elizabeth awake.

'Señora, señora,' she pleaded. 'Quickly. Señor Turner wants you, but he says to be quiet and not disturb the little señora.'

'What is it?' Elizabeth said, disoriented.

'I don't know. Señor Turner says I must listen outside the little señora's door and warn him if she stirs. You must go to him now. Please!'

Elizabeth, catching the panic, got out of bed and

had flung on clothes and was pulling shoes on to sockless feet before David stirred.

'Ed wants me,' she told him. 'Some kind of emergency.'

'Do you need me?'

Elizabeth tied the laces. 'I might. We're ordered not to disturb Alex.'

She ran along the corridor, her trainers making no sound on the carpet, and flung herself down the stairs. Ed – did the man ever sleep? – was in the hall. He grabbed her and hustled her through the door to the service area.

'The guy Clint. Where does he live?'

'You mean Clint Flanagan?'

'Find me his address.'

A voice to be obeyed. Elizabeth made for Alex's study and rummaged through the desk drawers searching for the address book she recalled Alex and the others using. It had been Ben's. She found Alex's and tossed it to Ed while she continued looking.

'No Flanagan,' he said.

'Here.'

He took the leather-covered book and made for the door. 'Tidy up. We don't want Alex getting suspicious until we're ready for her. See you in my office.'

He went out and Elizabeth, her mind full of questions and dread, shut the drawers of the desk and replaced the papers she had disturbed on the top.

'What's happened?' David in the doorway, as hastily dressed as she.

'I don't know. Something appalling.'

They hurried to Ed's office off the room where the surveillance equipment was housed. Diane left as they entered.

'She's getting someone to rouse Henry,' Ed said. 'I don't wish to hurt your feelings, ma'am, but he knows Alex the best of any of us.'

'Ed, just tell us what the hell is going on,' Elizabeth said.

He handed her three sheets of yellow lined paper. 'Flanagan comes from Miami, Florida, and that letter was mailed in Houston, Texas,' he said. 'It could be a hoax, but I don't think so. I think he's running and it's not as bad as it might have been.'

Elizabeth unfolded the letter and sat down.

'Dear Alex,' it began.

I have to tell you about me and Ben. You see, I thought he was like me. Even after he married I did. It's not so unusual. Anyway I was wrong and that's why he died. Alex, I have to tell you this.

I loved Ben. I was sure part of his trouble, the millstone, was because he hadn't realized he was gay and I'd have the chance to show him he was when we were alone together in Italy. Well, it didn't work out like that. Almost as soon as we got there all he wanted to do was come back. He kept saying he was cured and the only thing he talked about was you. Alex, he was so fucking happy. I was jealous, I guess, and suddenly there was no more time.

We were going to take the ferry to Elba and spend the night there, but when we got to Piombino Ben started to fidget, saying we should've headed for Rome and a direct flight to JFK. And can you believe it? Some guys from Pittsburgh U overheard us talking on the dock. They'd flown in from London to Pisa that afternoon, only it should have been morning but the air-traffic controllers were on strike in France. That did it. No Elba and to Rome next day.

Jeez, what a dump Piombino is! Those guys from Pittsburgh would've felt right at home there, only we figured the water couldn't be too polluted because kids were swimming in it. We were hot and it looked good. We found a hotel, checked in and headed for the Med.

To a boy from Florida that beach was a joke. About six foot by twenty of crappy grey sand, but the people with their umbrellas like it was the Riviera or some place. Well, you saw it, I guess.

Alex, I don't need to tell you this but you have a right to know.

We waded through the gunk and made it to the open sea. There were whitecaps and it was kind of exhilarating. We were a way from the shore and it came right out. There was no more time, see? I asked him if he'd ever thought he was gay because I had, I was, and he laughed at me. Worse, Alex, he wouldn't stop. He was on his back riding the waves, laughing and spitting out sea water and saying I was kidding, I couldn't be one of those. Something went in me and I jumped on him, got him on the chest and stomach and he didn't struggle or anything. He just sank. I know how to wind people. I knew I'd got it right but maybe I didn't expect it to work so well. I thought he was fooling and he'd pop up somewhere else, and if he had I'd have gone for him again. How can I explain it? At that moment I wanted to kill him, shut off that fucking laughter, but when I knew he wasn't fooling I wished I hadn't and I wanted to die too.

Elba was there and it seemed the place to aim for so I set off. It was further than it looked and the whitecaps weren't exhilarating anymore. I don't remember what I said when they picked me up and the people in the hospital didn't speak much English. I must have gabbled about Napoleon because when they found someone fluent to talk to me he fed me a story and I agreed with it and added some bits of my own. I was back to thinking

Ben had been fooling and had driven away and left me. I cried when they told me the car and his luggage were still there. They didn't suspect me. If they had I was ready to own up. I was sure they'd find Ben in the wrong place or there'd be marks on his body or someone on the beach would have seen it and said something, but nothing happened. I got away with murder.

I'm lighting out, Alex. I don't expect you to forgive me, but remember I'm writing this for you. I could have stayed silent. Thank you for inviting me to Ben's memorial service, but I won't be there or at dear old Suntan U next semester.

Alex, I'm sorry.

Clint.

'Murder,' Elizabeth said, staring unbelievingly at the signature. 'Murder! You said it wasn't as bad as it could have been. How in heaven's name could it be worse?'

Ed took the letter. 'When I first saw it I thought it was a suicide note. Still could be. And if it is and the press got to hear of it, which they would, what we've had so far will seem like a picnic.'

'You said it might be a hoax. What if it is?'

'Elizabeth, you're clutching at straws,' David said gently.

'How do we tell Alex,' she whispered, 'on the day

she begins the rest of her life?'

Ed shrugged. 'If we can keep it out of the papers does she have to know?'

'And a murderer goes free?'

Diane brought both Henry and coffee in. They were silent while the coffee was poured and handed round and Henry read the fatal letter. He rasped his hand along his unshaven chin and tossed the papers on to Ed's desk.

'It'll make Alex happy,' he said.

'Happy?' Elizabeth said. 'What on earth can you mean?'

'Happier,' he amended. 'In a curious way it's an honourable letter. As the man says, Alex has a right to the truth, except we must hope she doesn't demand revenge.'

'I don't understand.'

David put an arm around his wife. 'We're talking in riddles. Let's sum up in plain English. Ed, you thought – maybe still think – Flanagan has killed himself, and it's what he meant by lighting out.'

'Right, but now I believe he's lighting out to Mexico. Has lit.'

'Have you called the police?'

'No, sir. If he's dead there's not a thing we can do about it, and if we alert the cops all over the South – there's a lot of places he can get to from Houston, Texas – it's got to be done discreetly. Cops sell stories.'

'How is it done "discreetly"?'

'Marcus knows men in high places. He'll get working as soon as we tell him what's going on.'

'And you're not worried about Flanagan being dead or alive?'

'Only if he's dead and has left a suicide message naming names, and if a dozy sheriff from some one-horse Texan town goes public on it. But he's in Mexico.'

'You could confirm it,' David said, indicating the open address book, 'by ringing his parents. You have their number.'

Ed hit himself on the forehead, picked up the phone and flicked a switch so everyone could hear. Clint's mother – her voice at first sleepy; the phone had woken her – volunteered the information that her son was in Mexico. He had called them collect last night from there, she said when Ed, posing as a friend of Clint's, expressed surprise. She was beginning to be tearful about her son's abandonment of college when Ed cut her off.

'Case closed. Even if he rigged the call and was lying to her we know it wasn't a suicide note.'

'Shouldn't we tell the police, though?' Elizabeth said. 'He's admitted to murder.'

David motioned to the two lawyers present to take the floor.

'The crime was committed in Italy,' Henry said. 'First you have to persuade the Italian police to make it into a murder case when their own coroner ruled it as accidental death by drowning and there is no evidence to the contrary. Then they must apply for extradition, if a treaty exists between Italy and wherever Flanagan is. It would take years and fail.'

'And since he's hightailed it,' Diane added, 'it's obvious he doesn't intend to admit the murder to anyone else. The letter wouldn't hold him for more than five seconds, not if he had a halfway good attorney.'

'So he is safe in the USA and doesn't realize it?'

'Yup. Like he says, he's got away with murder.'

'I hope he hates Mexico, if that's where he is,' Elizabeth said. She picked up the letter. 'I'd better take it to Alex. You're right, Henry. She should know the truth. There's been enough deception in her life.'

It was nearly eight o'clock and Conchita reported no movement in Alex's room. Yesterday had been a strain and they had got to bed late. Elizabeth opened the door. As she put the cup of coffee she had brought on the bedside table the blonde head on the pillow shifted and Alex opened her eyes.

'Hello,' she said.

'Hello, darling.'

Alex frowned. 'Is anything the matter?'

'You've had a letter from Clint, a very terrible one.'

'Terrible. How?' she said, sitting up.

Elizabeth sat beside her. 'He – he says he killed Ben.' What other words were there to describe it?

She held her daughter until the sheets of yellow

491

paper dropped into Alex's lap and waited while Alex gazed into an unfathomable distance.

'Alex—?' Elizabeth began at last.

'It makes sense, doesn't it? More sense then Ben drowning by accident, than him doing something so silly as trying that swim. I'm not shocked or even surprised. Isn't that strange?' She fingered the letter, folded it along its already well-worn creases. 'Will Clint go to prison?'

Haltingly Elizabeth told her what Henry and Diane had said.

'So he won't?'

'They doubt it, even if you wrestled with red tape for years. And, Alex, it would be best not to tell too many people about this. The press . . .'

'Why shouldn't they know Clint killed Ben? It would punish him for what he did if he can't be punished any other way.'

'Darling, you'd be the one punished. He can change his name, become a new person and disappear. It will be you, who can't disappear, who will be tagged for ever as the widow of a homosexual killing. The details will be forgotten and the assumption made that Ben was homosexual.'

'Why can't I disappear?'

'Because you are going to do great things with the money you have. Remember?'

'Yes.' Alex relaxed against her for a moment, then she got out of bed and went to the dressing table. She opened the drawer containing her letter from

Italy and put Clint's in it. It belonged there. Ben had
died happy, died laughing. She would take comfort
from that and force herself to believe it did not
matter how he died.

'I'll get Frank on his own and tell him,' she
decided. 'It's up to him if he tells Joan. It won't help
them the way it's helped me but one of them must
know. And Betty and Austin because . . . well,
because. And Jess, of course. I'd like Mike and
Nancy to know but perhaps it wouldn't be fair on
them if they couldn't tell the others – not that any of
them would reveal it to the press but we mustn't
take any risks. Henry knows already, which is a
relief.' She turned to Elizabeth. 'Why? Why does
Henry know? What have you all been up to?'

'Worrying about you,' Elizabeth said.

'You don't need to.'

'We can't help it.'

Alex gave her mother an exasperated, affectionate
smile then gazed out of the window at the Sound.
'I'm worried about someone,' she said. 'Well,
people.'

'Oh dear. Who?'

'Daddy, but Jess more. I wish I hadn't made him
promise to tell her about the money. I'm glad you're
having lunch with her,' said Elizabeth's extraordinary daughter.

Jess was rendered speechless by the news that
greeted her when she arrived at the mansion and

Austin, who turned up a few minutes later – he was taking David for lunch at his club and a round of golf after – balled his fists and was about to yell in fury for action until Alex's calm demeanour restrained him.

'Do you want Betty over?' he said. 'You mustn't be alone.'

'Deprive my step-grandmother of a few hours under the total control of William and Annabelle?' Alex said. 'Certainly not. And I'm not alone. Henry's here.'

She pushed him and David towards Austin's car and delivered the same treatment to Elizabeth and Jess. 'Have a nice lunch,' she said, like the best New Yorkers.

Jess drove her mother's car to the restaurant her parents had recommended. 'It can't be true,' she kept saying. 'There was never any question of foul play. Clint's fantasizing.'

'He's left home and given up the chance of a college degree. He did it. It's Alex's acceptance I find hard to believe.'

They went into the restaurant and, mindful of the possibility of being overheard, though the idea of a press rat here seemed absurd, avoided the subject of Clint's letter. They ordered their meal and Elizabeth revealed David's theory about Alex and Henry.

'They'll marry?' Jess thought the scenario through. It was not impossible. This new Alex could be a wife to Henry, and Henry would be able to accommodate the presence of Ben in Alex's heart. As Elizabeth had done, 'Well, why not?' Jess concluded. 'Though given time and without,' she added, 'the help of manipulating hands.'

'Oh, I'm going to do some manipulating,' Elizabeth said cheerfully, 'and you'll help me. If she misses him as much as I think she will you may, for example, have to persuade him to let her pay for his flight over again. When she comes to see you at Montly you must make sure Henry isn't away on a retreat or at some high-level legal conference.' She smiled as she encountered Jess's shocked grey eyes. 'It's more or less what Richard did, isn't it? Provide opportunities.'

'But—'

'Yes, the motives are different but there's the same amount of free will. Alex and Henry could confound our best-laid plans, just as Alex and Ben could have done Richard's.'

Their food was brought to them – lobster salads of enormous proportions – and Jess picked up her fork.

'It's not only that,' she said. 'It's what he did – or didn't do about you and Alex, and what he's done about the money he owes. Our marriage is a fake. You said yesterday it was different, what he did to you and to me. From where I'm sitting it looks pretty much the same.'

'I didn't love him and he didn't love me. That's different, isn't it?'

Jess chewed on a chunk of lobster, swallowed it. 'I suppose so. In spite of everything.'

'We didn't want to sort it out. You do and so you must.'

'You make it sound easy.'

'It could be. It depends on how much forgiving and forgetting you're prepared to do.'

'Eight and a bit years. It's quite a lot.'

'No. Listen, Jess,' Elizabeth said, thinking how peculiar this was: her trying to save Richard's marriage. David had told her she was mad, but she wanted to help Jess. She liked her and wanted to take the despair from her; and she could not forget that it was because of Jess she was here on Long Island and in this restaurant. Why should she not help? 'Listen. I left Richard years before he met you. By that time there was a status quo as far as Alex was concerned and those are always hard to change. I was out of sight and mind. I don't blame Richard for not risking everything by raking over his sordid past, just as I never blamed him – well, not entirely – for how it turned out with Alex. That was my fault, and the beastly nanny's.'

'All she's done recently is cry and pray.'

'Her sins have come home to roost. May they keep her awake at night . . . So, Jess, how many years does that take away?'

'All but two, three maybe. However long Richard's been involved in this property speculation, and since Charman Trading went wrong. And when it did, and Frank told him how Franklin had changed his will, he decided to sell his daughter.'

'Free will, Jess. Alex has no regrets. Not a single one.'

'Richard should have confided.'

'He should have done.' Of course he should! He had behaved disgracefully and did not deserve to have this woman as his wife. 'But I'm glad Alex married Ben. If she hadn't who knows when I would have met her?'

'A long time ago if I'd been aware of the truth.' Fierceness appeared on Jess's face. Elizabeth found it moving.

'You've brought her up beautifully. I'm told how proud I should be of her, and of course I am, but it's your doing.'

'No,' Jess said sadly. 'I'm afraid it's not. The Alex you see now is entirely down to Ben. I had such doubts about him. All wrong, but I didn't know for sure until I heard the priest read out his own words yesterday. And then Clint's letter—'

'Hush,' Elizabeth said. 'We're here to talk about you and not that.'

A waitress collected their plates and asked if they would like dessert. They declined and ordered coffee.

'What shall I do, Elizabeth?' Jess said when it had arrived.

'If I were you I'd give him a second chance.'

'You were me, in a sense, and you didn't.'

'I didn't want to, Jess. You and Richard are right for each other and he and I were wrong. I went off and met David and we were right for each other and have been ever since. It still seems bizarre: me leaving Montly and David being at the hotel in Eastbourne, almost as though he had been waiting for me to come there. To this day he doesn't know why he decided to spend the night, for he could easily have returned to London.'

Elizabeth ran her hand through her hair. She still felt shaky when she thought of the sheer chance which had led to her sitting by the windows of the hotel lounge, staring out at the English Channel which had appeared as blue as the Mediterranean – or was that her memory colouring it so and making the day sunny and hot? A deep voice had enquired whether she had dropped this and a strong hand had held out an envelope. She had denied ownership and he had sat opposite her, offered her a drink and then dinner. He told her later he had been struck by the combination of exultation and sadness in her, like a bird leaving the nest and about to launch itself into the thermals but with a regret at what it was leaving behind. The diagnosis was stunningly accurate, and Elizabeth marvelled at it.

'I wanted you to launch yourself at me. In that instant I did,' he said.

Bizarre indeed. The envelope had been the hotel's, hastily written on and empty. He did not, he said, make a habit of picking up women using such a hackneyed means; or, when teasing, only because he hadn't realized it worked so well; or, when serious, because he hadn't been able to think of another way of attracting her attention.

'So you see,' Elizabeth said to Jess, having related this, 'it wasn't a matter of giving Richard a second chance. We'd given each other hundreds of them and they'd run out. Discovering what he had been up to was the excuse I needed. I should have taken Alex. It was a dreadful mistake and I've paid dearly for it, but what's the point of railing against the lost years? I have her now, thanks to you and Ben.'

'So you think I should go back to Montly and Richard as though nothing has happened?'

'How can you do that? You have to lay down new ground rules about how things are to be dealt with in the future. And,' Elizabeth said, her evil genius getting the better of her, 'make him suffer a bit while you do so . . . if' (her conscience reasserting) 'it would please you.'

Jess clinked her coffee spoon against her cup. 'Right now I have to say it would please me greatly, but I don't expect I could hold it up for long. Apart from anything else William and Annabelle's school starts next month. I took them out for weeks last term and we'll have the social services knocking on the door asking where they are if they don't reappear . . . Still,' she said, raising the cup to her lips, 'that's Richard's problem if I'm not there, isn't it?'

'The least of them. Jess, Richard should tell Alex not to ask Marcus Grimaldi for money. He won't give it, so spare yourselves the humiliation.'

Jess replaced the cup on the saucer with a sharp clatter. 'Will he not?'

'No way in my opinion,' and she told Jess of her brief conversation with the lawyer; of his suspicions about her and even – which she had not discussed with David – her base hope that Diane would report to her boss how David had paid for last night's meal, and thus show they were not sponging off Alex.

'It could be the lesson Richard needs,' Jess said. 'No handouts, no help. He can pull himself out of this hole on his own, even if it means selling a chunk of Montly.' The grey eyes began to gleam. 'Elizabeth, do you remember the Mountfield epergne?'

'Lord, yes. Richard was devoted to the whole caboodle.'

'Still is. Out the stuff has to come whenever there's a smart dinner party. It's very valuable. He can sell it.'

'Jess!'

'It will solve his problem and prove a point. I'll make him do it.

And William is *not* to go away to school next year. Why do the British send their sons off to be looked after by someone else, and when they're so very young?'

'To get them away from their mothers, perhaps,' Elizabeth said, amused by Jess's fighting talk.

'Well, I'm not having it. William will be looked after by me.' She called for the bill and selected a credit card. 'Lunch is on Richard.'

They left the restaurant and went out to the car park.

'Do you know Georgiana?' Jess asked as they got into the car.

'Georgiana who?'

'Mountfield. She loathed the epergne too. You never met her?'

'No.'

'I was jealous in case you had. How funny that seems now.' She swung the car on to the road. 'I'll give Richard a week. One week to decide what to do and after that we'll decide everything together. There's to be no more dabbling in things he doesn't understand. From now on he's a farmer and nothing else.'

This fighting Jess was quite terrifying behind the wheel of a car and Elizabeth asked her to slow down. Jess apologized and braked. Then she indicated right, slowed the car still more, stopped and kissed Elizabeth on the cheek.

'Thank you,' she said. 'I had to come to you even though it seemed crazy to want to. You haven't minded, have you?'

Elizabeth returned the kiss. 'Consider it from my point of view. A chance to advise someone on how to give Richard hell . . . Jess, he'll hate selling that bloody epergne. It was given to an ancestor by some grateful monarch.'

'Henry the Eighth,' Jess said, driving on, 'who got it from a monastery. It'll probably go to Japan or the Middle East or here to the US of A. The Mountfield epergne gracing the palatial home of a *nouveau-riche* tycoon. Yes, he'll hate it.'

They were recognized and waved through the mansion gates. New ones were being put up, more robust ones which could be opened and closed from the house and visitors scrutinized and interrogated from there. The number of men around Alex was being reduced but Ed said the level of protection would be the same.

'Will you really make Richard do it?' Elizabeth asked Jess.

'I certainly will, unless he can find another solution that doesn't involve begging Alex and her trustees for money.' Jess began to giggle. 'And if in future he undertakes to keep the thing polished.'

'Its every bobble and protuberance? Its every nut dish and sweetmeat dish and God knows what other kind of dish? Richard cleaning those?'

'You forgot the cruets. Twelve sets of 'em. They're the most fiddly. Yup, the whole caboodle as you called it. Once a month.'

Jess's giggle was infectious and Elizabeth caught it. They were both still laughing when Jess pulled up outside the mansion and their daughter ran down the steps from the front door.

'Are you drunk?' she asked, pretending shocked outrage.

'No! It's – oh, I can't explain,' Jess said.

'Well, you obviously had a good lunch. Jess, Daddy rang.'

'Did he?' Jess said, the mirth switching itself off.

Alex took her arm. 'He said I'm not to speak to Marcus about his affairs. He's worked everything out.'

'How? How in three days?'

Alex tucked her other hand under Elizabeth's elbow and walked her two mothers towards the rose garden. She had asked her father exactly that question. She had not been looking forward to requesting Marcus to cover Richard's debts but she didn't want Montly sold because of some lumps of concrete in London, though the solution he proposed indicated that had never been a serious threat. Alex did not want to delve into it, or into what had prompted Ben's Acres. All she wanted was Jess and Richard together again.

'He's worked it out,' she said. 'He hasn't actually done anything yet.'

'Did he say what he's worked out?'

'He's going to sell the Canaletto.'

'But I like that painting!' Jess exclaimed indignantly. Elizabeth spluttered and Jess's giggle resurfaced. 'Okay, what else? Will that cover what he owes?'

'I didn't really understand. Something about selling the London properties at a loss and using the money from the painting to pay off his partner and the rest of the loan. It doesn't seem very good economics,' she added. 'Do I have to go to college to learn that?'

'Not good but sensible, under the circumstances,' Elizabeth murmured.

'He'll explain better, I expect. He's coming over tomorrow to take you home.'

Both Elizabeth and Jess stopped walking.

'Why didn't you say so straight away?' Jess scolded.

Alex, grinning, urged them forward. 'I had to get you in a conciliatory mood. It's a good word, that. Are you conciliatory, Jess?' she asked.

Jess sighed. 'If you mean will I forgive him, then I suppose so. If he goes through with it and clears his debts and tells me things in future. But he has to do a penance.'

'What kind of penance?'

'Tell her,' Elizabeth said, laughter spilling out. 'She's one of us.'

Jess did so and Alex said, 'Once a month? Oh, poor Daddy!', and the three of them clung to each other, tears of laughter running down their cheeks.

'God, I feel better,' Jess said at last. 'Who's got a tissue?'

Alex found one in her shorts pocket and they shared it.

'Don't let me drive away with your handbag in the car,' Jess said to Elizabeth as Alex strolled them on again, wanting to prolong this time, this feeling of sisterhood, loving it.

'Is that where I left it?' And to Alex Elizabeth said: 'And where have you left Henry? Aren't we neglecting him?'

'He's by the pool. Donna's here, and Abe. Wasn't it kind of Abe to come for Ben's service? Mike's invited him to stay. He fell for Donna at a party here earlier this summer' – her voice faltered, recovered and carried on – 'and he fell again yesterday. He's suggested we meet up for a night out in New York, he, Donna, Mike and Nancy and Henry and me.'

'That could be fun.'

'Yes, except have you noticed Donna's a bit keen on Henry?'

'I have,' Elizabeth said. 'Is he keen on her?'

'I don't think so,' she said, and then after a moment's silence, 'I hope not. Anyway I'd like to help Abe, and for his sake it would be better if Henry was out of the way. I'll say I have to spend the evenings in New York with Frank and Joan, which is true—'

'Donna might reckon Henry's at a loose end and pounce,' Jess pointed out. She didn't dare meet Elizabeth's eyes.

'Henry has to as well. If he's staying with them it would be rude not to,' Alex said, her mind entirely on her scheme. 'That would give Abe three clear days to impress Donna, though there can't be a lot of future in it since she's at college in California and he's at Miami. . . ' She regarded her mothers with suspicion. 'What's so funny now?' she demanded.

'Oh, darling,' Elizabeth gasped, 'it's your manipulating hands.' And this time they refused to share with her the reason for their mirth.

David and Austin found Henry among the laurels that bordered the rose garden.

'How was your golf? ' Henry asked.

'Not very good,' David replied.

'You need practice, that's all,' Austin said.

'An understatement if ever I heard one. Henry, what are you doing?'

'Hiding,' he said. 'Donna is beautiful and perhaps I should be flattered, but frankly I'm terrified. And I was watching those three. Isn't it lovely to see?'

Two blonde heads and an auburn one laughing among the roses.

Austin moved into the open and called to Jess, who left the others and walked towards her father.

'We'd best get back. Your mom hasn't heard the news, remember?'

Jess had to think what the news was. It seemed hard to believe there was a shadow over this day. David plucked two red roses and held one out to Henry.

'Shall we go and claim our women?' he said.

'Sir!' Henry protested, his cheeks turning bright pink.

'Oh don't be so bloody coy, Henry,' David said crossly.

Henry took the rose.